LAST TALES

LAST TALES

Isak Dinesen

VINTAGE BOOKS
A DIVISION OF RANDOM HOUSE
NEW YORK

FIRST VINTAGE BOOKS EDITION, *November 1975*

*Copyright © 1957 by Random House, Inc.
Copyright 1955, 1957 by
The Curtis Publishing Company
Copyright © 1957 by Atlantic Monthly, Inc.
All rights reserved under International and
Pan-American Copyright Conventions. Published
in the United States by Random House, Inc.,
New York, and simultaneously in Canada by
Random House of Canada Limited, Toronto.
Originally published by Random House, Inc.,
in 1957.*

Library of Congress Cataloging in Publication Data

*Blixen, Karen, 1885–1962.
Last tales.*

*Translation of Sidste fortaellinger.
Reprint of the ed. published by Random House,
New York.
I. Title.*
[PZ3.B62026Las7]   [PT8175.B545]   839.8′1′372
75–9828
ISBN 0-394-74292-3

Manufactured in the United States of America

CONTENTS

Tales from "Albondocani"

THE CARDINAL'S FIRST TALE

W ho are you?" the lady in black asked Cardinal Salviati.

The Cardinal looked up, met the gaze of her wide-open eyes and smiled very gently.

"Who am I?" he repeated. "Verily, Madame, you are the first of my penitents who has ever asked me that question— the first, indeed, who has ever seemed to presume that I might have an identity of my own to confess to. I was not prepared for your question."

The lady remained standing up straight before him; without taking her eyes off his face, she mechanically pulled on her long gloves.

"Men and women," the Cardinal went on, "in the course of time have come to me and have asked my advice. Many of them have come in deep distress . . ."

"As I myself!" she exclaimed.

"In deep distress and anguish," he continued, "which, however, have never been deeper than my compassion with each of them—and have put their problems before me in all kinds of terms. Madame, the multitude of statements and arguments have been but so many variations of one single cry of the heart, of one single question: 'Who am I?' If I could but answer that question, if I could but solve that riddle for them, my consultants would be saved."

"As I myself!" she cried out for the third time. "When I first told you of the horrible conflict, of the cruel dilemma which was rending my heart, I put before you, I know, a number of details, in themselves unconnected and contradictory, and so jarring that I had to stop the ears of my mind to them. In the course of our talks together all these fragments have been united into a whole. Oh, not into an idyll—I am well aware that I am in for a *furioso*—but into a harmony without a discordant note to it. You have shown me myself! I might tell you that you had created me, and that I had come to life under your hands, and surely it would have been both happiness and pain to have been thus created. But it is not so; my happiness and my pain are greater still, for you have made me see that I was already created—aye, created by the Lord God Himself and issued from His hands. From this hour, what on earth or in heaven can harm me? To the eyes of the world, it is true, I am standing at the edge of an abyss, or walking in a blizzard in wild mountains, but the abyss and the blizzard are the work of God and are infinitely and magnificently beautiful!"

She closed her eyes, then after a second looked up again.

"Yet," she said, her voice soft, like the voice of a violin, "I shall be asking one more favor from you. I beg you to answer my question. Who are you?"

"Madame," said the Cardinal after a long pause, "I am not in the habit of talking about myself, and your demand makes me feel a little shy. But I do not want to see you go away—and maybe we two shall never meet again—without having granted you your last request. And indeed," he added, "I am beginning to take an interest in your question. Allow me, then, in order to save my modesty, to answer you in the classic manner, and to tell you a story.

"Take a seat, Madame. The story may be somewhat intricate, and I myself may be a somewhat slow raconteur."

Without a word more the lady sat down in the big armchair indicated to her. The library in which the two found themselves was cool and high up; the noises of the street only reached the talker and the listener like the carefree murmur of a calm sea.

A girl of fifteen, the Cardinal began, with rich gifts of heart and mind, and magnificently innocent, was given away in marriage to a brusque and bigoted nobleman three times her age, who took a wife to have his name live on. A son was born to them, but the child was delicate and had but one eye. The doctors, who found a reason for the sad misfortune in the mother's young age, advised her husband to allow a few years to pass before the birth of another child. Not without some bitterness, the gentleman decided to follow their advice, and in his own mind fixed the period of waiting at three years. So as not to expose his inexperienced wife, during these three years, to the temptations of a worldly life, he took up residence in a palatial villa of his, overlooking beautiful, lonely mountain scenery, and engaged an old, impoverished but proud-hearted maiden aunt as *dame de compagnie*. And so as not to have the daily anxiety for a feeble, threatened being affect the Princess' youthful vitality, he put his son out to nurse with a tenant family on another estate.

Possibly Prince Pompilio, who generally had firm faith in his own judgment, ought not this once to have yielded so easily to the old doctors' opinion. His young wife had accepted her circumstances in life, her marriage and her husband, her palazzo and her coach, the admiration of a brilliant society, and in the end her frail little son, exactly as in former days she had accepted the dolls and the rosaries presented to her, the regulations of the convent school, and her own transformation from child into schoolgirl, and from schoolgirl into maiden. Even the separation from her child she had suffered in the same way, as the ordinance of higher powers. During her pregnancy, while she had been watched over and petted by all who surrounded her, she had come to see herself as a fragile, precious vessel, within which a rare seed had been laid down to germinate, and at the end of the term it had been her husband's old name to which she had given birth. Her personal share in the venture was now but the slightly aching echo of a faint little cry. In the course of the three years by the mountain-lake she learned to dream.

The villa contained a fine library. Here its master passed most of the time that he could spare from the administration of his property and the visits of prominent ecclesiastics. Upon the library shelves tall tomes, with their backs to the world, preserved the ponderous knowledge of ages. But from time to time during three centuries, volumes of more frivolous thoughts, of longing and levity and words that rhymed, had happened to leap in amongst them. On a day when her husband was away, the mistress of the villa found her way to the library. The large cool room, which till now had known only black and bleak human figures, became the abode of a fresh young being in white muslin, whose rich tresses, as she was reading, tumbled forward and caressed the parchment, and who seemed to be lifted from her chair by her own deep sighs of sadness or delight, and to be blown by them to and fro on the marble floor. It fell in love with her; it became a bower above a fountain nymph, shaking down on its own the sweet fruits that her heart demanded.

Such excessive reading, the Prince reflected, might be harmful to his wife's health and mind; she should be other-

wise occupied. Princess Benedetta had a pure and sweet
voice, and within the second year of waiting the Prince ap-
pointed for her an old singing-master, who had once sung in
opera. She gave herself up to music, as she had given herself
up to books; her nature at first had listened, now it sang.
Here, she felt, was a reasonable human language, within
which things could be truthfully expressed. She was in good
understanding with the cadenza, both the full or perfect
cadenza and the deceptive cadenza, the *cadenza d'inganno*,
of which musical dictionaries will tell you that it makes every
preparation for a perfect finish and then, instead of giving
the expected final accord, suddenly breaks off and sounds an
unexpected, strange and alarming close. Here, quite obviously, the girl's heart told her, was the infallible rule of the
irregular.

A pleasant friendship soon united teacher and pupil. The
old maestro entertained the noble young lady with reminis-
cences of the opera, and within the third year of waiting he
obtained her husband's consent to escort her and the old aunt
to Venice to a performance of Metastasio's masterpiece
Achilles in Scyros. Here she heard Marelli sing.

How describe the beatitude into which, in the course of a
few hours, her whole being was transported. It was a birth,
the pangs of which were sweet beyond words, a mighty proc-
ess which needed, and made use of, every particle of her
nature, and in which, undergoing a total change, she triumphantly became her whole self. *Gratia*, Saint Thomas Aqui-
nas himself says, *supponit et perficit naturam*—Grace presup-
poses Nature and brings it to perfection. Any person of soul
and imagination will recognize the experience, every lover
in the world is a disciple of the Angelic Doctor. I shall leave
my analysis at that; I do not venture to compete with Saint
Thomas.

At the seventh recall, before the last drop of the curtain—
while the whole house was afoot and applauding madly—

from the stage-boards and from a nobleman's gilt box, a pair of blue and a pair of black eyes met across the pit in a long deep silent glance, the first and the last.

Smile not—not even in pity—at the fact that the youth, who called to life a young woman's heart, was a being of Marelli's kind, a *soprano,* formed and prepared in the Conservatorio of Sant' Onofrio, and once and for all cut off—no, laugh not!—from real life. But bear in mind that this whole love affair was of a seraphic order and went to a tune.

Old courtesans have confided to me that in their career they have met with young lovers, whose embrace had power to restore a long-lost virginity. Might there not likewise be young inamoratas with such genius for devotion that their glance will bestow upon its object the manhood of a demigod?

And all in all—that the emotion of longing, if suddenly and mightily aroused, should choose for its object the unrealizable—this may be a tragic or a grotesque phenomenon in life, but it is by no means a rare phenomenon. Among very young people it is even common, for with very young people the contempt of death and the love of death will be but one and the same heroic passion.

Their eyes met! Was, then, the unfortunate young singer, in the same way as the lady, wounded in the heart? All authorities agree that that year, in Venice, something happened to the soprano Giovanni Ferrer, who sang under the name of Marelli. His chief biographer, possibly out of tenderness for his ill-fated hero, interprets the fact differently, but does not deny it. The world-famous treble was changed. Till this hour it had been a celestial instrument, carried from stage to stage by an exquisitely elegant and graceful doll. Now it was the voice of the human soul. When, many years later, Marelli sang in St. Petersburg, the Empress Catherine, who had never been known to weep, sobbed bitterly all through the programme and cried: "*Ah, que nous sommes punis pour avoir le coeur pur!*" Poor Giovanni all his life remained faithful to the dark-eyed lady of Venice.

Alas, Princess Benedetta was less stable. In the course of her second, third and fourth youths not a few lively scandals came to be associated with her name. I myself am the only person to know that all the time a slim, gentle, grave guardian-angel was walking with her and seeing to it that there should ever be music in her heart. And now, if you feel like it, you are free to smile at the fact that this dazzling and beguiling, often-embraced lady had for her only true lover the Marelli, who was the lover of no woman.

Shortly after the episode of Venice the term of waiting stipulated by Prince Pompilio expired, and the husband once more with much dignity turned toward his spouse.

No man's hand during the three years had touched Princess Benedetta's lovely person, yet it was changed by more than time. By now she knew the nature and value of what she was giving into the arms of her husband, and in her second bridal night she shed tears different from those of her first.

The Princess became with child, but as long as possible kept the happy state of things to herself. "*Caprice de femme enceinte*," the Prince exclaimed, not a little piqued at an order of nature which would confide a momentous family matter to a lady, before informing her lord. Even afterwards she remained so strangely silent that it seemed as if she had given away only half her secret and had anchored her whole being in the other half. Her family physician had advised her not to sing, and she submitted to this recommendation as she had submitted to all other recommendations of his, for she meant her son to be glorious in strength and comeliness. In order to be secure against temptation she even dismissed her old singing-master. The old man, all in tears, blessed and kissed her at the parting hour, went back to his native village, lived on the pension granted him by his former pupil

and gave no more singing-lessons. But deep in her mind and
blood ran the lovely air of Metastasio's in which some day
that son was to proclaim to the world the triumph of beauty
and poetry as well as his own identity: "Ha! Now I know
myself Achilles!"

The change of surroundings had not meant as much to the
husband as to the wife, for at whatever scene of town or
country Prince Pompilio would gaze, he would see in it the
figure of Prince Pompilio. But the fall of dropping water, as
Lucretius tells us, wears away the stone. The monotony of a
country existence—without high duties at Court, without
prominent roles in grand church ceremonies or grim political
conferences—after a while began to tell on the master of the
villa. He looked round vaguely for something to bear out
the fundamental dogma of his own importance.

The villa had a chaplain and librarian, Don Lega Zambelli,
a short, paunchy man—I have seen him, and remember his
face—who in his career upwards from the humble position of
a swineherd's son had become skilled in the art of handling
great people, particularly in handling them by flattery. By
the time the princely couple took up residence at the villa,
Don Lega in his fat and secure office had begun to miss op-
portunities for practicing his talents, and he now welcomed
such a magnificent patron of the art as the Prince. The master of the villa, on his side, was pleasantly surprised to find
in the midst of wild lonely mountains a man of so much
virtue and discrimination. As he listened to Don Lega, he
came to realize that—unappreciated by his wife, unfortunate
in his son and heir, exiled from the elevated circles in which
he was wont to shine, and in the heyday of his manhood
condemned to celibacy—he had been favored with a particularly noble and precious cross. Before long he saw himself as
a chosen martyr on earth, and a saint in embryo. His visitors
noticed that with every month their host's waistcoats, and
his face, grew longer.

On a day six weeks before the Princess' confinement, he

formally asked her for an interview, and in her green boudoir, which overlooked the valley and the lake, made her a little solemn speech. He wished to inform her of a decision to which—in his long meditations upon the melancholy state of the world—he had arrived. If his patience was to be rewarded with the birth of a son, the infant should become a pillar of the Church. In order to find the right name for this future light of the family—for a name is a reality, and a child is made known to himself by his name—he had made his librarian go through the whole of the *Vitae Sanctorum*, and had settled upon the great Father of the Church St. Athanasius, who is known as "the Father of Orthodoxy." For sponsors to young Atanasio he had, after pious deliberation, selected the Cardinal Rusconi and the very holy Bishop of Bari.

The Princess during the address had kept her embroidering frame on her lap, and her eyes on it. When he had finished she looked up, and very quietly informed her husband that she too had been pondering the future and the name of her son, and had made up her mind. She had borne the house of her husband one son; now she was free. The child to come was to be the son of his mother, and the godson of the Muses. His name should be Dionysio, in reminiscence of the God of inspired ecstasy, for a name is a reality, and a child is made known to himself by his name—and for sponsors to her son she had selected the poet Gozzo, the composer Cimarosa, and the young sculptor Canova.

The Prince was first deeply surprised, then even more deeply shocked, to hear his wife, to his face, defy Heaven and him. Before he could find words to express his feelings, the Princess spoke again as quietly as before. She would remind him, she said, that at this moment the child was of one mind and body with her, and that it would follow her in whatever course she took. There was, indeed, nothing to prevent the two of them from walking out of the house and joining, say, a band of gypsies camping in the mountains or a troupe of jugglers giving performances in the villages. Under no circumstances, she wished her husband to understand, would he ever see the ghost of a pillar of the Church.

Having made this final statement the lady rose from her chair and took a small, very stately step toward the door, as if she meant to carry out her plan then and there. The Prince, seeing the sudden terrifying shadow of public scandal fall on his house, hurriedly placed himself between her and the door, and at her second little step forward, still speechless, took a desperate, awkward hold of her slim arm. The moment he touched her the Princess fainted. Her husband laid her on the sofa, rang for her maids and marched out of the boudoir.

In his own rooms he bethought himself that no wise man will attempt to reason with a wife in her eighth month, and so as not to risk a repetition of a painful experience, he ordered his coach and left for Naples.

Six weeks later, in the palazzo of Naples, he received the message that his wife had been brought to bed of twin sons, and that the doctors feared for her life.

During the hurried return journey to the villa, Prince Pompilio, in his coach and for the first time in his married life, gave himself up to reflections on the character and disposition of his wife. He remembered her childish freshness at their first meeting, the gracefulness of her movements, her little timid attempts at confidence—an echo, of her voice when she sang and of her trilling girlish laughter, rang with a strange perplexing sadness in his ear. Possibly, he thought, he himself had been lacking in patience with the pretty child he had made his wife. Indeed, if he found the Princess alive, he would forgive her. And since Providence, here, in an inventive mood, had miraculously supplied him with a means of being generous, he began to take pleasure in the idea of being so.

At the sight of her, in the enormous four-poster, transparently white, fixing unfathomable dark eyes on his face, he resolved to be even magnanimous. He touched her limp fingers with his hand, and slowly and solemnly, in a distinct voice so that she should be able to follow him, vowed to fulfill the wish that she had expressed in their last, turbulent meeting.

And in order to prove the worth of his princely word, he had the baptism of his sons take place in the chapel. The elder of the boys was christened Atanasio, and had for sponsors the Cardinal Rusconi and the Bishop of Bari. The younger boy was christened Dionysio, and his sponsors were the poet Gozzo, the composer Cimarosa, and the young sculptor Canova.

When the baptism was over, the old great-aunt of the children, not venturing to take liberties with the Prince-to-be of the Church, tied a pale-blue silk ribbon round the neck of little Dionysio in order to distinguish him from his brother, for the children were as like as two peas.

At the moment when the Princess was told that she was the mother of a live Dionysio, a faint flush rose to her white face. It was the beginning of an amazing recovery. Within a month she sat watching the children and their nurses in the rose garden. She had insisted on giving suck herself to her youngest son, and the repeated daily meetings between these two were—like kisses—reciprocal givings and takings of vigor and bliss.

You are a woman of the South, Madame, and you will not, like the more frivolous ladies of France, be amazed at the fact that a beautiful young creature, with the world at her feet, should find a full outlet for her emotional nature in her love for her infant. You will know that to watch our Southern mothers playing with and fondling their infants is to see the hearts aflame, and that an infant son, while still in swaddling clothes, may well be his mama's lover. It will be so, most of all, in the cases in which a divine power has condescended to take human form, and where the young mother feels that she is fondling or playing with a saint or a great artist. Why, we have before our eyes every day the image of that highest relation between mother and son, which includes all aspects of exalted, flaming love. A young maiden in love may seek sympathy and advice with the Virgin of Virgins, and the Queen of Heaven will not, like the austere virgins of the earth who know nothing of love, turn away from her confidence, but in the memory of a babe on her lap she will listen and answer in the manner of a *grande amoureuse*. I am not blaspheming, Madame, when I express the idea that any young mother of a saint or great artist may feel herself to be the spouse of the Holy Ghost. For it is a divinely innocent jest, and the Virgin herself may smile upon it, as upon a child toying with a bit of glass and catching in it the sun of the heavens itself.

The Prince now sent for his eldest son, and for a fortnight the life of the reunited family unexpectedly blossomed into an idyll, and only the Princess knew the happiness of the household to be radiating from the cradle of the infant of the pale-blue ribbon. Finding herself suddenly surrounded by a family of three—like a little girl all at once presented with three life-size dolls—she gave herself up whole-heartedly to the role of a materfamilias, distributing her tenderness equally to her three small sons, and generously washing her mind of past disagreements with their papa. She attended Mass every morning with the Prince in the chapel, and there patiently listened to the praying of Don Lega; of an afternoon she took the air with her husband in his light carriage round the lake and on the mountain roads, and in the evenings listened with sweet attention while he held forth on politics and theology. The Prince felt that his magnanimity had been rewarded with a genuine change of heart in his young wife.

Alas, the idyll was as short-lived as it was perfect.

Six weeks after the birth of Atanasio and Dionysio, while the Prince and Princess were out, the librarian of the villa placed his glasses on the window sill upon a pile of old missives from the Holy See to worthy ancestors of the Prince.

The rays of the sun hit the lenses and ignited the irreplaceable documents, the fire leapt to moldering papers and books and spread to wainscots and ceiling. The whole pavilion, which contained, on the ground floor, the library and, on the first floor, the nursery of the two babies, was burnt down.

The father and mother in their carriage from beyond the lake saw smoke rising from and soon enveloping the villa, and had the horses set into a gallop. As they swept up the avenue they took hope for a moment on seeing the fire partly conquered; indeed, the main part of the building still stands today. But rushing from the carriage they were received with dreadful news.

At the moment when the fire had reached the nursery, only one nurse was present there. She had snatched both children from their cradles, but upon the burning stairs, her clothes aflame and herself half choked with smoke, she had fainted. Other servants of the villa—headed by that dauntless old lady, Prince Pompilio's aunt, who cried out in a high voice: "Atanasio!"—had forced their way up and had dragged her out onto the terrace. Of her small precious charges one had been rescued from the pavilion alive, the other was laid down in the hall of the main building limp and lifeless, his guileless little soul borne upwards with the smoke. The pale-blue silk ribbon was gone.

I have been told that the Princess, as, wavering on her feet, she reached the group of weeping women in the hall, seized the surviving child from a lap, tore open her bodice and laid the baby to her breast, as if she meant to make him, in this one gesture, forever her own.

The Prince in a talk with a friend, on the evening of that same day, showed great fortitude of mind. "The hand of the Lord," he said, "has fallen heavy upon me, but I shall try to acquiesce in His will. Praise be to St. Rocco, the patron saint of my house—my son Atanasio has been spared to me."

A second tragic event trod upon the heels of the first: the

noble and brave old lady of the villa, who at first had not seemed to be fatally hurt in the accident, two days later succumbed either to some internal injury or to shock. It was a strange thing that on her last day she went on invoking the name of Dionysio, and in her incoherent talk gave vent to odd fancies which nobody could understand. "Do you not know," she cried, "that I am a nymph of the mountain Nysa, and the chosen guardian of this child!"

Princess Benedetta never attempted to argue the matter with her husband; in fact she never once touched upon the question of the children's identity. Along her small son's left cheek there ran a long burn, the scar of which showed for the rest of his life. His mother often, even when he had grown into a tall young man and was no longer her bambino lover, kissed this scar, as if seeing in it a proof that the burnt-up silk ribbon had once been tied round his neck. The son, as an old man, would also remember the little pet name of Pyrrha, by which she had called him in their most intimate hours of play and confidence. For a year she wore mourning with much dignity. Her calm made the Prince vaguely uneasy; at times he watched mother and child with a kind of strange misgiving.

To the household and to the friends of the house the little boy remained Atanasio. Only on a marble tablet in the family mausoleum was the name of Dionysio preserved.

As to Don Lega Zambelli, whose negligence had caused the disaster, his happy days as the Prince's adviser and comforter were over. He was dismissed from the villa, gave up his ecclesiastical career, and after many vicissitudes became accountant to an illustrious English milord. Atanasio happened to meet his father's former chaplain on the day before he was ordained priest, and mused upon the part which this fat man had played in his young life.

It was during the years which followed the catastrophe that Princess Benedetta's beauty, her talents and her rare gaiety of heart blossomed out. It has been said, earlier in this story, that at one time of her life she had learned to dream. By now she had done with dreaming and stood in need of reality.

Her son, who had known her in no other quality than that of a great lady of the world, later in life tried to form for himself a picture of the young Benedetta.

"Dear Mother," he thought, "you were ever a loyal and dauntless seeker of happiness. You willed the world to be a glorious place and life a fine and sweet undertaking. A man in your situation might have been perplexed and bewildered to the extent of losing confidence in his own judgment, giving up realities and taking refuge in illusions. But your sex possesses sources and resources of its own; it changes its blood at celestial order, and to a fair woman her beauty will be the one unfailing and indisputable reality. A very lovely woman, such as yourself, may indeed feel freest and most secure upon an edge or a pinpoint in life, with this reality as her balancing pole. You had been, till now, a small boat upon the great waters of existence, striving only, amongst its swells and breakers, to keep afloat and on an even keel, and looking to the stars for guidance. Now you set sail and stood out, gallantly making headway against tide and current, a full-rigged sailer. And O my dear Mother, in your arrogance and exuberance there was ever much deep humility!" He might even, here, with a sigh quote to himself the lines of a great poet: "Humility, and that I never had!"

So indeed daily life in the palazzo or the villa of the young Princess was gradually turned into a majestic and graceful regatta, with gay streamers flying. Its circle of friends grew to include all that the country contained of wit, splendor, elegance and romanticism, and outside the gate of the palazzo the poor of the streets would crowd to see its mistress stepping into her carriage, and cry out: "Bella! Bella!"

The Prince, at first watching the career of his wife with surprise and anxiety, before he knew of it was overpowered and laid low. In the course of years he came to accept, in sublime glow, the role of a saintly, dethroned king. Possibly his vanity even found a kind of melancholy gratification in the renown and glory of his palazzo and in the envy of other palazzos. To the eyes of the world the princely spouses from then on remained on befitting terms of stately amicability.

Little Atanasio grew up in this house, without realizing it himself, a highly important figure in it. Prominent tutors and preceptors to the two young Princes, of all subjects of learning, came and went in the halls. Ercole, the heir to the name and its future perpetuator, was trained in all accomplishments of a nobleman and a courtier, while Atanasio was schooled in Greek and Hebrew and the Fathers of the Church, and at times sent a longing glance toward the worldlier exercises. Still, as the elder brother wished to have the younger constantly by his side and was found to make faster progress when he partook of his lessons, the quick-witted and industrious little boy managed to become a fair horseman and to acquire skill on the harpsichord and in a minuet. He was a favorite in his mother's circle and at home in the great world; he was as happy on horseback as with the classics and, during the family's sojourns at the villa, he took delight in lonely wanderings in the mountains.

All the same, Madame, the task of existing and growing up was not an easy one to this child. It will never be an easy task to a child who, in the relation to father and mother, finds himself placed in the line of fire between two belligerent fortresses. But it was particularly exacting to the boy of whom we are speaking inasmuch as here father and mother did view his small person in totally different lights, did in fact see him as two totally different personalities.

To his father he was from the beginning the Prince of the Church and the glory of his name. While the Prince kept his son to his Latin and Greek and allowed him little freedom and no levity, there was ever in his extremely dignified manner toward the prelate-to-be a little touch of reverence. To the mother the pretty boy—apart from being his own ador-

able self—was the child-prophet of earthly beauty and delight. She spent much time in his company, was even annoyed
when her love affairs took her away from him, and in her
smiles and sighs made him her confidant, as if she wished
to see his little figure in the classical role of Cupid loosening
his mother's girdle. The child was thus at an early age
schooled in the art of equipoise.

He kept his small head by adopting and perfecting, in the
innocent manner of a child, the doubleness of his elders.
He saw the lovely and beloved form of his mother with the
eyes of the priest, the spiritual physician and gardener,
watching her with tenderness and forbearance, and at times
gently remonstrating with her and imposing upon her light,
graceful penances. He saw his father with the eyes of the
artist, and followed the stern figure with the attention and
approval with which a connoisseur follows the movements of
an accomplished actor or ballet dancer. To the perception of
this child-connoisseur his papa was the brilliant, finishing
coal-black brush stroke within the exquisite color scheme of
the palazzo. The papa himself, who had never been a picturesque figure to anyone, faintly sensed the fact; as the boy
grew up he became almost indispensable to his father.

In this way the hand of a child out of the elements of an
anomalous family life produced a reconciling synthesis.

It is seemly, here, to say a few words about Ercole. The
heir to the name—otherwise a taciturn and sullen boy, who
showed no partiality to any human being, and only distinguished himself by growing up to a most unusual height
—all through their childhood together displayed a staunch
and loyal friendship toward his little brother. In the life of
Atanasio he was, during that time, a support and a comfort,
possibly on account of the fact that he had but one eye.

At the age of twenty-one the young Prince was ordained
to the priesthood, and six months later his brother and
friend quite suddenly died from nothing more alarming
than a cold in the head caught at a levee. Out of the three

sons born to Pompilio and Benedetta, Atanasio was now the sole heir to the great name and wealth of the family. In the course of time the old Prince completed his role on the stage of life, draped his grandeur and loneliness round him in heavy folds of black marble, and lay down to rest in the mausoleum, at Dionysio's side. Even that fair lady the Princess Benedetta, like to a child at eventide, yawned and let go of her dolls. Her son, by then a bishop, had the happiness of administering extreme unction to her.

"I have seen your mother," said the lady in the armchair. "She was a friend of Mama's and, when I was a very little girl, from time to time came to the house—in the most lovely frocks and bonnets! I adored her because she could smile and weep at the same time. She made me a present of a bowl of goldfish."

"A week ago," said the Cardinal, "in going through the drawers of an old cabinet, I came upon a small flask of the perfume which she had made for her in Bologna—the recipe will have been lost by now. The flask was empty, but still gave out a faint fragrance. A multitude of things were in it, all in one. Smiles, as you say, and tears, dauntlessness and fear, unconquerable hope and the certainty of failure—in short: what will, I suppose, be found in the belongings of most deceased ladies."

"And so her son," said the lady after a pause, "early trained in the art of equipoise, was left to promenade in the high places of this world, in one single magnificently harmonious form, two incompatible personalities."

"Oh, no, Madame," said the Cardinal, "use not that word. Speak not of incompatibility. Verily, I tell you: you may meet one of the two, speak to him and listen to him, confide in him and be comforted by him, and at the hour of parting be unable to decide with which of them you have spent the day.

"For who," he continued very slowly, "who, Madame, is

the man who is placed, in his life on earth, with his back to God and his face to man, because he is God's mouthpiece, and through him the voice of God is given forth? Who is the man who has no existence of his own—because the existence of each human being is his—and who has neither home nor friends nor wife—because his hearth is the hearth of and he himself is the friend and lover of all human beings?"

"Alas!" whispered the lady.

"Pity him not, this man," said the Cardinal. "Doomed he will be, it is true, and forever lonely, and wherever he goes his commission will be that of breaking hearts, because the sacrifice of God is a broken and contrite heart. Yet the Lord indemnifies his mouthpiece. If he is without potency, he has been given a small bit of omnipotence. Calmly, like a child in his father's house binding and loosening his favorite dogs, he will bind the influence of Pleiades and loose the bands of Orion. Like a child in his father's house ordering about his servants, he will send lightnings, that they may go and say to him: 'Here we are.' Just as the gate of the citadel is opened to the vice-regent, the gates of death have been opened to him. And as the heir apparent will have been entrusted with the regalia of the King, he knows where light dwells, and as to darkness, where is the place thereof."

"Alas!" the lady again whispered.

The Cardinal smiled a little.

"Oh, do not sigh, dear and kind lady," he said. "The servant was neither forced nor lured into service. Before taking him on, his Master spoke straightly and fairly to him. 'You are aware,' he said, 'that I am almighty. And you have before you the world which I have created. Now give me your opinion on it. Do you take it that I have meant to create a peaceful world?' 'No, my Lord,' the candidate replied. 'Or that I have,' the Lord asked, 'meant to create a pretty and neat world?' 'No, indeed,' answered the youth. 'Or a world easy to live in?' asked the Lord. 'O good Lord, no!' said the candidate. 'Or do you,' the Lord asked for the last time, 'hold and believe that I have resolved to create a sublime world, with all things necessary to the purpose in it, and none left out?' 'I do,' said the young man. 'Then,' said the Master, 'then, my servant and mouthpiece, take the oath!'

"But if indeed," the Cardinal went on after a moment, "your kind heart yearns to melt in compassion, I may tell you, at the same time, that to this chosen officeholder of the Lord—so highly favored in many things—certain spiritual benefits, granted to other human beings, are indeed withheld."

"Of what benefits are you speaking?" she asked in a low voice.

"I am speaking," he answered, "of the benefit of remorse. To the man of whom we speak it is forbidden. The tears of repentance, in which the souls of nations are blissfully cleansed, are not for him. Quod fecit, fecit!"

He was silent for a second, then added thoughtfully: "In this way, because of his steadfast renunciation of repentance, and even though he be rejected as a judge and as a human being, Pontius Pilate took immortal rank amongst these elect at the moment when he proclaimed: 'Quod scripsi, scripsi.'

"For the man of whom I speak," he once more added, after a longer pause, "within the play and strife of this world, is the bow of the Lord."

". . . the arrow of which," the lady exclaimed, "each time strikes the heart!"

"An ingenious *jeu-de-mots*, Madame," said he and laughed, "but I myself used the word in a different sense and had in mind that frail implement, mute in itself, which in the hand of the master will bring out all music that stringed instruments contain, and be at the same time medium and creator.

"Then answer me now, Madame," he concluded, "who is this man?"

"It is the artist," she answered slowly.

"You are right," he said. "It is the artist. And who more?"

"The priest," said the lady.

"Yes," said the Cardinal.

She rose from her chair, dropping her lace mantilla over the back and arms of it, walked up to the window and looked out, first down into the street, then up into the sky. She came back, but remained standing, as in the beginning of the conversation.

"Your Eminence," she said, "in answer to a question, has been telling me a story, in which my friend and teacher is the hero. I see the hero of the story very clearly, as if luminous even, and on a higher plane. But my teacher and adviser—and my friend—is farther away than before. He no more looks to me quite human, and alas, I am not sure that I am not afraid of him."

The Cardinal lifted an ivory paper-knife from the table, turned it between his fingers and put it down.

"Madame," he said, "I have been telling you a story. Stories have been told as long as speech has existed, and sans stories the human race would have perished, as it would have perished sans water. You will see the characters of the true story clearly, as if luminous and on a higher plane, and at the same time they may look not quite human, and you may well be a little afraid of them. That is all in the order of things. But I see, Madame," he went on, "I see, today, a new art of narration, a novel literature and category of belles-lettres, dawning upon the world. It is, indeed, already with us, and it has gained great favor amongst the readers of our time. And this new art and literature—for the sake of the individual characters in the story, and in order to keep close to them and not be afraid—will be ready to sacrifice the story itself.

"The individuals of the new books and novels—one by one —are so close to the reader that he will feel a bodily warmth flowing from them, and that he will take them to his bosom and make them, in all situations of his life, his companions, friends and advisers. And while this interchange of sympathy goes on, the story itself loses ground and weight and in the end evaporates, like the bouquet of a noble wine, the bottle of which has been left uncorked."

"Oh, Your Eminence," said the lady, "do not speak ill of the new fascinating art of narration, to which I am myself a devotee. Those live and sympathetic persons of the modern novels at times have meant more to me than my acquaintances of flesh and blood. They have indeed seemed to embrace me, and when, reading by candlelight, I have wetted my pillow with the tears of Ellenore, this sister of mine—frail and faultful as myself—seems to have been shedding my own."

"Mistake me not," said the Cardinal, "the literature of which we are speaking—the literature of individuals, if we may call it so—is a noble art, a great, earnest and ambitious human product. But it is a human product. The divine art is the story. In the begining was the story. At the end we shall be privileged to view, and review, it—and that is what is named the day of judgment.

"But you will remember," he remarked, as in a parenthesis and with a smile, "that the human characters in the book do come forth on the sixth day only—by that time they were bound to come, for where the story is, the characters will gather!

"A story," he went on as before, "has a hero to it, and you will see him clearly, luminous, and as upon a higher plane. Whatever he is in himself, the immortal story immortalizes its hero. Ali Baba, who in himself is nothing more than an honest woodcutter, is the adequate hero of a very great story. But by the time when the new literature shall reign supreme and you will have no more stories, you will have no more heroes. The world will have to do without them, sadly, until the hour when divine powers shall see fit, once more, to make a story for a hero to appear in.

"A story, Madame, has a heroine—a young woman who by the sole virtue of being so becomes the prize of the hero, and the reward for his every exploit and every vicissitude. But by the time when you have no more stories, your young women will be the prize and reward of nobody and nothing. Indeed I doubt whether by then you will have any young women at all. For you will not, then, see the wood for trees. Or," he added, as if in his own thoughts, "it will be, at the best, a poor time, a sad time, for a proud maiden, who will have no one to hold the stirrup to her, but will have to come down from her milk-white steed to trudge on a dusty road. And—alas!—a poor and sad lover of hers who will stand by to see his lady disrobed of her story or her epos and, all naked, turned into an individual.

"The story," he took up the thread, "according to its essence and plan, moves and places these two young people, hero and heroine—together with their confidants and competitors, friends, foes and fools—and goes on. They need not distress themselves about material for the burnt offering, for the story will provide. It will separate the two, in life, by the currents of the Hellespont and unite them, in death, in a Veronese tomb. It provides for the hero, and his young bride will exchange an old copper lamp for a new one, and the Chaldeans shall make out three bands and fall upon his camels and carry them away, and he himself with his own hand shall cook, for an evening meal with his mistress, the falcon which was to have saved the life of her small dying son. The story will provide for the heroine, and at the moment when she lifts up her lamp to behold the beauty of her sleeping lover it makes her spill one drop of burning oil on his shoulder. The story does not slacken its speed to occupy itself with the mien or bearing of its characters, but goes on. It makes the one faithful partisan of its old mad hero cry out in awe: 'Is this the promised end?'—goes on, and in a while calmly informs us: 'This is the promised end.' "

"O God," said the lady. "What you call the divine art to me seems a hard and cruel game, which maltreats and mocks its human beings."

"Hard and cruel it may seem," said the Cardinal, "yet we, who hold our high office as keepers and watchmen to the story, may tell you, verily, that to its human characters there is salvation in nothing else in the universe. If you tell them— you compassionate and accommodating human readers—that they may bring their distress and anguish before any other authority, you will be cruelly deceiving and mocking them. For within our whole universe the story only has authority to answer that cry of heart of its characters, that one cry of heart of each of them: '*Who am I?*' "

There was a long silence.

The lady in black stood still, sunk in thought. At last, absent-mindedly, she lifted her mantilla from the chair and draped it round her shoulders and torso in most fashionable style. She took a step toward the man, and stopped. At this moment of parting she was pale.

"My friend," she said, "dear teacher, adviser and consoler. I see and understand, by now, that you serve, and that you are a loyal and incorruptible servant. I feel that the Master whom you serve is very great."

She closed her eyes, then after a second looked up again.

"Yet," she said, "before I go away—and perhaps we two shall never meet again—I beg you to answer one more question of mine. Will you grant me this last favor?"

"Yes," said he.

"Are you sure," she asked, "that it is God whom you serve?"

The Cardinal looked up, met her eyes and smiled very gently.

"That," he said, "that, Madame, is a risk which the artists and the priests of the world have to run."

THE CLOAK

*W*hen the great old master, the sculptor Leonidas
Allori, whom they called the Lion of the Mountains, was arrested for rebellion and high treason and condemned to
death, his pupils wept and stormed. For to them he had been
spiritual father, archangel and immortal. They assembled in
Pierino's hostelry outside the town, in a studio or in an attic,
where they could sob, two or three, in each other's arms, or—
like a big tree in a gale with its bare branches reaching up-
ward—crowded in a cluster could shake ten pairs of clenched
fists to the sky, in a cry for rescue of their beloved, and for
revenge on tyranny.

Only one out of all of them in those days continued to live
as if he had neither heard nor understood the terrible news.
And that one was the disciple whom the master had loved

above all others, whom he had called son, as the young man had called him father. Angelo Santasilia's schoolfellows took his silence to be the expression of infinite sorrow; they respected his pain and left him alone. But the real reason for Angelo's absence of mind was that his heart was filled with passion for the master's young wife, Lucrezia. The love and understanding between her and him just at this time had gone so far that she had promised him her total surrender.

In vindication of the faithless wife it must be pleaded that for a long time, and in deep agitation and alarm, she had resisted the divine and merciless power which held her in its hands. With the most sacred names she had sealed—and had made her lover seal—an oath: that never again should word or glance at which the master himself could not have rejoiced pass between the two. As she felt that neither of them could keep the oath, she entreated Angelo to go to Paris to study. Everything was prepared for his journey. It was only when she realized that this resolve could not be carried out, either, that she gave herself up to her destiny.

The faithless disciple, too, might have pleaded extenuating circumstances, even if these might not have been accepted by every judge or juryman. Angelo in his young life had had many love affairs, and in every single case had surrendered himself utterly to his passion, but none of these adventures had ever for any length of time left a deep impression on his being. It was inevitable that, someday, one of them must become the most important of all. And it was reasonable, it was perhaps inevitable, that the chosen mistress should be the wife of his teacher. He had loved no human being as he had loved Leonidas Allori; no other human being had he at any time whole-heartedly admired. He felt that he had been created by the hands of his master, as Adam by the hands of the Lord; from these same hands he was to accept his mate. The Duke of Alba, in Spain, who was a handsome and brilliant man, married a plain and simple-minded lady of the court and remained faithful to her, and when his friends, amazed at the fact, jestingly questioned him upon it, he answered them that the Duchess of Alba must needs, in her own right, and irrespective of personal qualities, be the most desirable woman in the world. So it was with the disloyal pupil. Once his strong amorous urge was joined with that great art which to him was the highest ideal of all—and was, moreover, coupled with a deep personal devotion—a fire was kindled, which later on he himself could not restrict.

Neither was Leonidas himself without blame in regard to the two young people. Day by day, in conversations with his favorite pupil, he had dwelt on Lucrezia's beauty. While making the young woman pose for his lovely and immortal Psyche with the Lamp he called upon Angelo to try, at his side in the studio, his hand at the same task, and did indeed interrupt his own work in order to point out the beauties in the living, breathing and blushing body before them, enraptured and inspired as in front of a classic work of art. Of this strange understanding between the old and the young artist neither of them was really conscious, and if a third person had spoken to them of it, they would have rebuffed him with indifference, perhaps with impatience. The one who suspected it was the woman, Lucrezia. And through it she suspected—at the same time with a kind of dismay and giddiness—the hardness and coldness which may be found in the hearts of men and artists, even with regard to the ones whom these hearts do embrace with deepest tenderness. Her own heart lamented, in complete loneliness, much as a lamb laments when led by its shepherd to the shamble.

As now, through various unusual occurrences in his daily life, Leonidas realized that he was being watched and followed, and as from this fact he concluded that he was in great danger, he was seized so deeply by the idea of his own death, and of the approaching end to his artistic career, that his whole being closed round it. He spoke no word of his danger to the people surrounding him, because these people, in the course of a few weeks, to him had become infinitely distant and thus, in accordance with the law of perspective, infinitely small. He might have wished to complete the work on which he was engaged, but soon his work, too, to him seemed an unreasonable and inconvenient distraction from the matter which really engrossed him. In the last days before his arrest, he stepped out of his isolation, unwontedly gentle and considerate toward all those around him. He now also sent Lucrezia away to the house of a friend, the owner of a vineyard, in the mountains a few miles from town. As, in order to give a reason for this arrangement—for he did not wish her to have any suspicion of the actual position—he explained to her that she looked pale and feverish, he himself believed that he was using a casual pretense to persuade her to leave him, and he smiled at the deep concern with which she received his command.

She at once sent word to Angelo and told him of her husband's decision. The lovers, who in anguish had been seeking an opportunity to meet and fulfill their love, looked each other in the eyes in triumphant certainty that now, and from now on, all powers of life were uniting to serve them, and that their passion was the loadstone which according to its will attracted and ranged everything around them. Lucrezia before now had visited the farm; she instructed Angelo as to how, by a certain path in the mountains, he could approach the house unseen, and come to her window. The window faced west, the moon would be in her first quarter, she would be able to discern the figure of her lover between the vines. When he picked up a pebble from the ground and threw it against the windowpane, she would open the window. As, in the course of their deliberation, they came to this moment, the voices of both faltered. To regain his equilibrium Angelo told her that for the nocturnal journey he had bought himself a large and fine cloak of violet goat's wool with brown embroidery, which a friend from the country, who was hard up for the moment, had offered him. All this they discussed in Lucrezia's room next to the studio where the master was working, and with the door to it open. The meeting, they decided, was to take place on the second Saturday evening.

They parted; and just as, all through the following week, the thought of death and eternity accompanied the master, the thought of Lucrezia's body against his own accompanied the young disciple. This thought, without having at any time really left him, constantly seemed to return to him anew like a forgotten, surprising, joyful message—"Open to me, my sister, my love, my dove, my undefiled: for my head is filled with dew, and my locks with the drops of the night. Thou art all fair, my love; there is no spot in thee. I am my beloved's, and my beloved is mine."

On Sunday morning Leonidas Allori was arrested and taken to prison. In the course of the week several interrogations of him followed, and possibly the old patriot might have justified himself in some of the accusations brought against him. But in the first place the government was resolved this time to make an end of such a dangerous enemy, and in the second place the accused himself was resolved not to upset, by any ups and downs, the sublime balance of mind he had attained. There was from the very beginning no real doubt as to the outcome of the case. Judgment was passed, and orders were given that next Sunday morning that most famous son of the people should be stood up against the prison wall, to fall against the cobbles with six bullets in his breast.

Toward the end of the week the old artist asked to be paroled for twelve hours in order to go to the place where his wife was staying, and to take leave of her.

His plea was refused. But such great strength had this man still in him, and with such an aura of radiance did his fame and his integrity of heart surround his person, that his words could not die quickly in the ears of those to whom they were addressed. The last request of the condemned man was brought up again and weighed by his judges, even after he himself had give up hope.

It so happened that the topic was raised in a house where Cardinal Salviati was present.

"No doubt," said His Eminence, "clemency here might set a dangerous precedent. But the country—and the royal house itself which possesses some of his works—is in debt to Allori. This man has often by his art restored men's faith in themselves—maybe men should now have faith in him."

He thought the matter over and continued: "It is said that the master—do they not call him the Lion of the Mountains? —is deeply loved by his pupils. We might find out if he has really been able to awaken a devotion which will defy death. We might, in his case, make use of the old rule which will allow a prisoner to leave his prison for a specified period, on the condition that he produce a hostage to die in his stead, if he does not return in time.

"Allori," said the Cardinal, "last summer did me the honor of executing the reliefs on my villa at Ascoli. He had with him there his beautiful young wife and a very handsome young disciple, Angelo by name, whom he called his son. We might let Leonidas know that he can obtain his freedom for a period of twelve hours, during which, as he wishes, he can take leave of his wife. But the condition will be that this young Angelo shall enter the prison cell as he himself leaves it, and that it will be made clear to both the old and the young artist that at the expiration of the twelve hours, at all events an execution will be carried out in the prison yard."

A feeling that in the circumstances it would be correct to decide on something unconventional made the powerful gentlemen with whom the matter rested accept the Cardinal's suggestion. The condemned man was informed that his request had been granted, and on which conditions. Leonidas sent word to Angelo.

The young artist was not in his room when his schoolfellows came to bring him the message and to fetch him to prison. Even though he had not paid any attention to the sorrow of his friends, it had nevertheless upset and distressed him, since at this moment he himself conceived the universe as perfect in beauty and harmony, and life in itself as boundless grace. He had kept apart from his fellows in a sort of antagonism, just as in respect and commiseration they had kept apart from him. He had traveled afoot the long way to the Duke of Miranda's villa to see a recently unearthed Greek statue of the god Dionysus. Still without really knowing it, he had wished and resolved to have a powerful work of art confirm his conviction of the divinity of the world.

His friends thus had to wait for him a long time in a small room high above the narrow street. When the chosen one finally entered, they pounced on him from all sides and informed him of the sad honor that awaited him.

So little had the master's favorite understood the nature and extent of the misfortune that had befallen himself and all of them, that the messengers had to repeat their tidings to him. When at last he comprehended, he stood petrified for a while, in the deepest grief. In the manner of a sleepwalker he inquired about the sentence and the execution, and his comrades, with tears in their eyes, gave him their answers. But when they came to the offer made to Leonidas, and the prisoner's request for Angelo, light returned to the young man's eyes and color to his cheeks. He asked his friends, indignantly, why they had not informed him at once—then without words he tore himself from their grasp to hasten to the prison.

But on the doorstep he stopped, seized by the solemnity of the moment. He had walked a long way and had slept on the grass, his clothes were covered with dust, and he had torn a rent in one sleeve. He did not wish to appear before his master like this today. He lifted his big new cloak from the hook on which it hung, and put it on.

The warders in the prison knew in advance of his coming.

He was led to the condemned man's cell, and let in. He threw himself into his master's arms.

Leonidas Allori calmed him. To make the young man forget the present, he turned the conversation round to the stellar heavens, of which he had often talked with his son, and in the knowledge of which he had instructed him. Soon his great gaze and deep, clear voice lifted his pupil up there with him, as if the two of them, hand in hand, had slipped back many years, and were now speaking together all by themselves in a lofty, carefree world. Only when the teacher had seen the tears dry on the pale young face did he return to the ground, and he asked his pupil if he was indeed prepared to spend, in his place, the night in the prison. Angelo replied that he knew he was.

"I thank you, my son," said Leonidas, "for giving me twelve hours which will be of boundless importance to me.

"Aye, I believe in the immortality of the soul," he continued, "and perhaps the eternal life of the spirit is the one true reality. I do not know yet, but I shall know tomorrow. But this physical world around us, these four elements— earth, water, air and fire—are these not realities as well? And is not also my own body—my marrow-filled bones, my flowing, never-pausing blood, and my five glorious senses—divinely true? Others think that I am old. But I am a peasant and of peasant stock, and our soil to us has been a stern, bountiful nurse. My muscles and sinews are but firmer and harder than when I was a youth, my hair is as luxurious as it was then, my sight is not in the least impaired. All these my faculties I shall now leave here behind me, for as my spirit goes forth on new paths, the earth —my own well-loved Campania—will take my honest body in her honest arms and will make it one with herself. But I wish to meet Nature face to face once more, and to hand it over to her in full consciousness, as in a gentle and solemn conversation between friends. Tomorrow I shall look to the future, I shall collect myself and prepare myself for the unknown. But tonight I shall go out, free in a free world, among things familiar to me. I shall observe the rich play of light of the sunset, and after that the moon's divine clarity, and the ancient constellations of the stars round her. I shall hear the song of running water and taste its freshness, breathe the sweetness and bitterness of trees and grass in the darkness and feel the soil and the stones under the soles of my feet. What a night awaits me! All gifts given to me I shall gather together into my embrace, to give them back again in profound understanding, and with thanks."

"Father," said Angelo, "the earth, the water, the air and the fire must needs love you, the one in whom none of their gifts have been wasted."

"I believe that myself, son," said Leonidas. "Always, from the time when I was a child in my home in the country, have I believed that God loved me.

"I cannot explain to you—for the time is now but short— how, or by what path, I have come to understand in full God's infinite faithfulness toward me. Or how I have come to realize the fact that faithfulness is the supreme divine factor by which the universe is governed. I know that in my heart I have always been faithful to this earth and to this life. I have pleaded for liberty tonight in order to let them know that our parting itself is a pact.

"Then tomorrow I shall be able to fulfill my pact with great Death and with things to come." He spoke slowly, and now stopped and smiled. "Forgive my talking so much," he said. "For a week I have not talked to a person whom I loved."

But when he spoke again his voice and mien were deeply serious.

"And you, my son," he said, "you, whom I thank for your faithfulness throughout our long happy years—and tonight —be you also always faithful to me. I have thought of you in these days, between these walls. I have frevently wished to see you once again, not for my own sake, but in order to tell you something. Yes, I had got much to say to you, but I must be brief. Only this, then, I enjoin and implore you: keep always in your heart the divine law of proportion, the golden section."

"Gladly, gladly do I remain here tonight," said Angelo. "But even more gladly would I tonight go with you, such as, many nights, we have wandered together."

Leonidas smiled again. "My road tonight," he said, "under the stars, by the grass-grown, dewy mountain paths, takes me to one thing, and to one alone. I will be, for one last night, with my wife, with Lucrezia. I tell you, Angelo, that in order that man—His chief work, into the nostrils of whom He had breathed the breath of life—might embrace and become one with the earth, the sea, the air and the fire, God gave him woman. In Lucrezia's arms I shall be sealing, in the night of leave-taking, my pact with all these." He was silent for a few moments, and motionless.

"Lucrezia," he then said, "is a few miles from here, in the care of good friends. I have, through them, made sure that she has learned nothing of my imprisonment or my sentence. I do not wish to expose my friends to danger, and they shall not know, tonight, that I come to their house. Neither do I wish to come to her as a man condemned to death, with the breath of the grave on me, but our meeting shall be like our first night together, and its secrecy to her shall mean a young man's fancy and a young lover's folly."

"What day is it today?" Angelo suddenly asked.

"What day?" Leonidas repeated. "Do you ask that of me—me who have been living in eternity, not in time? To me this day is called: the last day. But stay, let me think. Why, my child, to you, and to the people around you, today is named Saturday. Tomorrow is Sunday.

"I know the road well," he said a short while later, thoughtfully, as if he were already on his journey. "By a mountain path I approach her window from behind the farm. I shall pick up a pebble and throw it against the windowpane. Then she will awake and wonder, she will go to her window, discern me amongst the vines, and open it."

His mighty chest moved as he drew his breath.

"Oh, my child and my friend," he exclaimed, "you know this woman's beauty. You have dwelt in our house and have eaten at our table, you know, too, the gentleness and gaiety of her mind, its childlike tranquillity and its inconceivable innocence. But what you do not know, what nobody knows in the whole world but I, is the infinite capacity of her body and soul for surrender. How that snow can burn! She has been to me all glorious works of art of the world, all of them in one single woman's body. Within her embrace at night my strength to create in the daytime was restored. As I speak to you of her, my blood lifts like a wave." After some seconds he closed his eyes. "When I come back here tomorrow," he said, "I shall come with my eyes closed. They will lead me in here from the gate, and later, at the wall, they will bind a cloth before my eyes. I shall have no need of these eyes of mine. And it shall not be the black stones, nor the gun barrels, that I shall leave behind in these my dear, clear eyes when I quit them." Again he was silent for a while, then said in a soft voice: "At times, this week, I have not been able to recall the line of her jaw from ear to chin. At daybreak tomorrow morning I shall look upon it, so that I shall never again forget it."

When again he opened his eyes, his radiant gaze met the gaze of the young man. "Do not look at me in such pain and dread," he said, "and do not pity me. I do not deserve that of you. Nor—you will know it—am I to be pitied tonight. My son, I was wrong: tomorrow, as I come back, I shall open my eyes once more in order to see your face, which has been so dear to me. Let me see it happy and at peace, as when we were working together."

The prison warder now turned the heavy key in the lock and came in. He informed the prisoners that the clock in the prison tower showed a quarter to six. Within a quarter of an hour one of the two must leave the building. Allori answered that he was ready, but he hesitated a moment.

"They arrested me," he said to Angelo, "in my studio and in my working smock. But the air may grow colder as I get into the mountains. Will you lend me your cloak?"

Angelo removed the violet cloak from his shoulders and handed it to his teacher. As he fumbled at his throat with the hook, with which he was unfamiliar, the master took the young hand that helped him, and held it.

"How grand you are, Angelo," he said. "This cloak of yours is new and costly. In my native parish a bridegroom wears a cloak like this on his wedding day.

"Do you remember," he added as he stood ready to go, in the cloak, "one night, when together we lost our way in the mountains? Suddenly you collapsed, exhausted and cold as ice, and whispered that it was impossible for you to go any farther. I took off my cloak then—just as you did now—and wrapped it around us both. We lay the whole night together in each other's arms, and in my cloak you fell asleep almost immediately, like a child. You are to sleep tonight too."

Angelo collected his thoughts, and remembered the night of which the master was speaking. Leonidas had always been a far more experienced mountaineer than he himself, as altogether his strength had always exceeded his own. He recalled the warmth of that big body, like that of a big friendly animal in the dark, against his own numb limbs. He remembered, further, that as he woke up the sun had risen, and all mountain slopes had become luminous in its rays. He had sat up, then, and had cried out, "Father, this night you have saved my life." From his breast came a groan, wordless.

"We will not take leave tonight," said Leonidas, "but tomorrow morning I shall kiss you."

The jailer opened the door and held it open, while the towering, straight figure stepped over the threshold. Then the door was once more shut, the key turned in the lock, and Angelo was alone.

Within the first seconds he felt the fact that the door was locked, and that nobody could come in to him, as an incomparable favor. But immediately after, he fell to the floor, like a man struck by, and crushed beneath, a falling rock.

In his ears echoed the voice of the master. And before his eyes stood the figure of the master, illuminated by the radiance of a higher world, of Art's infinite universe. From this world of light, which his father had once opened to him, he was now cast down into darkness. After the one whom he had betrayed had gone from him, he was completely alone. He dared not think of the stellar heavens, nor of the earth, nor of the sea, nor of the rivers, nor of the marble statues that he had loved. If at this moment Leonidas Allori himself had wanted to save him, it would not have been possible. For to be unfaithful is to be annihilated.

The word "unfaithful" was now flung on him from all angles, like a shower of flints on the man who is being stoned, and he met it on his knees, with hanging arms, like a man stoned. But when at last the shower slackened, and after a silence the words "the golden section" rose and echoed, subdued and significant, he raised his hands and pressed them against his ears.

And unfaithful, he thought after a time, *for the sake of a woman. What is a woman? She does not exist until we create her, and she has no life except through us. She is nothing but body, but she is not body, even, if we do not look at her. She claims to be brought to life, and requires our soul as a mirror, in which she can see that she is beautiful. Men must burn, tremble and perish, in order that she may know that she exists and is beautiful. When we weep, she weeps, too, but with happiness—for now she has proof that she is beautiful. Our anguish must be kept alive every hour, or she is no longer alive.*

All my creative power, his thoughts went on, *if things had gone as she wished, would have been used up in the task of creating her, and of keeping her alive. Never, never again would I have produced a great work of art. And when I grieved over my misfortune, she would not understand, but would declare, "Why, but you have me!" While with him—with him, I was a great artist!*

Yet he was not really thinking of Lucrezia, for to him there was in the world no other human being than the father whom he had betrayed.

Did I ever believe, Angelo thought, *that I was, or that I might become, a great artist, a creator of glorious statues? I am no artist, and I shall never create a glorious statue. For I know now that my eyes are gone—I am blind!*

After a further lapse of time his thoughts slowly turned away from eternity and back to the present.

His master, he thought, would walk up the path and stop near the house, among the vines. He would pick up a pebble from the ground and throw it against the windowpane, and then she would open the window. She would call to the man in the violet cloak, such as she was wont to do at their meetings, "Angelo!" And the great master, the unfailing friend, the immortal man, the man sentenced to death, would understand that his disciple had betrayed him.

During the previous day and night Angelo had walked far and slept but little, and the whole of the last day he had not eaten. He now felt that he was tired unto death. His master's command: "You are to sleep tonight," came back to him. Leonidas' commands, when he had obeyed them, had always led him right. He slowly rose to his feet and fumbled his way to the pallet where his master had lain. He fell asleep almost immediately.

But as he slept, he dreamed.

He saw once more, and more clearly than before, the big figure in the cloak walk up the mountain path, stop and bend down for the pebble and throw it against the pane. But in the dream he followed him farther, and he saw the woman in the man's arms—Lucrezia! And he awoke.

He sat up on the bed. Nothing sublime or sacred was any

longer to be found in the world, but the deadly pain of physsical jealousy stopped his breath and ran through him like fire. Gone was the disciple's reverence for his master, the great artist; in the darkness the son ground his teeth at his father. The past had vanished, there was no future to come, all the young man's thoughts ran to one single point—the embrace there, a few miles away.

He came to a sort of consciousness, and resolved not to fall asleep again.

But he did fall asleep again, and dreamed the same, but now more vividly and with a multitude of details, which he himself disowned, which his imagination could only have engendered when in his sleep he no longer had control of it.

As after this dream he was once more wide awake, a cold sweat broke out over his limbs. From the pallet he noticed some glowing embers on the fireplace; he now got up, set his naked foot upon them and kept it there. But the embers were almost dead, and went out under his foot.

In the next dream he himself, silent and lurking, followed the wanderer on the mountain path and through the window. He had his knife in his hand, he leaped forward, and plunged it first in the man's heart, then in hers, as they lay clasped in one another's arms. But the sight of their blood, mingled, soaking into the sheet, like a red-hot iron, burned out his eyes. Half awake, once more sitting up, he thought, *But I do not need to use the knife. I can strangle them with my hands.*

Thus passed the night.

When the turnkey of the prison awakened him, it was light. "So you can sleep?" said the turnkey. "So you really trust the old fox? If you ask me, I should say he has played you a fine trick. The clock shows a quarter to six. When it strikes, the warden and the colonel will come in, and take whichever bird they find in the cage. The priest is coming later. But your old lion is never coming. Honestly—would you or I come, if we were in his shoes?"

When Angelo succeeded in understanding the words of the turnkey, his heart filled with indescribable joy. There was nothing more to fear. God had granted him this way out: death. This happy, easy way out. Vaguely, through his aching head one thought ran: *And it is for him that I die.* But the thought sank away again, for he was not really thinking of Leonidas Allori, or of any person in the world round him. He felt only one thing: that he himself, within the last moment, had been pardoned.

He got up, washed his face in a basin of water brought by his guard, and combed his hair back. He now felt the pain of the burn in his foot and again was filled with gratitude. Now he also remembered the master's words about God's faithfulness.

The turnkey looked at him and said, "I took you for a young man yesterday."

After some time footsteps could be heard up the stone-paved passage, and a faint rattling. Angelo thought, *Those are the soldiers with their carbines.* The heavy door swung open, and between two gendarmes, who held his arms, entered Allori. In accordance with his words the evening before, he let himself be led forward with closed eyes by the warders. But he felt or perceived where Angelo was standing and took a step toward him. He stood silent before him, unhooked his cloak, lifted it from his own shoulders and laid it around the young man's. In this movement the two were brought close, body to body, and Angelo said to himself, *Perhaps, after all, he will not open his eyes and look at me.* But whenever had Allori not kept a given word? The hand which—as it put the cloak round him—rested against Angelo's neck forced his head a little forward, the large eyelids trembled and lifted, and the master looked into the eyes of the disciple. But the disciple could never afterward remember or recall the look. A moment later he felt Allori's lips on his cheek.

"Well, now!" cried the turnkey with surprise in his voice.

"Welcome back! We were not expecting you. Now you must take potluck! And you," he added, turning to Angelo, "you can go your way. There are still a few minutes to six o'clock. My lords are not coming till after it has struck. The priest is coming later. Things are done with precision here. And fair —as you know—is fair."

NIGHT WALK

*A*fter Leonidas Allori's death a sad misfortune came upon his disciple Angelo Santasilia: he could not sleep.

Will the narrator be believed by such people as have themselves experience of sleeplessness, when he tells them that from the beginning this affliction was the victim's own choice? Yet it was so. Angelo walked out through the prison gate, behind which he had for twelve hours been hostage for his condemned master, into a world which to him contained no direction whatsoever. He was totally isolated, an absolutely lonely figure in this world, and he felt that the man whose grief and shame—like his own—exceeded that of all others must at the same time be exempt from the laws which governed those others. He made up his mind not to sleep any more.

On this day he had no feeling of time, and he took fright when he realized that darkness had fallen, and the day was over. He was aware that his friends, other pupils of the dead artist, were tonight keeping watch together, but on no account would he join them, for they would be talking of Leonidas Allori and would greet him as the chosen disciple, upon whom the eye of the master had last dwelt. *Yes*, he thought, and laughed, *as if I were Elisha, the follower of the great prophet Elijah, on whom the passenger of the chariot of fire threw his mantle!* So he betook himself to the taverns and inns of the town, where casually collected people roared and rioted and where the air was filled with strumming and song, and was heavy with vapors of wine and the smell of the clothes and sweat of strangers. But he would not drink like the others. He left one inn to proceed to another, and both in the taprooms and in the streets he told himself, *All this does not concern me. I myself will not sleep any more.*

In such a tavern, on the night between Monday and Tuesday, he met Giuseppino, or Pino, Pizzuti, the philosopher, a small man shrunken and dark of hue as if he had been hung up in a chimney to be smoked. Pizzuti had once, many years ago, owned the noblest marionette theater in Naples, but later on his luck had left him. In prison, and in chains, three fingers of his right hand had withered, so that he could no longer maneuver his puppets. He now wandered from place to place, the poorest of the poor, but luminous, as if phosphorescent, with love of humanity in general and with a knowing and mellifluous compassion for the one human being with whom he just happend to be talking. In this man's company Angelo passed the next day and night, and while he looked at him and listened to him he had no difficulty in keeping awake.

The philosopher at once realized that he had a desperate man before him. To give the boy confidence he for a time spoke about himself. He described his puppets one by one, faithfully and with enthusiasm, as if they had been real friends and fellow artists, and with tears in his eyes, because they were now lost to him. "Alas, the beloved ones," he moaned, "they were devoted to me and they trusted me. But they are dispersed now, limp of arms and legs, with moldering strings; they are thrown away from the stage to the uttermost parts of the sea. For my hand could no longer lead them, nor my right hand hold them!" But presently —as ever in the vicissitudes of his existence—he turned his mind toward life everlasting. "That is not a matter for grief," he said. "In Paradise I shall once more meet and embrace them all. In Paradise I shall be given ten fingers to each hand."

Later on, after midnight, Pino led the conversation to Angelo's own circumstances, felt his way in them, and soon had them all at his seven fingers' ends.

In this way it happened that next night Angelo told him his whole story, as he would not have been able to tell it to any person in the world other than this crippled vagabond. At that the old man's face lit up in high, solemn harmony. "That is not a matter for grief," he said. "It is a good thing to be a great sinner. Or should human beings allow Christ to have died on the Cross for the sake of our petty lies and our paltry whorings? We would have to fear that the Saviour might even come to think with disgust of His heroic achievement! For exactly this reason, as you will know, in the very hour of the Cross, care was taken that He had thieves by Him, one to each side, and could turn His eyes from the one to the other. At this moment He may look from you to me, and mightily recognize and repeat to Himself, 'Aye, verily it was needed!' "

After a while Pino added, "And I myself am the crucified thief Demas, to whom Paradise was promised."

But early on Thursday morning Pizzuti quite suddenly vanished, like a rat into a gutter hole. He left the room on a necessary errand and did not return, and not till seven years later did Angelo again see this excellent man. And as the silence behind him grew deep and, as it were, conclusive, the outcast man realized that he no longer needed to hold on to a decision. It would not happen to him again to fall asleep.

For some time he walked among people, still absolutely lonely, like an unproved but ambitious young ascetic with a hair shirt next to his skin. So as not to meet his friends of the past he changed his lodgings, and found for himself a small closet high up under the roof in the opposite quarter of the town. During the first time he was surprised at the fact that his sleepless nights did not appear long, but that time simply seemed to have been abolished—night came, and then again morning, and to him it meant nothing.

But, just as unexpectedly, his body rose in rebellion against his mind and his will. The moment came in which he gave up his pride and prayed the great powers of the universe: "Despise me, cast me away, but allow me to be like the others, allow me to sleep."

He now bought himself opium, but it did not help him. He also purchased another strong sleeping draught, but it only conveyed to him a row of novel, quite confused sensations of distance, so that objects and times which were far away were felt by him as quite near, while such objects as he knew to be within reach—his own hands and feet and the stone steps of the stairs—were infinitely far off.

His brain by this time was working extremely slowly. One day in the street he saw Lucrezia, who had returned to the town and was living with her mother. But only late at night, when the church towers had rung out midnight, did he tell himself, *I saw a woman in the street today, it was Lucrezia.* And after another while, *I once promised to come to her. But I did not come.* For a long time he sat very still, handling this thought, and at last he smiled, like a very old man.

It was shortly after this day that he began to turn to other people and to look to them for help. But when he begged their advice, he was in such deadly earnest that he made the persons he addressed smile, and they answered him in jest or altogether dismissed his questions.

One morning he bethought himself of Mariana, the old woman in whose tavern he had met Pizzuti. She had, he knew, given friends of his good advice—it was not impossible that she might be able to help him. But the lack of seriousness in his counselors till now had frightened him out of asking straightaway, and he searched for a pretext for going to her house, until he remembered that he had left there his purple cloak with the brown embroidery. At that he went straight to her house.

Old Mariana looked at him for a while. "Well, well, Angelo, pretty death's-head," she said. "We Christian people should bear one another no grudge, and I forgive you, today, that you did reject my fond love, and kept thinking of another woman, when I wanted you. I shall help you. Now listen well, and afterwards do exactly as I tell you. Walk from the broadest street of the town into a narrower one, and from this narrow street into one still narrower, and go on like that. If from your narrowest alley you can find your way into a tighter passage, enter it, and follow it, and draw your breath lightly once or twice. And at that you will have fallen asleep."

Angelo thanked Mariana for her advice, and pushed it down to the bottom of his mind. Only when it was quite dark did he make up his mind to test it.

His own room was in an out-of-the-way alley. He had to proceed into the broadest and best lighted of the boulevards. For a long time he had not been in this part of the town, and he was surprised to see how many people there were in the world. They walked faster than he, they were intent on their errands, and as far as he could judge an equal number were walking in each direction.

How, he asked himself, *has it become necessary for all people who live east of the boulevard to come west, as well as to all who live west to come east? It might make one feel that the world was badly managed. The whole city of Naples is now set up as a big loom, men and women are the shuttles to it, and the weaver is busy tonight. Yet this great pattern,* he reflected as he walked on, *is no concern of mine—others will have to look after it. I myself will keep my thoughts carefully collected on what I have got to do.*

At this he turned from the Via di Toledo into a smaller street, and from that into one still narrower. *It is not impossible,* he thought, hope strangely dawning in his heart, *that this time I have been well advised.*

After a while he found himself in a lane so narrow that, looking up, he saw above him only a handbreadth of evening sky a little lighter than the eaves. The paving was here very rough, and there were no lamps; he had to place his hand on the wall of a house to walk on. The contact with solid matter did him good; he felt grateful toward this wall. It suddenly vanished under his palm. There was a doorway here, and the door was open. It gave into an exceedingly narrow passage. *I am in luck tonight,* he thought, *I am lucky to have come upon such an exceedingly narrow passage.* He proceeded until he came to a small door. Underneath this door a faint light shone.

Now for a while he stood perfectly still. In there sleep awaited him, and with the certitude of sleep memory came back to him. He felt, in the dark, his hard, drawn face smoothening, his eyelids lowering a little like the eyelids of a happy, sleeping person. This moment was a return and a beginning. He stretched out his hand, took care to draw his breath lightly twice, and opened the door.

By a table in a little, faintly lit room a red-haired man was counting his money.

The sudden entrance of a stranger did not seem to surprise the host of the room, he looked up casually and then sank back into his former occupation. But his guest felt the moment to be formidable.

The man by the table was ugly, and had nothing kind

about him. Yet in the fact that even while counting his money he left his door unlocked, to be entered by a stranger, there was a kind of friendliness which might hold great possibilities. *But what am I to say to him?* Angelo thought.

After a while he said, "I cannot sleep."

The red-haired man waited a moment, then he looked up. "I never sleep," he declared with extreme arrogance.

After this short interruption he resumed his work. He carefully arranged his coins in piles of two, scattered them with his big hands and re-collected them in piles of five—to scatter these once more, and build up, absorbed in the task, new piles of six, of ten and fifteen, and at last of three. In the end he stopped, and without taking his hands off the silver leaned back in the chair. He gazed straight before him and repeated, with deep scorn, "I never sleep.

"Only dolts and drudges sleep," he took up his theme after a while. "Fishermen, peasants and artisans must have their hours of snoring at any cost. Their heavy natures cry out for sleep even in the greatest hour of life. Drowsiness settles on their eyelids. Divine agony sweats blood at a stone's throw, but they cannot keep awake, and the whizzing of an angel's wings will not wake them up. Those living dead will never know what happened, or what was said, while they themselves lay huddled and gaping. I alone know. For I never sleep."

Suddenly he turned in his chair toward his guest. "He said so Himself," he remarked, "and had He not been so hard driven, with what high disdain would He not have spoken! Now it was a moan, like the sea breaking against the shore for the very last time before doomsday. He Himself told them so, the fools: 'What, could ye not watch with me one hour?'"

For a minute he looked Angelo straight in the face.

"But no one," he concluded slowly, in indescribable pride, "no one in the world could ever seriously believe that I myself did sleep—on that Thursday night in the garden."

OF HIDDEN THOUGHTS AND OF HEAVEN

It was a lovely spring day, and the almond trees were blossoming, delicately pink and coral like flamingo feathers, down the slope in front of the white villa. From the terrace at the top there was a wide view over the landscape, and all shapes and colors within it—the far-off, air-blue mountains, the greenish-gray olive groves on the nearer slopes; the serpentine, dust-gray road through the valley below; the free, fleeting groups of big clouds; and the noble, mathematically straight, darker blue line of the sea on the horizon—in the cool of the evening were as beautifully harmonious as if an angel had stood behind the shoulder of the observer and poured out it all from his flute.

Angelo Santasilia, the famous sculptor who owned the villa, was sitting on the terrace, shaping tiny figures in clay.

His long workday was over, and he was satisfied with his work. But his three children—two fair-limbed little boys and a little girl with a skin as transparent as an almond blossom and big, childishly unfathomable dark eyes—before consenting to go to bed had demanded that these three equestrian statues should be ready by the next morning. No one horseman was to be superior to another, yet they all were to be so different that each of the children could immediately pick out its own from among them. The task had gripped the artist's imagination, so that he was now deeply engrossed in it. His wife, Lucrezia, wrapped in a crimson shawl, sat a little behind him, and smiled at her husband's gravity.

A nightingale sang in a distant thicket, and all of a sudden another struck up, enraptured, quite close by.

Angelo was still in his working smock. His great beauty since we last saw him had become richer, almost blooming like that of a woman.

A small man came from the house down toward husband and wife. He did not carry his hat in his hand, for he had no hat, but his attitude was as dignified and deferential as if he had been sweeping the ground with the panache of one. Lucrezia first caught sight of him, and drew her husband's attention to him—but Angelo, who was just about to shape a rearing horse, did not want to be interrupted. Still when he turned his head, and recognized in the approaching figure the wanderer, Giuseppino Pizzuti, a friend of old times, he waved his hand to him.

Giuseppino greeted his host as if their parting had taken place that very morning. All the same, the years had not passed over him without leaving their mark. He was even leaner than before and more poorly dressed. His eyebrows were raised high on his forehead, as if a permanent deep amazement had placed them there. He seemed to be without weight, like a withered, rolled-up leaf.

At first he seemed quite unaffected by the changed circumstances of his old companion in misfortune; indeed, he hardly seemed to notice them at all. But when he was introduced to Lucrezia and saw what a lovely wife Angelo had, he was so deeply impressed that he styled him "Signor Santasilia" and "Maestro."

"Nay," Angelo interrupted him, "speak not so. I am no fine gentleman and no master. Do you remember where we last spoke together?"

"Yes," Pizzuti answered after some deliberation, "it was at the inn of Mariana-the-Rat, the good home of thieves and smugglers, down by the harbor."

"Aye, and let us talk together as we did there," said Angelo.

Lucrezia after a while noticed that her husband's guest had three fingers missing on his right hand, and turned her face away. She was expecting her fourth child, and feared any impression of ugliness which might put its stamp upon the unborn baby. She therefore rose as quickly as with courtesy she could, remarked that the wanderer must be in need of something to eat and drink, and walked back to the villa to prepare something. The two men followed her with their eyes until she disappeared through the door.

"And how, Pino," asked the host, "have you been doing since I saw you last?"

The old man began to tell his story. He had traveled far and wide, had seen famous places and people and witnessed remarkable natural phenomena. He had also consoled the distressed and set on the right path those who had strayed from it. Suddenly he gave himself up to tears.

"Why do you weep, Pino?" asked Angelo.

"Oh, my friend, weep with me," Pino answered. "I have loved since last we met."

"Loved?" Angelo repeated, slowly and with astonishment, as if he were repeating a word of a foreign tongue.

"Oh, loved, loved!" cried Pino. "Life's sorest pain has

penetrated and torn asunder even this heart of mine. A woman, radiant, triumphant like a song, smiled upon me—and went away again!"

"Life's sorest pain?" Angelo repeated as before.

"She was a great lady traveling from England," said Pino. "Three years ago, in Venice, as she got into her gondola, she gave me such a deep, friendly, animated glance, such a goddess glance, that thereby heaven came down and walked on earth! I followed her, we met again, and each time her eyes gave me the same greeting out of her soul's inexhaustible riches. Once she spoke to me. She was tall like a statue, she wore a silk robe that rustled gently, her hair was like red-golden silk!"

Pizzuti raised his right hand to the sky. "But I," he cried out, "I lack these my three fingers, and will nevermore make my puppets dance! When she had gone away, the world was a void—and yet how full of pain! I had just one thing left to me in my infinite destitution: to talk with somebody who might possibly, just once in the course of the day, speak her name. I remained in Venice for two years, solely to sit with her gondolier, a plebeian who could neither sing nor play, hoping for this: that he would pronounce her name, as if waiting for sweet music to come from his lips. But he married, and his wife forbade me her house. O Angelo Santasilia—all life that I have in me consumes itself!"

Pino let his head fall onto his breast; tears poured down his face onto his greasy black cloak.

"You must not let that worry you," said Angelo. "It is a good thing to have a great sorrow. Or should human beings allow Christ to have died on the cross for the sake of our toothaches?"

After a while he continued: "Tell me her name, Pino. Then you will stay on in my house, and I will speak it once a day."

Pino closed his eyes, made two attempts to speak, but remained silent. He whispered, "I cannot."

Lucrezia's red-cheeked maid came from the house, smiling, with a tray containing wine, cheese and bread, and a cold chicken. Angelo poured out wine to his friend and to himself. The old wanderer was obviously hungry, yet he ate and drank slowly, as now he did everything.

"And you, Angelo," he said, "how have things gone with you?"

It was now Angelo's turn to report on his life in the seven years that had gone. He told Pino of the works he had completed since they had seen each other, and of the large orders he received from princes and cardinals, of the pupils who flocked to his school and of his children. When he stopped, Pino's gaze met his, and for some time they sat thus in silence. It seemed strange to Angelo to be sitting again with Pizzuti.

"Yes, you see, Pino," he at length said slowly. "All this—art, a lovely wife, beautiful children, renown, friends, wealth—all this will constitute a man's happiness, my happy life. But you know that there be rivers which at one place in their course disappear into the ground and run beneath it for a couple of miles. Woods and rose gardens grow in this ground, but beneath them runs the river. In that same way a river is running beneath my happiness, and only to you can I speak of it. That river is the secret which Lucrezia bears and keeps from me. For I do not know what happened on the night when I was hostage for Leonidas Allori in prison.

"She has never spoken of it. Many times I have waited for a word from her lips which would solve the riddle. On our wedding night I waited for it—and the river ran deep below our bridal bed. One day when we walked together along the seashore, and there was an offshore wind, and she gazed at me, I waited for it. But she has never spoken, her full sweet lips have always been sealed over the secret. While I was still young, I felt that I might have to kill her if she continued to keep silent.

"But I have reflected," he went on, "that I have no claims

on her. For the entire being of a woman is a secret, which should be kept. And one more deep secret to her becomes part of it, one charm more, a hidden treasure. It is said that the tree under which a murderer buries his victim will die, but the apple tree under which a girl buries her murdered child does blossom more richly and does give more perfect fruit than others—the tree transforms the hidden crime into white and rosy, and into delicious flavor. I must not expect her to part with this secret either."

He gazed out over the valley.

"And I have further thought," he said, "that in the moment when at last I should be asking Lucrezia, 'Tell me, for I suffer, what happened that night that Leonidas Allori came to you, in the house of the vintager, in the mountains? Did the master learn, then, that you and I had betrayed him?' she would turn her face toward me, her clear eyes dark with sorrow, and answer me: 'So you have known that your master went to the vintager's house in the mountains, and you have never told me that you knew! For seven years, day and night, you have hidden your knowledge from me, and even my kisses have not been able to make you speak!' Maybe, after that, she would leave me forever. Or again, maybe she would still stay with me for the sake of the children, and because my great fame gives her pleasure. But she would never again be my happy, smiling wife.

"And I have come to understand that she would be in the right. For in the mind and nature of a man a secret is an ugly thing, like a hidden physical defect. And thus," he finished, "the river runs beneath my life."

Pino remained silent for a while, glanced at his friend and then gazed at the mountains. "And how goes it?" he asked. "Can you sleep now?"

"Sleep?" Angelo repeated, as before, as if from its sound he was repeating a word from another language, "Aye, do you remember when I could not sleep? Yes, thanks, now I can sleep."

Again there was a silence.

"No," Pino said suddenly, "you are mistaken, and things are not as you imagine. I happen to know. A person who—because of you—did have this matter at heart, might—for your sake—ask Lucrezia, 'What happened the night your lover pledged his life for your husband? Did the great artist then get to know that you two, whom he had held dearest of all, and whose hearts and fates he had directed as by strings on his fingers, had betrayed him? Did the blow then break his great heart? Or did he stand up to it, even if staggering, trusting to the law of the golden section?' She would then look up at the inquirer, her eyes so clear that he would be ashamed to doubt even for a moment the truth of her words, and answer him, 'I am very sorry that I cannot tell you. But I do not remember. I have forgotten.' "

"Do you mean to tell me," Angelo asked in a low voice, "that you have asked her?"

"I have seen your wife for the first time today," answered Pino. "But you forget that I have once written marionette plays. I had then a lovely puppet, the *jeune première* of my theater, with rosy cheeks and white bosom, and with eyes of clear dark glass, who resembled Lucrezia."

When after a pause the old man again looked at Angelo, he noticed that he was smiling a little. "What are you thinking of, Angelo?" he asked.

"I was thinking of those small instruments that we call words, and by which we have to manage in this life of ours. I was thinking of how, by interchanging two everyday words in an everyday sentence, we alter our world. For when you had spoken, I first thought, 'Is that possible?'—then secondly, after a moment, 'That is possible.' "

They now for some time talked of other things, and to give Giuseppino pleasure, Angelo made him tell of his marionette theater. But from time to time the smile left the face of the old theater director, and he sank back into melancholy.

"But listen now, Pino," said his friend. "Today your

heaven is seven years nearer to you than when we last met. There you will see again both your puppets and your milady. For I take it that you are still Demas, the thief on the cross who had Paradise promised him?"

"Well, Angelo," said Pizzuti, scratching his head with his two fingers, "there you bring up something to which I have been giving a good deal of thought. I certainly still do believe that I am that great sinner to whom hope was given. But how, now, did things really go with this thief on the cross?

" 'This day shalt thou be with me in Paradise,' the Saviour said to him. But when on the evening of Good Friday Demas presented himself at the gate of Paradise, Christ was not there, and as you know, forty days passed before He came home in all His splendor. Very likely the young King of Heaven, in those days of great events, gave not much thought to an invitation. But I myself—better than most people—will know with what confusion and anxiety the poorly dressed guest did approach the gate.

"And I have pondered," Pino went on, "who will really have been present behind the gate at which Demas was staring, with the authority to let a thief into Paradise? The Rock of the Church, the great Fisherman Peter, at this dark hour crouched at the back of the high priest's house, farther away from Paradise than ever before or after. Saint Mary Magdalene, whom Demas knew from Jerusalem, was sobbing into her long hair and had not yet made up her mind to go to the grave. Those friendly saints with whom we are now familiar—Francis, Anthony and sweet Catherine—came upon the heavenly stage only many centuries later. The gentle Blessed Virgin, had she by that time been Queen of Heaven, would have understood all that was going on in Demas' heart, and so would have come to the gate herself, with her crown on and her retinue of angels—but even her strong heart could not hold or bear any more on that Friday night. Yet after a long time, I have imagined, the little children whom King Herod had had put to death in Bethlehem came running along to throng around the newcomer. No doubt they laughed at the sorry figure collapsed in a small heap over his sundered bones, perhaps they did even point their little fingers at him, as children will do at a ragged cripple. But in the end two of them ran in to fetch Saint Anne, Christ's blessed grandmother. And as this worthy woman now appeared at the gate and spoke to him, Demas suddenly realized how everything is explained and made clear to the blessed in heaven, for even after the happenings of Good Friday, she was mild and bright as a lighted candle.

"I have now imagined the following conversation to take place between the two of them.

" 'Come in,' the lady says, 'come in, my good man, you are expected. But my grandson has been delayed, for He has found it necessary to descend into hell.'

" 'O Lady,' Demas answers, much ashamed, 'there will have been some mistake, just as I expected, and it is down there that I am to see Him once more. May I make so bold as to ask the way, for I want nothing better than to be where He is.'

" 'Certainly not,' said Saint Anne. 'You must do as you are told. And I myself very much want to speak with one who has seen Him so recently.'

" 'O Lady,' says Demas again, 'how can one such as I discourse with you on that which no man on earth can describe?'

" 'I know, I know,' says the holy grandmother. 'Who would know better than I? My good man, you did not see Him when He first learned to walk. I myself held one of His little hands, and His mother held the other—never have I seen a child so like his mother! No, it is as you say—it is indescribable!'

"And led by Lady Saint Anne's hand—that same hand of which she had spoken—Demas stepped across the threshold of Paradise."

Angelo laughed at his friend's story.

"Aye, if I had still got my theater," said Pizzuti, carried away by his own eloquence, "I should have played this scene on the stage. Might it not have been sublime and thrilling, dear Angelo? Now it must content itself to become reality someday.

"And you yourself now," he said after a minute. "Are you going to Paradise? And shall we meet and talk together there, as we do here now?"

Angelo for a long time found no answer. He took up one of his small clay figures and set it on the balustrade, a little to the left.

"A man is more than one man," he said slowly. "And the life of a man is more than one life. The young man who was Leonidas Allori's chosen disciple, who felt that at his hand he would become the greatest artist of his age, and who loved his master's wife—he will not go to heaven. He was too light of weight to mount so high."

He set up another figure on the balustrade, at some distance from the first and to the right of it.

"And this famous sculptor, Angelo Santasilia," he went on, "whom princes and cardinals beseech to work for them, this good husband and father—he will not go to heaven either. And do you know why? Because he is not at all eager to go there."

He placed his last figure in between the two others, farther back on the balustrade.

"Do you see, Pino?" he said softly. "These three tiny toy figures are placed to mark three corners of a rectangle, in which the width is to the length as the length to the sum of the two. These, you know, are the proportions of the golden section."

He let his skilled hands fall to rest in his lap.

"But," he finished very slowly, "the young man whom you met at the inn of Mariana-the-Rat—the good home of thieves and smugglers down by the harbor—the young man with whom you talked there at night, Pino—he will go to heaven."

TALES OF TWO OLD GENTLEMEN

Two old gentlemen, both of them widowers, played piquet in a small salon next to a ballroom. When they had finished their game, they had their chairs turned round, so that through the open doors they could watch the dancers. They sat on contentedly, sipping their wine, their delicate noses turned up a little and taking in, with the melancholic superiority of age, the fragrance of youth before them. They first talked of ancient scandals in high society—for they had known each other as boys and young men—and of the sad fate of common friends, then of political and dynastic matters, and at last of the complexity of the universe in general. When they got there, there was a pause.

"My grandfather," the one old gentleman said at the end of it, "who was a very happy man and particularly happy in his married life, had built up a philosophy of his own, which in the course of my life from time to time has been brought back to me."

"I remember your grandfather quite well, my good Matteo," said the other, "a highly corpulent, but still graceful figure, with a smooth, rosy face. He did not speak much."

"He did not speak much, my good Taddeo," Matteo agreed, "for he did, in accordance with his philosophy, admit the futility of argumentation. It is from my brilliant grandmother, his wife, that I have inherited my taste for a discussion. Yet one evening, while I was still quite a young boy, he benignly condescended to develop his theory to me. It happened, I remember, at a ball like this, and I myself was all the time longing to get away from the lecture. But my grandfather, his mind once opened upon the matter, did not dismiss his youthful listener till he had set forth to him his entire train of ideas. He said:

" 'We suffer much. We go through many dark hours of doubt, dread and despair, because we cannot reconcile our idea of divinity with the state of things in the universe round us. I myself as a young man brooded a good deal over the problem. Later on I arrived at the conviction that we should, more easily and more thoroughly than we now do or ever have done, understand the nature and the laws of the Cosmos if we would from the beginning recognize its originator and upholder as being of the female sex.

" 'We speak about Providence and announce: The Lord is my shepherd, He will provide. But in our hearts we know that we should demand from our own shepherds—'

"—for my grandfather," the narrator here interrupted himself, "drew most of his wealth from his vast sheep farms in the province of Marche.

" '—a providential care of our sheep very different from the one to which we are ourselves submitted, and which appears mainly to provide us with blood and tears.

" 'But say instead, of Providence: "She is my shepherdess"—

and you will at once realize in what way you may expect to be provided for.

"'For to a shepherdess tears are convenient and precious, like rain—as in the old song *il pleut, il pleut, bergère*—like pearls, or like falling stars running over the firmament— all phenomena in themselves divine, and symbolic of the highest and the deepest spheres of human knowledge. And as to the shedding of blood, this to our shepherdess—as to any lady—is a high privilege and is inseparably united with the sublimest moments of existence, with promotion and beatification. What little girl will not joyously shed her blood in order to become a virgin, what bride not hers in order to become a wife, what young wife not hers to become a mother?

"'Man, troubled and perplexed about the relation between divinity and humanity, is ever striving to find a foothold in the matter by drawing on his own normal experience. He will view it in the light of relations between tutor and pupil, or of commander and soldier, and he will lose breath— and heart—in search and investigation. The ladies, whose nature is nearer to the nature of the deity, take no such trouble; they see the relation between the Cosmos and the Creator quite plainly as a love affair. And in a love affair search and investigation is an absurdity, and unseemly. There are, thus, no genuine female atheists. If a lady tells you that she is an atheist, she is either, still, an adorable person, and it is coquetry, or she is a depraved creature, and it is a lie. Woman even wonders at man's perseverance in questioning, for they are aware that he will never get any other kind of answer than the kind which King Alexander the Great got from the Sibylla of Babylon. You may have forgotten the tale, I shall recount it to you.

"'King Alexander, on his triumphant return from the Indies, in Babylon heard of a young Sibylla who was able to foretell the future, and had her brought before him. When the black-eyed woman demanded a price to part with her knowledge, he let a soldier bring up a box filled with precious stones which had been collected over half the world. The Sibylla rummaged in the box and picked out two emeralds and a pearl; then she gave in to the King's wish and promised to tell him what till now she had told nobody.

" 'Very slowly and conscientiously, all the time holding up one finger and begging him—since she must never speak any word of hers over again—to give his utmost attention to her words, she explained to him with what rare woods to build up the sacred pile, with what incantations to kindle it, and what parts of a cat and a crocodile to place upon it. After that she was silent for a long time. "Now, King Alexander," she at last said, "I am coming to the core of my secret. But I shall not speak one more word unless you give me the big ruby which, before your soldier brought up the box, you told him to lay aside." Alexander was loath to part with the ruby, for he had meant to give it to his mistress Thaïs at home, but by this time he felt that he could not live without having been told the final part of the spell, so had it brought and handed over to her.

" ' "Listen then, Alexander," the woman said, laying her finger on the King's lips. "At the moment when you gaze into the smoke, you must not think of the left eye of a camel. To think of its right eye is dangerous enough. But to think of the left is perdition." '

"So much for my grandfather's philosophy," said Matteo. Taddeo smiled a little at the account of his friend.

"It was," Matteo went on after a while, "this time brought back to me by the sight of the young ladies before us, moving with such perfect freedom in such severely regulated figures. Almost all of them, you will know, have been brought up in convents, and have been taken out from there to be married a few years, a year—or perhaps a week—ago.

"How, now, is the Cosmos made to look to a girl in a

convent school? From my cousin, who is Mother Superior of the most ancient of such schools, I have some knowledge of the matter. You will not, my friend, find a mirror in the whole building, and a girl may spend ten years in it and come out not knowing whether she be plain or pretty. The little cells are whitewashed, the nuns are dressed in black and white, and the young pupils are put in gray smocks, as if there were in the whole world but the two colors, and the cheerless mixture of them. The old gardener in charge of the convent garden has a small bell tied round his leg, so that by the tinkling of it the maidens may be warned of the approach of a man and may absent themselves like fawns before the huntsman. Any little sisterly kisses or caresses between school friends—light and innocent butterflies of Eros—by the alarmed nuns are chased off the grounds with fly-flaps, as if they were wasps.

"From this stronghold of unworldliness our blossoming virginal ascetic is fetched out into the world and is married. What is now, from the very first day, the object of her existence? To make herself desirable to all men and the incarnation of desire to one. The mirror is given her as her chief instructress and confidante; the knowledge of fashion, of silks, laces and fans, becomes her chief study; the care of her fair body, from the brushing and curling of the hair to the polishing of the toenails, the occupation of her day; and the embrace and caresses of an ardent young husband is the prize for her teachability.

"My friend—a boy brought up for his task in life in an equally incongruous manner would protest and argue, and storm against his tutor—as, alas, all men do protest, argue and storm against the Almighty! But a young girl agrees with her mother, with her mother's mother and with the common, divine Mother of the Universe, that the only method of turning out a dazzling and adorable woman of the world is a convent education.

"I might," he said after a pause, "tell you a story which

goes to prove in what good understanding a young girl is with the Paradox."

"A nobleman married a girl fresh from the convent, with whom he was deeply in love, and on the evening of their wedding drove with her to his villa. In the coach he said to her: 'My beloved, I am this evening going to make some alterations in my household, and to hand over to you a proportion of my property. But I must tell you beforehand that there is in my house one object which I am keeping to myself, and to the ownership of which you must never make any claim. I beg you: ask me no questions, and make no investigation in the matter.'

"In the frescoed room within which he sat down to sup with his wife he called before him the master of his stables and said to him: 'Listen to my order and mark it well. From this hour my stables, and everything in them, are the property of the Princess my wife. None of my horses or coaches, none of my saddlery or harness, down to the coachman's whips, in the future belongs to me myself.'

"He next called up his steward and said to him: 'Mark my words well. From this hour all objects of value in my house, all gold and silver, all pictures and statues are the property of the Princess my wife, and I myself shall have nothing to say over them.'

"In the same way he had the housekeeper of the villa called and told her: 'From today all linen and silk bedding, all lace and satin curtains within my house belong to the Princess my wife, and I myself renounce all rights of property in them. Be not forgetful of my bidding, but behave according to it.'

"In the end he called in the old woman who had been maid to his mother and grandmother, and informed her: 'My faithful Gelsomina, hear me. All jewelry, which has before belonged to my mother, my grandmother, or to any former mistress of the house, from tonight belongs solely to the Princess my wife—who will wear it with the same grace as my mama and grandmama—to do with what she likes.'

"He here kissed his wife's hand and offered her his arm. 'You will now, dear heart,' he said, 'come with me, in order that I may show you the one precious object which, alone of all my belongings, I am keeping to myself.'

"With these words he led her upstairs to her bedroom and set her, all puzzled, in the middle of the floor. He lifted the bridal veil from her head and removed her pearls and diamonds. He undid her heavy bridal gown with its long train and made her step out of it, and one by one he took off her petticoats, stays and shift, until she stood before him, blushing and confused, as lovely as Eve in Paradise in her first hour with Adam. Very gently he turned her round to the tall mirror on the wall.

" 'There,' he said, 'is the one thing of my estate solely reserved for me myself.'

"My friend," Matteo said, "a soldier receiving from his commander-in-chief corresponding instructions would shake his head at them and protest that surely this was no strategy to adopt, and that if he could, he would desert. But a young woman, faced with the instructions, nods her head."

"But," Taddeo asked, "did the nobleman of your tale, good Matteo, succeed in making his wife happy?"

"It is always, good Taddeo," Matteo answered, "difficult for a husband to know whether he is making his wife happy or not. But as to the husband and wife of my tale, the lady, on the twentieth anniversary of their wedding, took her husband's hand, gazed archly into his eyes and asked him whether he still remembered this first evening of their married life. 'My God,' she said, 'how terrified was I not then for half an hour, how did I not tremble. Why!' she exclaimed, throwing herself into his arms, 'if you had not included in your directions that last clause of yours, I should have felt disdained and betrayed! My God, I should have been lost!' "

The contradance before the two old gentlemen changed into a waltz, and the whole ballroom waved and swayed like a garden under a summer breeze. The seductive Viennese tune then again died away.

"I should like to tell you," Taddeo said, "another tale. It may go to support your grandfather's theology, or it may not."

"A nobleman of an ambitious nature, and with a brilliant career behind him, when he was no longer quite young decided to marry and looked round for a wife. On a visit to the town of Bergamo he made the acquaintance of a family of an ancient, great name but of modest means. There were at the time seven daughters in the tall gloomy palazzo, and at the end of the pretty row an only son, who was still a child. The seven young sisters were fully aware that their individual existence might with reason be disputed or denied, since they had come into the world as failures in the attempt at acquiring an heir to the name, and were—so to say—blanks drawn by their ancient house in its lottery on life and death. But their family arrogance was fierce enough to make them bear their sad lot high-handedly, as a privilege out of reach to the common people.

"It so happened that the youngest sister, the one whose arrival, he felt, to the poor Prince and Princess would have been the hardest blow of all, caught our nobleman's eye, so that he returned to the house, and again returned.

"The girl, who was then but seventeen years old, was far from being the prettiest of the group. But the visitor was a connoisseur of feminine loveliness, and spied in her youthful face and form the promise of coming, unusual beauty. Yet much more than by this, he was attracted by a particular trait in her. He guessed behind her demure and disciplined bearing the fruit of an excellent education, an ambition kin-

dred to his own, but more powerful because less blasé, a longing—and an energy to satisfy the longing—a long way out
of the ordinary. It would be, he reflected, a pleasant, an
entertaining experience to encourage this youthful ambition, still but faintly conscious of itself, to fledge the cygnet
and watch it soaring. At the same time, he thought, a young
wife of high birth and brought up in Spartan simplicity,
with a nostalgia for glory, would be an asset in his future
career. He applied for the girl's hand, and her father and
mother, surprised and delighted at having their daughter
make such a splendid match, handed her over to him.

"Our nobleman had every reason to congratulate himself
on his decision. The flight feathers of his young bird grew
with surprising quickness; soon in his brilliant circle one
would not find a lady of greater beauty and finer grace, of
more exquisite and dignified comportment, or of more punc-
tilious tact. She wore the heavy ornaments that he gave her
with as much ease as a rosebush its roses, and had he, he
thought, been able to set a crown on her head, the world
would have felt her to be born with it. And she was still
soaring, inspired by, as well as enraptured with, her successes.
He himself, within the first two years of their married life,
acquired two supreme decorations at his native and at a
foreign court.

"But when he and his wife had been married for three
years he observed a change in her. She became pensive, as if
stirred by some new mighty emotion, obscure to him. At
times she did not hear what he spoke to her. It also seemed
to him that she would now prefer to show herself in the
world on such occasions where he was not with her, and to
excuse herself from others where she would have to appear
by his side. 'I have spoilt her,' he reflected. 'Is it indeed
possible that, against the very order of things, her ambition
and her vanity now make her aspire to outshine her lord, to
whom she owes all?' His feelings were naturally badly hurt
at the idea of so much ingratitude, and at last, on an eve-

ning when they were alone together, he resolved to take her to account.

" 'Surely, my dear,' he said to her, 'you will realize that I am not going to play the part of that husband in the fairy tale who, owing to his connection with higher powers, raised his wife to the rank of queen and empress, only to hear her, in the end, demanding to have the sun rise at her word. Recall to yourself the place from which I took you, and remember that the response of higher powers to the too indulgent husband forwarding his wife's claim was this: "return, and find her back in her hovel." '

"His wife for a long time did not answer him; in the end she rose from her chair as if about to leave the room. She was tall and willowy; her ample skirts at each of her movements made a little chirping sound.

" 'My husband,' she said in her low, sonorous voice. 'Surely you will realize that to an ambitious woman it comes hard, in entering a ballroom, to know that she is entering it on the arm of a cuckold.'

"As, very quietly and without another word, she had gone out of the door, the nobleman sat on, wondering, as till now he had never done, at the complexity of the Universe."

THE CARDINAL'S THIRD TALE

*A*nd I, too," with these words Cardinal Salviati broke the silence that followed upon the Spanish Ambassador's story. "I, too, can tell a tale which may somehow illuminate our theme."

As ever he spoke slowly and gently, and as ever the sweetness and authority of his voice captured the circle round him. He sat leaned back in his deep chair, so that his face with the ugly scar was in shadow. But his two hands, the beauty of which the great painter Camuccini has immortalized in his Christ praying in the Garden of Gethsemane, rested on the arms of the chair, in the light of the candelabra, and from time to time, in an almost imperceptible movement, accompanied the modulations of his speech.

"I myself," he continued, "have not been in a position to

follow from beginning to end the happenings which I shall have the honor of relating to you. But I am as firmly convinced of their veracity as if they had been part of my own experience. For they were told me by the friend of my childhood, Father Jacopo Parmecianino, who was the most honest and candid human being I have ever known. Aye, he was more than that—of humble birth and appearance and hampered by a defect of speech, a slight stammer, he was in reality a saint, in whose modest dwelling miracles were at home. The heroine of my story, too, I have met. Her name was Lady Flora Gordon.

"I first made this lady's acquaintance in one of the drawing rooms of Rome, at a time when she was, I believe, in the middle forties. Her apparition in our party was the sensation of the evening. Many tales were told of her great wealth, which was exceptional even among her countrymen, those headstrong, restless milords who travel through our land and with their swarms of attendants occupy our palazzos. On that evening I was told that she was one of the three richest women in Britain. And for other reasons than that the Scots lady was bound to impress anyone with whom she came into contact.

"The Lady Flora was by no means ugly. But all the same a presence like hers would be difficult for any lady to carry. For she was a giantess, mightier than any of those whom, as a child, I have seen shown in our fairs. Wherever she went, she stood head and shoulders above the men with whom she conversed. She was correspondingly vast of hips and chest. Her hands and feet, in themselves beautiful, were of a size to match those of the marble angels in my own chapel, and her white teeth compared with those of the faithful dapple-gray on the back of which I have passed many happy hours of my youth. Nose, jaw, ears and bosom, as well, in this lady were of goddess-like dimensions. She had rich red hair, but her grandly swung eyebrows and her thick eyelashes were almost colorless. Her skin was fresh and white, although slightly freckled. Her voice was full, clear and harmonious

"As if Lady Flora meant to show that under all conditions she owned to her nature and her worth, she carried herself exceedingly straight, her head high. Her attire was always costly, but severe in color and style and never embellished with a silk ribbon, a bow or any of the falbalas by which our own ladies do manifest not only a charming disposition, but the wish to charm. Her only jewels were a single row of pearls, an heirloom in her family, the match of which, according to rumor, was not to be found among the regalia of Britain. From time to time she donned garments of particular color and pattern, of which she was very proud. For, strange to say, such fabrics, down through the ages, to the noble houses of Scotland have held the significance of a coat of arms.

"Lady Flora had traveled in many countries, but till now had not visited Rome. She spoke our language freely and fluently, as she spoke French and German, even if with that particular accent which her countrymen cannot or will not put off. She had great connections all over Europe, and she was as much at her ease talking to a cabman as to a prince. At the same time something in her manner would remind her partner that the motto of her country is *Noli me tangere*. She also declined to follow the British custom of shaking hands in meeting or parting.

"On the evening in question I only exchanged a few words with Lady Flora. From our short conversation I gathered that she had come to Rome, by no means attracted by the beauty or holiness of the Eternal City, but on the contrary in order to confirm by personal observation her deep distrust of all that its name implies—from the Holy Father himself and us, his humble servants, to the music of our churches, the art of our museums, and the customs of our simple Roman people. Lady Flora had been brought up in one of those North-European denominations which most of all despise and abhor beauty, and when later in life she rejected its teachings, she at the same time, through her own experience, adopted a still harder view of life. In the course of our talks I felt that she had, wherever she had traveled, inspected the loveliest and most famous countries and cities of our poor earth with this same purpose: to corroborate her essential suspicion of both Creator and creation. The lady inspired me with profound pity, but at the same time with profound respect. For in everything she said and did there was nobility and truthfulness.

"She was, moreover, an exceptionally witty woman; indeed her rare gift of repartee during her stay in Rome made her a highly welcome, if somehow feared, guest in all drawing rooms. Still here as elsewhere she preserved a peculiar quality which set her apart from our own wits. Whenever a sensational event or a scandal in society touched on an *amorette* or did in the slightest way taste of *la belle passion*, to her eyes it lost any kind of interest, and she turned away from it as from something altogether beneath her dignity.

"My friend, the Prince Scipione Odescalchi, who at that time was more than ninety years old, said to me: 'Oh, that I were only seventy-five years younger! For our young Roman beaus of today are nothing but a handful of *petit-maîtres!* They have lost sense of the sublime, and they see not that this Lady Flora is a goddess. Sweet Cupid, God of Love, deign to let the shadow of one of your pinions fall upon our guest, for it is a disgrace to all of us that she should leave the Eternal City the same as she came!'

"Later on from Father Jacopo I learned some of the lady's history.

"Lady Flora was an only child, and sole heir to her father's wealth, which had been increased by her mother's great dowry. This virtuous and noble lady, her mother, had been as tall as the daughter and had weighed as much. But on the other hand the maiden's father—around whom a multitude of gay and gallant anecdotes had grown up, so that to his countrymen he had become a kind of mythic figure—was below medium height and slight of build. Yet at the same time the Scots nobleman had been so harmoniously proportioned, with such big radiant eyes, such rich locks, and such perfect gracefulness in all his movements, that till his death he was reckoned to be the finest-looking man in the Kingdom. He had made use of his rare beauty, as well as of his many talents, to enjoy to the full the delights of this earth—and above all the delights of love! It seems that he was ever irresistible to the ladies of his own country, as well as to those of other countries, for like his daughter he had traveled much. His consort, who was deeply in love with him, and jealous by nature, suffered much in her married life."

The Cardinal made a short pause, then continued:

"Are you, my amiable audience, familiar with the name of the great English poet and philosopher Jonathan Swift? Without doubt he was a man of true genius. But he was also, sad to say—and, to us, incomprehensibly—filled with a strange and terrible loathing of the earth and of humanity as a whole. In his most celebrated book, *Lemuel Gulliver's Travels*, with almost satanic cleverness he manages to ridicule human conditions and functions, simply by distorting their dimensions. Military valor and glory, the grandeur and pathos of the battlefield he holds up to laughter by making officers and soldiers, horses and cannon, present themselves *en miniature*, the size of pins and thimbles.

"But the immortal passion of love, with all its attributes, he burlesques by magnifying to a monstrous, a fabulous scale the persons of the lovers and their mistresses, and such charms of the human body as are elsewhere praised and sung. His adventurous traveler, Gulliver, ascends the bosoms of the amorous *dames d'honneur* as an alpine climber scales a snow-white mountain. Under their languishing sighs he totters as under an earthquake, and he comes near to drowning in the beads of sweat which the rapture of the rendezvous makes start out on their skin. The faint per-

fumes which surround a woman's body are turned into ex-
halations which nearly stifle him; nay, I will not detail to
you, my graceful and gallant listeners, this poet's sinister
representation of what other poets have made the subject
of sonnets.

"Father Jacopo more than once, he told me, discussed this
remarkable book with Lady Flora. She evidently knew it
by heart, and made use of it to deride in toto the Almighty's
work of creation.

" 'Look, Reverend Father,' she said to him, 'how little is
needed, what slight transposition of dimensions suffices to
reveal to us the true nature of your noble and beautiful universe!'

"Father Jacopo in his heart was horrified at her heresy, but
he answered her, as he always did, discreetly and meekly.
'Unless, Signora,' he said, 'these same observations will reveal
to us with what subtle precision the harmony of our universe
is adjusted and balanced. Unless they will tell us with what
reverence we must eye the ordinance of the creator, so
that not even in imagination do we presume to alter or
transpose any jot or title thereof. The shortening or lengthening of a single string of an instrument may enable us to
distort, aye, to annihilate its music. But surely, surely the fact
does not justify us in blaming that master who built the
violin.'

"It now appears as if Lady Flora's father, when exasperated
by his lady's jealousy, was wont to quote to her the book of
this English poet, and that he would even with cruel fantasy
and wit add to it and invent and recount new adventures of
Lemuel Gulliver. Verily, when we consider the lady's situation we cover our eyes, as if invited to gaze into an abyss of
suffering and injury. A small young woman, who had her
slightness and scantiness made an object of mockery and
complaints from her husband, might well feel personally
hurt and mortified. Yet in her case it would not be the
insignia of womanhood itself which were blasphemously dis-

cussed. This Scots lady, to whom her husband would recite
hexameters describing the adventures of the Prophet Jonah,
his tremblings and final engulfment, will have suffered not
only in her personal dignity, but in that of her sex. It is not
to be wondered at that through the years she was changed,
until the friends of her childhood and youth no longer
found in her any trace of the maiden's or the new-married
wife's rich and innocent nature. The incessant, burning wish
to grow smaller had acted as a corrosive on her heart.

"It furthermore appears that Lady Flora's mother, while
heroically keeping silent on her misfortune to the whole
outer world, in the end failed to suppress all articulation of
her misery. She made her daughter her confidante! Young
Flora, while growing up, and month by month approaching
the measures and weight of the elder woman, had heard her
father's sallies repeated by the mouth of her mother. And
yet the girl was like her father in courage and wit, and this
handsome and gay father of hers, at the time when she was
still a pretty, nimble little girl, had taken pleasure in galloping with her across the Scottish heather and in training
her to the arts of dance and sword-play. She could not possibly
wish him any ill. But with the lamentations of her mother
in her mind she yearned to annihilate the small, slim wanton
women who seduced him, and with the flippancies of her
father in her mind she longed to annihilate that same sacred
body, which was just now budding into its season of rich
flowering. Undoubtedly at an early age she vowed never
through a marriage or a love affair to repeat her mother's
misery, and this in itself was a barren and desolate destiny.
But her reason for the resolution, of which she could not
speak, was a still heavier burden. What sad condition in a
young virgin to grow pale with shame at the very same
thoughts which will make her sisters blush deeply with sweet,
delicate modesty!

"Thus daily life at the ancient Scottish castle, between
the two mighty ladies and the small gentleman, to the eyes

of the world passed nobly and harmoniously. But within this same existence a young heart day by day hardened, until it could find comfort but in one single thing—absolute loneliness. The maiden shrank from any touch, physical or mental. Her great wealth and high rank, far from making her lot easier, seemed to render her even more lonely. Her isolation became her pride, and by the time when, after the death of both her parents, she first traveled in Italy, her arrogance was boundless.

"Father Jacopo made Lady Flora's acquaintance without at first suspecting in the presence of what misfortune and of what obduracy he found himself. These two, who in the future were to signify so much to each other, met for the first time in a small village of Tuscany, where Lady Flora had rented a villa for a couple of months, and where Father Jacopo on his way to Rome had fallen ill with a sudden fever, and was laid up at the inn. When Lady Flora was informed that an old priest was lying at death's door in the miserable tavern, she had him fetched up to her own house and saw to it that he was nursed and nourished until he had regained his strength. The priest already in the inn had learned of the lady's exceptional wealth; his primary feelings toward her were gratitude and admiration. But in his simplicity he had knowledge of the human heart, and before long he looked deep into the condition of her soul. Undoubtedly the sight struck him with awe; without doubt, too, her impenitence itself did tie him to her, so that at no price in the world would he have let go of her.

"They were brought closer together by the fact that she soon left to him to distribute the rich alms which she dealt out, without ever, in her general contempt of man, bothering who received them. And when she made up her mind to continue to Rome, she invited Father Jacopo to keep her company in her comfortable English coach, while her British and Italian attendants followed in two other carriages.

"In the Eternal City the friendship between the noble-woman and the priest was continued and confirmed; for three months they met almost daily. Father Jacopo's manner in his intercourse with his fellow creatures was so naturally winning that most people, almost unknowingly, disclosed to him their feelings and their doings. It must have been the same in the case of Lady Flora. I cannot imagine that she did ever confide in him, still less complain to him. Her communications about her past life were given gaily and with a high hand. But his mysterious intuition had its effect even on this haughty lady; step by step she was led to speak to him with absolute frankness.

"A particular circumstance made itself felt in the relation between them. Lady Flora had known many clergymen, high and low, of her own country, but till now had not conversed with a priest of our church. It had amused her to shock and scandalize the British ecclesiastics by her utter disbelief and her utter contempt of Heaven and Earth. She now took it for granted that it would be still easier to give offense to a Roman Catholic priest; she lost no time trying her hand at Father Jacopo. This task, however, she did not undertake out of malice, but out of a kind of hard jocularity peculiar to her nature. But there was no scandalizing Father Jacopo. He was, as he himself told me, by no means a courageous man, and in the confessional while he listened to the reports of evil doings and thoughts his hair would often stand on end. But he could no more take offense at such things than he could take offense at a stroke of lightning or at an avalanche. In the one case as in the other he would at once endeavor, in every possible way, to stop or repair the havoc worked by the savage powers of nature; but in the one case as in the other he would accept the catastrophe without the slightest personal rancor. This attitude in a servant of the Church surprised Lady Flora; she carried her blasphemy further and grew coarser and harder of speech. Father Jacopo's imperturbable peacefulness under this persecution in the end forced from her a kind of respect which she can rarely, if ever, have felt toward any human being.

" 'In my dealings with Lady Flora,' Father Jacopo said to me, 'I sometimes felt that she had donned a heavy armor, which she had till now, quite rightly, considered impenetrable. She had taken pleasure in seeing all bullets glance off from it. And yet it is not impossible that within her proud heart she had at times vaguely desired to meet an opponent worthy of her.'

"Now Father Jacopo in his quality of priest had a peculiar trait. It went against him to set forth in his prayer any particular request; he disliked pestering Heaven with a specified petition. Nor did he ever pray directly for the salvation of his penitents. Lady Flora a couple of times challenged him: 'I suppose, Father Jacopo, that you will now be praying for my conversion?' And guiltily he would have to confess that this he had never done. Whenever the weal and woe of any individual human being lay heavy on his heart, he was wont, he told me, before he began to recite his breviary, to center his thoughts upon that person, and during the prayer to hold him or her, as it were, upon his arms until they ached from the weight. 'And then,' he used to explain, 'it came to me that I must act in such and such a way.'

"Lady Flora was a strong and healthy woman, and had never in her life been hindered from an undertaking by ill health. But it so happened that on her first day in Rome she slipped on a marble stair of the palazzo on the Piazza del Popolo of which she had rented two floors, and sprained her ankle. For some time she had to keep to her sofa, and the doctor enjoined her to refrain from all excursions, even by coach. During these weeks Father Jacopo in spite of his many duties found time to visit her. And the thought of her filled his whole mind even when he did not see her.

"So here they sat, two human beings of unique honesty, both singularly free of ever having wronged a fellow-creature, talking together. In one of them the uprightness and the blameless conduct had produced a sovereign arrogance, in the other an unconditional humility.

"Within the lofty *salon* they went over both the phenomena of earthly existence and the ideas of Paradise and Hell. Lady Flora was skilled in such debates, and was never at a loss for an answer, while on his side Father Jacopo was often struck dumb by her heart-rending irreverence. It seemed to him that were he to answer her at all he must shriek out loud, and he was only able to stifle the shriek by pressing his lips hard together. Neither would he let himself be driven by her to make the sign of the cross, and he therefore during their conversations sat with his hands firmly folded in the lap of his old soutane. But it happened that on his return to his own small room he crossed himself time after time, so vividly did he feel the presence of the demons evoked by her words; aye, it would seem to him that for hours he had conversed with Lucifer himself. In spite of all this, on the morrow he went back to the palazzo, meek as ever.

"In his heart Father Jacopo decided that the unequaled loneliness of the woman and her unequaled arrogance were one and the same mortal sin. For a long time he pondered in what way to encounter her, and he called himself an unworthy priest because he could not find a solution. He fasted and watched in the hope that he might thereby fortify his weak nature and hit upon the right spiritual weapon in their trial of strength. Empty and exhausted, upon his knees on the stone floor, he fought his battle for the woman who at that moment was supping on dainties and generous wine, or sleeping placidly behind the silken hangings of her four-poster.

"For a moment Father Jacopo imagined that Lady Flora's inconceivable isolation in itself might be a road to salvation. What a hermitess of the desert, what a stylite, famous through the ages, might he not make of her! But he rejected the thought as a dangerous temptation. It was, he felt, a once too easy and too bold. In his mind—for he was a man of vivid imagination—he saw the Scots noblewoman on top of her pillar, straight and colossal, never giddy, one with the marble on which she stood. From her altitude she would glance down at the men and women round the pillar's foot, confirmed in her conviction of their pin-size, or she would gaze tranquilly skyward, at last confirmed in her conviction of the emptiness of the heavens. Terrible, terrible the hermitess with the gay, grim smile would be up there!

" 'Nay,' Father Jacopo thought, 'it is by the low, rough roads of humanity; it is by the streets, lanes and highways trudged by the feet of human beings that my high-flying lady must walk to Heaven.'

"So he spoke to her, first of all, of the oneness of all creation.

" 'I know,' said the lady, 'your evangelists of oneness will proclaim first of all that one must not be oneself. My own oneness is my integrity. I have not married, I have taken no lover; the idea of children repels me—all because I want to be one, and alone in my skin.' "

" 'I have not expressed myself well,' said Father Jacopo, 'I was thinking of the brotherhood of all human beings.'

" 'What!' Lady Flora exclaimed, 'are you, my good, pious Father Jacopo, in reality a Father Jacobino? Is it the maxim of *Liberté, Egalité, Fraternité*—in the name of which the Government of France did so merrily play ball with the heads of my father's good French friends—which you are preaching to me?'

" 'I know but little of politics,' said Father Jacopo. 'The equality of men of which I talk is the likeness of one man to the other—a family likeness, if you want, of which phenomenon you know more than I. We speak of one thing being like another without disparaging the integrity of either; nay, on the contrary, in doing so we acknowledge their essential difference, for nobody will compare two identical things. I do not comment on the likeness of one button of my cassock to another, but I may well allow myself to hold forth on the likeness between the diamond in your ring, which measures not half an inch, and the clear star in the sky, which according to the astronomers is a sun, if not a whole solar system!

" 'This likeness between all things within creation does not, like the *egalité* of which you spoke, claim that they all be treated in the same way. For I cannot set the sun in your ring, and however rare and fine your diamond, it would not, if placed in the sky, shine far about. No, this equality of mine has no claims to make. But it yields proof that all things of this world are issued from one and the same workshop; it is in each thing the authentic signature of the Almighty. In this sense of the word, Milady, likeness is love. For we love that to which we bear a likeness, and we will become like to that which we love. Therefore, the beings of this world who decline to be like anything will efface the divine signature and so work out their own annihilation. In this way did God prove His love of mankind: that He let Himself be made in the likeness of men. For this reason it is wise and pious to call attention to likenesses, and Scripture itself will speak in parables, which means comparisons.'

" 'Yes, in pretty comparisons,' said Lady Flora. 'King Solomon, I have been taught, prophesies on the relation between Christ and His Church, and tells of the bride—who symbolizes the Church—that she is like a rose of Sharon, and then again that her teeth are like a flock of sheep about to lamb, whereof every one beareth twins, and that her belly is like a heap of wheat!'

"Father Jacopo folded his hands. 'A rose of Sharon,' he said. 'Aye, and does not the rose clearly exhibit to our eyes the signature of the workshop from which she is issued? And does not the heap of wheat, too, exhibit it?'

"And as he realized to what extent his own soul was the lover of the woman's soul, he added slowly, in a voice which trembled a little because he was clasping his hands so hard, these lines from the Song of Songs: 'Set me as a seal upon thine heart, as a seal upon thine arm, for love is strong as death; jealousy is cruel as the grave. Many waters cannot quench love, neither can the floods drown it: if a man would give all the substance of his house for love'—and for a moment he called to mind Lady Flora's great wealth—'it would utterly be contemned.'

"On another day he once more dwelled upon the idea of human fellowship and said: 'The third article of our creed itself speaks of the Communion of Saints—'

" 'Thank you, I know it, I know it by heart,' Lady Flora interrupted. 'The Communion of Saints, the Resurrection of the body—'

" 'And the Life everlasting,' Father Jacopo finished tranquilly. 'Of the Communion of Saints because—amongst human beings—without communion no real sanctity will be obtained. A hand, a foot or an eye only gains the divine signature when integrated into a body. We are all branches on the same tree—'

" 'I have always liked trees,' said Lady Flora, 'and make no objection to talking about them. But I am a tree in myself, Father Jacopo, and no branch.'

" 'We are all,' Father Jacopo continued, 'limbs of the same Body.'

" 'Oh, do spare me, just for once, your limbs and bodies,' Lady Flora exclaimed. 'And do stick to botany, and to that heap of wheat of which the other day you talked so beautifully.'

" 'That is not possible,' Father Jacopo declared with much force. 'That the wheat is transformed into Body—in this lies the inmost mystery of our communion! You doubt,' he went on, carried away by his theme, 'that we be all one!— and yet you are aware that one is dead for us all!'

" 'Not for me,' Lady Flora said briskly. 'I beg to be excused! Never in my life have I asked any human being— much less any god—to die for me, and I must insist that my own personal account be kept altogether outside this statement. A great deal of rubbish,' she went on, 'in the course of my life I have had foisted upon me—especially here in Italy —and have been paying for it too, in good sound sterling. But what I have neither ordered nor paid for I will not receive.'

"At that Father Jacopo realized that Lady Flora's great sin was not that she ever refused to give—for more than anyone he was acquainted with her exceptional generosity and beneficence—but that she refused to receive, and he grew heavy at heart. He sat immovable and dumb for such a long time that in the end she turned round toward him in her chair.

"'Alas, Lady Flora, my child,' he at last said, 'allow my frail reason time to comprehend the extent of your heroic unreason! I cannot at this moment, not tonight, speak to you of your relation to Heaven. I am an unworthy priest, and it appears as if Heaven will not employ me as its spokesman; when I make the attempt, it withdraws itself from me!

"'But I am a man,' he continued very slowly and in great agitation of mind, 'let me speak to you of your relation to mankind.

"'There are many things in life which a human being— and in particular a highly talented and privileged human being like you, my daughter—may attain by personal endeavor. But there exists a true humanity, which will ever remain a gift, and which is to be accepted by one human being as it is given to him by a fellow human. The one who gives has himself been a receiver. In this way, link by link, a chain is made from land to land and from generation to generation. Rank, wealth and nationality in this matter all go for nothing. The poor and downtrodden can hand over the gift to kings, and kings will pass it on to their favorites at Court or to an itinerant dancer in their city. The Negro slave may give it to the slave-owner or the slave-owner to the slave. Strange and wonderful it is to consider how in such community we are bound to foreigners whom we have never seen and to dead men and women whose names we have never heard and shall never hear, more closely even than if we were all holding hands.'

" 'Bah, this is theology,' said Lady Flora. 'It is very amusing to discuss theology with you, Father Jacopo. But in my family we have always been practical people.'

"Father Jacopo now realized that he would never by words or arguments prevail against the obstinate lady. Yet here in Rome he was somewhat more hopeful than he had been in her villa in Tuscany. For as he walked about the old squares and streets and entered the churches—ever carrying her with him in his mind—he reflected that the Eternal City itself must possess the remedy against her ailment, and must itself know when and how to use it.

"One day Father Jacopo sat for a long time in the basilica of San Pietro. In here he felt that the dimensions of the mighty building, as if on their own and without our reflecting upon it, would swallow up and do away with all difference of size between human beings. And it came to him that this would be the right place to take Lady Flora.

"So as soon as her invalidism permitted, he asked her to visit San Pietro in his company.

"He had planned beforehand what round to make, and in what order to point out to his companion the treasure of the basilica. But he did not carry out his program.

" 'For as by the side of the lady I entered the church,' he said as he told me his tale, 'it seemed to me that I was seeing it with her own eyes! This was the very first time that its vault rose above me and that its walls embraced me. And my happiness at the idea that such glory was to be found on earth made me dumb.'

"Nor did Lady Flora speak. For more than three hours she dwelt in the church, and as very slowly she finished her round it seemed to Father Jacopo that her step grew lighter.

"In the end she stood still in front of the statue of St.

Peter himself, and for a long time remained standing before it. She paid no attention to the worshippers, who walked past her in order to kiss the foot of the figure. She raised her eyes to the head of the great Apostle, and for a while looked him gravely in the face. Thereupon she lowered her gaze to the hand of bronze, which holds the key of heaven, and to Father Jacopo it looked as if she compared it to her own, which was clutching the ivory handle of her parasol. The moment to her faithful friend was solemn and strangely joyful. His tongue was loosened, almost without knowing it he broke into the proclamation of the basilica itself: *'Tu es Petrus, et super hanc petram ædificabo ecclesiam meam!'*

"In the coach Lady Flora said, smiling: 'Is that something great, now—to let oneself be crucified head downward? One would not be able to help laughing!'

"After this day San Pietro became the favorite goal for Lady Flora's drives in Rome. Her coachman, when she had taken her seat in the carriage, without waiting for orders would steer his team toward the big square, and each time she terminated her walk in the church in front of St. Peter's own figure.

"One early morning, while the church was still almost empty, Father Jacopo happened to enter it and to see Lady Flora standing, erect as ever, lost in contemplation of the statue. He did not approach, but silently observed the group which the two formed.

"'Is the woman now,' he asked himself, 'for the first time in her life, filled with reverence and transported by the greatness of a human form? Her pride of birth is boundless,' he further reflected, for through his noble penitents he was acquainted with aristocratic arrogance. 'In disdain even of royal houses she reckons her ancestors, the Scots chieftains, back to heathen ages. Does she, now, dare to feel consanguinity with the fisherman from the lake of Genesareth?' He could not tear himself from the sight of the immovable seated and the immovable standing figure. His thoughts ran on, for he was, as I have already said, a man of intuition and imagination.

" 'Is her courage,' he asked himself, 'boundless too? Does she fancy that at this moment the Dark One before her perceives a consanguinity with a person of flesh and blood? The great scholars will have it that this bronze St. Peter has once been the Jove of ancient Rome, enthroned on the Capitol, and that he is only in so far recast as the thunderbolt in his hand has been replaced by the key. Of this a simple priest can know nothing. But if it be so, then surely a divine energy has passed through the bronze, so that now all lines and forms therein are those of Peter himself. Surely, then, the transformed will have power to transform. And surely the woman who sets her pride in denying all, will find help with him who, before the cock crew the third time, three times had denied!'

"Lady Flora's sojourn in Rome now, according to her plans for the journey, approached its end. From Rome she would go southwards, first to Naples and Sicily and later on to Greece. Since the time when the great and beloved poet Lord Byron glorified, and died for, this country, its soil to his countrymen has become both sacred and familiar, and it is to them a new colony, which the mighty British kingdom has acquired, this time by spiritual arms.

"It was at this stage of events that Father Jacopo looked me up, in considerable agitation of mind, and told me his and Lady Flora's story.

" 'And now, my Atanasio,' he said, 'you will have to come to my aid, and to give me your advice.

" 'A couple of evenings ago I sat with Lady Flora in her red salon. Suddenly she turned toward me, with more hardness and mockery in her face than I have ever seen there, and asked me: "How, Father Jacopo, have you come upon the idea that I be afraid of you?"

" 'Any such thought had been far from me, and I told her so. "Oh, do not beat about the bush now," she said. "For indeed you permit yourself to believe that the hocus-pocus of your Rome, its holy water and rosaries and saints' bones—in the twinkling of an eye, and whether I myself consent or not —shall change me into a meek little lamb within Saint Peter's fold. You permit yourself to believe that I have already, in some alarm, experienced a need to go down on all fours, and that this alarm is the real reason for my departure—aye, for my flight—from Rome! But you are a simpleton, good Father. You are wasting your time pouring water on a Highlander, and no Gordon willl ever be bitten by the teeth of your holy skulls. I warrant you that they would crack in the attempt! For no outside touch will ever leave a mark on us, but it is we, my friend, who mark and stamp the things that touch us.

" ' "Look here," she continued, "in order to please you, and in gratitude for your kind guidance in Rome, I am still willing to go down on all fours. On my knees"—here she struck one of her mighty knees—"I shall ascend your holy stair, the Scala Santa! And you will see for yourself, then, that while my weight may have polished or worn your steps a bit, I my-self"—and here she struck her mighty bosom—"shall be no softer and no more polished on the top of the stair than I was at the bottom of it! Come, my kind and wise friend, I shall order my carriage, and we will go there at once, and together!"

" 'I had to think,' said Father Jacopo, 'before I answered her: "Indeed, Milady, if—without any human companion, in the depth of night, and with the night of unbelief in your own heart—you would imitate this act of penance of the believers, I should feel that it was all done in vain. Aye, I might tremble to imagine who was now in reality accompanying you. But if you would consent to carry through the act as a common member of the long row of humble, poor sinners, I should feel that you might still partake of the blessing of human fellowship."

" 'She looked at me and laughed again. "O la la," she said, "a fox and a priest—the two will always have one more way out than you expect, and it is hard for decent people to run them to earth. How often have I told you that the breath of your humble sinners is odious to me!"

" 'She recited some lines out of a book:

> "....... *mechanic slaves*
> *With greasy aprons, rules and hammers, shall*
> *Uplift us to the view;—in their thick breaths,*
> *Rank of gross diet, shall we be enclouded,*
> *And forc'd to drink their vapor* ...

" ' "Nay, give me an honest Scots northwestern! We two have got much in common, and can speak to one another.

" ' "For the blessing of your human fellowship, Father Jacopo—what does it mean but that one man leans on another, because none of the whole crowd has energy to stand on his own legs. Your long row of humble poor sinners squeeze together, body to body, to keep warm. Oh, let them be cold, and keep their self-respect!

" ' "I shall tell you something, Father Jacopo," she continued slowly. "While, formerly, the human body, with its vapors, to me was the most unpleasant; lately, here in Rome, it is the face that I loathe, because of the dishonesty and hypocrisy which I read in it. In the City of Rome there is but one honest face, and that is fifteen hundred years old."

" 'She said no more, and I left her and walked away.

" 'But when I was alone,' Father Jacopo finished, 'I bethought myself of many things, and a question was put to me, which I myself cannot answer. Therefore I have come to you. Am I not committing a double wrong by allowing a haughty and unbelieving woman to share in the devotion of the humble and faithful? Shall I not thereby be blaspheming against the sacred act and against the sacred idea of community?'

"Like Father Jacopo himself," the Cardinal said, "I had to think before I spoke.

" 'My Jacopo,' I said at last. 'Be you without fear. It is

not impossible that, in the wisdom of your simplicity, you have found the surest means of hindering the purpose of this woman, whom you call haughty and unbelieving. I cannot see her taking her stand in your humble and faithful row. Her *dégout* of human touch is very deep; she shakes hands with nobody. Very likely the great lady, in the countenance of a person to whom she gave her hand, has read amazement at the size of that hand. And, my friend, what handgrip would she find, in all Rome, to respond to her own?

" 'But if, in spite of all, she should take you at your word, then you may trustfully lay the responsibility for the blasphemy on my shoulders. For I tell you, Jacopo: there will be no blasphemy.

" 'There are in Rome—and in the world—so many poor wretches who yell and whine over the worthlessness of the world, and their own wretchedness, as over a toothache, and who cry out for salvation as for a hot poultice—or out with the tooth!—that one may well wonder at the patience of the Lord. But the human being, who in such dead earnest challenges—not Heaven, for Heaven is not to be challenged—but her own nature, Heaven will not let down. Through her own nature it will mightily answer her.

" 'She is right: she is a noblewoman, and it is she who will transform the things that touch or strike her—not the outside things that will ever transform her.

" 'The matter now stands between high powers. You and I, Jacopo, can but wait and see.'

"Father Jacopo let himself be consoled by my words, he thanked me and walked away.

"I did not see him again. Some time after our talk together I was informed that Lady Flora, in accordance with her plan, had left Rome. I much regretted not to have seen her before her departure, for I should have been happy to thank her for her very handsome donation to the Basilica of St. John Lateran.

"A few months later I learned that Father Jacopo had applied for and obtained the modest office of parish priest in his native parish, a long way from Rome, in Piemonte."

The Cardinal here made a long pause.

"The last chapter of—or the epilogue to—the story which I have had the honor to tell you, I know from the heroine.

"In the following spring I paid a visit to the Bath of Monte Scalzo, in Ascoli.

"Oh, how live and soothing is the air of that neighborhood to breathe! How exquisite in its pureness! With what noble force and mastery does it blue the distant mountains! This is the real country of my childhood. The austere, medieval castle, my father's residence, stands far away from here; it is the dowry of my mother, the Villa Belvicino, which is pasted like a swallow's nest between the long slopes and the endless olive groves. When I was a child she often took me with her here, and we were alone together and perfectly happy.

"In Monte Scalzo I looked up one of the guests of the Bath, an old friend.

"The human misery for which people resort to this particular Bath is that which has been named after the goddess of love of our own Roman ancestors. And the treatment which the Bath offers them, follows the old saying: '*Hora cum Venere, decem annu cum Mercurio.*' Yet the visitors of the Bath never blab about their intimacy with the goddess, but they very courteously inquire after one another's facial erysipelas, migraine or rheumatism.

"Their circle was naturally amiable, unprejudiced and fearless, and I felt content and easy in mind in their company. Many pleasant hours were passed at the card table, others were dedicated to music or to philosophical discussions. The lively conversation would also run on common friends and acquaintances, but would always be free of malice.

"This season it had become a fashion among the ladies and gentlemen of the Bath to designate both present and absent friends by fictitious, romantic names—frequently taken from mythology, history or the classics. Until the newcomer in their circle had become accustomed to the pleasantry it might cause him some embarrassment.

"A lady of the coterie, who was away at the moment, and who obviously was sincerely missed by everyone, was referred to as Diana, or at other times as Principessa Daria, or as just Daria—and always with quite exceptional affection and respect. I was therefore surprised when I realized that this name was in fact an abbreviation of the word dromedaria, which seemed to me a gross nickname for a woman of high rank and—as I gathered—past the prime of youth. But a gentleman of the society, a famous orientalist, smilingly undertook to enlighten me.

" 'Think no ill of us, Your Eminence,' he said. 'For if we allow ourselves to name a highly esteemed friend after a somewhat disregarded beast of burden, the appellation is derived from an old revered Arab legend.

" ' "Do you know," the Arab asks the foreigner, "why the dromedary, while carrying her hard and heavy loads, does still carry her head so high, and does turn it from right to left with such haughty disdain of all other creatures? I shall tell you the reason. Allah, the Almighty, confided to the Prophet the ninety-nine of his hundred names, and all these are set down in the Koran. The hundredth name, though, he withheld even from the Prophet himself, and it is known to no human being on earth. But the dromedary knows it. Therefore she gazes round with pride and keeps aloof, conscious of her superiority as keeper of the secret of Allah. She says to herself: *I know the name*."

" 'The lady of whom we are speaking,' he added, 'in mien and carriage displays the pride of one initiated, of the Keeper of the Seal. And this is why we have given her the name which offends you.'

"I had been staying at the Bath for a few days when one evening a lady entered the room and at once was surrounded and greeted with joy. My orientalist and the other gentlemen gallantly and respectfully kissed her hand. The lady's unusual height allowed of no mistake. I at once recognized Lady Flora. She had become extremely thin, and so looked still taller. She no longer had her brilliant red hair, but bore a most elegantly dressed wig. Her silk frock, costly as ever, had a choice and tasteful trimming of ribbons and lace.

"She carried herself with the same nobility and truthfulness as at our first meeting, and during the conversation of this evening I learned that her wit was as live and sparkling as ever, and that there was moreover now added to it a gentle and delicate irony, of which I had no remembrance. In the course of the evening the talk of the circle, which did generally brush everything between Heaven and Earth, a couple of times turned to events of an amorous nature. Lady Flora then joined in with a fine, gay equipoise, and promptly and pleasingly inserted quotations from a couple of poets. Alas, her full clear harmonious voice of former days was gone. But in her present broken, low and hoarse voice, like to the cackle of an old wise raven or a cockatoo, there was a new joviality, a mirthful forbearance with and benevolence toward the frailty of humanity. The bold verse of Zoram Moroni she delivered as frankly as a young boy, but at the recitation of a sublime and moving love poem a deep, delicate blush mounted to her face.

"And one thing more. I could feel no surprise at the fact that her friends at the Bath had named her Diana. When at an earlier time I had occupied myself with Lady Flora, in my thoughts I had characterized her as a person of high birth and great wealth, as a native of Britain and a great traveler, and as a mind equal or superior to my own; but hardly ever as a woman. Now through the fellowship with the libertines of Monte Scalzo she was changed; mystically she had become a maiden—an old maid.

"When her eye fell upon me, she amicably came forward to greet me, and almost at once inquired after Father Jacopo. As she learned that he had altogether retired from Rome and was now living among poor and simple people, she was silent for a while.

"'Poor Father Jacopo,' she said. 'He took upon himself to tackle things and people that he had not been born to meddle with. However, he was a good, kind man, and I hope and trust that by now he too will be happy.'

"I could not ask her how she had come to be at Monte Scalzo, but the thought occupied me.

"One evening we were sitting on the western terrace, and together were silently watching how the air above us and around us was slowly emptied of the light of sunset, how night filled the valley, and the stars, one by one, came out in the vault of the sky.

"'What a sweet and fragrant wind,' she remarked.

"Our talk fell on poetry, and in the course of it I named the English poet Swift.

"She did not speak at once.

"'I wish that he were here,' she said. 'I have often, lately, wanted to talk with him. A fine poet, my friend. But, alas, ill-advised to give up his noble mind and precious time to the question of size, when even persons of true genuine dullness will know every body and soul in our universe to be infinite!

"'Du reste,' she added after a moment with a little smile, 'I love the Dean—(and lead a heart)!'

"Then she told me what had happened to her after I had last seen Father Jacopo.

"'The evening before I left Rome,' she said, 'at a very late hour I drove to St. Peter's. The church was empty and almost dark. Lights were burning in front of St. Peter's figure. In the dusk it looked very big. I gazed at it for a long time, knowing that this was our last meeting. When I had stood so for a while one of the candles flickered a little; it looked as if the face of the Apostle changed, and as if his lips moved faintly, and parted. A young man in a brown cloak came into the church, went by me and kissed the foot of the statue. As he passed me

I felt a smell of sweat and stable, a smell of the people. I first paid real attention to him after he had passed me, because he stood still so long with his mouth against St. Peter's foot; in the end he walked on. He was slight of build, with a perfect gracefulness in all his movements. His face I never saw. I know not, Cardinal, what in this moment drove me to follow his example. I took a step forward and, like him, kissed St. Peter's foot. I had thought that the bronze would be ice-cold, but it was warm from the young man's mouth, slightly moist —and that surprised me. Like him, I held my lips against it for a long time.

" 'Four weeks later, as I was staying in Missolonghi, by the Bay of Patras, I discovered the sore on my lip. My English doctor, who accompanied me, at once diagnosed the disease and named it to me. I was not ignorant, I knew the name.

" 'I stood, Your Eminence, before the glass and looked at my mouth. Then I bethought myself of Father Jacopo. To what, I thought, does this bear a likeness? To a rose? Or to a seal?' "

THE BLANK PAGE

*B*y the ancient city gate sat an old coffee-brown, black-veiled woman who made her living by telling stories.

She said:

"You want a tale, sweet lady and gentleman? Indeed I have told many tales, one more than a thousand, since that time when I first let young men tell me, myself, tales of a red rose, two smooth lily buds, and four silky, supple, deadly entwining snakes. It was my mother's mother, the black-eyed dancer, the often-embraced, who in the end—wrinkled like a winter apple and crouching beneath the mercy of the veil—took upon herself to teach me the art of story-telling. Her own mother's mother had taught it to her, and both were better story-tellers than I am. But that, by now, is of no consequence, since to the people they and I have become one, and I am most highly honored because I have told stories for two hundred years."

Now if she is well paid and in good spirits, she will go on.

"With my grandmother," she said, "I went through a hard school. 'Be loyal to the story,' the old hag would say to me. 'Be eternally and unswervingly loyal to the story.' 'Why must I be that, Grandmother?' I asked her. 'Am I to furnish you with reasons, baggage?' she cried. 'And you mean to be a story-teller! Why, you are to become a story-teller, and I shall give you my reasons! Hear then: Where the story-teller is loyal, eternally and unswervingly loyal to the story, there, in the end, silence will speak. Where the story has been betrayed, silence is but emptiness. But we, the faithful, when we have spoken our last word, will hear the voice of silence. Whether a small snotty lass understands it or not.'

"Who then," she continues, "tells a finer tale than any of us? Silence does. And where does one read a deeper tale than upon the most perfectly printed page of the most precious book? Upon the blank page. When a royal and gallant pen, in the moment of its highest inspiration, has written down its tale with the rarest ink of all—where, then, may one read a still deeper, sweeter, merrier and more cruel tale than that? Upon the blank page."

The old beldame for a while says nothing, only giggles a little and munches with her toothless mouth.

"We," she says at last, "the old women who tell stories, we know the story of the blank page. But we are somewhat averse to telling it, for it might well, among the uninitiated, weaken our own credit. All the same, I am going to make an exception with you, my sweet and pretty lady and gentleman of the generous hearts. I shall tell it to you."

High up in the blue mountains of Portugal there stands an old convent for sisters of the Carmelite order, which is an illustrious and austere order. In ancient times the convent was rich, the sisters were all noble ladies, and miracles took place there. But during the centuries highborn ladies grew less keen on fasting and prayer, the great dowries flowed scantily into the treasury of the convent, and today the few portionless and humble sisters live in but one wing of the vast crumbling structure, which looks as if it longed to become one with the gray rock itself. Yet they are still a blithe and active sisterhood. They take much pleasure in their holy meditations, and will busy themselves joyfully with that one particular task which did once, long, long ago, obtain for the convent a unique and strange privilege: they grow the finest flax and manufacture the most exquisite linen of Portugal.

The long field below the convent is plowed with gentle-eyed, milk-white bullocks, and the seed is skillfully sown out by labor-hardened virginal hands with mold under the nails. At the time when the flax field flowers, the whole valley becomes air-blue, the very color of the apron which the blessed virgin put on to go out and collect eggs within St. Anne's poultry yard, the moment before the Archangel Gabriel in mighty wing-strokes lowered himself onto the threshold of the house, and while high, high up a dove, neck-feathers raised and wings vibrating, stood like a small clear silver star in the sky. During this month the villagers many miles round raise their eyes to the flax field and ask one another: "Has the convent been lifted into heaven? Or have our good little sisters succeeded in pulling down heaven to them?"

Later in due course the flax is pulled, scutched and hackled; thereafter the delicate thread is spun, and the linen woven, and at the very end the fabric is laid out on the grass to bleach, and is watered time after time, until one may believe that snow has fallen round the convent walls. All this work is gone through with precision and piety and with such sprinklings and litanies as are the secret of the convent. For these reasons the linen, baled high on the backs of small gray donkeys and sent out through the convent gate, downwards and ever downwards to the towns, is as flower-white, smooth and dainty as was my own little foot when, fourteen years old, I had washed it in the brook to go to a dance in the village.

Diligence, dear Master and Mistress, is a good thing, and religion is a good thing, but the very first germ of a story will come from some mystical place outside the story itself. Thus does the linen of the Convento Velho draw its true virtue from the fact that the very first linseed was brought home from the Holy Land itself by a crusader.

In the Bible, people who can read may learn about the lands of Lecha and Maresha, where flax is grown. I myself cannot read, and have never seen this book of which so much is spoken. But my grandmother's grandmother as a little girl was the pet of an old Jewish rabbi, and the learning she received from him has been kept and passed on in our family. So you will read, in the book of Joshua, of how Achsah the daughter of Caleb lighted from her ass and cried unto her father: "Give me a blessing! For thou hast now given me land; give me also the blessing of springs of water!" And he gave her the upper springs and the nether springs. And in the fields of Lecha and Maresha lived, later on, the families of them that wrought the finest linen of all. Our Portuguese crusader, whose own ancestors had once been great linen weavers of Tomar, as he rode through these same fields was struck by the quality of the flax, and so tied a bag of seeds to the pommel of his saddle.

From this circumstance originated the first privilege of the convent, which was to procure bridal sheets for all the young princesses of the royal house.

I will inform you, dear lady and gentleman, that in the country of Portugal in very old and noble families a venerable custom has been observed. On the morning after the wedding of a daughter of the house, and before the morning gift had yet been handed over, the Chamberlain or High Steward from a balcony of the palace would hang out the sheet of the night and would solemnly proclaim: *Virginem eam tenemus*—"we declare her to have been a virgin." Such a sheet was never afterwards washed or again lain on.

This time-honored custom was nowhere more strictly upheld than within the royal house itself, and it has there subsisted till within living memory.

Now for many hundred years the convent in the mountains, in appreciation of the excellent quality of the linen delivered, has held its second high privilege: that of receiving back that central piece of the snow-white sheet which bore witness to the honor of a royal bride.

In the tall main wing of the convent, which overlooks an immense landscape of hills and valleys, there is a long gallery with a black-and-white marble floor. On the walls of the gallery, side by side, hangs a long row of heavy, gilt frames, each of them adorned with a coroneted plate of pure gold, on which is engraved the name of a princess: Donna Christina, Donna Ines, Donna Jacintha Lenora, Donna Maria. And each of these frames encloses a square cut from a royal wedding sheet.

Within the faded markings of the canvases people of some imagination and sensibility may read all the signs of the zodiac: the Scales, the Scorpion, the Lion, the Twins. Or they may there find pictures from their own world of ideas: a rose, a heart, a sword—or even a heart pierced through with a sword.

In days of old it would occur that a long, stately, richly colored procession wound its way through the stone-gray mountain scenery, upwards to the convent. Princesses of Portugal, who were now queens or queen dowagers of foreign countries, Archduchesses, or Electresses, with their splendid retinue, proceeded here on a pilgrimage which was by nature both sacred and secretly gay. From the flax field upwards the road rises steeply; the royal lady would have to descend from her coach to be carried this last bit of the way in a palanquin presented to the convent for the very same purpose.

Later on, up to our own day, it has come to pass—as it comes to pass when a sheet of paper is being burnt, that after all other sparks have run along the edge and died away, one last clear little spark will appear and hurry along after them —that a very old highborn spinster undertakes the journey to Convento Velho. She has once, a long long time ago, been playmate, friend and maid-of-honor to a young princess of Portugal. As she makes her way to the convent she looks round to see the view widen to all sides. Within the building a sister conducts her to the gallery and to the plate bearing the name of the princess she has once served, and there takes leave of her, aware of her wish to be alone.

Slowly, slowly a row of recollections passes through the small, venerable, skull-like head under its mantilla of black lace, and it nods to them in amicable recognition. The loyal friend and confidante looks back upon the young bride's elevated married life with the elected royal consort. She takes stock of happy events and disappointments—coronations and jubilees, court intrigues and wars, the birth of heirs to the throne, the alliances of younger generations of princes and princesses, the rise or decline of dynasties. The old lady will remember how once, from the markings on the canvas, omens were drawn; now she will be able to compare the fulfillment to the omen, sighing a little and smiling a little. Each separate canvas with its coroneted name-plate has a story to tell, and each has been set up in loyalty to the story.

But in the midst of the long row there hangs a canvas which differs from the others. The frame of it is as fine and as heavy as any, and as proudly as any carries the golden plate with the royal crown. But on this one plate no name is inscribed, and the linen within the frame is snow-white from corner to corner, a blank page.

I beg of you, you good people who want to hear stories told: look at this page, and recognize the wisdom of my grandmother and of all old story-telling womer!

For with what eternal and unswerving loyalty has not this

canvas been inserted in the row! The story-tellers them-selves before it draw their veils over their faces and are dumb. Because the royal papa and mama who once ordered this canvas to be framed and hung up, had they not had the tradition of loyalty in their blood, might have left it out.

It is in front of this piece of pure white linen that the old princesses of Portugal—worldly wise, dutiful, long-suffering queens, wives and mothers—and their noble old playmates, bridesmaids and maids-of-honor have most often stood still.

It is in front of the blank page that old and young nuns, with the Mother Abbess herself, sink into deepest thought.

New Gothic Tales

THE CARYATIDS,
AN UNFINISHED TALE

On a summer afternoon in the forties of the last century, two carriages and a couple of riding horses were making a halt within the glade of a forest near Sarlat in the Province of Dordogne, in France. The coachmen and grooms stood beside the horses, feeding them with bits of bread. The one carriage had four horses to it, the other was a light and elegant little phaeton. Of the saddle horses one was black and one gray.

A little river was running through the glade. Near the place where the carriages had stopped it grew wider and shallower, and the grassy banks were trodden down by the cattle that came here to drink.

The sky was high and blue; all round the horizon large, immovable, gray and delicately rosy clouds were towered up, which might forebode thunder on the morrow. But the afternoon was clear and fine. The little river came out gaily from the thicket, through the dark foliage of which the sprinklings of sunlight dropped into it like a drizzle of gold, and here in the open it reflected the blue and gray hues of the summer sky as frankly as a mirror.

Of the people who had come in the carriages and on horseback, two ladies and a couple of nurses were occupied in bathing three young children in the river, and were talking loudly and laughing over it. The children's clothes were strewn upon the grass, together with the ladies' sunshades, thrown upside down, as fine as a flower bed. The young ladies in their slim bodices and voluminous skirts were themselves like peonies on slender stems, gracefully flung upside down upon the riverside.

The mother of the three children, a tall and willowy young woman with a narrow face and big starlike dark eyes, had tied a lace handkerchief round her head, and was holding her naked little son down in the water, and scolding a sturdy young woman in the peasant's dress of the province, who was standing barefooted in the middle of the stream to receive the child. The little boy stared at his mother with her own big dark eyes, very skeptical about the undertaking, and wondering whether the women really did mean him to go.

The two bigger children, little girls of five and six, the one fair and the other dark, were running laughing down the river, their hair all done up in curl papers. The one of them was pulling off the shaggy dark pink flowers of the wild hemp that grew on the sides of the stream, the other was splashing down the river, from time to time throwing herself down flat on her stomach, and beating the water with her feet.

The second young lady, who for driving her smart phaeton had put on an elegant frock in tartan colors—which were highly fashionable—and cut somehow in the style of a young cavalier's costume, walked alongside on the sward like a hen with ducklings, laughing at the children and holding her handkerchief to her mouth. She was a school friend of the young mother, and the widow of a neighbor, and had come from her own house to join the party in the forest.

Meanwhile the two men of the party, who were the husband and the young brother of the dark lady, had walked together slowly to the farther end of the glade. They were neighbors, and had met here to discuss a question of their boundaries, which a change in the course of the river had slightly altered. The ladies had profited by the occasion to make a picnic in the woods. They were talking about poachers, and were waiting for the arrival of the old keeper whom they had summoned here to meet them. A gang of gypsies and poachers had for some time given them much trouble.

"If only," said Philippe, the eldest, "we could get rid of the miller's widow at Masse Bleue. I remember the first time I saw her, eight years ago, when she was only a child. I met her in the forest, and because she was such an uncommonly graceful child I tried to stop her and make her talk with me. It really seems to me now, when I think of the scene, that I was holding out my stick to a smooth little viper that was trying to get round it, indeed she was hissing at me, maneuvering to the right and the left."

As he was speaking, the old keeper arrived, accompanied by the two spotted long-haired dogs. He had to cross the river; in the middle of it he took off his cap to them. They walked down together, and came from the mellow golden light of the glade into the green and cool shade of the forest. After they had discussed the question of the stream, Philippe addressed a few questions to the old man on the gypsies. The old servant's face grew dark.

"If only," he said, "we could get rid of the miller's widow of Masse Bleue. It was a strange thing in the old miller to go and marry a gypsy girl, and the whole pack is thick as inkle-weavers. Where a snake gets its head in, it will soon get the whole body. They all know that she will shelter them if they get into trouble, and she has many guests down at the old mill." He stole a glance at Philippe, not daring to give course to his feelings about the gypsies, fed by a life-long struggle, for he knew that the young lady of the manor held a protecting hand over the tribe. The gypsies possessed a position of their own on the estate. Although they came and went, and had no real home, a certain section or tribe reckoned themselves, and were reckoned by the masters of Champmeslé, as belonging to their land. They gave much trouble, but still their lords would have allowed no one from the outside to interfere with them, as if they were a nuisance strictly their own.

"Tell me, Claude," said Philippe thoughtfully, "do you believe that the people had anything to do with the disappearance of old Father Bernhard?"

The keeper wiped his face. "As God liveth, my lord," he said, "they caused his death. But if you can say that they killed him, that the devil only knows. This is how it was: These people, who do not believe in the Lord, do no more wait for His hour, but when they are tired of their life, they just finish it, as it pleases themselves. They dig a grave in the forest, and before sunrise they go to it with their sons and friends, and some of them even blow airs on a flute, and they lie down in it. They spread a goatskin over their face, and as the sun comes up, the others fill in the earth. They will remain there, lying on the grave, without eating or drinking, with their face upon the sod, till the sun is down, for they do not believe that the old man in the grave will have died till then. Then they go back, and eat and drink, having buried their father, and think no more of it.

"Now it was said that they had buried, in this way, an old woman who came from a country in the East, and indeed I think that she was the grandmother of the miller's widow. Father Bernhard also heard of it, and was terrified that such ungodliness should be going on in the parish.

"I said to him: 'It is the same to me whether, of the people, the living are buried or the dead choose to walk about. As to its happening in my forest, I do not like it, but many things go on in a forest which you may not like.'

"Then he went to the people himself. 'Father Bernhard,' they said to him, 'you settled people chase us from one place to the other. You fine us and whip us and put us in prison and hang us. Do you now also grudge us a little earth to put into our mouths? Wait a little, and you will yourself come running after us, to ask us to bury you for the sake of your peace.'

"Shortly after this, as it was that time of the year, they all went away, and I did not see any one of them for a long time. Now you know, sir, that Father Bernhard, who was a pious man, was not learned, and had difficulty in reading. From this time he began to read all day, and to carry his book with him everywhere. One day, when I was out, it was the market day of Sarlat, and they were driving pigs to the fair. I found Father Bernhard at the side of the road, very pale and panting.

"'Who do you think, Claude,' he said, 'just passed me? You would never guess. The swine of the Gadarenes,' he said, 'all the herd of them. Why, they may arise as well as other things in the Scripture, and the people have sent them here. The devils are in them still, but they are tired by now of being in swine, and are looking for someone to enter into. It is hard that an old man like me shall have to be, now, night and day in the mountain, cutting myself with stones.'

"I said nothing to him; what can one answer to things out of the Holy Book?

"Then, again, a fortnight later, I met him. 'Will the people not be back soon, Claude?' he asked me. 'When will they be back?'

"Only the Thursday of that same week he was gone altogether, and nobody saw him after that. And you will remember, sir, that as he had last been seen near the mill, they swept the seine for him in the mill pond. There were then two little gypsy children, who stood by. 'Sweep with a harrow,' they said." The old man stopped, swore an oath deep in his chest, and sighed.

"But Claude," said his master, smiling a little, "they can have nothing to do with the misfortune of poor Father Bernhard. You tell me yourself that they were far away by that time."

"Yes, they were certainly not here," the old man said with deep bitterness. "They would take care about that, the crafty devils. But what is she about at night, at Masse Bleue, making the wheel turn, when she has no grain to grind? Is that right, to have the water and the wheel work for her for nothing, just making fools of them? Ask her yourself, my lord."

Seeing the young woman in the tartan frock coming down toward them the men changed the subject of their talk, and the keeper again took off his cap.

"Am I interrupting an important debate?" she asked them, smiling. "Childerique sends me to ask you to take a glass of wine with us. You too, Claude." She nodded to the old man.

They all walked up to where the young mother, having finished the task of bathing her children, still blushing from the effort, was instructing the servants to spread a tablecloth upon the turf, and to bring wine and glasses. Out of the carriage the groom lifted baskets of cherries, deep orange speckled with crimson, and rich black, through the skin of which the red blood shone. The children had milk and cake served to them upon a rug, a little way off, and were silent under the novelty of the treat.

The conversation of the party ran upon horses. They were all of them horse-breeders and traders, and keen equestrians. Childerique had given up hunting after the birth of her little boy; she had lost her own mother when she had been a baby, and would not have her children run any risk. But it had been a great sacrifice, and a horse was still to her what a bottle is to an old reformed drunkard; also her team of horses was only a substitute. She was driving it today to break it in, in the hope of selling it well to a very rich neighbor, who had lately come to the district. The old nobility of the Province was much taken up with this man, as with the first person capable of making a fortune whom they had never met face to face. They founded many speculations upon him.

"Surely, Delphine," said Childerique to her friend, "you could sell Paribanu to Monsieur Tutein for me. You are his formulary in the manners of good society, and have only to tell him that a true gentleman is ever known by his off thill-horse."

The young widow blushed a little. "If I really have the honor," she said, "of playing mentor to Monsieur Tutein's social Telemaque, I shall have more conscience than to drive him straight into the arms of Circe. You must ask him to your birthday party at Champmeslé, and do the bewitching yourself."

They began to discuss this party, which was to be given in honor of Childerique's twenty-fifth birthday, and was to take place in a week. Childerique got up with her husband and went off to look at the children, leaving the two others to discuss various festival arrangements, which were to be a surprise for herself.

On the way she squeezed her husband's arm a little, and said, low: "There is a bite."

She was planning a match between her brother and her friend. That the young widow was five years older than the projected bridegroom she thought a fortunate circumstance. She was six years older than the boy herself, and would have disapproved and been jealous of any quite youthful feminine influence in his life. Her mind was running pleasantly on the prospect of presenting to the young couple a green set of Sèvres porcelain, which had come to Champmeslé nearly a hundred years ago with a young bride from Delphine's own estate of Azat. She came near to communicating her thought to her husband, but restrained herself, suspicious of his laughter at her old manner of anticipating the course of events.

The nurse was teasing the little boy by pushing him back on the rug every time he tried to get up; the child was hiccoughing with laughter, clear as a shrill little bell. At the sight of his father he gave such a shout of exultation as did, in the mast, Columbus' watchman at the first sight of a new continent. The young man lifted him onto his shoulders, and the child looked down majestically at the green world below him, and at his big sisters, suddenly so very small.

Children whose parents have been very much in love develop a fearlessness toward life unknown to the breed shot in cold beds. They are indeed like those cherubs of old Relievi who are represented riding on lions, spurring the mighty lord of the desert with their little rosy heels, and pulling his dark mane. The dangerous powers of life have kept watch round their cradles; the lion has been their guardian and friend, and when they meet him again in life they recognize him, laughing, as their old playmate.

"What was Claude preaching about?" Childerique asked her husband. "I suppose it was of the gypsies."

"There are so many of them just now," said Philippe, "he wants us to chase them off the land, and tells me that Monsieur Tutein has done so on his estate."

"Yes, Monsieur Tutein," said she with disdain, "what does he know about them? Grandmama once told me that in '93 they hid Grandpapa from the soldiers when he came back home to see his wife. At that time Monsieur Tutein's people were very likely with the troops of the mountain. When I was a little girl I often wished to be a gypsy child and to wander about with them. Did you never want that?"

"But I did it," said her husband, "when I was living in Canada, with my father. As a child, I was friendly with many of the red Indians, and went about with them for long whiles.

They were good people, kind to me, and taught me many things. Sometimes these people remind me of them. It is curious, for instance, about that young woman of the mill. I knew an old Indian woman, whose tribe believed her to be a witch. She was a hundred years old, and hideous to look at. Still those two are alike. I have wondered whether it is the brand, the witch's mark, which they have in common. An old Indian told me that once a woman has turned to witchcraft there is nothing in the world that can turn her off it, not love, children, nor virtue. I have wondered . . ." he stopped.

"I know," said Childerique, "you have been told that old Udday, her father, once laid a curse upon my father and all his descendants. But my mother liked them." This was always the last word with her. Her piety to the memory of her dead mother tolerated no argument.

"And besides," she cried, "where is the curse on me? Where is the curse?" Laughing she dragged down her little son from his father's shoulders, played with him and blew into his face. "Where is our curse?"

"Childerique," cried Delphine from her seat on the grass, "I must go back or I shall be too late. The two old sisters De Maré are coming to play cards, and I must pick up the Abbé on my way to make a fourth."

"And why not Monsieur Tutcin?" asked Childerique.

"Oh God," said Delphine, "the old ladies would never believe that a man who is not of the old nobility could keep from revoking."

The party broke up, first seeing Delphine off in her phaeton. From the entrance to the dense wood she waved her hand with the whip; her gay colors were swallowed up by the somber deep.

Childerique got herself and her family into the landaulet; she let the coachman drive the horses for the return journey. The little boy grew sleepy on his nurse's knees.

"Give him to me, Marie," said the mother.

No sooner was he seated in her arms than he dropped off to

sleep, his dark curls—luminous as the black cherries that they had been served—toward her bosom. She became absorbed in the delight of the pressure of his firm little body against her own, and sat silent, thinking of the struggle she had had with her stepmother, before she got the old woman's consent to nurse her babies herself. "What obstacles people do make for our happiness," she thought.

The two riders trotted on, a little behind the carriage, their horses here in the forest much worried by the gadflies and prancing on the narrow road; they did not talk. The young boy, red-haired, tall and slim on his tall horse, was pushing his mount on impatiently, as if he could not stand this state of things one moment longer. Philippe had his eyes on the carriage, and that air of listening and keeping watch which rarely left him.

On his return to France from America nine years before, his neighbors had been impressed and a little frightened by his new ideas and schemes of reform, but he had quite settled down by now, and seemed to form himself like a ringwall round the little world of his domestic life. It had indeed taken him some time to get used to the abundance growing up around him. It seemed to him that he had done nothing but take to himself a lovely young girl of his native province, and from that one step had resulted the richness of life on all sides, the multiplicity of color and melody in his house and garden, the activity everywhere, laughter and crises of tears, the sweetness of young lives and alternation of work and hopes, the whole solar system of Champmeslé.

He watched the figure of his wife, sunk in musing in the carriage seat. He recognized the thoughtful mood which had come over her, the wave-motion of her being, following the rhythm of the moon like the tidal waves of the sea. It was as if a weight were being gathered grain by grain, within the depth of her, balancing down her vitality into a new calm and a deeper understanding. Sometimes she would disappear from him altogether for a day or two, but only to come back, radi-

ant, as from a flight into a distant world from which she
brought with her fresh flowers to adorn her home.

II

The young master of Champmeslé himself had had an uncommon destiny.

He was born in Dordogne, but when he was seven years
old his father had gone away from the country, and had taken
him with him, to live in Canada, on an estate near Quebec,
upon the river of Maskinongé, which had been in his family
for a long time. The boy never quite knew what quarrels
about politics and religion had driven his father into exile.
His mother had died two years before.

For some reason his father took up, in the new country, the
life of a hard-working farmer, and left the interest on his
capital to accumulate in France, and to keep up and improve
his estates there. Philippe was told that they were rich, but he
never knew in practice what it meant to be rich.

He became conscious of himself and of the world in a rough
new country. Still the old province, these same hills and
valleys, woods and old towns which now encircled him, were
with him during all his childhood, as God is ever present to
a child piously brought up. The names of the old places were
on his father's tongue, and the boy would not forget how the
rivers ran and the roads turned, what were the signs of the
changing seasons, or how the old people on the farms were
related to one another. The records of stags killed and horses
bred in France were kept on the Canadian farm. Most often
of all would come back the name of Haut-Mesnil and of the
people who lived there.

His boyhood, lonely in a strange country, in the company
of a melancholy man, had shone all the same with rainbow
radiance from a lost, a promised land.

Time after time in the course of these years his father would
take up the idea of going back to France. The life of the child
then reflected the terrible struggle within the soul of the

ordinarily collected, quiet man. He saw him thrown off his balance, upset and stirred to the bottom of his being. The occupations of their daily life were than left and forgotten as if they had not existed. For weeks the agony would go on; the man would decide to go and give it up ten times within one night, or he would imagine them already on the way, wake up and find himself in the Canadian home, and despair. These outbreaks became a yearly returning rite, an equinoctial gale in the existence of the boy. One thing he would notice: as soon as there was any plan of going back to France the names of Haut-Mesnil and its inhabitants would disappear from the vocabulary of his father. Then, in the end, the mood passed, always in the same way, and the Baron de La Verandryé never went back to France.

When his father fell ill, the conflict of his life suddenly dissolved itself in his plans and hopes of his son going to France when he himself should be dead. During his last months he talked much of all that the boy was to do there, with such gay hopefulness as Philippe had never known in him. The boy would find him feverish in his bed, waiting for his return to instruct him how to put out carob in a pond of Champmeslé. On his last day his mind was swarming with the names of old servants and dogs; to the son listening it was as if the world of Champmeslé were rushing out to meet him.

Six months after his father's death, when he had settled the affairs of their estate, Philippe started on his journey home.

He had his first real feeling of freedom at the sight of the ocean. But one moonlight night, when he was on the deck of the ship, in the dark-brown, transparent shadow of the large sails, it was to him suddenly as if the cold gray wandering waters spoke to him, warning him not to go, but to turn back. The feeling did not last long, but he remembered it long.

On his return to France, for a time he forgot everything. The promised land more than kept its promises. Strange as it was to him to travel toward his home, to meet, one after the other, the blue hills and rivers, and the towns, and to find them so much smaller than he remembered them—for in Canada the problem of distances had been one of the serious phenomena of life, but with the fertility and smooth roads of the French land all seemed to be one neighborhood and distance nonexistent, and this was much like a dream, and from the first made everything dreamlike to him—conditions were soon, in a much stranger way, changed entirely. He was no longer acting himself, but was being received and handled by something stronger than he. Just as it had come to lift up his dying father, the country came out to meet him, put its arms round him and held him. He learned that his father had been dear to people here in a way which he would never himself have guessed; they talked of him with smiles and tears. A new picture of the lonely man was here forming itself for his son.

This extraordinary happiness of his first year in France was, even now, sometimes brought back to Philippe, unconsciously, in an old tune or a scent. And when he thus got the whole fullness of the nights and days of that year, of friendships, hunts, journeys, meals and dreams, distilled and in one draught, the strongest flavor within it was still that feeling of belonging to something, and of having been taken into, and made one with, a life outside himself, in which he had still a more perfect freedom than he had known before. It had the sweetness of a first union of love. Consciously he could never recall it, it had lasted too briefly.

In due time he also called at Haut-Mesnil. There he found things much changed, for the master of the house had died, his widow was a second wife, whom his father had never known, and the present head of the family, her son, was a boy of ten. The daughter of the first marriage, with whose name he was familiar, was in a convent at Pirigueux. But he was received as kindly there as everywhere, and in time, in spite of the place being so unlike the Haut-Mesnil of his childhood dreams, he came to feel more at home there than in any other house. So much power is there in lifeless things, in houses, roads, trees and bridges. Also there was a particular influence at work in the place, for which, later on, he came to find a name.

From the Countess he learned a thing which surprised him, namely, that the heads of the houses of Haut-Mesnil and Champmeslé had not been on friendly terms. This did not affect the benevolence of the Countess toward him; in fact it seemed that this lady had made it a line of conduct to take, in life, the opposite side from her husband. Thus she had taken, on her marriage, the side of her stepdaughter against her father, and even, when her own son appeared on the stage and was made much fuss about, against him. She did not come from Dordogne, but from the Province of Geneva; she was a highly bigoted, dry woman, with little knowledge of the world or the heart, no imagination and no faculty for loving. Life was dull to her, and she welcomed, with a passionate gratitude, the few phenomena in it which were capable of awakening her imagination. Probably it was her grudge against her husband that he had never been able to do so—even her son, when he had once been born, had failed. For scandal she had no taste; the world of sentiment lay too far off her domain. Religion had often shown a fatal tendency to dry up under her hands, from the ecstasy which, upon the best of authorities she had expected of it, into sawdust of moral principle. But adventure she appreciated. When Philippe would talk to little Childerique of red Indians, of bear-hunts, or of canoe expeditions, she would listen, as spellbound as the child; for these last she had even a particular preference, being terrified of water herself. Something of the picture of the little boy who had grown up, motherless, far from France, in the company of wild redskinned men, struck her heart and brought out one of the rare little wells of feeling in it. Philippe found in the narrow-minded woman, who could not love, a rare talent for being a friend, which, toward him, lasted all her life.

Many things at Haut-Mesnil were explained by the strange luster which was still spread everywhere by the memory of the Countess Sophie, Childerique's mother. The remembrance of this beautiful young woman seemed to live in all the province, like an afterglow of her rich vitality. People talked about her as if she were still alive, and little tales of her grace and generosity were hurried upon him, as if he could not be accepted as a true child of the community until he shared this creed. He heard of her curious taste for disguise, so that she would, like a neat female Haroun al Raschid, become acquainted with the poor and outcast of the land in her maid's apron, or even dressed up as a horse-dealer's boy, for she was an exquisite horsewoman; and of her impulsive heart, when, on finding a poor tenant's household lamenting a dead mother and a new-born baby, she had shifted her own little daughter to the arms of the nurse, and laid the forlorn child to her full breast. The present Countess herself, who had never seen Madame Sophie, had a special feeling toward the frail figure, a mixture of admiration and pity. In Childerique, while she strove to graft into her the strictest principles of prudence, her true devotion went toward those imaginative, defying sides of her nature which recalled the dead woman.

When Childerique came from her convent she found the new young neighbor a persona grata of Haut-Mesnil, so much the friend of her little brother that to begin with she did not like him. Philippe afterwards wondered whether the stepmother had not, before the girl's return, planned—as much as she had it in her to plan anything in life—to unite sense and romance by marrying off her stepdaughter to the largest estate of the province as well as to the blood-brother of the Mohicans. The heart of the young man needed no encouragement; it was prepared for love for this girl as a field, plowed and harrowed, for the spring rains. Virginal and generous, Childerique seemed to him, from the beginning, the incarnation of France and of all there that he had dreamed of as a child. At times it was as if he had known her first, and as if the country were imitating the girl in sweetness and ease of heart. Now even had the old woman and the young man been scheming together skillfully; the prey would not have been easy for them to come up to.

Childerique was at this time intoxicated with her freedom, but not at all with her power. She had grieved as a child because she had not been born a boy; for the sake of her mother's honor, she was indignant that her stepmother should have accomplished, without any effort, the exploit which her beloved mother had failed to achieve. She was also at this period of her life troubled by being unusually tall for her age. Toward both these worries of her existence she took up the same attitude; she seemed to feel that as the truth could not be concealed, the world might as well have it point-blank. On this account she carried herself erect in her full height and also allowed herself the full freedom of being a girl, following all her own whims and frankly keeping from the society of males. In spite of her conventual education she was a Diana of Dordogne, a kind deity, but with bow and arrows. She might well, had she been bathing in her favorite forest pool, and had Actaeon approached, sweaty from the hunt, congratulating her on her choice of a bathing place, have invited him to join her in a swim. But had she found him spying on her secretly she would not have been behind the goddess in loosing her fierce hounds on him, or in her enjoyment of the sight of his dismembering. She had no desire to be desired, and her woman's kingdom of longing, rapture and jealousy seemed to her all too vast; she did not want to take up the scepter at all. Like a young stork which considers that it runs very well, and does not care to fly, she had to be lured into her element. But once in it she gave proof of great powers. After his first kiss and words of love, she fluttered up audaciously into flight; it was, in their honey-moon an ecstatic, easy soaring, and as the children were conceived and born a succession of majestic wing-strokes.

They were married in the month of June, and Philippe took his young wife by her own team of four horses, which were his wedding present to her, the dreamlike easy distance from Haut-Mesnil to Champmeslé. The house to which he brought her was inferior to her old home, for the manor of Champmeslé had been burnt down during the Revolution. The family had since lived in a long white house, formerly the habitation of the inspector of the estate. But it lay very finely, surrounded by the terraces, gardens and woods of the old chateau; and within, it was richly furnished with choice old things and tasteful modern furniture.

Up under the roof of this house there was a large room, light in itself, but darkened by shutters. Upon the day-week of his wedding the young husband, a little giddy with happiness, roaming about in the house of which many corners were still unknown to him, came up here, and on finding the place filled with old furniture, mirrors, pictures, books and papers, sat down for half a lazy hour, going through old letters in the chiaroscuro of the room, and scattering them round him. Really he was looking for some trace of the little boy Philippe who had wandered about in the same house twenty years before, and might have left a reflection in some dim and dusty old looking glass, into which no one had since gazed.

Out of an old, tortoise-shell box, which opened by the touch of a spring, a packet of letters, tied together with a pale blue ribbon, came into his hand. They were love letters, written by a lady to her lover, by Childerique's mother to his father. Afterwards he remembered how he had, after the first glance, got up to destroy them, when his eyes had been caught by his own name.

The young mistress wrote: "Your clever and adorable little Philippe, who, when I sat with him on the garden seat, and had closed my eyes to think of you, poked his little finger into my face and said: 'Light your eyes, Madame.' "

Here was the child of Champmeslé then, no longer lonely; a young woman had sat with him in a garden, had smiled at him, and repeated his little sayings in a letter to her lover.

He read all the letters through, only once, but he found later that he knew many passages of them by heart, and could have passed an examination on the correspondence of the dead lovers. The last of them was a crumpled bit of paper, unlike the others in form as well. It ran: "Dear Baron de La Verandryé. Just a word. I am sorry for what I said to you yesterday. The bearer, the gypsy Udday, has got my message and will give it to you correctly, it is too long for me to write, as I am not well. Good-bye, good-bye."

Philippe looked at the date, it was the day of Childerique's birth. This letter was written to deceive anybody into whose hands it might fall; the lovers had quarreled, and unable to bear the burden of their disagreement at this moment, Sophie had sent the gypsy with a verbal message, and the little note as a credential.

As soon as he understood the sense of the letters, Philippe got up and locked the door. It was as if he had found his father in here, defenseless and exposed to danger.

Here, then, was the central point and the heart of his world, even from childhood, and of his father's wanderings, exile and death, run to earth at last in the attic of Champmeslé. This sweetness and this fire had hurled people to and fro across the ocean. He looked round him, so strongly did he feel the presence of the man in the grave over the sea, and the woman in the mausoleum of Haut-Mesnil. How was it possible that he had not known till now? His heart was squeezed by pain as he thought of the companionship and comfort that he might have given his father had he only understood that when he said "France," he meant "Sophie."

He made a heap of all the letters together with the same

ribbon, struck a light and watched them flame up and come
to ashes upon the cold fireplace.

So Childerique was his father's child. There was no doubt
about it, the young impassionate mother had informed her
lover of the happiness and danger, and had come back to it
many times. It seemed natural enough, and that rare sympathy and feeling of home which he had with her was real
and sprang from a source deep in their blood. He had had
the sensation, when they had laughed and jested together, of
being with someone whom he had known well and loved all
his life, and now he understood that too: he had then been
playing with his father as a child.

He smiled at the thought that he and she were works of
the same artist. He had met, in his father's nature, a deep
conflict between his sense of duty and the strong and wild in-
clinations of the heart. He himself was then a product of the
man's conscience, his respect of, and resignation to, outward
forces, but Childerique was what his father could do when he
was left free, where he wanted to be.

Suddenly the thought of Childerique filled the room so
completely that it drove away all the shadows, and he rose to
go to her when he remembered that he had locked the door.
He was struck by a great wave of terror. It seemed to him
that he had separated himself from her forever. That gray
and cold ocean upon which he had looked down from the
ship, he had laid it between him and the young wife down-
stairs whom he had lately held in his arms, and had left ar-
ranging bouquets for their home.

Frightened to death, he could not bear the silence. "Father!" he cried, his hands to his head, and in a moment, as
there was no answer: "Sophie—Madame Sophie, what have
I done?"

Why had they not told him, but let him walk straight into
this misery? Still, he knew now that his father had told him,
had he only understood. But, he thought again, the day be-

fore his wedding a bridge had given way as he rode across it, and he had been in danger of his life. Why had the dead people not helped him there, and let him die? Now they had left him here, all alone.

He sat for a long time in the room, to make up his mind. Had it been the week before, he thought, he could have told her, or he could have gone away without ever telling her; it would have been better to have done that. Now he could do nothing. In the end, before he left the room again, he had sealed his mouth and his heart forever; she should never know that anything had been changed between them. He thought: It would bring down all the world around her, the sacred memory of her dead mother, her strong faith in honor and virtue, her joy and hope about their future. Was it not then for him to guard her against such disaster? In his heart he knew well that all these reasons were of no account, and that the true motive for his silence was that he could not, he would not suffer her to think with horror of his embrace.

His longing for her, as he got up, was so strong that his arms and hands ached. "Let it be as it will," he thought. "Let them even separate our souls forever, if it be as they tell us. Our bodies they shall not separate at all."

As life went on at Champmeslé during the following seven years, and his existence grew up on all sides, this same thought was ever with him. Their home became, round Childerique, a little world of its own, through all of which one line and spirit ran. The horses and dogs, the servants of the house, the furniture and the books of the library, the lilacs on the terrace, the drive up to the door, the silhouette of the roofs as you came home late in the dusk, and the tunes that she played—all belonged to one another, and were each of them part of a greater whole. If they were scattered by another revolution, or if, their earthly career finished, they were to meet again in another world, wherever two or three of them were gathered together they would recognize each other and cry "Hail, there is one more of us. We, too, were there. We, too, were part of Champmeslé."

When the first two children were born, he was glad that they were daughters. He thought that it would be wrong should a child of incest carry forth the name of La Verandryé. After the birth of his first little girl he had even gone to their old doctor to ask him whether there was any sure way of deciding the sex of children beforehand.

The old man laughed at him. "Oh, Monsieur le Baron," he said, "you are too impatient. Do not refuse to plant us a few roses at Champmeslé, for the joy of the province, before you graft the oak."

Childerique herself had been on the watch for any sign of disappointment in her husband, but she thought that the loveliness of the children had conquered their father's heart. When the boy was born she made all the house and land of Champmeslé clap their hands at this master-stroke of hers.

She had wanted the child named first after his father and then after hers. To him neither choice had seemed seemly, he thought: "Let each of the dead men have that peace of the grave now, which they have more and less deserved."

He often wondered what would happen to her should she come to know the truth now. He imagined that she would go into a convent; she would have to throw herself away from them all into the arms of Heaven for her salvation. It was not her actual fate either which took up his thoughts, but the transformation which, at a word, all her world would undergo. He had seen grass fires, and the black and waste land which they leave behind them; her flowering world would come to look like that. When he had been a boy he had been the friend of an old Indian horse-trader, who had assured him that he was, at the very same hour as he was trading horses in the marketplace of Quebec, even as well, in the strong and shaggy shape of a timber wolf, hunting and sleeping in the mountains. Thus, he thought, the white house of

Champmeslé was even at this time at once the pride and refuge of her heart and to her mind a house of crime against the law of God, a place of shame. The three children, playing under her eyes on the terrace, were both the flowers and the crown of a proud, old race, and, more terrible than the cubs of the timber wolves, nameless offspring of dishonor. And he himself—like to his friend Osceola, who, while he was grooming his sleek horses and tying up their tails, was also trotting upon a trail in the woods or sitting in the snow and howling at the terrified mares and foals—he was at the same time the head of the corner of her happiness, and her enemy, the destroyer of it all.

In the beginning of their married life his consciousness had made him a little unsteady in his relations with his wife. He would leave her then, to come back begging for her love, as if he thought that they were soon to be separated for life. Childerique, who had no means of comparing him to other young men in love, took this as the normal expression of a man's passion; it did not affect her; her strength and resilience of heart could have stood out against a heavier weight thrown at it. Sometimes she felt a slight compassion for him because he was still a stranger to many things which seemed to her foundation stones of existence. He was at home neither in the old nonsense rhymes of the nursery nor in the Divine service of Church, and he hardly remembered his First Communion.

One trait in the nature of his wife made Philippe wonder if she had in her an instinct which knew more than she did herself. With him, while she was such a devoted wife, radiant with love, her feelings seemed to be more those of a sister or comrade than of a woman in love, as if she knew his love to have been born with him, and to be hers by right of nature. Many women, he was aware, will buy their supremacy over their lovers at the price of much self-denial, and will submit to servitude through all the hours of the day to hold, within one hour of the night, triumphantly, the highest power of life and death. This, in a woman, had always made him uncomfortable; he distrusted both the servitude and the triumph. Childerique would be prepared to buy his appreciation of her as a housewife or a mother, and his admiration of her wisdom, justice and virtue, at the cost of her greatest efforts, and of a good deal of persuasion. For his desire and adoration, which were her happiness, she would give nothing at all, as if holding that within their sphere there can be neither sale nor purchase.

But with the young Lord of Haut-Mesnil, six years younger than herself, she showed all the attributes of a passionate and jealous mistress. She could not live without his adoration, and would humor and coax him into it; in her relation to him she never ran short of coquetries and artful flattery. She was vain about his appearance and about her own when he was near, and melancholy when he was melancholy, like one of his own dogs. And with him she was also capricious, zealous of attention, hurt by negligence and ever on her outlook for a rival, be it only one of his friends from school. She rarely gave her husband any caress on her own accord, but she would take trouble to keep near the boy, fondling and petting him, holding his hands and playing with his fingers or running her own fingers through his red locks.

III

There was in the forest a large oak near which the roads divided and went off, the one to Haut-Mesnil and the other to Champmeslé. Here Childerique had her carriage stopped to take leave of her brother.

But the boy rode up to her and said: "I will dine at Champmeslé if I may. I have something to talk to you about." She smiled at him very tenderly.

Still during dinner she decided to make him ride home

early. He caught hay fever easily, and tonight he looked tired and restless; his face was pale and his eyes and nose red and swollen.

After dinner the brother and the sister walked up and down the terrace. Her husband watched them from the window of the library as he went through his papers and letters. He was starting in a day or two on his annual trip to La Rochelle, where he was to arrange the business of his Canadian property, and this time meeting some people of his from over there. A letter from Canada, received the same day, and not yet read, was on his table before him. The couple on the terrace walked into and out of his range of sight. Childerique had let down her hair, still moist from the children's splashings. It was very thick and soft, and wafted round her neck and shoulders as she moved. Philippe remembered having seen pictures of deities with hair of snakes, rays of sun or zigzagged lightning, and he could well believe the personality of the bearer forcing itself thus even into the hair. These dark tresses, dead stuff which you might cut off or burn without her feeling it, just because at one point they were attached to her head, would twist, shine and fill the air with fragrance. As she turned and came toward him, the sun behind her, her head was wrapped in a dark cloak, within which red fires were smoldering.

The boy was silent for a while, gazing not at her but far away over the landscape. In the setting sun it was filled with strong and live colors, the shadows lengthening across it on all the eastern sides of slopes and forests. The glinting river wound along in the distance, in and out between groups of trees and rushy margins. The sister did not speak either; she had picked a rose and from time to time touched her lips with it.

Suddenly the boy stopped and spoke. "Remember this afterwards," he said, "I need not have told you. I have told no one else, nor shall I do so. But one time, long ago, out in the forest, I said to you that I should probably always tell you everything that I was doing. In three days' time I am marrying the miller's widow at Masse-Bleue,"

His sister made big laughing eyes up at him over her rose, confident of some jest. On meeting the ice-cold, bloodshot eyes of an antagonist, she stood dead still and looked at him, and the color of her face slowly deepened to dark crimson; her eyes even seemed to water from the heat of the fire on her forehead and cheeks. It was as if, on finding her brother murdered and plundered in a dark forest, her first feeling should have been that of shame on seeing him naked. Soon her silence became intolerable to him.

"Yes," he said, "this is Udday's curse. We are lost. But I am free to be lost, if I choose, whatever all the world, whatever you say of it."

It hurt her mortally that he should speak of all the world and of her in the same breath; still she dared not give in to her emotion, lest she should fall down dead, when she could not afford to fall, for she was standing up here to fight him.

"Why," she said, gazing straight into his pale, agonized face, "are you doing this?"

Her question seemed to calm him; he looked back at her. So many times had he explained his whims and difficulties to her, to get her influence in their home on his side, that her words were to him like a bugle call, which he could not disobey. After a moment he sighed deeply, and spoke to her, very slowly and brokenly.

"You know," he said, "that people live on the moors and the waste land where the vipers are. There is not one of them who has not been bitten by vipers at some time. They have become immune to the poison; not only do they not die from it, as we do, nay it harms them not at all. You know, Childerique, how frightened I have been, all my life, of vipers and snakes—even now, when I set eyes on one of them I feel as if I should die. Well, I should like to be invulnerable to their bites, too. I will be with the people who cannot be hurt by vipers," after a moment he added, "who play with them, and make them dance."

It was her weakness that she understood him so well. His mother, she thought, would not have grasped the meaning of a single word he was saying; she would have met him with an absolute, heroic lack of understanding, which would have swept all he had said into nothingness. Her own fatal insight into his soul was like a weight round her neck. Still she disdained pretending not to understand. She was aware that all their common past was behind his words. They brought up a swarm of pictures of him and of herself, out on travels in the woods, in those moors or marshes of which he spoke, where they had strayed against the orders of his mother and their nurses. They had seen vipers there, and had been looking for wolves, which they knew to have lived there many years ago. They had been out in search of other things as well, of the dangers and horrors of the world. She had then egged the delicate boy on, indignant of his timidity, and she had triumphed when in the end she had called forth his foolhardiness. Their dangers had caused her great delight. But on what wild track was her little dog now running? She could not follow him, and she would not let him get away.

"Ah, indeed," she cried, "you talk like a man! It is the right thing for the lord of Haut-Mesnil to go to the people of the moors, to be taught to make vipers dance, to be taught witchcraft, and treachery. It was thus that you went away, in the old days, to learn the ways of Turks and infidels, and left the women to guard your land. But what about us? Might we not also want to try the taste of poison, to sleep in the woods at night?" She was surprised at her own words; they rushed to her lips on their own. What was she saying?

"Might we not also," she went on, "marry, at our pleasure, someone who could make vipers dance? But we did not do so. We did not forget our honor, or the honor of our houses, when you went away. There is not one, no not one, of the women of Haut-Mesnil, who has disgraced her name, the name of our father. Is it forever, then, the task of the women to hold up the houses, like those stone figures which they call caryatids? And are you now, Lord of Haut-Mesnil, going to pull down all the stones of our great house, upon your own head, and upon mine, and the heads of all of us?"

He looked at her with a strange, cold and hard curiosity. "What about you?" he repeated. "You, women of the great houses, who are holding up the houses upon your arms? You believe, Mama and you, that you are the finest things in all the world, but then it is, perhaps, easier to make fine things out of stone than in flesh and blood."

Childerique drew in her breath in a long deep sigh. It was easier to her to hear herself, in his mouth, compared to his mother than, as before, to all the world, for she loved her stepmother, and had great respect for her.

"You curse us, when we leave you, you say," the young man went on, "but what have you got to do with us, when you can never get your arms down? You know what you want; that is a good thing to you. But what do we want? No one thinks of that. Father never liked Mama, how could he, when she was made out of stone, a caryatid, as you say, on the house of Haut-Mesnil? Why should I want more stones, a son of stone, with a heart of stone, which you must break with a hammer, and throw on the road? A weight, that's what you want to give us, always a weight. The devil take it," he cried, having worked himself into a childish fury, "if the loveliest things in the world be made of stone, we must be free to go and play with those that are less lovely."

She was as furious as he was, and it seemed to her that some huge black shadow, of such depth as she had never known, was stealing upon her from all sides. But she spoke calmly. "When you were a baby," she said, "and we were out in the forest together, I watched Rose-Marie nurse you, and when the milk ran from the corner of your mouth I wished that I had been grown up like her, and able to nurse you myself. Now I think it would have been better had I forced the juice of gall-apples into your little mouth, so that you should never have grown up to shame us. How have you come to turn from all our old ways like this? What has the mill witch," she cried out, "given you, so that you must forget me?"

"Who?" he asked, staring at her as if he had forgotten what they had been talking about.

She stared back at him contemptuously. "The mill witch," said she.

As if his thoughts were, by her words, forced back to a resting-place, his eyes fell, and slowly his distorted face was smoothed out, as if someone had kept stroking a hand over it. "I do not know," he said, "but she knows."

The darkness and the pain were now closing all round the sister. "Let us go away together, you and I," she cried. "We will sleep in the marshes, we will walk on the moors. Shall we not, in time, become immune, we two, to the vipers' poison? Come."

He stood straight up and looked at her for a moment. Then he sighed deeply. "Childerique," he said, "do you always dream of me? At night, I mean, when you are asleep?"

"Dream?" she asked. "No."

"No, you do not," said he, with deep, bitter emotion. "But I, you see—it is only in the mill, in my dreams, that you have never been. When I dream of the mill, that I am in the mill, you are never there. I have gone to the mill, I chose it for myself, now it is too late to go back. Now it is too late for you and me to go together. I wish, now," he went on very slowly, "that you would never think of me again. I should like to know for certain that you were never to think of me."

For a second her knees, within her voluminous skirt, swayed, as if she meant to throw herself down upon them to him, but her movement took another direction; she cast herself toward him, folding his slim figure in her arms with the

energy of a protecting mother or of a drowning woman, looking with radiant eyes into his face.

"Oh, my brother, my dearest love," she said, "I will never
let you go. Do you not think that I know more than you, that
I can also open up a new world to you? Oh, I can teach you
dances too, darkness, magic too." While she spoke she lifted
her hand and pressed up his chin.

The boy turned so deadly white under her touch that he
frightened her. He drew back a step, and as she followed him,
with strong hands he freed himself of her. "No, do not do
that," he said, "Simkie has held me, holds me, like that."

The sister stood where he had left her, as white as he. She
thought: "That was the last time that I ever held him in my
arms."

Suddenly he walked away.

At that moment a strange and terrible thing happened to
her, which she had never experienced. She saw herself,
clearly, as with her own eyes. She saw her own figure standing before the house, with her loosened hair; she even saw it
grow smaller and smaller, upon the terrace, as he walked
away from her.

The young Master of Haut-Mesnil rode away quickly,
making his horse trot down the long avenue of sweetly smell-
ing lime trees. But as he got onto the road he thought: "At
this pace I shall be home in three-quarters of an hour," and
drew in his reins. He saw before him the long crimson drawing room, and his mother below her lamp, looking up from
her cross-stitch to welcome him. He blew the air through his
nostrils and turned his horse from the road to a narrow path
which ran through the woods; after half an hour's ride it
brought him out in the open, and to the moors.

He rode slowly now, down the slope from the forest to the
open land, first through a thicket of nettles, raspberries and
crane's bill, then through the deep undergrowth of bracken
that crushed under his horse's hoofs. The sound of the break-

ing branches and the strong and bitter smell went to his head and heart; it seemed to him that this was his fate: to crush and destroy everything where he went. As he got out, the wide stretch of moor lay before him.

The sun was just setting; the air was filled with clear gold. The heather was not yet in flower, but the long hills had in their somberness a sweet promise of bloom. Along over the dark moor ran a floating line of fine golden dust that was the dry grass flowering in the wagon track across the dark land.

Into the head of the boy, riding on in deep thought, ran the often playfully repeated sentence of his old Swiss tutor about him: "Homo non sum, humanum omne a me alienum puto." He wondered what it was that these human people named human. It seemed to him that there was a curse upon him—of human beings loving him, and claiming love from him in return, when he could not, would not love! He thought of his mother, who from his early childhood had ever been hoping for some richness of life through him and his love of her; of his friends at school, who had liked him, and wanted him to like them. He was sorry for them all. But all this love—it was like the cravings of vampires, with their large wings, asking for your blood and offering you, with deep sighs, their own thick hot blood in return.

He rode alongside a long slope that ran from north to south, and was suddenly struck by seeing, upon a lower parallel hill, east of him, his own shadow and that of his horse, accompanying him as he rode, upright, huge and long —a giant horseman stretching himself as far as he could over the land.

"God," he thought, "oh God! Save the world from me."

The sun went down, and with the setting of it, the hills that had blushed in its last slanting rays in a soft shine of grayish purple, suddenly cooled and darkened, like steel withdrawn from the furnace; the world became indescribably somber and severe. Immediately after, an owl flew past him on noiseless wing-strokes.

He tried to follow its flight in the glass-clear air. He remembered the joy which the sight of the big night-bird always caused to the heart of Childerique. "I count that a great stroke of luck, a great happiness, to see an owl," she had said to him. He had asked her if she believed that the birds were omens of happiness. "I do not know," she said, "I think it a great happiness, in itself, to see them."

Just as he was thinking of this, his ear caught the sound of music, the notes of a flute, played at a long distance. His face changed. He turned his horse's head round and rode down the track of live gold-dust, now extinguished, toward the mill of Masse-Bleue.

Down here he had soon to ride through long milk-white stripes of mist, which rose from the damp meadows near the river. Below them the sward was still bright green. In the midst of a grass field a gate rose straight before him, dark in the dark. He did not care to get off to open it, but made his horse walk back a little, and, hurrying it on, he jumped the gate. It was a risky thing to do in the dusk; the horse had become wild by it; he himself grew warm and comfortable from his success. A strong smell of marsh-whortleberry and bog-myrtle contracted his nostrils. The stars came out one by one.

IV

The lady of Champmeslé came out of the shade of the forest to the white road, and walked onto the bridge leading across the lock of the mill pond to the mill. The smell of running water and water-weeds was fresh and quelling here. The hour of noon was absolutely still, not a soul about, and the heat heavy as lead, the whole landscape was somber with it as if seen through a pair of dull blue glasses. Even the mountain-high white clouds had a sort of dusk in them. Childerique paused on the bridge. Nobody knew that she was here, and that thought itself was inspiring to her; this had not happened to her since she had been married. She had been in such uproar all night, now, if she hesitated it was neither from fear nor irresolution, but just to gain her breath. She had been filled with wrath, and had started from the high terrace of Champmeslé like one of those great white clouds, sweeping down with thunder and lightning upon the mill of Masse-Bleue. But this dead silence, these smooth rapid waters rushing away under her feet—were they hers or the miller's widow's—and with whom were they in league?

The miller's widow opened the door of the mill house, and appeared on the threshold as if she had been expecting her. She was wiping her round arms, that had flour on them, on her skirt. The women of her tribe, Childerique knew, often smile very sweetly and coaxingly, but laugh out only in triumph or amorousness.

The gypsy was eighteen years old, broader than Childerique and more rounded in all her lines, and singularly light of movement. She was barefoot and had on nothing more than a shirt and a closely folded, faded blue cotton skirt. Although both married and widowed she, here in her own house, wore her thick hair in two pigtails; between them at the nape of her neck a coarse tatter of hair bristled out, a sign of strength.

At the nearness of this strong and fresh young body Childerique's fury came back; she felt in her hands the desire to seize the rich round amber-colored throat and to strangle this creature who defied her, and a deadly nausea at the thought of touching her, as if she had had a snake in front of her—and the latter feeling was the strongest.

"You come to me, my lovely lady," said the gypsy, "all the long way, in the midday heat! Please God you will not regret it. Come in, come in now." She held open the door, and as Childerique was about to walk in, she kissed the palm of her hand and deftly placed it for a moment upon the threshold.

Within the room of the old wooden mill house it was hotter and closer than outside. A stripe of golden dust of light lay across it from the small window. The miller's wife had been taking her new bread from the oven; it was arranged upon shelves along the wall. She lifted a three-legged chair into the middle of the floor for her guest. Childerique sat down because a tiredness and giddiness had come upon her. She thought: "I would as well sit down in a viper's nest."

"I am informed," she said slowly, "that your dogs are again, in your old manner, running mad down here." The gypsy stared at her, clear-eyed, patient as a child. "That is your affair," said Childerique, "but you may not snap at anyone outside your own pack. You, you have bewitched the young Lord of Haut-Mesnil. Get you gone." As she pronounced her brother's name she held on with both hands to the seat of the chair. "Get you gone," she repeated. She remembered having been told how the pious old miller had used to birch his young wife. "This creature," she thought, "is used to more brutality than I can even think of." She tried to remember the old modes of punishment of which she had, as a child, been shown the instruments, at Haut-Mesnil.

The gypsy sighed, and shifted onto a position customary to her, standing upon one little foot, with her other naked ankle in her hand. "Ah, ah," she said, "how hard they speak, how hard! Ah, stop it, you cut the heart of the poor girl, you fine lady."

Childerique looked hard at her; she felt her own face under her wide summer bonnet burning. The air of the room, filled with the fragrance of flour and new bread, was heavy for her to breathe. She was at this moment held by a queer fancy. She remembered how she had been taken, as a child, to see the Queen as she had been passing through Pirigueux, and how at the sight of the ceremonial she had thought: "Whatever happens, happens because it pleases the Queen." Even when it had begun to rain the little girl had felt that it did so because the Queen allowed it, because the rain pleased the Queen. Now, in the presence of the young gypsy the fancy, long forgotten, was recalled. "This woman," she thought, "is pleased with whatever happens," and this seemed to her to be a strange treachery at the hands of fate. "But my God," she thought, "what is the matter with this Simkie? Why on earth is she like a queen, this slut on her bare feet? Is it really the queens and the gypsies who have all that they want, and only we, the women of the great houses and the estates, who have to work to hold up the world?" The words of the Scripture came back to her: "And we know that all things work together for good to them that love." Her thoughts shied at the name called forth to her. Could it be the same with the Devil as with God? Would he have the equal reward to give for being loved? "Yes," she thought, "yes, it is so. It is all because Simkie is really a witch, this extraordinary content in her, like that of a child. It is the witch's happiness; this is what she sells herself for to the Devil." And somewhere at the bottom of it, as if at the bottom of the mill pond, she saw the doom of the witch, the sadness and dreadfulness of her fate.

"Are you God, beautiful lady?" asked the gypsy, watching her face. "Are you to manage all the world?"

"Yes," said Childerique with all the strength of her heart. "I am to manage the world here, at Champmeslé. God himself has placed me here to do so. You know that too, all of you. Beware of me."

"But how can it be, my mistress," said the young woman in the slow and lisping voice, the mellifluous drawl of her tribe, the fortune-teller's voice. "How can it be? If I have indeed bewitched the lord of Haut-Mesnil, how can I undo it now? You, you know yourself that young men are after women with long hair, who speak sweetly to them, who sport with them. If it be only that, say so, my sweet lady, for you know that a young woman can again make a young man leave her, whom she has made to come to her. But if there have been

spells and magic there, and the Devil has helped me—why!
the Devil is on to the work even now, and you and I cannot
stop him, indeed we cannot, my dear, dear mistress."

She was out of breath with speaking so insinuatingly, and
stood as if she waited for a decision, very still.

"Yes," said Childerique hoarsely, "you have bewitched
him. You brought him to you by spells, you know it well."
At this the gypsy woman began to sway and rock her body as
in pain; all her movements were graceful and fascinating.

It occurred to Childerique that her brother had held the
girl in his arms. A strong pain and alarm ran through her;
she looked away and down. At the same time, as if even the
idea of a gentler and sweeter human relation, brought into
this place of harsh judgment, was softening the air of it, the
terrible hardness which had been like a pain in her entrails
these twenty hours seemed to loosen. As often, when she was
suddenly and strongly moved, her thoughts ran to her
mother; she remembered her good-will to the foreigners
within her land.

"Simkie," she said, looking again at the gypsy, and for the
first time calling her by her name, "release my brother of
this magic, and I will forgive you and do you no harm."

Simkie wrung her hands. "Oh, Madame," she said, "the
Devil is not to be jested with. We shall have to make a
stronger magic, you and I now, to break the power of the
one which has been made."

"Yes, yes," said Childerique. "If you have made one
charm, you must be able to make another."

At the very moment she thought: "What is this that I am
saying? How do I get this into my head? I have got fever,
surely."

"And what shall I do it for, my lady?" asked Simkie. "If
my lord marries me I shall sleep in a silken bed. Why shall I
undo my work? What are you going to give me for it?"

Childerique could not answer; she sat dumb. "For honor's
sake, for the honor of Haut-Mesnil"—these words had been

strong in her heart all day. But she was ashamed to speak them to the gypsy. She could not tell her that she was really here on her mother's errand, for the sake of that young heir of Haut-Mesnil whom she had failed to bear, and that the strength and courage of the dead woman were bearing up her own, in the service of their house. She looked round in her mind for something to promise the sorceress.

"Let it be for nothing, then," said Simkie and sighed. "Who knows, who knows, I may get my reward for serving you still, in some way. Only repeat this, which you said, that you will not harm me afterwards nor will any of your people."

"No, that we will never do," said Childerique.

"But what shall the words of the witchcraft be now, my lady?" asked the gypsy. "What am I to demand of the Devil of the water, if he will come to us? For what shall he have come?"

Childerique felt again the blood in her face. "For this," she said, "that the lord of Haut-Mesnil turn entirely. . . "

"No, no," the gypsy quickly interrupted her, placing a finger on her lips. "Names must never be spoken, that is against the rules of witchcraft. No, wait, I shall speak for you and you will tell me if I am right in what I say, if it be to your good pleasure. This," she went on after a moment, speaking very slowly, and looking down, "shall be a charm to turn the heart of your brother, your father's son, entirely away from the woman whom he now loves, and thinks of as his wife. This shall be a charm to separate the two forever with the help of our guest, whom we have called for."

"Yes," said Childerique, staring into the gypsy's face.

Simkie stood again for a while in deep thought. "It can be done," she said at last, "but not now. You must come back for it. Come this time tomorrow, and it will be for you to speak the words, for if I have once spoken a charm I cannot myself speak against it again. And you must bring with you. . ."

She stopped herself. She seemed to change and grow heavier. All her lightness of limb and movement had gone from her; she looked worn like a woman with child. "Madame," she said after a long time, "you must bring your little son to help us make the spell. A male child, who has in him blood common to you, who will speak the charm, and of him about whom we speak it. Blood, Madame, such noble blood is precious in magic."

Childerique thought: "My little son? How am I to bring him here if nobody may know? I shall have to carry him all the way through the forest except where he can run a little." The idea itself was charming to her; it was rare that she had the child to herself without the nurses. "But what am I to tell them," she thought, "to get away without anybody knowing?"

Simkie saw that she hesitated. "Come, come then," she said, speaking all the time now in the same heavy and strained way, as if a great weight had been laid on her. "You do not quite have faith in Simkie? Come, I will show you a little magic to make you believe, a little only today."

Childerique looked round her bewildered. "Come this way," said the gypsy, and opened the door to the mill room. Childerique stopped on the threshold for a moment. She had need of her courage now. It was not that she was afraid of what might befall her in there, but she felt the fatality of this one step which took her from the daylight of her life till now into the play with unknown powers. What made her, after a second, walk on was not the convocation of her strength, but her love of danger. The unknown called to her. And she would now know more of witchcraft.

Everything within the large old building was wry and crooked, and from this room to the other, three high steps led down. The huge room of the water wheel was much older than the rest of the mill, and built all in timber, now black with age. The room was dim; the panes of the windows were green and covered with cobwebs. Down here it was suddenly quite cold. The room had an atmosphere of its own, made by the presence of the water; its breath met you on the threshold. The river ran below the heavy floor boards. Childerique felt all at once cool and fresh, her face and hands all bedewed like a silver cup quickly filled with ice-cold water. She followed the miller's widow across the floor. This was the room in which the gypsies were said to have their dancing and singing at night. The floor was smoothed and polished with the dragging about of heavy sacks, the sweeping away of grain, and the steps of two hundred years.

This, Childerique thought, was the only room which, within the dreams of her young brother, she had not entered. Well, she was here now. If within his dreams of the future she should still not be there, his dreams would not be true, not in accordance with reality.

In the middle of the room rose the wooden walls of the water wheel's house. "We shall call the magic of the wheel," said the gypsy, "which is the most honest of all magics. Come, my little wheel, my full moon, I let you loose; you shall have all the river to turn you, and no grain to grind."

Her bare feet made no noise as she went to loose the wheel. With an effort she heaved up the ponderous bolt which connected the wheel with the water.

At once the room became alive. Above and below a hundred little voices whispered and groaned, the timber creaked and moaned, heavy iron sang and snarled, beyond all the voices rose the roar of the wheel and the splashing of water.

The sweat had sprung out all over the gypsy's face, and as she stood now close to her, Childerique was again struck by her sudden disfigurement. She dragged herself along laboriously, and she had the stiff and empty face of a woman near her confinement. Childerique felt quiet and strong now, her own body light as when she was a child. She was victorious at last, her adversary prostrate before her; she was even, with all the honors of war, being taken into the heart of the fortifications of the enemy. In her triumph her heart was ready for forgiveness, and beating loudly.

The gypsy let up the door to the wheel's shed. "Look down," said she.

Childerique walked out on a little gangway near the wheel, holding onto the rail. She was at once splashed all over by a delicate sprinkle of fresh drops—this was a joke on the part of the water. At this moment, she thought, for the last time: "How can I be so foolish? There will be nothing there but just water."

She had indeed to wait long, before anything else showed itself to her. Then it was as if by a sudden jerk her own position was changed; she was no longer gazing down, or there was no longer any up and down in the world. At this, and all at once, the noise round her changed; it had sense; it spoke.

Before her a great pattern of glowing red sparks was forming itself. First it was like a wheel, then settled into a sort of fixity, but what it was she could not tell. From time to time it was blurred, some of the lights were put out. A strange smell, alarming to her, and a new noise, a grunting or rummaging, spun round her head.

Now again she saw clearly. The sparks were not a pattern on a dark ground, they were themselves the background, that of a flaming evening sky. The black lines, and stripes upon it, were the lower branches of a fir thicket; these branches were dead and bare because the growth was so dense that no light reached down here.

The large moving forms amongst the trees were a troop of huge black boars, some of them quite close to her. They were all busy grunting and rooting up the earth, buffeting one another and rubbing their flanks and backs upon the mighty fir trunks. A sow with her young passed her; a terrible old boar with terrible tusks turned and fixed his little red eyes on her, and afraid that he would come for her she flinched back. It was all gone. She was in the mill again, giddy and out of breath.

She found herself staring, with a queer delight, into the face of the gypsy. "What is that? What was all that?" she asked.

"That was the old forest of Haut-Mesnil," answered the miller's widow. "That was just the place where the great house stands now."

Enraptured and transported Childerique turned again to the water wheel. She no longer asked herself what it all meant, or why the gypsy was showing it to her. She felt only a deep ecstasy about this new world opened to her. Had anybody tried to drag her away from the wheel, her mind would have been deranged by grief. The water was now foaming under the buckets of the wheel. "Look again," said the witch.

Again the noise changed; this time it grew fainter, as if melodious. A great and sweet, fresh calm came upon Childerique.

Before the landscape had shown itself, she knew that it was lovely. It was again the wood, and the picture was dark; she could distinguish the depth, and the stems of the trees by the lighter green of the grass and the undergrowth only. It was either after sunset, or very early morning, before sunrise. Just in front of her lay a vast space of water, and upon it hung a thin milky mist. She heard wild ducks a little way off, between the rushes. It was all dim around her, like a big bouquet of foliage, reflected within a thick silver mirror. But she herself—to get this view of it all, she must be in the water, the clear surface up to her chin, and she remembered for a moment the dragonfly on a broad green leaf which she had watched from the mill bridge. What a deep pleasure it was to sit upon the water like this!

In the dusk on the shore she saw a form moving, curious to her at first. It was a woman in white, but as she was swathed in a dark shawl, the upper part of her body become one with her surroundings, the white skirt swept on as on its own. This amused Childerique; she clapped her hands. But as the lady passed out into the glade, she distinguished clearly her little dark head, the curls arranged *à la coup de vent,* and a great wave of tenderness and pride exalted her whole being. She knew this lady. Who was she? Immediately after she recognized the spot; it was the outskirts of the park of Haut-Mesnil, and she saw also, at that same moment, the reflection of a star, the first or the last of the summer night, shiver in the lacteal surface of the water. There was a seat in the wood; the young lady sat down on it, and leaned her head upon her folded hands at the back of the seat.

Suddenly Childerique noticed a change in the mirror of the pond; it was broken into an outstretched pattern of little chopped, luminous ripples. And what was this? She saw it the next moment: the ducks had been disturbed by something, and came rushing across the water toward her; in the dusk she could not see their tawny bodies, but only the long lines made upon the surface by their hurried retreat. She thought: "It is early summer here; the young wild ducks are not fledged yet." But what had disturbed them? A young man came along the forest path, from the opposite side to the woman, hastened up to her and took her in his arms; she sank into his embrace.

At the moment when the lady gave herself up to her lover's adoration, Childerique knew her. It was her mother, the fair and cherished Sophie, younger than herself and bright with beauty and happiness. "Oh, dear Mother," she thought, "apple of my eye, I see you at last." The young man must then be her father, so much younger than she remembered him, really just like Philippe when he had first come to France. Her mother, she thought, had come out to meet her father in the park. Childerique remembered her father only as a cold man, coming in silent from the work of the estate, or from hunting. How much she had wronged him; he had come back, in the old days, like this. She saw that the two wanted nothing in the world but one another; they clung together, pressed their faces together, and sought and held each other's hands; the woman took the man's face between her hands and lost herself in contemplation of it. Again they sank into each other and made one figure only in the half-light. The gestures were all so familiar; it was indeed as if she had seen herself and Philippe in a looking glass, younger and fairer. She had often been told that she was like her mother, and surely her father had had something of the beauty of Philippe, or it was only that all young men were alike, making love. She remembered an evening, a month perhaps after their wedding, when she herself had gone to meet her husband in the forest, and he had made love to her there, half against herself. At times then he had alarmed her by the violence of his love for her, as if there were no moment to lose, as if death were threatening to separate the two. Now she knew that that was just the way of her father and mother.

Had she in real life come upon a pair of lovers like this, she knew that she should have turned her eyes away. Not so here, although she felt the blood in her cheeks; not so with her own mother, in this world of sweet witchcraft. Here everything had a deeper meaning and heart, and the mother and daughter could well do service to the gods hand-in-hand. Nor was she sorry that her mother did not turn and look at her, or notice her at all, although at the first moment she had felt a burning longing for that. This was a lovelier confidence and intimacy; this was as it should be.

The picture was blurred to her as if her eyes had been filled with tears. She again found herself clinging to the wet rail of the gangway in the mill. The miller's widow was before her, with drops of sweat in her eyebrows. Childerique sighed deeply as she realized that the visions were all gone.

"I have shown you true pictures," said the gypsy laboriously.

"Yes, yes," answered Childerique, wringing her hands as the miller's wife had done before.

"I shall show you more tomorrow," said Simkie.

"Yes, tomorrow, tomorrow," said Childerique, feeling

how long it was till tomorrow, and how the time would be filled with longing.

Now she herself walked slowly, and she stopped on the threshold to take one more look at the room, and listen once more to the music of the water wheel.

"The wheel has been turning on your behalf, Madame," said the gypsy. "The water that turned it has gone a long way already, and will not come back to turn it the other way."

On the bridge she paused. She thought: "How much have I learned since I stood here last! How much wiser I am!"

She looked round, and was surprised at the change in the earth and air. That high sky had paled, as if bleached, drenched of all its rich blue, so much so that the large clouds, which had appeared light against it now, without having themselves changed their hue, floated like dark, slate-colored clots on a white metal ground. It was cold. Gusts of wind rushed through the trees which swayed and bent. The dust of the road whirled up in little spires.

As she walked through the forest, heavy drops of rain came down through the tops of the trees; they felt lukewarm in the cold air. She heard thunder in the distance, but no heavy shower followed—probably there was a great storm somewhere off. She herself, who had rushed down to the mill, now walked with difficulty, although she meant to hasten, like a honeybee, carrying the collected sweetness of moors and gardens through the rain to her hive, heavy and a little unsteady on the wing. In the darkness of the forest path she seemed to feel the nearness of a young lover, and when the twigs and tendrils caught her dress it was as if she had to stop to give him time for a sweet word or a kiss. She thought of her husband, and for the first time in her life she felt an overwhelming longing for his embrace. She calculated how long it would be until she could be in his arms, and pictures of lovemaking swarmed at her from all sides, like gadflies on the narrow road, and made her face glow and her knees weaken under her.

Where the forest path joined the drive of Champmeslé there grew, curiously, a very old, crooked wild mulberry tree. She mused under it, and thought: "This terrible, sweet drowsiness which makes my limbs so heavy, which lies like honey on my tongue and runs so soothingly in all my veins— can it be a poison, a drug? Does the poppy-juice confuse you like this?" She remembered having spoken to her brother of the sweet taste of poisons and was surprised at her own wisdom. She thought: "I shall never get home," and was astonished when, immediately after, she saw before her the white house of Champmeslé.

Her husband, who had seen her approach from his window, came out to meet her. "Where have you been?" he asked her.

Childerique breathed heavily. "Oh, do not ask me," she exclaimed.

"Why not?" said he, and struck by her looks he added: "My dear, you are not well." He took her hand. "Have you got fever?" he asked her.

"What an idea," said she. "I walked fast to get home. I am a little chilly."

She was frightened herself because at the sight of her husband she felt disappointment and insecurity. It was as if he, the house and garden of Champmeslé and all the life awaiting her there were pale and cold in comparison with the world of witchcraft, as the landscape was pale and cold now compared to the glowing earth and air of an hour ago. Had the warmth and color gone from her live husband to remain with the vision lovers, even with the vision animals of a burning sky and a forest of a thousand years ago?

"Where do you come from?" he asked her again.

"Oh, why do you go on asking me," she cried, "when I would rather have died than told you? I come from the mill, from the miller's widow, Udday's daughter. But you, you know nothing of all this."

"Yes," he said, "I know of Udday. What had you got to do there?"

"Oh, she knows a thousand times more than we do," said Childerique. She took his hand, eager to prove to herself that he was, after all, the lover of the forest path, but let it go again, staring into his face. His hand seemed to her changed, and hot; it burnt her cool fingers. He had asked her if she had got fever, but had he not fever?

"You are quite wet," said he, laying his hand on her shoulders and bosom. "Be sensible now for once and take off your clothes. You should go to bed, my dear. You were looking feverish last night already."

From her window Childerique, never thinking of changing her clothes, looked toward the horizon and at the figure of her husband, small in the foreground. He had walked onto the end of the terrace and stood there, his hands in his pockets, quite still. She found time to wonder, in the whirl of all her thoughts, what he would be thinking of. "He walks there," she said to herself, "like a sentinel. He thinks: Will the storm come up here? It is well that I have got my wheat garnered. Will the lightning strike in the forest of Champmeslé?"

As she followed him with her eyes her heart softened to him; tears pressed against her eyelids even while she kept moving up and down her room.

ECHOES

In the course of her wanderings Pellegrina Leoni, the diva who had lost her voice, came to a small mountain town near Rome. This happened at the time when she had fled from Rome and from her lover, Lincoln Forsner, whose great passion for her threatened to place her, and to hold her fast, within a definite, continued existence. She came to the town toward evening, in a cart drawn by a horse and a mule, which had carried chestnuts and wool down to the plain, and as she was about to pay her fare she found that she had brought no money with her. She did not worry, for she had never given much thought to money, and she knew that her friend, the Jew Marcus Cocozza, would before long have traced her dwelling place and would provide her with all she needed.

On her left hand she had a ring with a big diamond; she took it off and gave it to the wagoner.

It was autumn. Dark fell almost at once, and the thin mountain air cooled suddenly; the wanderer seemed to feel the breath of snow in it. The houses round her faded, as if they were withdrawing into themselves and relinquishing the world.

Pellegrina walked through the narrow street with her small, hastily packed traveling bag in her hand. She had grown fat in Rome, on heavy, sweet food and much wine, behind walls baked by the sun and in the continuous turmoil of talk and music. She had to stop to catch her breath; as she stood still she felt the cold and the loneliness up here as a happiness. She thought: "This is a remarkable town, one feels as if one may stay on here." In a while she felt that she was hungry after her hurried departure and her journey. As a child she had often been hungry; through the faint ache in her stomach she once more became the light-footed ferocious wench who had sniffed in smells of food in the evening air, lonely with the loneliness of very young beings, and in a strange way safe. She thought: "I shall have to find a place to sleep in tonight. I shall have, tonight, to beg bread and shelter from the people in this town."

She here realized that she had for some minutes been following on the heels of a huge form: a man in a cloak. He slowed up and stopped outside a small baker's shop, which was open to the street and upon the counter of which an oil lamp was burning. She caught up with him and stood still. Before the man entered the circle of light he sighed deeply, all anonymous in the dark. But when the light fell upon him she saw that he was a very old man, heavy of body; his face was not wrinkled but hardened and as if polished, like a big old yellow bone; his eyes were pale. She reflected, in the kind of fancy which might have run through the head of the girl of twelve: "He is a dead sailor, who has been long in the water. He stands up straight because, as is the custom with dead sailors, they have tied a weight to his feet. But he is still swaying a little with the current."

He did indeed stand as still and patiently as a dead man before the counter of the shop until the ruddy baker's wife behind the lamp turned and caught sight of him, and without wasting words on the business, as if in accordance with an old habit, reached out for a loaf of bread from the shelf, rubbed it on her bare arm and handed it to him. The old man received it, likewise without a word, placed a small coin on the counter and continued his way.

"Good night, Niccolo," said the baker's wife. "Good night," he answered in a toneless voice.

Pellegrina, as has been told, was a baker's daughter and would know that in a baker's shop there may be bread left over from yesterday which is given to beggars. But since she never thought of the past she walked on. Also in the old man's figure and bearing there had been a namelessness akin to her own. If now she added her own loneliness to his, would not the two together reach a rare, a remarkable pinnacle of loneliness? She hastened her steps a little.

"Forgive me," she said. "I have eaten nothing today and have no money with which to buy bread. I saw you just now buying a loaf in the baker's shop. Will you, out of compassion with the poor of this earth, give me a piece of it?"

The old man turned all round toward her, so helplessly surprised at being spoken to that she smiled. Her old habit of charming everybody she met got the better of her in the lonely village street in which she was begging her bread.

"I ask for nothing more," she said in her husky, insinuating voice. "Many people, I am told, are happy to have a bit of bread for supper. I ask for nothing else. If you have a dish of meat waiting for you in your house, I shall not claim to share it."

The man, who had stood immovable before her, at these words suddenly lifted his elbow, as if to deal a blow or to cover his face.

"Do not strike me," she said gently. "Cannot you and I be friends? Be not afraid that I shall stay too long with you. I am a woman who is always traveling farther."

After a silence the old man said: "Come with me."

They walked on side by side, all through the village, until they came to the old man's house standing at the end of a lonely narrow road with a low wall running along it.

Here the man stopped and opened the door to the hut.

"Wait," he said. "I shall light a dip. I myself most often sit in the dark. But I shall light a dip for you tonight."

She kept standing on the threshold while he raked the ashes from the embers on the fireplace, blew on them and lighted a tallow dip by a shaving. "Come closer to the fire," he said slowly and hoarsely, pointing to the only chair of the room. She, however, would not take her host's seat, but pulled a wooden stool up to the fireplace. The old man took down a heavy key from a nail and locked the door.

"How is it," she asked, "that you leave the door to your house open when you are out and thieves may come in, but that you lock it when you are in it yourself?"

The old man looked at her, then looked away. "I do that," he said.

The small room was filled with the rank smell of goats and sheep, and was indeed only divided from the cattle-shed by a half-door. She heard the animals moving and munching in the dark. The room was so low that the head of the big man brushed the joists of the ceiling.

Little by little the glimmering of the dip and the fire gained power over the shadows of the room, and in their light the old host stared at his guest for a long time. A fine lady in black silk in the street had asked a piece of bread from him and had sat down on the stool in his room.

At last he asked: "Why, Lady, have you come to this town?"

"I have come to this town," Pellegrina answered, "because

there is no reason whatever why I should come. And that is the way in which I always travel."

The old man said: "I have heard of many kinds of people. I have heard of unhappy, moon-stricken people, who are running from place to place for no reason. Those people one must not mock, but must give them shelter and bread. But I know not if you be one of them."

"No," said Pellegrina, "I am not one of the moon-struck people, and you, and all others, are free to mock me. But you see, Niccolo, some travelers are drawn forward by a goal lying before them in the way iron is drawn to the magnet. Others are driven on by a force lying behind them. In such a way the bowstring makes the arrow fly."

"In such a way," said the old man heavily, "the hunted and pursued travel."

"Yes," said Pellegrina, "but you seamen also name it: running before a following or a fair wind."

"Why," he asked, "do you call me a seaman?"

She answered: "I am in the habit of observing the looks and ways of my friends. You walk like a seaman, and you have the eyes of a seaman, which are used to gazing over great distances."

"And who will your friends be, Lady?" he asked.

"All people are my friends," said Pellegrina. "I have not got an enemy in the world."

He was silent again, and a couple of times sighed as deeply as he had done in the street before the baker's shop.

"It is sixty-five years since I saw the sea," he said.

"A long time, Niccolo," she said. "Yet surely you might see the sea again from these mountains."

"Yes," said he, "I might see it. If I walk up two hours by the path behind the house, I shall see it from there. By the time when I had first got the house, and had built the chimney and the shed to it, I walked up those two hours and came to a flat bit of ground, and from there I saw it—gray."

"All the same," she said, "it has had a strong grip on you, to have flung you up as high as here. You have lived in one house for sixty-five years, Niccolo, and yet you are a traveler of my own kind. And while those who travel toward a goal before them are traveling in fear of never reaching it, alas, I have myself lately left an unfortunate young man, who for a long time still will be rushing toward a goal that he will never reach, and his name, Niccolo, was Lincoln—we, who are running before the wind, may be without fear, for what will we have to fear? Therefore you must not fear me, no more than I fear you."

"I do not know," he said after a pause, "how it comes to be that a hunted and pursued traveler should look so joyous?"

Pellegrina answered: "It is like this: joy is my element. Therefore do I also wish that tonight I might give you joy."

"In what way would you give me joy?" he asked, surprised and as if angered.

"It is like this," she said again, "that just as it is forbidden me to remain long in the same place, remembrance is forbidden me. But you, my friend, who are free to remember things, look you back sixty-five years, or ten or fifteen years more, and tell me whether there you will find an hour in which you were happy."

"It is not good to remember things," said he.

"I have forgotten," she said, "what it is like to remember things."

"And it is not such hours as you speak of that I remember," said he.

He sat on for a long time. In the end—as from the bottom of a deep draw-well and by the aid of a heavy and rusty chain —he heaved up a recollection. When he had been a very small child among his brothers and sisters, it seemed that in the evening, and as she had got all her children put to bed, his mother had sung to them.

"I do not much like," he said, and looked in front of him into space, "to listen to people talking. Maybe it is better to hear them sing. Maybe you would give me joy, as you say, if you would sing to me."

"I would fain do so, dear Niccolo," she said, "but unfortunately I cannot sing."

Now Niccolo could think of no more things which would give him joy. But he called to mind that besides the bread he had onions, cheese and wine in his house, and brought forth these.

"I have not," he said, "during those years of which I have spoken, had anybody come into my house. I have not shared a meal with anybody. I have forgotten how, in sharing it with other people, one breaks bread. Do you this for me."

She did as he required and handed him half of the loaf. "Is not this a fair hand?" she said as he took the bread from her. "The mouths of many fools have kissed it."

"I do not like to touch people," he said. "I do not like hands."

"But if I am to break the bread with you," she said, "I ought, I think, to say grace as I have heard it said. 'Dear Lord,' I should say, 'help us that we may with happy hearts administer to the wants of this our flesh, which you have destined for the glory of the resurrection.'"

"But that is a lie," said the old man. "There is no resurrection of the flesh. Or tell me, Lady, how that flesh would ever rise again which the fish have eaten?"

Pellegrina smiled at him. "I am no priest, Niccolo," she said, "but we will pretend that I be one. I shall answer you, then, that the dumb fishes, too, are pious creatures of God, and that our flesh, if it be eaten by them and be committed to their keeping until the Lord decides otherwise, the while is safe and well with them."

The old man sat on in silence, munching his onions.

"And if," he asked suddenly, "one man has eaten of another man's flesh? If an evil man, a boy with no good in him, has eaten of the flesh of a good and holy man? And many years have passed, so that it has become one with his own?

How would it come to happen that this flesh should rise?"

"Alas, Niccolo," she said. "Life is hard, and sad things happen round us in the world. Yet I can tell you that the Lord likes a jest, and that a *da capo*—which means: taking the same thing over again—is a favorite jest of his. He may have wanted, now, a sailor stuck on the top of a mountain, such as was Noah, whose name begins with the same letter as yours. It is a very sad thing that for the olive leaf I can only bring you a twig of laurel, all dry. But I shall tell you, to make up for it, that the Ark upon its rock may well have been laughing at the weightless flotsam from the deluge, running about from one place to another."

"You have not answered me," he said and stared at her.

"In my heart I have answered you," said she. "But I shall answer you over again:

"Alas, Niccolo, I guessed it when in the street you raised your hand against me—to strike or to hide your face—as I spoke to you the word of meat. Sad things happen in the world round us. I have heard of people shipwrecked in a boat, and the one of them might well be a good and holy man, and the other of them might well be a boy with no good in him, who saw no other way of saving his life than eating of the flesh of his dead companion."

"Yes, it was like that," Niccolo said after a pause. "We had got away from the ship in a boat, the two of us, I myself and the old chaplain of the ship, the *Durkheim*, all alone for a long row of days, on a long row of gray waves. And when he had died, I saw no other way of living on than by eating of him. I would not touch his face, and I would not undo his clothes. His left hand lay beneath his body; I ate the flesh of his right hand. On the evening of that same day I was picked up by a Spanish ship.

"I have told nobody," he said after another silence, "what I have now told you. If, when you go away, you tell it to the people of the town, they will chase me out of my house and away from the mountain by throwing stones at me."

"And then," she said, "I shall have no house to offer you instead, as you have offered me yours."

"Are you going to tell them, then?" the old man asked, his pale eyes on her face.

At that she became so sad that she dropped her head and her long hair fell forward.

"I told you that I was your friend," she said. "Should I then, always, be betraying my friends?"

"I have got no friends," said Niccolo. "I know nothing of the ways of friends. Are you going to tell your friends what I have now told you?"

"No," she said, "it is to you that I shall tell something. The right hand of that good man, the ship's chaplain, when the hour of resurrection comes, will grip you by the hair—and that, Niccolo, is why you have still got such long, thick hair—or will hold on to the very entrails and bowels of you, to lift you up with him. And you shall see before you the flesh, the thought of which has followed you in the dark, radiant like the sun."

"From where do you know this?" he asked.

"I have come from far away," she answered, "and I have got far to go. I am nothing but a messenger sent out on a long journey, to tell people that there is hope in the world."

"Are you an angel then?" he asked.

"I was an angel once," she answered, "but I let my flight feathers wither and fall off, and as you see I can no longer get up from the ground. Yet, as you will also see, I can still flutter a little, from one place to another. But we will not speak any more of me. Tell me instead of the shipwreck. And the more things you can tell me about it, Niccolo, the more joy you will give me."

The old man after a while set to telling his long tale, with the breaks and searchings for words of a man who has lost the habit of speaking, and with the keen recollection of details of a man whose thoughts have time after time gone over his theme. The *Durkheim* had caught fire and had gone down, in open sea, south of the Cape. The crew had taken to the boats; at the last moment the ship's boy had dragged the old ship's chaplain through the fire and the smoke, and had tumbled with him into a last boat that had been overlooked. In this boat the two had suffered great distress, until one morning the chaplain died.

During this account Pellegrina, who had come in from the cold, on her stool close to the fire grew sleepy. Yet when it was finished, and the narrator had sunk back into silence, she asked him to tell her more about his life. Niccolo told her slowly and unevenly as before that he had been a wild boy and that, while quite a small child, he had broken his little sister's nose with a stone. As he related his life on board the ships and in port, she asked him if he had ever had a sweetheart. "No," he said, "when the *Durkheim* went down I was but fifteen, I had never kissed a girl. And afterwards I thought my mouth too rare a thing to give to kissing women."

In the end her eyes twice fell to. "Niccolo, my friend," she said, "I could spend the whole night sitting up here and listening to you. But I am tired after a long journey, and I must needs sleep. Show me a place where I can lie down for a couple of hours."

Niccolo looked at her, looked round the room, and got up from his chair. There was no bed in the room, but only on the floor a couch made up of goatskins. "I have got but this bed to give you," he said, "and you will be used to a silken bed. But lie down there and fear not me. I shall do you no harm."

"And where will you sleep yourself?" she asked him.

"I never sleep a whole night through," he answered and sighed. "I wake up many times, go out and see whether it is south wind or north wind, east or west wind, and come back again. I shall look after the fire, so that the room shall not be cold when you wake up tomorrow."

The touch of the goatskins on the hard floor was pleasing to her after her soft bed in Rome. But as again she looked at the old man, blowing on his fire, she called to mind the fools who had shared that bed with her, and once more felt his loneliness akin to her own.

."Nay," she said, "lie down with me here. You have told me that I need not fear you. The dip is burning down. Leave the fire, and lay you down to sleep as peacefully as, when you were a small child, you lay down by the side of your mother, who could sing to you."

Laboriously the old man obeyed her order, first going down on his knees, then stretching himself out. Vaguely, for a short moment, the face of Lincoln, who had last lain close to her, ran through her mind. "Why must pity of human beings," she asked herself, as again she chased away the picture, "forever suck the marrow from my bones?"

She said in the dark: "My small son Niccolo, I know that you have stolen apples, broken your little sister's nose with a stone, and eaten human flesh. But all is still well between us, and our two heads can rest on the same pillow."

A mighty, mute movement ran through the huge and coarse male body by her own; it was as if the bones in it were beginning to break. He raised one arm and dropped it heavily across her breast. His big head followed it; he bored it down into the freshness of her hair and the softness of her bosom beneath it—indeed, for a minute, like a babe seeking and pressing toward his mother's nipple. At the moment when the spasm of his limbs dissolved, and he loosed himself from her, he was asleep. A short while after, she slept herself. Two or three times in the course of the night she woke up and heard him snoring lowly and deeply.

When she awoke it was light. She looked round to find out where she was. A basin of fresh water stood by the side of the couch, and she washed her face and combed her hair. At that the old man returned with a jug of hot goat's milk and bade her good morning.

She looked up at him while she drank. "Now I am going away, Niccolo," she said, "and I thank you for bread and onions, for wine and milk and shelter."

"I would rather you stayed on," he said.

"Speak not so," said she. "Those are words that hurt my ears, and have hurt them too many times."

"What words, then," he asked, "should I speak to you that will not hurt your ears?"

"If you be my friend," she said, "and if you wish to help me, you will answer the question which every day comes back and makes life burdensome to me."

"If I can, I shall answer it," he said.

"Tell me then," said she, "whether to go to the right or to the left."

He thought her question over. "And if I tell you, will you follow my advice?" he asked. "Will you care to know, as you are walking on and in the place you come to and where you sit down: Niccolo sent me here?"

"Yes," she answered him. "Add now, Niccolo, you who are still allowed to remember, your weight to the weight of the forces which are sending me forth. It will do me good to think, wherever I go and in whatever places I sit down to rest: Niccolo sent me here."

He again thought the matter over. "You are a lady," he said, "unused to walking in the mountains. You will soon wish to sit down within a house. But in any house you walk into people will ask you who you are. And you will not tell who you are."

"I cannot tell who I am," she said.

"I know but of one house," he said after a while, "into which people may go, and nobody will ask them who they are."

"What house is that?" she asked.

"It is a church," he said.

She laughed. "Are you a churchgoer, Niccolo?" she asked him.

"No," he answered. "I have not been inside a church for sixty-five years. But when I was a child my mother took me there, and sometimes in the ports the ship's chaplain also took me to church with him."

"And what kind of houses, then, are those churches?" she asked again.

"They are strange houses," he said, "for they are called the houses of God, yet the doors are always open to people, and they have got seats for people in them. And in there someone is waiting for people to come. His name is Jesus and Christ, both names, and He is God and man, both."

"Alas, the hard lot," said she. "I, too, have heard of Him. He will have been pleasant to talk with, for He was highly urbane, and said things to people which they must have been happy to hear. He said: 'Be ye therefore perfect!' And I tell you, Niccolo, there is not a singer in the whole world who is not longing to hear those words spoken. Yet He went through much, even more than we. For He will, in His quality of God, have known man's dreadful obstinacy, which may well be incomprehensible to a God. And He will also, in His quality of man, have known God's terrifying fancifulness, incomprehensible to man."

"Hush," said the old man, obviously scared. "You must not speak like that. Such words as yours are called heresy, and if the people of the town heard them, they would throw stones at you too."

"Nay, Niccolo," said Pellegrina. "I have said these things to God. I may say them to men as well."

"Think not so," Niccolo said, more alarmed than before. "One may take many liberties with God which one cannot take with men. One may allow oneself many things, toward Him, which one cannot allow oneself toward man. And, because He is God, in doing so one will even be honoring Him."

"We will not quarrel about theology, Niccolo," said she. "Tell me, instead, whether the church of which you speak stands to the right or to the left."

The old man took down the key from its nail, unlocked the door and walked outside the house with his guest of the night, to explain to her what way to take. There was a fine drizzling rain. Pellegrina, listening to him, with her left hand lifted up her skirt to start on her way down the muddy road.

When Niccolo had finished his directions, he stood silent. "You told me last night," he said at last, "that the mouths of many fools had kissed your hand."

"Yes," said she, "many foolish mouths, filled with frivolity and flattery."

The old man fumbled for her right hand and lifted it to his mouth. "And this mouth of mine, which you have made speak the truth to you," he said, "has now kissed it."

"Farewell," she said.

"Farewell, Lady," said he.

It was a Sunday morning and the Feast of the Rosary. Up in the rainy air the church bells were swinging and ringing, and people going to church carried umbrellas, and here and there in the narrow streets knocked against one another. Pellegrina walked along with them and came to the small square on which the church stood. In the porch to the church she stopped for a moment, the nave before her in spite of its candles looked a dark place to enter. But she bethought herself that she had for once been advised where to go, and that she ought to follow the advice.

The boys' choir struck up the *Kyrie*, and on her chair she began to feel the cold of the room and the smells of damp clothes and of human bodies round her, and to wish that the service would come to an end.

But as, at the offertory, the shrill, innocent braying of many young singers ceased, one single clear boy's voice took up the opening notes of the *Magnificat*. All alone, abandoned by the other voices and leaving them behind, it rose to the low ceiling of the church and reverberated from it.

A minute later a lady in the congregation fell forward on her knees, her head on the ledge of her prie-dieu. A couple of

women near her stirred on their chairs, believing her to be
suddenly taken ill, then, looking at her silk gown, reflected:
"A great *peccatrice*, of the great outside world, up here in
our church has been struck down by the weight of her sins,"
and sat on.

But Pellegrina was not struck down by any weight. Her
body fell from her like a garment, because her soul went
straight upwards with the tones. For the voice that gave them
out was known to her. It was the voice of young Pellegrina
Leoni.

At the sound of the first notes she did not believe her ears,
but lifted her fingers to stop them. Then, as, in the "from
henceforth all generations shall call me blessed," she took in
the ring and the timbre of the singing, she was filled with
immense joy and was floating in light. After a long time she
cried in her heart: "O Sweet. Sweetness of life! Welcome
back." And again after a very long time she laughed. Aware
that it was unseemly to laugh in church she brought up her
handkerchief to her face; when she took it back she found
that it was drenched with tears.

Even when the young singer had long finished his solo, and
her soul was slowly returning to her body, she remained on
her knees. As in the end she looked up and gazed around her,
the priest had read the last gospel, and the church was almost
empty. But a little girl with two long black plaits, who had
sat on a chair to her left, kept standing beside it, troubled by
the idea that the fine, unknown lady might be dead. As
slowly she got to her feet, her eyes met those of the child, and
so radiant with happiness was the face of the woman that the
little girl's face, like a reflection in a mirror, broke into a
smile.

"Who was it," Pellegrina asked her, "that sang the *Magnificat?*"

"It was Emanuele," the child answered in a low, sweet
voice.

"Who is Emanuele?" Pellegrina asked.

"Emanuele is my foster brother," said the little girl.

Here the row of choir boys on their way out of the church passed the two. The girl indicated one of them. "That is Emanuele," she whispered. Pellegrina tried to see the face pointed out to her, but things were swimming before her eyes; it passed by and was gone.

The little girl was still by her side. "What is your name?" Pellegrina asked her.

"Isabella," the child answered.

"I shall be staying on here a little, Isabella," said Pellegrina. "I became giddy a while ago, I know not why."

In the afternoon of that same day Pellegrina took lodgings in the town with an old spinster by the name of Eudoxia, the very last of a family who had lived in their tall narrow house for two hundred years. Eudoxia sewed lace, and after she had come to be alone in the house and her old legs had grown too stiff to carry her up the stairs, she slept and cooked her meals on the ground floor, where she had her shop. The top flat of the house stood empty, furnished with worm-eaten and faded beds and chairs of ancient days. From its windows there was a wide view over the neighboring mountain slopes and the low land at their feet.

For a week Pellegrina sat by these windows and looked out. Many thoughts ran through her head. She reflected: "It is a strange thing that I should have known on my first arrival here that this town is the place in which one may stay on." And on another day, recalling the row of village boys amongst whom Isabella had pointed out to her the singer of the *Magnificat:* "So you have, lost voice of mine, taken abode in a young breast, the breast of a peasant boy of the mountains whom, as he was herding his father's goats on a slope, I might have passed in my carriage without noticing him. The gods disguise themselves cunningly, and will also, in their own time, don goatskins and sheepskins."

Her landlady's big gray cat took a fancy to Pellegrina and came up to lie on her window sill; he brought the old maid herself up the stairs. To Eudoxia her lodger named herself Signora Oreste and explained that she was the widow of a world-famous singing master of Rome, who in his day had taught both great singers and princes and had traveled from court to court in Europe. Now, she said, she had been ill for a long time, and on the advice of the doctors had traveled up to the mountain town because of the excellency of its air and water, maybe she would some day make its name as famous as that of her husband.

After a while Pellegrina inquired about Emanuele. The old woman started upon the theme with unexpected solemnity. Emanuele, she said, was a brand plucked out of the fire. His father, who had been a distant cousin of Eudoxia's, and his mother, who had come from Milan, once had owned a farmstead some way out of the town. Twelve years ago, when the boy was but a baby, a mountain slide had crushed the house with its stables and outbuildings. The husband and wife with their two little daughters, and their donkeys, cattle and goats had all perished, and the wife's young brother, who was living with them, had had both legs smashed under the stones. But in the morning the child was found, unhurt and yelling for food, in the midst of the ruins. One might call it a miracle.

In very old days, Eudoxia explained, the town had possessed a priest who worked miracles, and whom the townspeople had wished to be made a saint. A deputation had traveled the long way to Rome to see the Pope on the matter, but nothing had come of it. From her account Pellegrina understood that since those days a bitterness had remained in the hearts of the town, together with a mystic hope of rehabilitation. Now many people felt that this child had been spared and chosen by Providence for great things in life, and that the village might still come to have a saint of its own. The pious Podesta, whose name was Pierro Rossati and who was a widower, had taken the small boy into his house and had him brought up with his own, only child. Emanuele,

Eudoxia thought, might become a priest. But he might also come to marry Pietro's daughter—if so, he would make a greater match than he had been born for, but Pietro would not hold back the hand of his daughter from a husband picked out by the hand of the Lord. From the window Eudoxia pointed out the place where the lost farm had stood.

When she had gone, Pellegrina sat on, gazing toward the spot.

"I have heard," she thought, "the story of the Phoenix which burns herself up in her nest and has her one egg hatched by the heat, because there must never be more than one Phoenix in the world. It is an old story. But God likes a *da capo*. Twelve years ago this boy was still a baby. He may well have been born at the hour of the Opera fire in Milan. Was, then, that fire in reality kindled by my own hand? And was the flaming death of the old Phoenix and the radiant birth of the young bird but one and the same thing?"

So she was to take up her voice of olden days and to make it perfect as it had once been. She was to teach the boy Emanuele to sing.

She knew that she would have but a short span of time before her, for within three or four years the voice would break. It was before the end of that time that the voice of Pellegrina should be heard again by the world, in that heavenly *da capo* which is also called resurrection. Christ Himself, she remembered, when risen from His grave had dwelt for only forty days among His disciples, yet upon these forty days the whole world had built up its creed. Her audience, her gilt boxes and her pits and her beloved galleries would hear Pellegrina sing once more, would bear witness, with its own ears, to a miracle, and would build upon it its hope of salvation. Would she herself, she wondered, on the first night of Emanuele's appearance, be hidden away in the gallery, an old unknown woman in a black shawl, the corpse in the grave witnessing its own resurrection?

She again wondered: "Have I been for thirteen years

traveling, not as I told Niccolo, in flight, but in reality—and in a beeline—toward a goal?"

Slowly and carefully, as in former days with Marcus Cocozza for her counselor she had gone through and taken possession of a new part of hers, she went through and took possession of the task before her. For this last part bestowed upon her by the director of her theater was the greatest of her repertoire and in itself divine. In it she must allow herself no neglectfulness and no rest. Were she to die at the end of the respite granted her it would be but a small matter.

She had a piano sent from Rome. It arrived on the same cart, with a horse and a mule to it, which had brought herself to the town, had to have its legs unscrewed to be taken up the stairway, and caused a stir in the street below. She looked at it for some time and struck a triad. Within the next few days she took to playing on it; then small crowds would gather on the narrow terrace behind the house to listen.

She still sat waiting up in her rooms. She, whose nature held so little modesty, was timid at the idea of facing the child from the church with her own voice, and was preparing herself for the meeting by cleansing her nature of any hardness unworthy of that refound voice.

At the end of the week she made up her mind to act and, in all she did, to behave like a reasonable person.

She wrote to the Podesta that she would pay him a call, put on a fine frock and bonnet and walked to his house. She gave him her name and her situation as she had given it to Eudoxia, and told him that she had heard his foster son sing in church, and that she was, for the length of her stay in the village, offering to take on the boy as a pupil, free of charge. For it would, she said, be a great thing to him, should he become a priest, to sing well in church. She spoke in the light manner of a great lady from Rome, and the Podesta listened to her in the reserved and respectful way of a villager. But with the importance of her errand in her mind Pellegrina wondered whether Emanuele's foster father was not, deeper down in his own mind, aware that the two of them were here closing a bargain upon the possession of a chosen vessel. She made him promise to bring the boy to her house.

So Pellegrina and Emanuele met in the room of the piano. For the first few minutes she spoke without looking at him, steadying herself with her hand on the table and keeping her eyes on Pietro. When at last she turned her eyes to the figure who had lived so intensely in her thoughts, and there had had existence partly as a singing voice and partly as a divinity, she saw that he was a child. He had a round, clear face, blue eyes and a mass of dark hair. He was sturdily built, with long arms and short hands, and held himself straight. He was, she felt, less timid of her than she herself was of him.

But as again, after having talked to Pietro for a while, she took a longer glance at him, a deep and sweet satisfaction filled her. She knew that before starting their lessons she would have to find out whether the chest of her pupil was wide enough, his mouth large enough and its palate high, the lips sufficiently soft and sensitive, the tongue supple and neither too long nor too short. She saw now that in all these things the young singer before her was without blemish. His chest was like an osier basket filled with lettuce and herbs; his throat was a strong column. She felt her own lungs drawing breath in his body and his tongue in her own mouth. A little later she made him talk and made his eyes meet hers, and she sensed, as she had often done before, the power of her beauty and her mind over a young male being, her heart cried out in triumph: "I have got my talons in him. He will not escape me."

In this their first meeting she struck a number of notes on the piano and made her pupil take them up. The sound of his voice moved her as deeply as it had done in the church, but this time she was prepared for it, it fell like rain on parched, plowed land. A day was fixed for Emanuele's first lesson, and the man and the boy, still with their caps in their hands, walked down her stairs.

After the second lesson Pellegrina thought: "I am like a virtuoso who takes up a unique instrument—he knows it all through; his fingers are one with its strings and he will not mistake it amongst a thousand, yet he cannot tell the volume of its capacity, but must be prepared for anything."

At the end of the third lesson Emanuele, when about to leave, lingered by the door and stood up straight there, his eyes on Pellegrina's, but without a word.

"Do you want to ask me anything?" she asked.

He had a way of shaking his head, as if to himself.

"No," he answered, "not to ask you anything. To tell you something."

"Tell me, then," she said.

"I know who you are," said he.

"Who am I?" she asked.

"You are not Signora Oreste, from Rome," he said. "You are Pellegrina Leoni."

These words, which for thirteen years Pellegrina Leoni had dreaded more than death, now in the mouth of the child had lost their bitterness.

She said: "Yes, I am she."

"I knew," said he. "My mother's brother, Luigi, told me of her. He spoke of her to nobody else. He had been a servant in her villa near Milan, and he said: 'People believed Pellegrina Leoni to have died, but it is not so, for she cannot die. And I shall see her again.' Later on he again spoke of her and said: 'Nay, I know now that I have been mistaken. I shall never see her again. But you will see her.' He explained to me how I was to recognize her. 'By the way she walks. And by her long hands. And by her kindliness toward all low and poor people. And when you see her, think of me.' I have remembered, too, to think of Luigi," the boy concluded, "now that at last you have come up here, to me."

"Luigi," Pellegrina repeated. At this moment she realized, in surprise, that the ban on remembrance was lifted when she was with Emanuele. "Yes, Luigi was my servant. He laughed, all my servants laughed. He put my flowers in water when I came home from the Opera. I recall his face now, laughing, above big heaps of roses. Indeed, Emanuele, you are a little like him. But this is a secret among the three of us."

"Nay," said the boy, "Luigi is dead. Now I shall be Luigi. And no one but I will know."

In the course of the next few months two forgotten kinds of happiness came back to the exiled woman and grew upon her day by day.

The first of the two was this: that hard work had once more come into her existence. For Pellegrina was by nature a sturdy, indefatigable old workwoman, and in the days when she had still been free to make a choice, idleness to her had been an abomination. Now, after those many years in which her one concern had been to leave no tracks in the ground that she fled over, she was again allowed to set her feet in deep and to pull her weight, and toil healed her heart and set it free.

Her singing lessons with Emanuele and her planning of them took up most of her days and kept her awake at night. The very difficulties she met were inspiring to her, and she laughed to herself as she recalled old sayings of Marcus Cocozza: "Sorrow is turned into joy before her. Her heart is as firm as a stone, aye, like the nether millstone. Out of her nostrils goeth fire, and a flame goeth out of her mouth." She did not, though, meet with many difficulties, her instrument gave itself into her hands unrestrainedly. At times its ready response to her touch even alarmed her a little as a symptom of too much softness in its nature. "Bear in mind, Emanuele," she admonished the boy, "that only hard metals will give out a ring."

She no longer worried about the briefness of her respite. For up here in the mountains time itself, like the air, was of a richer substance than in the lowlands, and the more of it she gave away the more she had. It happened that Emanuele brought the little girl Isabella with him to her house. She then talked and played with the child, and the hour of the lesson was not shortened. Old Eudoxia began to feel proud of her rich and distinguished lodger, she talked much about her to her friends and introduced some of them to her, and the great lady from Rome found time to speak kindly to them all. From Eudoxia's explanations about her neighbors and their relationship, Pellegrina gathered that the citizens of the small town had been intermarrying for many hundred years. As she got to know them she saw that they had all of them become alike, their skulls slowly growing narrower and their faces more wooden; many of them squinted a little. One day the old squinting parish priest himself paid her a call, and became eloquent on the needs of his poor and sick, on his way down the stairs the old man was filled with bitter regret that he had not asked for twice as much from a person of so much wealth, and so ready to give.

Once she saw Niccolo in the street, walking along slowly and evenly in the cloak that he had on when she first met him. But he did not see her.

The second happiness which, up here in the wide mountain landscape, came to Pellegrina, was her love for her pupil.

It had in it both adoration, triumph and an infinite tenderness. All obsessed by her longing to give, she behaved to the child who was to receive like a lioness to her cub. She could not keep her hands from his thick hair, but pulled it and twisted it round her fingers; she folded his head in her arms and pressed it to her breast. Pellegrina had never yearned to have children of her own, but had, long ago, jested with Marcus Cocozza about the idea of the mighty singing bird surrounded by a nestful of young squallers with open beaks. Now she thought: "It is, then, in this mountain village that I am to lay babes to the breast and to give suck. But what curious sucklings have I got up here: an old toothless shark, and a cygnet!" Then after a fortnight the boy grew to her eyes

and became her young brother, the precious Benjamin
whom she was to lift up into the splendor of Egypt. During
this period of brother- and sisterhood she was struck by a
new family likeness between herself and him—from the beginning they had had but one voice. As now the voice day by
day pervaded Emanuele's whole being his face took on a
sweet and pathetic resemblance to her own. Again he grew,
and she thought: "In three years we two will be one, and you
will be my lover, Emanuele."

A few times a particular trait in the boy's character puzzled her or vexed her: his fondness for laughter. She was herself a laughing person, and Marcus Cocozza had quoted
Homer to her, on the goddess Aphrodite, who loved to laugh,
but she would find, or create, something to laugh at. Emanuele, now, might laugh for no apparent reason and appar-
ently without being able to stop, like a kind of music box run
riot. Sometimes these golden peals of laughter charmed her,
like the exuberant warbles of a bird in a tree; at other
times, when each word spoken by her or by himself set him
laughing she frowned at him and told him: "Stop that laughter, it is silly. It means nothing, and turns you into a clown"
—in her heart adding: "You village idol—are you in reality
nothing but the village idiot?"

The boy abandoned himself to her tenderness as he did to
her teaching, without surprise or reserve. In spite of the wild-
ness of their embraces there was ever in them great dignity
and deep mutual reverence; the giving and receiving was a
mystic rite, and an initiation.

Once, at the end of a lesson, she thought: "If he were to
die now, I should die with him." At that same moment he
went down on his knees before her, raised his eyes to her face
and said: "If you were to die, I should die too."

All the same she would from time to time find herself wondering as to how well she did in reality know her pupil.
There was always in his bearing and in his attitude to his
surroundings the grandeur of that faith in which he had

grown up: that in all his world he was the Chosen and Elect. In such a young person it was curiously impressive and moving. Behind it was his rare gift and feeling for music, the thorough, extraordinary musicalness of his nature. She could not tell whether there was much more, neither could she tell whether she herself wished for more to be there.

She had heard his voice before she had heard his story; to her from the first the two had been one, and his singer's career his vocation. But she came to doubt whether it was so to him himself. Possibly he would have welcomed any call from outside with equal frankness and candor, and would innocently have expected a fanfare to await him in whatever field he entered. Once, when he had sung with particular sweetness and purity, he told her that he wanted a flute with silver keys.

During these months of work and love, in which she was rendering her pupil ageless, Pellegrina became ageless with him. At one hour she would look bent, withered and infinitely wise like an old grandmother, at others she had the face of a girl of seventeen.

One day she spoke to Emanuele of the greatness and glory awaiting him. Since the day when he had told her that he knew who she was, although none of them had pronounced the name of Pellegrina Leoni, she had talked to him freely of the past, had compared his voice to her own, and his work to her own at the time when she had been taught to sing. But the child Isabella on this day happened to be present, so she spoke in an impersonal way of the triumphs of a great singer, of his power over the mighty of the earth and of the gold and the flowers flung before his feet. She recounted to the children how an enthusiastic audience had unspanned the horses from a beloved singer's coach and had drawn it through the town themselves. She saw that her visions of his future fascinated and amused the boy, but that they did not really mean much to him. He had no knowledge of the big towns that she named and but little of the worlds of princes, cardinals, and courts, the mountain town to him was the world, and it was up here that he meant to fulfill his destiny. With Isabella her words went deeper, she grew pale under them and her dark eyes were very big. Maybe, Pellegrina thought, the child was alarmed at the idea of a mighty lady carrying her foster brother with her away from her own world. "But let her go with him!" she thought. "Let her follow him about wherever he goes. Her innocence and gracefulness will make a sensation at all the courts of Europe!"

In order, now, to give Isabella a taste for such courts Pellegrina set to making up a big elegant doll for her. From Eudoxia she purchased lace and silk ribbons and made the doll's frock a replica of the frock of her own greatest role. In old days she had been clever with her needle, she lost herself in embellishing the wax doll, with beads and spangles on its long train like stars on a winter sky, and in the end placed a tall golden crown on its head. She was looking forward to sending for Isabella and handing her over the doll, when, just as she was endeavoring to put the crown straight, the little girl knocked at the door. She had never come to her house alone before; she was grave, and before she spoke she smoothed the folds of her skirt with her hand.

"I have come up here, Lady," she said, "to say good-bye to you. For I am going far away."

"Where are you going to, Isabella?" Pellegrina asked in surprise.

"To Greccio," Isabella answered.

Pellegrina smiled at the idea of Greccio being far away, for she could see the town from her windows. But Isabella went on gravely, informing her that in Greccio she had an aunt who was a nun, and that the nuns of Greccio ran a girls' school. She wanted to enter that school. "And when I am big enough, in five years," she announced, "I shall become a nun too."

"A nun?" Pellegrina exclaimed. "What makes you want to become a nun?"

"I shall be a nun," Isabella said, "so that I may pray all day for someone."

"For whom?" Pellegrina asked.

"For Emanuele," answered Isabella.

Pellegrina let her hands sink onto the doll in her lap. "How wise you are," she said. "How wise you are, Isabella. That is the one thing of which I have not thought: that somebody must be praying for him. Surely it will help him. You are wiser than I am."

She lifted the doll onto the table.

"Look," she said. "I have made a doll to go with you to Greccio. Much love of mine will go with her, now that I know you are going to pray for Emanuele."

Isabella left the doll untouched on the table, but beneath her long lashes her eyes ran like dark drops from its crown to its small shoes. She drew a long sigh of adoration.

"Maybe," she said sadly, "I shall not be allowed to have a doll with me in Greccio, not a big, elegant doll like her."

"But do you not see," Pellegrina asked, "that this is no ordinary doll? It is Saint Cecilia, the patroness of music, with a heavenly crown on her head. By her all human hearts are uplifted and blessed."

Isabella still did not move, but she looked from the doll to Pellegrina's face.

"I am not," said the child, "in Greccio, going to pray for Emanuele only."

"For whom more are you going to pray, Isabella?" Pellegrina asked.

The little girl shifted her feet. "The other day," she said, "when you told Emanuele of all the great things that happen to a great singer, and what sweet presents he gets, and how a thousand people love him, I thought by myself that maybe you could describe all these things so well because they had happened to you yourself."

"No," said Pellegrina gently, "all these things, dear child, have never happened to me myself. For I cannot sing. But I have in my time met many such famous singers; from that I can tell others about them."

"I thought by myself, Lady," the little girl went on, "that after you had seen and known all the glory of the world you had come up here to our town to find your soul again and to save it. Therefore I resolved that in Greccio, when I pray for Emanuele, I shall pray for your soul too."

Pellegrina put her arms round the child. "Yes, Isabella," she said. "It is all true, and pray you for my soul."

After a moment she asked: "Does Emanuele know that you are going away, and that you want to be a nun?"

"I have told it to him," Isabella answered.

"And what, then, did he say to you?" Pellegrina asked.

Again Isabella shifted her feet, she turned her face away a little. "He said the same as you did now," she answered in a little sad voice as before, "that it was good. That it was wise."

By this time it began to grow cold in the town. The days drew in, and in the mornings and evenings clouds hung heavily round the mountain tops. Pellegrina caught a cold, and for a few days was so hoarse that she could not speak. But she consoled herself: "Isabella is praying for me."

The particular softness in the nature of her pupil, which had at times upset Pellegrina, came out as well in a fear of physical pain, unknown to her herself. It did not displease her, for by now nothing in the boy could possibly displease her, but she could not hold herself back from trying to rid him of it. One day, playing with his hand, she said to him: "I am going to prick you with my needle in three of your fingertips, till I draw a drop of blood from each of them, and you must not withdraw your hand." Emanuele looked up at her with doleful eyes and trembling lips, but managed to keep his hand steady. She wiped the three drops of blood off on her small handkerchief, one by one, then, as she looked at the three little scarlet spots she lifted the handkerchief to her lips.

The next day Emanuele did not turn up for his lesson. Pellegrina wondered what might have happened to him, but she did not send for him, since his will was her law. She kept sitting by her window, doing a little needlework and meditating: "It is happiness, even, to sit here and wait for him."

When he came back on the morrow he seemed to expect an inquiry about his absence, and as it did not come he said: "I was ill yesterday." He turned pale under his own words.

Yet he went through his scales more nobly than before; his voice to her had a new, deeper ring to it. Once more she was filled with the reverence or awe that she had felt before, and as at their first meeting, she sat on for a while in silence.

"Do you know, my little Emanuele," she said at last, "that you are now singing with my own voice? This is my great secret. My heart is swelling on to my lips as I tell it you. You have got Pellegrina Leoni's voice in your chest, and verily Pellegrina Leoni herself till now did not know how beautiful it was."

She could not tell whether he was listening to her praise of him with a new, deeper attention, or whether he did not hear a word of what she said.

But as he was about to go, he lingered by the door, as he had once before done, and asked her: "Where did you get your gold ring?"

"Of what gold ring are you speaking, Emanuele?" she asked him.

He answered: "Of the gold ring which you gave to Camillo, the wagon-driver, when he brought you up here."

She remembered the ring and called to mind that while she had bestowed many gifts on old Eudoxia and her friends, and on the poor of the priest, she had never made Emanuele a present, and she wondered if the heart of the village boy was yearning for some possession.

"Oh, I have got many rings, Emanuele," she said, "and other things as well. Would you like a ring? Or a gold watch? Or would you like silver buttons for your coat? I shall get them for you."

"No," said the boy, "I want no ring. No gold watch. No silver button either. But Camillo believed that it was just a trinket you had given him, a toy to play with. Then, last week, he showed the ring to a friend of his in Rome, who is a goldsmith, and his friend told him that it was worth as much as his whole house. You have given Father Jeremiah gold too. There is nobody up here who has got things like that. There is nobody up here who would, if they had such things, give them away as you do. Where did you get your gold?"

Pellegrina, as has been told, had never troubled herself much about money; she thought his question silly and was at a loss how to answer it. She said: "I have told you that I am a rich woman. I have got a friend who gives me all I want."

The boy shook his head. "But your friend," he said, "has never come up here to see you. Nobody here has seen him."

"Nay, he has not been up here," she said. "My friend does not show himself much to people."

"Shall I see him?" Emanuele asked.

"Nay," she again answered. "You will not see him. But my friends are his friends. Tell me what you want, and I will make him send it to you."

"I want nothing from him," said the boy.

But he still did not go away. He gazed round the room slowly, letting his eyes rest on one thing after the other, at last he looked back at her.

"What are you looking at?" she asked him.

"I was looking at this room," he answered, "and at all the things here. At the green lamp, and the piano. I was thinking of them all."

"What were you thinking of them?" she asked him.

"I was thinking," he said, "that here I have been happy."

The words in his mouth sounded so curiously grown-up that they made her laugh. He, generally so touchy at being laughed at, remained grave.

"Happier," he said, "than in other places. I think that here I have heard my own voice coming to me from somewhere else, I know not from where."

With a strange childish dignity he again took his glance off the room and off her.

For three days after this he did not come. This time she grew alarmed, wondering if he had really fallen ill. In the early morning of the fourth day she left her house to find him.

She went to the Podesta's house, and was told there that he was not ill, but that he had been away on his own much these last days, and was so now. She went to the house of Pietro's sister, whom, she knew, he was wont to visit, but he was not in her house either. She went to a small square, where she had once seen him playing ball with other boys. Boys were playing ball there still, but he was not among them. She went on from there to the houses of two or three friends of his, the names of whom she had learned from him, but he was not with any of them. She could not give up her search, but walked on at random. She had grown slim and light-footed once more up here in the mountains. When she had been a girl her walk had always been faster than that of other people; she walked so now, and the comb fell from her head so that her long hair was loosened and floated after her.

Suddenly, on the outskirts of the town, she came upon him, standing immovable, his back half-turned to her and gazing into distance. At once, at the very sight of him, order and benevolence returned to the world, and she stopped to breathe them in and let them fill her. At this moment, and just as she was going to call out his name, he unexpectedly turned and walked away, at first slowly, then quickening his step. She walked after him, as quickly as he.

A pale silvery winter sun showed itself in the sky; the varying gray tints in the house walls round her and in the landscape below them came out tardily in its light; the scarf round the fleeing boy's neck was a burning red spot in the cool picture.

All of a sudden the slight figure before her swerved off into a steep side street ending, high up, in a flight of stone steps. She had almost caught up with him, but on the stairs her long ample skirts were in her way, and she stopped.

"Emanuele!" she cried. "Stay! It is I."

At the sound of her voice the boy began to run.

It flashed upon her that he might really, for some reason unknown to her, have been running away from her. Although he had not turned his head, he had sensed her approach and then taken to his heels, and Pellegrina Leoni had been running through the town in pursuit of a truant pupil. The idea made her laugh where she stood.

"Nay, stay, come down, Emanuele!" she cried up to him, her voice half-stifled with laughter. "Come down, and come back with me."

Emanuele turned round and faced her. He was trying to speak, but either he was breathless with his quick walk, or otherwise some violent emotion was holding him back, no sound came from him.

She wondered whether she had somehow overworked or scared him. He was not as hard as she; his heart was a long way from being like the nether millstone. She must be careful now; she must lure the bird back.

"You dearest child, come here with me," she called up to him, her husky voice enticing and insinuating like a stringed instrument. "We will play the loveliest games together. I have got velvet from old Eudoxia wherewith to make you a fine new coat. I have got the flute with silver keys. I have got many new songs and airs for you to sing. Dances."

At that he found his voice.

"No!" he cried. "No. No. No. And it is going to be no, I tell you, every time, whatever you try to make me do."

She stood without a word. She looked up at him to take in

his face, and she did not recognize it or feel sure that it was the face of the child she had taught. This face seemed to have been all flattened out, the eyes themselves washed away and half disappearing in the flatness, pale like the eyes of a blind person below his twisted brow. It was the face of a little old woman.

"No!" he shrieked out in furious triumph at being able to speak, and she felt, in her own hands, that his two hands were hard clenched, "I know who you are. You are a witch. You are a vampire. You are wanting to drink my blood."

He stopped as if terrified by the sound of his own words, then cried on:

"You sucked my blood from your handkerchief. I saw it myself. You have got gold, diamonds, the flute with silver keys. You have sold your soul for them to the Devil."

She tried to make his words a jest. One said such things, at times, to one's lover.

"Oh, no, Emanuele," she cried back. "I have never in my life sold a thing. Whatever my friend the Devil has got from me, he has got as a present."

His answer came down as from very high up: "It is the same to me. You want my blood, all the blood that is in me. Witches live on forever by drinking children's blood. You want the soul of me, now, to make the Devil a new present!

"Luigi told me so," he went on. "He told me that you could not die, that you were immortal. All people thought that you were dead, but you were not dead. You had found, then, another boy whose blood you had drunk."

He stopped, and again went on: "It is true that you are old. But there is no help to me in that. For a witch will live till she is a hundred years old. She will live till she is three thousand years."

As now she did not answer a word, her silence stemmed his own speech. For a moment he stood dead still and closed his eyes.

"Once," he then cried out, "I thought that I should die if

I were to leave you. Now I know that I should die if I went back to you."

She stood as still as he, for in this long wail of farewell, and of doom, his voice had rung out as it should ring when at last she had made it what it was meant to be. It was Dido's lament, Alceste's heroic sacrifice, in Pellegrina Leoni's voice.

The boy again opened his eyes and stared at her. Up where he stood he could get no farther. For the steps were here barred by a stone fence with a gate to it. For a minute he was immovable, a wild animal at bay; then he fumbled among the stones of the fence by him, heaved a stone from it and pressed it to his breast.

"If you do not stay where you are," he cried, "I shall throw the stone at you."

She, however, would not or could not stay where she was. In a wild and blind hope that the struggle might still be turned into an embrace, with two fingers she lifted up her skirt in front and, as in a dance, took a light step upwards.

As she moved, Emanuele hurled the stone. She had seen him throw stones before, very accurately. It must be his terrible tumult of mind which now made his hand unsteady or made him misjudge the distance. The stone brushed her head, and her thick hair somewhat warded off the blow. Yet she staggered under it and came down on one knee, and she felt the warm dampness of her blood as it trickled over her forehead and her left eye.

Before she got up, a second stone whirled past her ear.

Then she became furious. She had not been angry during the thirteen empty years of her flight; now in a second she was thrown back twice that length of time. She sent her indignation upwards in the dialect of her native village, as eager for battle as a small wench with a boy using unfair means of fighting.

"You clod!" she cried. "You stumpy peasant boy! So you are throwing stones, are you! So you will be biting too, will you, when I get hold of you!

"Do you know at whom you are throwing stones!" she went on. "A thousand men, a Pope, an Emperor, Princes, gondolieri and beggars, if I but lift my voice, will be here to avenge me on you, you fool."

She fetched her breath. "Yes, I am a witch," she cried. "A great witch, a vampire with bat's wings. But what are you, who dare not come down to play with a witch? What is a coward's soul worth? Must you sit on that soul of yours as a young miss on her maidenhood, with all your wooden, squinting friends sitting round you, praying that it may be preserved! The one amongst them who knew what a soul is, you sent away. I tell you, you are being poisoned by your soul. It is a bad tooth, have it out!"

She would have gone on, and would have been happy to go on, now that she had got her strength back and her blood up. But she stopped short, for her ear had caught her own voice. What should have been the roar of a lioness was the hissing of a gander and a pain in her throat and chest. For a minute she steadied herself with a hand against the wall beside her; then she turned and walked down.

On the second step down her foot struck the stone that had been thrown at her. She took it up, rubbed it into the scratch on her forehead and turning once more flung it up lightly, so that it fell at the feet of the boy who had thrown it.

"Keep it, you!" she said. "Pellegrina Leoni's blood is upon it."

She began to walk back through the streets and her mind was as dumb as her breast. On the way she fumbled at her hair and wiped the blood off her face with it. At last she stood still. She gazed round her to recognize the street, then crossed it to where, on a corner, there stood a low stone trough for watering donkeys and cattle, and sat down. The leaden sky once more had closed over the town, a thin, chill wind came running along.

Pellegrina sat on her trough for a long time and let many reflections run through her head.

She first thought:

"I was right. I was right when I told Niccolo that joy was my element. The people of this earth who have it in them to suffer so deeply, and to fear, will get the better of me every time. I cannot hold my own against them." She called up before her the faces of the townspeople, one by one. Here was Eudoxia's face, furrowed with care and worry, here were the faces of Eudoxia's neighbors, strained and anxious, and the tallow-colored face of the parish priest, blunt and stolid, as if blind. "Joy may come to them," she told herself, "as a surprise, for an hour or two, but none of them feels at home in it." The idea of the overwhelming majority of unhappy people in the world closed in upon her from all sides. "I cannot stand up against all of them," she told herself. "Not against all."

She next thought:

"Emanuele was mistaken; he was all wrong. But one cannot blame him for that. I myself have been told about the mingling of blood between two people. But he has never heard of such things. To him the mingling of blood will mean the drinking of it. He saw me sucking his blood from my handkerchief, and he ran away before me in fear of his life. But it is difficult to tell, in a mingling of blood like ours, who gives and who receives. You ought to have known, Emanuele, that I should not have brought the drops of your blood to my mouth if it had not been that I was longing to give all my own blood to you."

She again thought:

"And then, maybe, he was not as much mistaken as all that. Or can you honestly vow, Pellegrina, that you yourself, who have so often been begged to stay on, who have been held back and have been pursued, did not, today, take pleasure in being the pursuer?"

She here became conscious of people passing her or coming toward her in the street, and it seemed to her that they looked at her with grief or in fear. She remembered that she had on her forehead the mark of Cain. She also remembered Niccolo's words: that if people knew what she was thinking they would throw stones at her. She dipped her long tresses in the water of the trough and washed her face with them.

"But it will still be there," she reflected, "and I shall have to get up and away from here. For it must be a sorry thing to be stoned." She called to mind how, on the evening of her coming to town, she had told herself that this was a place in which one might stay on. "But there I was wrong," she thought.

She wanted, before rising and going away, to think once more of Emanuele. It would, she knew, be the last time, for on parting from him she must again give up remembering. She sat gazing down in the water of the trough, but she saw his face as he had lifted it to tell her that if she died he must die too, and as he had lowered it like a small angry bull-calf when he had thrown the stone. "Must pity of human beings," she cried in her heart, "forever be sucking the marrow out of my bones?"

She thought at last:

"Oh, my child, dear Brother and Lover. Be not unhappy, and fear not. It is all over between you and me. I can do you no good and I shall do you no harm. I have been too bold, venturing to play with human hands on an Aeolian harp. I beg pardon from the north wind and the south wind, from the east and west wind. But you are young. You will live to weigh more than I do, half as much again, and to prove yourself the Chosen and Elect; you may live to give to your town a priest-saint of her own. You will sing too. Only, dear heart, you will have to work hard to unlearn what you have learned from me. You will have to take great care so as not, when you are singing the Gospel, to introduce *portamento* effects.

"And the voice of Pellegrina Leoni," she concluded her long course of thought, "will not be heard again."

As she got up from the trough and stood on her feet she asked herself: "Shall I go to the right or to the left?"

She bethought herself of Niccolo, who had taken trouble to give her his advice on the matter, and reflected that she ought to follow the advice once more, and go into the church. For in a church, she remembered having been told, people will not stone anybody.

She again had to look round to find the way to the church, then walked along to it.

She had expected to find the church empty. But the day happened to be a Sunday, as had been the day of her first visit there, and when she lifted the heavy leather curtain of the porch she saw that there were people in the room behind it. It was the latest Mass of the day, a silent Low Mass. Without making any noise she sat down close to the door, and she soon came to feel that she was already on the road again, and that the quiet in which she sat was but a pause.

In a while the communicants, who had been up by the altar, came back and again took their seats. She cast a glance at the face of her neighbor, a very old woman, to see if there she would find any fear of her. The face had no expression at all, but she saw that the wrinkled lips and toothless gums were still moving and munching a little with the consummation of the Host.

"You too, Niccolo," she thought, "spoke the truth on that evening when we talked together. One can take many liberties with God which one cannot take with men. One may allow oneself many things toward Him which one cannot allow oneself toward man. And, because He is God, in doing so one will even be honoring Him."

New Winter's Tales

A COUNTRY TALE

There was a wood path running along the stone fence at the western edge of a wood. Outside the fence the open landscape lay calm and golden, already marked by the hand of autumn. The large fields were empty, the harvest was gathered in and only the rakings were left, set up here and there in low stacks. Some way off, on a field road, a last cartload was rolling toward the barn in a cloud of golden dust. The distant woods to the north and south were brownish-green, gently and gravely gilt or rusted by the sun of long summer days. The woods to the west were deep blue; from time to time a faint blue tinged the fields as well, where a flight of wood-pigeons rose from the stubble. Along the fence the last honeysuckle, upon limp stalks, was giving out its farewell fragrance, and the bramble already had scarlet leaves and black, ripe berries. But the depth of the forest was still green, a summer vault, and where the beams of the afternoon sun fell through the verdure it became luminous and filled with promise, like May foliage. The path wound in and out, and up and down, the forest slopes. It swerved toward the fence, as if it meant to unite the wood world with the open country, then shrank back again as if in fear of giving away a secret.

A young man, bareheaded, in a riding coat, and a young lady in a white summer frock came walking along the path. Her frock, Greek in drapery like that of a dryad, with the belt just below the breasts, trailed lightly on the ground and, as she walked on, rolled a dry beechnut of last year along, as a wavelet plays with a pebble on the beach. She let her dark eyes under long lashes glide lovingly and happily over the forest scenery, like a young housewife going through her house and finding everything in good order.

They walked along slowly and easily; they were at home in the wood and belonged to it. Their clothes and carriage told that they were a young squire and squire's lady of the fair, rich green isle.

Where the path took off and ran over the fence toward the fields she stood still and gazed out into the distance. To her companion, who stopped with her, it was as if he did not himself see the landscape before them, but only through her knew that it existed, and what it meant. It became infinitely lovely within her eyes and mind, lovelier than itself, a silent poem. She did not turn toward him; she rarely did so, and very rarely on her own offered a caress. Her form and color, the fall of her rich dark hair and the lines of her shoulders, her long hands and slim knees, in themselves were caresses; her entire being and nature was to enchant, and she craved for nothing else in life. On his way to the wood he had pondered the problem of the vocation of man; now he thought: "The vocation of a rose is to exhale scent; for that reason do we plant roses in our garden. But a rose on its own exhales a sweeter scent than we could ever demand of it. It craves for nothing else in life."

"What are you thinking of now that you tell me not?" she asked.

He did not answer at once, and she did not repeat her question, but, climbing the smooth-worn path across the fence, for a moment shaded her eyes with her hand against the light, then seated herself where she stood, her hands folded round her knees. From far away her frock, catching the sun, would now be visible like a golden-white flower in the green. He sat down in the shade of the trees, where his eyes could rest on her form. The air here at the edge of the wood was clear and warm, the light full and timeless, the stubble fields breathed a generous sweetness. A pale-blue moth came and settled upon a sun-baked stone beside her.

He did not want to break up their happy hour in the wood, and remained silent for a while.

"I was thinking," he said at last, "of the old people who lived here before us, and who cleared and broke and plowed this land. They will have had to begin their work over and over again. In very old days they had bears and wolves to fight, then Wendish pirates and invaders and then, later again, hard and unsparing masters. But were they to rise from their graves, on a harvest day like this, and to look out over the fields and meadows before us, they might still consider that it had been worth their while."

"Oh, yes," she said and looked up toward the blue sky and the clouds. "And they will," she added, "have had real fine hunting, with those bears and those wolves." Her voice was as clear as a bird's, with a faint ring of the island dialect, like a melody, to it. She talked as if she played.

"And they might then, today," he said, "forget the wrongs done them."

"Oh, yes," she said once more. "It is all a long time ago." She smiled a little to herself. "Now you are thinking of a peasant," she said, "since you talk of wrongs."

"Yes," said he, "I was thinking of a peasant."

"And why," she asked, "are you digging your old peasants out of the mold to bring them with us into the wood today?"

"I might tell you why," he said, but sat on silent.

"You are a clever, wise, learned man, Eitel," she said. "Your land is better worked and looked after than the land of your neighbors. People talk about you and your reforms and inventions. The King himself has said that he would there were more like you in his country. You give more thought to your peasants' welfare than to your own. You have been away for years in foreign countries to study new farming systems and how to make their lot easier and happier to them. And yet you speak as if you were in debt to them even now."

"I may be in debt to them even now," he said.

"I remember," she said thoughtfully, "that one day when we two were children and were walking together in the wood —just like now—you began telling me of the wrongs done, in old times, to the peasants in Denmark. I was older than you, but you spoke so gravely that I forgot my dolls for your tales. I almost believed, then, that the Lord God must have decided to create our whole world over again, and that you must be one of the angels whom He had chosen to assist Him in the task."

"You were the angel, I think," he said, and smiled a little, "who had the patience to listen to the fantasies of a lonely boy."

They sat in silence for a while, thinking of the time of which they were talking.

"Today," she said, "I know a little more about the world, and I do not think that it is going to be created over again— not in our time. I do not know, either, that one must think it unjust that there are both noblemen and peasants on the earth, any more than that there are both pretty and plain people upon it. May I not brush my own hair without grieving for the sake of the women who have got thin, dull hair?"

He looked at her long silky ringlets, and called to mind the many times that he had loosened them and wound them round his fingers.

"But to you," she went on, "it is as if it were all your fault that there are poverty and distress in the world. It is as if you were tied with a rope to those old peasants of whom you talk."

"Yes, I may be tied to them with a rope," he said.

She sat silent for a long time, her hands round her knees. "If I had been a peasant's wife," she said lowly and happily, "you would not have taken me."

He did not answer her. He was seized and transported, as often before, by the fact of her nature being so entirely without shame. She blushed easily, with joy or pride, but never with guilt. And that, he reflected, was why he found peace with her as with no other human being. He had heard and read, and he knew from his own experience, that a man's love of a woman never for a long time outlives possession. But he had been the lover of this young lady, his neighbor's wife, for two years. Her little daughter, up at her husband's house to which the wood belonged, was his. And his desire and his tenderness were stronger today than two years ago, so strong that he had to hold himself back so as not to draw her to him or to kneel down before her and kiss her hands in sweet, wild gratitude. It would be the same, he felt, were they to live to old age. And it was not by her beauty or her gentleness that she did hold this happy and painful power over him. It was because she knew not shame nor remorse, nor rancor. After a while he also reflected that in her last words to him she had spoken the truth.

"You," he said at length in a changed voice, low as her own, "you have never wronged the people whose lives were in your hand. Your family, your fathers, have lived in good understanding with the peasants on their land, as with the land itself."

"My family and my fathers were like others, I think," said she. "Papa had such a temper! When he had taken something into his head, it would have to be done; he did not worry much whether it was reasonable or not."

"But the name of your fathers," said Eitel, "has not been loathed by the people who served you. Your harvesters have sung while they reaped their fields."

She thought the matter over. "Have you got the barley in, with you?" she asked.

"Yes, it is in," he answered, "except for a little in the lower field and a bit in 'Milady's Paddock.' "

"It would not make much difference to you, I do not think," she said after a moment, "whether they sang or not while they reaped for you. That is what I have been wondering about many times, Eitel: what have you gained by your toils and your travels and your studies? It has made you a stranger among your equals. You do not take much pity on your friends, be they ever so unfortunate in cards or in love. And if you sell them a horse, you will know what price to ask, and stick to it. But when you are trading with a peasant you will feel, I think, that you must give him the whole horse for nothing. And for all that, there is no great affection for the peasants in your heart.

"Those old men," she continued slowly, "those old lords of the land whom you cannot forget—maybe they took more pleasure in having their servants about them than you do. They felt that those people belonged to them; they made merry with them and were pleased and proud when they were comelier or shrewder than the servants of their neighbors. But you, Eitel, you do not want your own valet to touch you; you dress and undress without him; you ride about without a groom; you go out with your gun and your dog all alone. Why, when that old tenant of yours, to whom you forgave his lease, wanted to kiss your hand, you would not let him do so, and I had to give him mine to kiss, so as not to let him go away empty! It is not out of love for your peasants that you rack your brain and allow yourself no rest. It is out of love for something else. And what that is I know not."

"Nay, you are mistaken," said he. "I love this land of mine, every acre of it. In foreign countries, in the big towns there, I have been sick with longing for this very soil and air of mine."

"I know," said she, "that you love your land as if it were your wife. But you are not the less lonely for that. And I wonder, Eitel," she added with a vague mockery or pity in her voice, "I wonder whether in all your life you have really loved any human being except just me."

At her words he looked back searchingly into the past. She herself, he reflected, wherever she had been had found something to love.

"Nay," he said once more after a while, "I have indeed loved very deeply a human being—a long, long time ago. But at the same time you are right. It is not out of love for my servants or my peasants that I do, as you say, rack my brain and allow myself no rest. It is out of love for something else. And the name of that thing is justice."

"Justice," she repeated wonderingly and became silent. "Eitel," she said at last, "we two need not worry ourselves about justice. Fate is just, God is just. Surely He will judge and retribute, without our assistance. And we human beings may leave off judging one another."

"And yet," he said, "we human beings take upon ourselves to judge one another. Yet we take upon ourselves to sentence one another to death.

"Did you ever know," he asked after a pause, "that my father had a man put to death?"

"Your father?" she asked. "A peasant?"

"Yes," he answered, "he was a peasant."

"I believe that they told me so," she said, "when I was a little girl."

"They told you so, Ulrikke," he said. "They told an old story, a nursery tale, to a little girl. But to me it was a different tale, for my own father was in it."

"It seems to me that I remember your father," said she,

"and that he set me on his knee and played with me. And yet that can hardly be. But Mama has talked about him many times, and has told me that he was a handsome, gallant, gay gentleman. A very fine horseman and afraid of nothing—like you."

"My father died before I was born," he said. "That, to me, has seemed to mean that he did, from the very beginning, wish to give all that was his into my hands."

"You need not grieve at that," she said and smiled.

"I need not grieve at that," he repeated slowly. "You are thinking of his land and of his fortune. That inheritance of mine has been growing with me myself, during my minority. But he left me more. His own guilt and that of his fathers, that dark shadow which they cast wherever they walked— that, too, is an inheritance which may also have been growing until today."

"Until today?" she asked.

He caught the vague echo of resentment in her voice— their happy day together darkened by ancient incomprehensible shadows. His heart ached a little at it.

"Listen," he said, "I have never spoken to you of my father. Today if you would hear me, I should like to speak of him.

"I have never seen his face or heard his voice, yet in my small world when I was a child he was ever with me. His portrait on the wall showed the face of a handsome, gallant, gay gentleman, and the people round me have talked to me of him as your mother did to you, for who speaks ill to a child of his dead father? How did it then happen that this dead father came to his child, a dark figure looming over the little boy, wrapped in a black cloak of guilt, gloom and shame, formidable? Yet I was never afraid of him. It does, I believe, happen like that with children: the grown-up people will tell them of a troll or hobgoblin, and the child will become familiar with the troll and will, in its own way, make it belong to him. In the peaceful house, filled with gentle women, my father and I belonged to one another, and if he was formidable I was formidable as well.

"As I grew older," he continued, "and on my own or by the hand of my tutor began to think and reason more abstractly, my ideas of a moral order of the world, of right and wrong and of justice, all grouped themselves round his figure as if they did indeed come to me through him. It was then that I realized the nature of our partnership. He had a claim on me; there was something that I must do for him; he required me to pay his debt.

"As then I read the story of Orestes, I reflected how much easier was his task than mine, since he had a virtuous father to avenge. As I was taught my catechism, the words that stuck in my mind were these, 'I am in my father and my father is in me.'

"In the end, five years ago, when I was eighteen and his land and fortune were given into my hands, when I was known to the world no longer as Master Eitel but by the name of my fathers, it became clear to me what I had to do. So I made up my mind to go to foreign countries, there to study how to make the lot of the people on my land happier.

"This is what I have thought of, Ulrikke," he continued. "The Christian religion will tell us of our duty toward our brothers and our neighbors, the people living round us to-day. It bids us take up the cause of the abandoned, destitute and downtrodden among them. It was first preached by artisans and fishermen.

"But there is another kind of religion which speaks not of brothers or neighbors but of fathers and sons. It proclaims our duty toward the past, and it bids us take up the cause of the dead. To that religion the nobleman is priest. And for this reason are we noblemen and bear old names, for this reason is the land given into our hands: that the past, and the dead, may put their trust in us. My brother or my neighbor, after all, if I strike him may return the blow, and the oppressed around us, if too hard tried, may rebel. But if we are not there, who will look after the past? And who will then be abandoned and destitute and in very truth downtrodden as the dead? For this reason do I bear my father's old name, which has been known in the country for many centuries, that my dead father in his grave, who can trust in no one else, may trust in me.

"To cut away from the past," he said very slowly, as if to himself, "to annihilate it, is the vilest of all breaches of the laws of the cosmos. It is ingratitude, and running away from your debt. It is suicide: you are annihilating yourself in it. I have heard it said, or have read somewhere," he added and smiled a little, "that a thing is not true until it is twenty-five years old—almost my own age. I shall not, at the moment when I have become, truthfully, what I am, in cutting off my roots, turn myself into a shadow, into nothingness.

"You tell me," he went on, "that it is not out of love for my people that I am working, and you are right. For in this I am doing the work of my father. I will him to be able to speak some day to the man he wronged, 'Now your death has been paid for, Linnert.' I have been told—a very long time ago, and I do not remember by whom—that for eleven years, the last eleven years of my father's life, the peasants on his land did not speak his name, but in speaking of him used other names, of their own invention. I will them to name him again, some day, as they say, 'The son of this man dealt fairly with us and was just to us.'

"There can be," he said after a while, "there can be no lawful love between me and them while they do still fear and distrust my father in me. And I cannot allow them to touch me while I still know them to be shrinking from his blood within my veins. When I have paid off my father's debt, it will be time for me to stretch out my hands and let them kiss them."

"I do not think, though," said Ulrikke, "that any of the families round here are afraid of your father's name or of his blood. If you had not gone away to foreign countries, while we were both so young, I think that Papa and Mama would have been well pleased to have you and me marry. I was told that they did indeed talk about it, even before you were born."

He sat silent, once more checked in his course of thought by her mysterious light-heartedness. Her words brought him back to Germany and to the time, five years ago, when letters from home had informed him that she was married. Until that hour he had felt sure that he and she belonged to one another, and had been too simple to know or to reckon with the forces which had stepped in and had carried her off. Later on, after his return to Denmark, he had understood. Her mother, a beauty and *bel-esprit* of European fame, at this time had had her eyes opened to the fact that her daughter was nineteen years and sweet and graceful, and in haste— in jealousy, or in a fit of wild motherly tenderness, and in order to save that daughter from her own tempest-tossed career —had married off the maiden to an old man. Now, for a few moments, he called to mind those dark nights in which, from his wet, burning pillow, he had stormed against the gods, and had seen the playmate of his childhood as the central figure in a classic group: the white-robed virgin upon the sacrificial altar of a non-human power.

But she, who had been the dedicated victim of his picture, today sat in the wood, ever white-clad, and talked of their disaster as if it had been the tragedy of a hero and a heroine in a book. For a long time he remained silent, with the ring of her voice in his ear.

"And what was now," she asked, "the story of your father and the peasant? I do not quite remember it. You might tell it to me."

"I have never told it to anyone," he answered.

"Who, then, told it to you yourself?" she asked again.

He searched his mind and was surprised to find that he could not answer her question.

"I do not remember," he said, "that it was ever told to me. I must have heard it when I was a very young child."

"But it has been in your thoughts all your life," said she. "It is time that I should hear it, here in the wood."

It took him some time to fetch up a recollection which was stored so deep down in his being. When at last he spoke, his words came slowly, and more than once in the course of his tale he had to stop to collect his thoughts.

"There was," he began, "on my father's land a peasant named Linnert. He came of a very old peasant family, which had always belonged to us, and it is believed that many hundred years ago the farmstead of his people had stood where our house does today stand, and that the foundations of it were still existing deep down in the ground. Through the ages these peasants had all been handsome, ingenious and deep, and many tales were told about their extraordinary physical strength. For these reasons my own people had been proud of them—such as you said just now that the old lords of the land would be proud of their peasants—yet none of them had ever been in service in our house. This Linnert was born the same year as my father, and since my father had no brothers or sisters, the peasant boy was taken on as a playfellow to him.

"Now," he went on slowly, "in telling you this tale of mine I can give you no explanation why things in it happened the way they did. I have tried to find an explanation. I have been wondering if there might be found, deep down, some reason for the happenings. I have imagined that there might be a woman at the bottom of them. For the maidens of that old peasant stock were cow-eyed and red-lipped, as its young men were hardy and chaste, and my father was a lusty youth, and might well have cast his eye upon a pretty girl on his own estate. But I have found nothing of the kind, nothing at all. I can only, in going through my story, state that things happened in this way—that it was so.

"There was at that time," he took up his account, "south of

the manor house and overlooked by its windows, a stretch of grassland on which the peasants' cattle were wont to graze together with my father's. Later on the peasants ceased to bring their cattle there, and my father had the land included into the park.

"Now one summer the rain failed, the grazing dried up, and the peasants suffered much loss. My father himself had to take home his young stock to feed it in the byre, and upon this occasion his cowmen by mistake took with them a small black bull-calf that belonged to Linnert. Linnert on the next day walked up to the manor and claimed his calf back. My father, when it was reported to him, laughed. Linnert, he declared, was a clever fellow, to charge his master's cowmen with theft, and so increase his stock. He would have to be rewarded for his inventiveness. So my father had a fine big calf brought from his own byre and handed over to Linnert. Here, he made his people tell him, he had his calf back. But the peasant refused to take it, declaring that it was not his, and remained standing by the byre all day waiting for his own calf.

"Next morning my father had a fine young bullock led down to Linnert's lot and once more made his cowmen tell the peasant that here he had his calf back. But it fell out as the first time. Linnert came back with the bullock on a rope. 'This fat young bullock is not mine,' he said. 'There shall be justice on earth. My small calf was not half so big, nor half so handsome. Give me back the small black bull-calf of mine.' And just as the day before, he remained standing in the farmyard till late in the evening, waiting for his calf.

"My father by that time had a very magnificent full-grown bull, which he had bought at a high price in Holstein, but the animal was vicious and had gored a cowman to death. His neighbors had warned him that he would have to part with it, but he had answered them that he did still have people on his land who could manage a bull. Now he bid three men—for a lesser number dared not take on the job—

to lead the bull down to Linnert's byre, and sent a message with them. 'If this,' he had the peasant told, 'is your own animal, which I have unlawfully taken from you, it is hereby returned to you with my apology. But if it is not yours, and if you yourself are such a great man as to know that there shall be justice on earth, surely you will be great enough to bring it back to me on Sunday evening.' For Sunday was my father's birthday, and as was his custom he was giving a dinner party to ladies and gentlemen of the neighborhood. And he thought it not impossible that Linnert might indeed bring home the bull before the eyes of his guests.

"All these things happened in the month of August, and for a week the weather had been exceptionally hot and sultry.

"Already on Saturday morning, while my father was being powdered, the people in the farmyard cried out loudly: 'Here comes Linnert riding on the Holstein bull!' My father ran to the window to see a sight, the like of which he had never seen, for Linnert came through the farmyard gate and up the courtyard, astride the bull as if he had been a hack. The bull was covered with dust and froth, his sides went in and out like a pair of bellows, and blood ran from his nose. But Linnert sat up straight on his back, his head high. He reined up his mount in front of the tall stone stairs, just as my father came out of the front door, his head only half powdered.

" 'You are the bonny horseman,' my father cried, 'and I shall have you rechristened, for a peasant's name no longer befits you, but you will have to be named after him who brought the wild bull of Crete alive to Peloponnesus!' He took a step down the stairs and added: 'But why do you come to-day? I bade you come tomorrow, when I should have had all the fine people of the isle here to see you.' 'I thought,' Linnert answered, 'that when your bull and I had got you to look at us, we needed no more people.' My father went down the last steps. 'Then this is like one of our earliest games,' he said, 'and I shall drink a cup of wine with you, Linnert, and have you take home the silver cup filled with rigsdalers.' 'And one of our last games, I think,' said Linnert. And with that he did indeed turn the bull and make him walk down the courtyard to the byre door. My father had his powdering finished.

"But one hour later the cowherd came up from the byre and reported that the bull had died. As the herd had set him in his stall, the blood had run thicker from his nose, he had sunk on his knees, and a little later he had laid his head on the floor. And then he had died.

" 'And what is Linnert doing,' my father asked, 'for whom I have been waiting here to drink with him?' The cowman answered that Linnert, just like the other day, was waiting in the farmyard.

"My father had Linnert brought before him.

" 'You have ridden a bull to death,' he said. 'It is a deed of which people will be talking for a hundred years to come. If now he is your own bull, it is all your own affair, and the meat and the hide will be yours. But if the bull was mine, you will have to pay me for him. To whom of us, now, did the bull belong?' 'It was not my bull,' Linnert answered, 'and I did not come up here to get a bull, but to have justice.' 'You shame me, Linnert,' said my father, 'for I thought that in you I had not only a strong man, but a shrewd one. But here you tell me that I have given you more than your due, and yet you go on asking me for what I cannot give you, seeing that it is not to be found on earth. Now I ask you again, for the last time: To whom of us did the bull belong?' Linnert answered: 'That big bull was yours, and it is the small black bull-calf that is mine.' 'Have it your own way,' said my father. 'You have then killed my best bull on me, and you will have to pay for it. And since you are so keen on riding, you shall ride once more today.'

"The timber-mare, which had not been used for many years, was still standing in front of the barn. My father had Linnert lifted onto it. It was a hot day, and in the course of the afternoon it grew still hotter. When the shadow of the barn reached the timber-mare, my father had it dragged out into the sun."

Eitel for a moment stopped in his tale. "My father," he repeated, "had it dragged out of the shadow into the sun.

"It was the habit of my father," he again took up the story, "in the afternoon to go for a ride in the fields. As this afternoon he passed the timber-mare and the man upon it, he pulled up his horse. 'Say the word, Linnert,' he said. 'When you call to mind that the bull was yours, my men will take you down.' Linnert answered not a word, and my father lifted his hat to him and rode out of the yard.

"Once more, as my father came back from his ride, he stopped by the timber-mare. 'Have you had enough, Linnert?' he asked. 'Yes, I believe that I have had enough,' the peasant answered. At that my father had him lifted off the timber-mare.

"'Are you then,' he asked him, 'going down on your knees to kiss my hand and thank me for my mercy?' 'Nay, not that,' answered Linnert. 'My small black calf I could touch and smell, but I smell no mercy on your hand.' At that same moment the clock on the stable struck six strokes. 'Then set him up again,' said my father, 'and let him sit until he splits in two.'

"As now the dusk fell," Eitel continued, "my father looked out of the window and saw that the peasant had fallen upon his face on the plank. 'Go, Per,' he said to his valet, 'and have Linnert taken down.' The valet returned. 'They have taken down Linnert,' he said. 'He is dead.'

"It was found that the bull had gored Linnert and broken two of his ribs. There was blood standing under the timber-mare.

"This matter became known and talked about, and it caused my father some trouble. For things were no longer, in his days, what they had been in the days of my grandfather or my great-grandfather, when the masters could do as it pleased them with their servants. A complaint was put before the King himself. But my father had not known that the man had been gored by the bull. And so in the end no more was done about it.

"That is how it happened," said Eitel. "I have told you the story you wished to hear."

Both the young people were silent for a while. "But that story," said Ulrikke, "happened many years before you were born."

"Yes," said Eitel. "It happened ten years before I was born."

"How is it then," she asked, "that you come to think of it today?"

"I can tell you that too," said he. "I have come to think of it today because this morning I was told that the grandson of the peasant Linnert had been sentenced to death for the double murder of a keeper and his boy, and is to have his head cut off in Maribo tomorrow, at noon."

She shuddered slightly at the gruesome news. "Alas, poor creature," said she. "But what," she asked after a moment, "has that got to do with your father and the peasant?"

"I shall go on with my story," said Eitel, "and tell you what it has got to do with my father and the peasant.

"As you know," he said, "my mother was gentle and kind to everyone. She had, I believe, been grieving over this matter, although it happened ten years before she was married to my father. It came to pass about the time when I was born that Linnert's daughter was left a widow with a babe at her breast, for the peasants, as you know, marry young, and Linnert by the time of his death had been married for ten years. My mother then may have bethought herself of the old story. For she sent for the peasant woman who like herself, was nineteen years old, and took her on as a nurse to her own child. I have been told that my mother's lady friends did warn her, fearing that Lone might have kept her own father's death in mind, and now might be hard to my father's child. But my mother answered them that she thought too well of human nature to fear any such thing. If that was finely spoken, it was a fine thing as well that her trust was never betrayed. I told you, just now, that in my life I had loved one human being besides you. It was of this woman, of Lone that I was thinking."

"Is she still alive?" Ulrikke asked. "And is it for her sake —poor woman—that you grieve today?"

"Yes," he answered, "as far as I know she is still alive. She stayed with us until I was seven years old, and they took on a tutor for me. Then she married our parish clerk, and later on she went with him to Funen. Yes, it is for her sake too that I grieve today.

"For in telling you of Lone," he went on, "I am, as I said just now, only going on with my story. Lone was well treated in our house, she had fine clothes and a pretty room next to the housekeeper, and among all the servants she was my mother's favorite. And Lone repaid my mother's kindness according to her means. Those two young widows, the mistress and the servant-woman, were, I believe, truly devoted to each other. When my mother died, Lone, they say, did not speak a word for a week, so deep was her sorrow. My mother's friends by that time had had to take back their words of misgiving about the peasant woman: when I grew up so strong, they now said, it was Lone's milk that I had got to thank for it, it was Linnert's strength that she was passing on to the child she nursed, and I, too, might come to ride home a bull some day! I have not thought of Lone for a long time; today I have thought of her. She was always with me, since my mother was too delicate to have me about her, and I have seen her in my mind like a big hen covering me with her warm wings, sitting by my bedside when I was ill and concocting strange sweet and bitter medicines for me, and I have remembered the songs that she sang and the fairy tales that she told me. For in her family they all had a gift for poetry, and the young men made up ballads, as the old women preserved the myths and legends of the isle."

"We ought to be grateful to Lone then, you and I," Ulrikke said gently.

"Yes, we may well be so," said Eitel, "you and I. But there is one more character in the story, and he has no reason to be grateful to anyone. Those happy years of mine were not happy to Lone's own son."

"Her own son?" she asked.

"Yes," said he, "the one who is to end his life tomorrow at Maribo. I have known little about him. Lone can never have spoken his name to me; he was named after her own father: Linnert. Today I have asked people about him, and have found out more. Lone, I was told, sent him away, a long way off. She was loyal to her duties, and may have feared that the nearness of her own child might make her less zealous in fulfilling them. While he was still a child, he became shepherd boy on a farm of which they tell me that the farmhands were starved and eaten up by vermin. When he grew up he was apprenticed to a keeper at another place, and that was the ruin of him, for there he learned to handle a gun, and so took to poaching. I was told that he was ever a wild boy, given to drink and brawls. And now in the end he has become a manslayer and has forfeited his life.

"It is because of this boy that I have today dug the old peasants out of their graves and brought them with us into the wood. Or they may themselves have risen from the grave and have come with us, because this my milk-brother is so soon to join them there.

"You once believed, you tell me," he said with a faint smile, "that the Lord God, were He to create a juster world, might deign to choose me to assist Him. But it looks to me now as if the Lord God, through all this, has meant to impress on me that an injustice once done can never again be rightened. My mother wished to righten an injustice when she took Linnert's daughter into her house and made the peasant woman her friend, but all the good she did thereby was to take away the very mother's milk from that woman's own child. I myself have dreamt that with my own life and my own blood—a nobler blood, in spite of all—I might wash away the blood that ran under the timber-mare. But it has all come to this: that more of that same blood will be running at Maribo tomorrow. All my life I have felt my father to be a prisoner in the chains of guilt and hate, and I have believed that the moment would come when I would hear him say to me: 'It was well that you set me loose.' But when, now, will these words be spoken?"

"Oh, Eitel," said Ulrikke, "we cannot tell. There may be another justice than ours, which in the end will set all things right."

"Think you so?" he said, and after a moment: "Listen now. This morning a rumor spread that the prisoner had escaped from prison. I thought then that he might look me up, to lay his curse on me and on my father's memory. If he had come—if he comes tonight—can I comfort him with the words with which you try to comfort me: 'There may be another justice than ours, which in the end will set all things right?' "

Once more there was a long silence. In the midst of it, suddenly, the quick persistent little tap of a woodpecker was heard in a tree close by.

"I know the one of whom you are speaking," said Ulrikke.

He tore himself from his train of thought. "You know him?" he asked in surprise.

"Aye," she said. "Once upon a time we were friends. I was a girl of thirteen, and it was to our keeper at home that he was apprenticed. I now understand that it must have been the same boy, for his name was Linnert. I was alone at home that summer; Mama was in Weimar. He and I were often together in the wood. We searched for birds' nests, and he taught me to imitate the cuckoo so that I could call it to me, and to troat to a buck. Nobody knew of it. I remember that I once tucked up my skirts and walked with him hand in hand down the brook, all the way from where it runs into the wood to where it comes out of it. He was strong and light of movement, and he had got the thickest, softest hair. Once," she went on, her voice clear and happy at the memory, "he fell down from a tall tree and scratched his face, because he would not let go a wood-pigeon's nest and eggs that I had wanted to get. We walked down to the brook, so that he could wash off the blood, and there, all of a sudden, he dropped down as if he were dead. I sat with his head in my lap, there in the wood."

She sat sunk in her own thoughts, gazing into the distance. "I gave him a kiss," she said, "when he woke up. His skin was as smooth as my own. I said to him: 'You must never cut off your hair, and you must never grow a beard.' "

It was as if in her words she had held a flower to her face. A queer little pang of jealousy was in the sweet smell of it. He looked at her, took in her person and poise. A hundred kisses he had had from those red lips. Well, twelve years ago the lost, bleeding boy had had one too. Tomorrow the head which had lain in her lap was to be cut off by the hangman, he would lift it up to the crowd to see by that pretty hair which was never to be cut off.

"When I imagined," he said, "that the hour was to come when I might say: 'Now your death has been paid for, Linnert,' I was thinking of the man whom my father killed. I have known nothing till today of young Linnert. I tell myself, now, that that hour will never come, but that, instead, this boy will be passing sentence on me."

She turned toward him, gave him in one single movement her whole face, the dark smiling eyes and the trembling lips.

"On you!" she cried. "When I love you!"

She sank from the fence into his embrace, like a flower turned by the wind. They lay breast to breast, and the moment closed over their heads like a wave of the sea, washing away past and future. She lightly put two fingers under his chin and lifted up his face.

"Oh, you upholder of the past!" she said. "Soon, soon all these things round us will be things of the past. Soon, soon I shall be poor old great-grandmother Ulrikke, who is now in the churchyard, but who did once meet her lover in the wood. Did her lover love her there?"

"Did he love her there?" he whispered down into her hair. "Paradise, to him, was in her arms!"

"Alas," she whispered back against his collarbone. There was a laughter and a sigh in the whisper. In such a way smiled and sighed the famous beauties of that great world which was hers by birthright, but which she had never known, because she was a flower grown up in the shade. In her lover's arms, in jest, she mimicked those heroines whom her mother worshipped and imitated.

"Why does my heart sigh?" he asked.

"Alas," she whispered once more. "Paradise! People like you will never go to Paradise. You will only be happy in Hell."

Now it was he who tenderly forced her face up. "What do you mean, sweet?" he asked.

She looked him in the eyes solemnly and archly. "Oh, yes," she whispered as before, "there you would be at peace to forget all about your justice. For there nothing can become any worse than it is. And there nobody will be any worse off than you yourself."

Once more she laid her face on his shoulder. He would have spoken, but her nearness, the light weight of her body against his own, overthrew his reasoning. The silent forest depths all around him, and her own deep silence so close to his heart, became one to him, and unresistingly he let himself sink into them.

A while after she said: "I must go," and did up her hair. She had insisted on giving suck herself to her youngest child, her lover's daughter, and now the child was drawing her back to it by invisible bonds.

As she put in her comb she said: "You know that Mama is staying with us?"

He said: "I shall walk with you as far as the forest gate."

They walked together, happily, without words. By the forest gate she turned round to him. "Remember," she said, commandingly and imploringly, her eyes at the moment of parting filled with tears, "that you are to live."

He, who remained leaning on the gate in the deep green shade, let his gaze follow the white figure as it walked on lightly and grew smaller. "Is she thinking of me at all?" he wondered.

The great park of the house joined the wood; the tall forest trees gradually withdrew to give place to lawns, shrubs, gravel paths and flower beds. The mistress of the garden followed the path leading to the house.

Afternoon sun and shade shared the garden between them. Crimson and purple asters glowed in the beds. Two gardener's boys were raking the paths; the old head gardener himself from a distance caught sight of his lady, took off his cap and approached to show her a big scarlet and yellow dahlia, which he himself had forced and now wanted to name after her. She praised the flower and fastened it in her fichu. By the big garden stair her small son freed himself from the hand of his nurse and ran to meet her. As she lifted him up he grasped at the bright flower at her breast. She teased the child with the flower, brushing his face with it and holding it up out of his reach. When he sulked she pressed him to her, patted his cheek and pulled his hair. But she did not kiss him; her lips still belonged to the wood. She handed him over to his nurse and hastened on, impatient in her errand.

As an hour later she entered her mother's rooms she found the curtains drawn, tables and chairs covered with a multitude of scattered garments, and her mother herself in violent agitation pacing the floor like a lioness in her cage. For a moment the older woman stared, as if horrified, at the younger. Immediately after she hurried toward her, broke down altogether and wailed lowly. Ulrikke looked round the room for the cause of her mother's despair. The lovely Sibylla had put on a long, floating riding habit of black velvet with a short coat of green cloth to it, and had not been able to button the coat.

"Oh, Rikke," the mother cried out, "I have grown old."

In a sudden fierce movement she turned to her own image in the long, dim looking glass within the darkened room. The curls of the image were tousled and its face was swollen with weeping. Accusingly the woman of flesh and blood cried out to it in a low hoarse voice, "I was lovely once!"

Ulrikke in general would find words of comfort when her mother bewailed the loss of her great beauty. Today she said nothing, but only clasped the doleful figure in her arms, holding her so close that she could not again gaze into the glass.

"If I had grown thin!" Sibylla moaned on her daughter's breast. "If I had become a skeleton, a skull, a memento mori to the trivial crowd, who refuse to think of time or eternity! Then I should still be an inspring figure to them! And upon my entrance into a ballroom I should still strike sparks from them all: epigrams, poems, heroic deeds—and oh, passion as well. I should at least inspire them with horror, Rikke, and I should expect to inspire horror. But I am fat!"

The fatal word, actually pronounced, struck her dumb for a few moments.

"It is not death," she again took up her theme, this time speaking slowly and solemnly, "it is not death which I do personify to them. It is dissolution and decomposition. There is an odious abundance of this body, which was once so perfect in its proportions. There is too much of these arms, these hips, these thighs—of this bosom! Rikke, my bosom makes people laugh!

"If a human being had done this to me," she cried out suddenly, "I should have had my revenge; I should have had the men who adored me stand up to avenge such cruelty. For picture to yourself what it means: to take a young woman—happy, innocent, trustful—and slowly, slowly to draw out her teeth and her hair, dim her eyes, distort her body, crack her skin and her voice, and then to exhibit her to the world as if all naked—'*Voilà la belle Hélène!*' It is not right! It is not just! My God, there is no justice on earth!"

The aging *lionne* had drawn the curtains of her window, because powder and rouge no longer sufficed to hide the decay of her loveliness. She, who had loved sunlight and candlelight and the light of surprise and adoration in all human eyes that met her own, now like a hunted animal fled from all light, took cover in a dark room, and within the darkness raved about a future among the blind.

In her daughter's arms she still held herself back, a hard-tightened knot. She felt the warmth and strength of the young body so close to her own, shut her eyes and groped for a way out of her misery. Her friends, other ladies of her own age, did find comfort, she knew, in the youth and happiness of their daughters. Could she possibly do the same thing? The answer came immediately: No. She divined that Ulrikke had a lover, and before today she had wondered whether the harmony of a youthful idyll might have power to turn her mind from the disharmony of her own stormy, insecure affairs of the heart. The answer, now as before, came immediately: No. In growing distress she asked herself whether this incapacity might be her punishment because five years ago she had deliberately sold the girl's happiness for a short postponement of her own death sentence.

"And would I then," she asked in her heart, "have foregone my respite of five years?" Once more the answer came unappealably: No. "If today," she said to herself, "things were what they then were, I should do as I then did. I could do nothing else. So help me God, I could not!" The old nursery tale of the vampire which gets a new lease of life by drinking the blood of young creatures ran in her mind. Bewildered by the idea she lifted her daughter's hand and set her teeth in one of the slim fingers, then, horror-struck, dropped the hand. She opened big glassy eyes, eyes which had once been sung by great poets, and stared at Ulrikke.

"Oh, you know not," she whispered, "what it is to have been loved with passion, with the proudest that a man has got in him! And then in the end to be loved out of pity. You too," she added, her stiff gaze still on her daughter's face, "you too do love me out of pity!"

Ulrikke went on gently caressing her. Across her mind, like shadows of clouds across a sheet of water, ran the shadows of that woe and fear that seemed to darken the lives of all human beings. In her mother's wild lament at her breast she heard an echo of her small daughter's furious weeping an hour ago, of her lover's melancholy monologue in the wood, and at last of the bitter loneliness, far away, of her doomed playmate. All, all of them seemed to grieve and fear. Was there so much to grieve at and to fear in the world? Was death ever sad and fearful? For the first time in her life she realized that she, too, was to die. But while to the others death seemed to look like a dark bottomless sea, to her herself, she imagined, it would be a shallow water into which she might wade, her skirts tucked up, with a serene face.

"What a goose I am," she thought, "to give myself up to such silly fancies!"

"Oh, what a goose you are, my little Mama," she said, loosening her arms from her mother's form. "You are just as lovely now, when you look like the goddess Juno, as ever you were when you were as slim as a reed! Come, your stays are too tightly laced, let me undo them for you and set you loose!"

As if all the lines of the elder woman's face had been held together by that same silk cord which her daughter was now undoing, they were suddenly smoothed out, and a little childlike smile ran over the face. At the cessation of physical torture her mental misery, too, lessened, and hope rushed to her heart. She might still be loved!

Once more she lifted Ulrikke's hand to touch it with her lips.

"Oh, dear Mama," said Ulrikke, "if today you and I went down to bathe in our old place, where the river bends—as when I was a little girl—the five weeping willows there would, just as then, bend down to kiss your white shoulders. Look," she added, taking her flower from her fichu and fastening it upon the lapel of that same green riding coat which had caused such bitter tears, "this flower old Daniel gave me. It is a new dahlia which he himself has forced. Nobody on the whole isle has got the like of it. He begs you to let him name it after you, 'Sibylla,' because it is so sweet and so big. Gaze at yourself now, gaze at Sibylla! It is truer than that silly glass."

Eitel rode home from the wood across the stubble fields. When he came onto his own land he set his horse into a canter and made it jump some low stacks of rakings.

His mind was still resting in the happiness of the forest meeting, tranquilly, like a trout between two stones in a brook, keeping its stand by the slightest movements of its fins. His eyes strayed over the landscape. By this time flights of wild ducks began to draw their thin lines low down on the sky; big, light rosy clouds were towering up above the horizon; far away to the west the sea met the sky in a stripe of grave blue. His ears caught many distant sounds round him: a cart rolling along the road, people shouting as they were driving home their cattle. But he kept his own being collected, he would think of nothing but her.

He called to mind how, three years ago when he and she

had met again, they had dreamt of the time when she would once more be free again, and to the eyes of all the world the two should belong to one another. Now he no longer knew whether, were that time to come, he should be any happier than he was now. There was infinite sweetness in their secret intimacy. To love her, he thought, to him was like washing his face and hands, or like diving down, in a clear, evenly running stream, which was ever renewing itself, and it was fitting that his path to the stream and his bathing place itself should be hidden to all the world.

When above the trees he caught sight of the tall roof and proud gables of his house, he slowed down his steaming mount. He did not ride up the broad stately lime avenue to the courtyard, but took the narrower poplar avenue which led to the farmyard. Here ears, straw and thistledown from the harvesting lay in the deep wheel tracks and stuck high up in the branches of the poplars.

Within the house, in the long library, the light of the sunset fell through the windows as the light of the afternoon had been falling through the tree crowns onto the spot where they had been sitting together. The old oak floors shone in it like dark forest pools; the gilt frames of the portraits, the tints of silk and velvet became alive and luminous like tree stems, foliage and mosses. This last deep glow of the day was her trembling smile at their parting, her compassion and the promise of a next meeting.

He was shortly expecting the visit of a learned old man from Copenhagen, a prophet of the new reforms, and was looking forward to their talk together. When he had had supper he told his young German valet, whom he had brought with him from Hanover, that he was not to be disturbed, and fetched down a number of heavy books to look up such matters as he would discuss with his guest. He could still, in the window recess, read by the last daylight, and he sat down with a book on his knee and other books on the window sill.

While he was reading his valet came into the room to place a three-armed candlestick on the table, remained standing by it and announced: "There is a person outside who asks to have speech with gnädiger Herr."

His master did not look up from his book. "It is late," he said after a moment.

"That is what I said myself," said the valet. "But this person has come afoot, in great haste, and will not be turned off."

Eitel closed his book and again was silent. "Let him come in then," he said at last.

"It is a woman, gnädiger Herr," Johann said, "She tells me her name is Lone Bartels. The housekeeper seems to know her, and assures me that she has once been in service in the house."

"A woman," said Eitel. "Lone Bartels. Bring her in."

Presently he heard his old housekeeper talking lowly to somebody outside the door. It was opened, and his guest entered.

She dropped a curtsy by the door and stood still there. She was not dressed like a peasant woman, but had on a white cap and a black silk apron, beneath which she kept her hands. She was a heavy woman with a pale, as if mealy, skin— a parish clerk's wife, who had not needed to do hard work. She looked straight at him.

He had felt an immediate deep relief and happiness on learning the name of his visitor of this late hour. But as now his and Lone's eyes met, against all reason he was seized with a kind of cold, deadly fear, which made his hair stand on end. It was not, here, a distressed mother come to plead for the life of her son. It was the old dark ages, eternity, destiny itself entering his room.

He was terrified at his own terror. Only after a long silence did he take a step toward the woman before him. And when the candlelight was no longer between him and her, he recognized the face once so well known, and beloved by the child above all other human faces. Almost without knowing what he did he folded her in his arms, he felt her big soft body filling them, and smelled her clothes. It was as if he had lain at her breast yesterday.

"So you have come to me, Lone," he said, surprised at the sound of his own voice, which rang almost like the voice of a child.

"Yes," said the woman. "Now I have come."

She spoke as in old days, lowly and slowly. During her years in a nobleman's house she had laid off her peasant's dialect, she spoke like an educated woman. They looked each other in the face.

"It is good that you have come," said he.

"I wished to see my dear master," said she.

"Nay, Lone," said he, "do not call me master. Say 'Eitel' as you did in the old days."

A faint, slow blush mounted into her pale face. Otherwise it remained immovable, the lips pressed together, the eyes very clear.

"How is it with you, Lone?" he asked.

"Now it is well with me," she said and drew her breath deeply. "Now that I see you again."

The familiar ring of devotion in her voice went to his heart. And at the same moment his sudden deep terror at her arrival was explained to him. It was she, he now knew, who long, long ago had told him the story of his father and Linnert.

Had she now come to give him the means of making up for it? For a while he kept as still as she. He would allow himself a few minutes in which to speak to her as he had done when he was a child, before he let her name her tragic errand to him.

"You ought to have come earlier," he said. "Why have you not come to see me, Lone, these many years?"

"Nay," she answered, "there was no need for that. I knew

that things were going well with you." Her bright eyes did not leave his face. "I have been waiting," she said after a short pause, "to hear that you had married."

"Would that have pleased you, Lone?" he asked.

"Yes, that would have pleased me," she answered.

His thoughts strayed far away, then came back to her.

"But I have had news of you," she said, "every year."

"You have had that?" he asked.

"Why, yes," she answered. "I heard that you had gone far away to foreign countries. Once the weaver from here came to a wedding in Funen, and he told me that you had become a very learned man. And two years ago you came to Funen yourself, and bought a pair of horses at Hvidkilde."

"Yes," he said, searching his mind, "I bought the two bay wheelers there."

He led her to a small settee by the wall, beneath the portrait of his father and mother, and sat down with her, her hand in his.

"Aye, you were always the one for horses," said the woman. "When you were a small boy you had a hobbyhorse with you wherever you went."

"I had that, Lone," he said.

"In those days we rode many miles together, you and I," she said and smiled a little without parting the wrinkled lips, "right up to the King's castle. I sewed all your horses for you, out of leather and wool and bits of silk ribbons."

"You did that," Eitel said again, his thoughts with those mounts of long ago; if now he searched his memory he would find their names there. "Nobody could do it as well as you."

For a while the two sat silent, hand in hand. He thought. "But it is of her son that she means to speak to me."

"You had to have them in bed with you," said Lone, "so that they, too, might listen when I was telling you a story."

"You knew many stories, Lone," he said.

"Do you still remember them?" she asked.

"I think I do," said he.

"It was only this morning," he said after a while, "that I heard of your son, Lone."

She stirred a little in her seat, but did not speak at once. "Yes, now he is to die," she said at last.

This calm, collected resignation moved him, as if he and the humble mother were mourning together over her child.

"He has been in my thoughts all day," he said. "I have considered begging the King's mercy for him in Copenhagen. I would fain have gone to Copenhagen to do so, Lone."

"You would fain have done so?" she said.

"But he is a manslayer, my poor Lone," he said. "He has killed a man. I fear that it would be no good begging the King's mercy for him."

"Yes, he has killed two men," said Lone.

"Then it may be the best thing for him," Eitel said, "to atone for his guilt. Then nobody can bear him any grudge."

"No," she said, "then nobody can bear him any grudge."

"But I can get you leave to see him in prison tomorrow morning," said he.

"That is not needed," said she.

"So you have already seen him there?" he asked.

"No," Lone answered, "I have not seen him there."

"They have not dealt fairly with you, then," said Eitel. "They should have let you see each other, and speak to each other. But I shall go with you to Maribo and see to it that it be done. We will go together tomorrow, you and I."

"We went to Maribo, too," said the woman, "the time we took our rides together."

Eitel did not know how to go on. "Have I forgotten," he asked himself, "the way the simple, deep mind of an old peasant woman works? Or does she feel that she had to speak to me of old days in order to make me help her?"

"In return for that, Lone," he said gently, "should I not now drive you to Maribo, so that you may see your son?"

Once more she waited a while before answering. "I have not seen him for twenty years," she said.

"For twenty years?" he asked in surprise.

"Yes," she said, "It is twenty years since I saw him last."

"Why have you not seen him for twenty years?" he asked after a pause.

"There was no reason why I should see him," she said. Her voice was so low that he was not sure she had spoken.

"How did it come to pass," he said, "that your son did fare so ill?"

"It had to be so, I think," she said.

"But you might have fetched him back when you married and got a house of your own," he said. "Was it your husband who would not let you do so?"

"No, the clerk would have let me do as I liked," said Lone.

"Did you never help him," Eitel asked, his voice low like her own, "when he got into trouble?"

"No," the woman answered.

A dull alarm and pain made him rise from his chair. His own words to Ulrikke came back to him with a keener edge, now that he sat beside the heavy, close mother. It was true, then, that with her milk he had sucked the very mother's love from the peasant woman's breasts.

"You ought to have done so, Lone," he said slowly. "He has been lonely and friendless. I myself ought to have remembered him before today. You were as good to me as if I had been your own child. I should have stood by your son."

"There was no reason why you should do so," said Lone.

He went to the window, but felt her eyes following him and came back to her. He thought: "When I heard that she had come, I believed that she had come to judge me. But it is harder still that she should have come to acquit me."

"Yet he is still your son, Lone," he said, "be his trespasses ever too grave."

"No," said Lone.

A sort of sorrowful resentment blended with his compassion for the woman. He thought: "She cannot lay all this on me." It seemed to him that he must at all costs reawaken in the heart of the mother some kind of love for her doomed son.

"You are a woman, Lone," he said. "You will remember the time that you bore him. He is the child that quickened in your body, even now when he has forfeited his life."

"No, it is not so," she said. "It is you who are my child."

He was so deeply absorbed in his own thoughts that at first he did not hear what she said. It was only when once more he found her eyes upon him that he caught her words.

"Me?" he said, and after a few seconds, "Of what are you speaking, Lone?"

"Aye, now I shall speak the truth," said Lone.

"The truth?" said he.

"Yes," she said. "Linnert is the master's boy. I took away the child and put my own in his stead, when I was giving suck up here."

The door opened, and Eitel's valet came in with the evening wine, as he was wont to do when his master sat up to read. He placed the silver tray on the table, looked at his master and the woman and went out.

When the door had closed behind him, Lone rose, and remained standing up before Eitel.

"I can bear witness to God and man," she said, "that what I have now told you is the truth."

"You do not know what you are saying," he said.

"Yes, I know what I am saying," said she. "Well may I remember the time that I bore you, and the time when you quickened within my body. For you are my child."

He thought: "Anguish and distress have upset her reason," and waited a little to find the right words to speak to her.

"It is an ancient nursery tale that you are telling me here, Lone," he said. "The tale of the changelings, so old that one smiles at it. You mean to help your son by telling it me. But you are mistaken. I shall do what I can for him without it."

"It is not to help him that I tell it you," she said. "It is all one to me whether they cut off his head or not."

"Why do you tell it me then?" he asked.

"I did not know for certain, till the day before yesterday," she answered slowly, "that he was to die. When I knew, I thought: 'Now this has been brought to an end.' And then I came to see you once more."

"Why did you wish to see me once more?" he asked.

"I wished to see how great and happy you were," she answered.

"There is no one in the whole world," she went on, "who has known of this except myself. And now you know too. The clerk has never known of it. I shall not tell it to our parson on my deathbed. But now I have come to tell you how it all happened."

"Nay, you shall tell me nothing," he said. "All this is but what you have dreamt, my poor Lone."

She stood up straight before him.

"I have got no one in the whole world," she said, "to tell it to except you, I have been waiting to do so for twenty-three years. If my tale is not told now, it will never be told."

She brought out her hands from beneath her apron and slowly smoothed it down, and this had been a familiar gesture of hers in his childhood, when he had been obstinate, and she was talking sense to him. "But if it be your wish," she went on, "that I shall go away without saying more, I can do so too."

He was silent for a while. "No," he said. "You may speak, to lighten your heart. I shall hear you." He seated himself in the armchair by the table, but the woman remained standing up.

"Aye, now I shall begin," she said very slowly, "and I shall forget nothing.

"It was on the very first evening that I came up here that I changed the master's child for my own. The child up here had been born three days after mine. He was small, and he cried much. I sat by his cradle and sang to him until I had made him sleep. Then I got up and made up a doll out of a pillow and of silk ribbons in the room, just as later I made up horses for you, and laid it in the cradle, and I drew together the cradle curtains. I told the maid of her sweet ladyship that I was now going home to my own house to fetch my Sunday shawl and two new aprons of mine, but that she was to leave the child alone the while, for now it had been fed and was quiet. But I took the child with me under my cloak and kept it warm, and I could do so because it was so small. On the stairs of the western wing I met the housekeeper, and she stopped to talk to me, and asked me if I had got plenty of milk. 'Aye,' I answered her, 'the child that I lay to my breast will thrive, and will not cry.' But I was telling myself as we stood there, that if the child now cried, it would be all over with me. But it did not cry, not that time.

"I laid the child in my own old cradle within my own house, but you I took out of it, and I hid you in a basket that I was taking with me and covered you up with my Sunday shawl and two aprons of mine."

"Nay," Eitel interrupted her. "Speak not like that. Speak not, in this tale of yours, the word *you*."

Lone stood still and looked at him. "Do you mean me," she asked, "not to speak of you, or of what I did for you?"

"If you will tell me your story," Eitel said, "tell it like any other nursery tale."

Lone thought the matter over and again began.

"I laid, then," she said, "my own child, my son, in the basket, and I walked up to the house, and I had to stop from time to time, for my own child was heavier than the other. There was a full moon, so that the road was clear and light all the way. The next morning I told the maids in the house that the child was not well, and that nobody must come into our room, and in this way I was alone with him for a week. Her sweet ladyship had me called before her bed every day, so that I might tell her how things were with the child, and I told her that it was well with the child. She asked me if I wished to go home to see my own child, but I answered her that I had already sent it away from my house, to the house of people of mine.

"The week after," she went on, "the christening was to be held. On that day a lot of great people came to the house, and the old Countess of Krenkerup bore the child to the font. I drove to the church in the same coach as her, with four horses. I held the child on my lap, and only in the porch did I give it over to her. And as now I heard my son christened Eitel after the master's father, and Johan August after the master himself, in the name of the Father and of the Son and of the Holy Ghost, I said to myself: 'Now that is done which cannot be undone.'"

At these last words the woman colored faintly as in pride or triumph.

"And why should you have wished it done," Eitel asked.

Lone laid her right hand upon the table. "For this reason," she said. "When her ladyship first sent for me, to give suck to the child, and I walked up through the farmyard, I passed the timber-mare."

"The timber-mare?" said Eitel.

"Yes," said Lone. "It was still standing there, in front of the barn. Her sweet ladyship had wanted it taken away, but the master had said no. I had never till that day been up to the house, but as I walked past it, by the side of her ladyship's lackey who had been sent to fetch me, I remembered how, when I myself was ten years old, they had brought back my father from it. And on the evening of the day when my child had been christened in church, when all the fine guests were gone and the house was dark, I once more walked down to it. I laid my right hand upon that hard wood, as now I have laid it on your table, and spoke to my dead father and said to him: 'Now your death has been paid for, Linnert.'

"And do you believe me now?" she asked.

"No, I do not believe you," he answered. "I could not believe you if I wanted to."

Lone drew her breath deeply, looked round the room and again looked at him.

"This is the one thing that I had never thought of," she said slowly and dully, "that when I told you my tale you were not to believe it. I had thought that you yourself would remember how I carried you from our own house to the house of the master."

She stood sunk in her own thoughts. "That house of the clerk's in Funen," she went on, "I was never really in it. It seemed to me that all the time I was over here, with you. But it was not in this great house of the master's that we lived together. It was in that old farmhouse of ours, the old people's house, which is standing deep down below. Down there I held you in my arms, and we spoke together sweetly. Is that what you tell me now, that you have never been down there?"

"You know yourself," he answered her, "that I have never been down there."

Once more she was silent. "There was one more, though," she said, "who at the time guessed something of this, and who might bear out my tale. That was the woman who took over the master's child and kept him with her. It was Maren in the marshes."

"Maren in the marshes?" Eitel repeated. "I have heard of her. I have seen her once. She was a gypsy, all black to look at, and it was said that she had killed her husband."

"Yes," said Lone, "she was a bad woman. But she could hold her tongue."

"Where is she now?" he asked.

"She is dead," Lone answered.

Eitel rose from his chair. "And if all other things within your tale had been possible," he said, "would it be possible, Lone, that a good woman like you could have behaved so to a friend who trusted you, to my mother?"

Lone took a step toward him, and although she still looked straight at him, she seemed somehow to be groping her way. "Do you call her gracious ladyship your mother even now?" she asked. As she came nearer, he drew back a little, and she followed him slowly in the same half-blind way. "Do you flee me now?" she asked.

He stood still, realizing that he had indeed meant to flee from the woman before him.

"Lone," he said, "once you were dearer to me than any other human being. At this hour it seems to me that you may still be so, aye, as dear as if you were indeed my own mother. Or that I should hold you in horror, like one of the witches in whom old people believe, gloating over a crime against nature, as one mad with wickedness, wishing to drive me mad with her."

So he and the woman remained standing face to face.

"And shall there be no justice on earth?" she at last asked.

"Yes, there shall be justice on earth," he answered.

"But justice," Lone went on in a low wailing voice, "justice, with you and me, cannot mean that when I did carry you up to the house, in danger of my life, so as to give it all to you, it was the house and the people up here who took you over and made me one of theirs! Justice," she wailed on lowly, her body doubling up as in great pain, "cannot mean that I am never once to call you my son, and never once to hear you call me mother!"

Eitel stood gazing into the woman's pain-quivering face.

"I have been off my mind," he thought. "I have spoken hard to an old sorrowful peasant woman, who has taken refuge in my house. I have said that I must loathe and fear an old parish clerk's wife from Funen." He went up to Lone and took her hand.

"Yes, my poor Lone," he said, "you are to call me your son, and to hear me call you my mother. We did so many times, years ago. And nothing has changed between you and me since then."

Lone very slowly with her right hand fumbled along his arm from wrist to shoulder and back again, then let the hand sink. "I have come a long way to see you tonight," she said.

"And I have not looked after you, Lone," he said. "You should have had something to eat and drink. Now I shall have it brought for you. You shall sleep tonight in your own room. And tomorrow," he added after a pause, "as I said before, I shall drive with you to Maribo. You shall come back with me from there, to stay in my house as long as you choose."

He stood with her hand in his. Wonderingly he felt, deep down in his mind, a reluctance to put an end to a talk which had been filled with such ugly confusion, and heard, there, a voice cry out sadly: "Never more, never more." He put off the parting for a moment.

"At this time of night, Lone," he said, "it happened that I would wake up from a bad dream. Then you would sing to me till I fell asleep again. I remember now, too, that one of the horses which you made for me was sewn of crimson silk, with a name of gold fringe from one of my father's court coats, and that his name was Guldfaxe."

"Yes, that was his name," said Lone.

Her eyes still met his, but they were now without expression, the eyes of a blind woman.

After a long silence she whispered: "May you sleep well."

"And you, Lone, little mother," he said.

He listened to her steps down the long corridor.

When the sound had died away, he took the heavy candlestick from the table, walked up to his father's portrait on the wall, and lifted the candlestick up high, so that the smiling face was fully illuminated. "Hullo, my father," he said, "did you hear that? You were a handsome, gallant, gay gentleman. What now, if the nursery tale that the clerk's old wife has told us had been true? You would then have seen the grandson of the servant whom you wronged and killed giving up his life and his thoughts and his happiness even, in your service, to clear your name and wipe out your guilt. Would that seem to you the crowning joke of the whole affair—a fine extravaganza? Would it be at that that you are now laughing?"

He was still standing so, the candlestick in his raised hand, when the door behind him opened once more, and his old housekeeper came in noiselessly.

Mamzell Paaske had been in his father's house before he had married, and it was a privilege of hers to enter the son's room unannounced, when she had matters of importance to communicate or discuss.

In her young days she had been a beauty and had had offers of marriage from all parts of the isle, but she had refused to give up her spinsterhood. Now in her old age she had become extremely pious. There was still a pathetic loveliness in the very small, delicate figure, and she was light and graceful like a lady of high birth. At the moment she was deeply moved, and was wiping her eyes with a small folded handkerchief.

"Another old woman," Eitel thought as he set down the candlestick. "This one may be twice the age of the first. Can it be that she will bring me twice as strange a message?"

He told her to take a seat, and she sat down on the edge of a chair, her old head nodding and shaking a little all the time.

"Dear me, how sad, how very sad," she began.

"What is it that you want of me?" he asked.

"Oh, me, it is of Lone that I am thinking," said Mamzell Paaske. "So Lone came back to the house once more, after all. The way up here has been heavy for her to walk this time. She was so proud here in the old days, in the fine clothes that her ladyship gave her. Dear master, will you, now, be able to obtain mercy for that poor unhappy son of hers?"

"Mercy," Eitel repeated, in his own thoughts. "No, Mamzell Paaske, I fear that it cannot be done."

"Nay, I understand, I see," said the old housekeeper. "Justice must have its way. And he was caught in the act, I am told, and has been sentenced to death by the learned, venerable judges themselves.

"In other ways Lone is well preserved, I am bound to say," she continued. "She has had easy days with the parish clerk. I remember him well, he was a peaceful man, if a little stingy. You will know, dear Master, that he is somehow related to the Paaskes. It is hard on him that his stepson should fare so ill."

"What is it you want of me?" he again asked.

"Take it not in bad part, dear Master," she said. "I wished to hear a little more about this great misfortune and about poor Lone."

"You might have spoken to her yourself," he said.

She wiped her small mouth with her handkerchief.

"I dared not do that," she said. "You will know yourself that at times Lone is not right in her head."

"I never heard of that," he said.

"But it is so all the same," said Mamzell Paaske and again nodded her head. "We were well aware, all of us up here in the house, that she was not like other people. All her folks were queer. In the village they will tell you that in old days there were witches among them. Lone was a good, faithful servant all her time, to her ladyship and to you yourself, Master. But by a full moon she was not herself."

"By a full moon?" Eitel repeated.

"Yes, by a full moon, like tonight," said she. "She would say many strange things then, and make people believe them.

"I knew Linnert too," she added after a moment.

"Did you know him?" he asked. "How did he look?"

"Oh, they were all fair folks," she answered. "But they were all of them queer. They would not fall in with the world such as it is."

"Still my mother will have thought well of them," he said, "since she took Lone into her house when I was born."

"No, no, not at the time when you were born, dear Master," said she. "It was not till after you had been christened, and when it was found that the first nurse here had too little milk, that her ladyship sent for Lone."

"Not till after I had been christened?" he repeated. "Do you remember that for certain?"

"Oh, dear Master," said she, "how would I not remember for certain everything from that good old time? Those were the happy days, when all in the house was put into my hand. The fine linen, the plate, the china and glass, the things even that had been given to the lords and ladies of the house by the King. And as to the servants of the house, too, it was I who took them on or sent them away. Aye, this your first nurse, Mette Marie, it was I who engaged her, and later on—since her ladyship was not well enough to look after things—it was I who found that she had too little milk, and sent her away. Then Lone came up here to be your nurse."

"Were you here, too," Eitel asked after a while, "at the time when Linnert brought back the bull and died?"

"Yes, said Mamzell Paaske, "I was here then, too. And in my humble way I warned my dear master to let him off. 'My dear noble Lord,' I said to him, 'do not go on with this. There may be blood in it.' "

They were both still for a minute.

"You were here," Eitel then said, "when my father was my own age. Was he a hard man even then?"

"Nay, nay," said she. "My lord was a handsome, gay gentleman; he was never hard. But he was bored. Great lords are bored, that is their grief, just as the peasants have got their cares and worries in life. I myself, by the grace of God, have been lucky. I have never been bored, nor have I had cares or worries."

"Look after Lone well tonight," Eitel said after another silence. "Let her be short of nothing, now that in her misfortune she has come to my house."

Mamzell Paaske had been looking away, thinking about

the time of which she had spoken. Now she turned her face round toward him in a little birdlike movement. "I cannot do that, dear Master," she said. "Lone has gone."

"Gone?" he repeated.

"Aye, indeed she has gone," said the old woman.

"When did she leave?" he asked.

"Just after she had come from you," she answered. "I met her on the stairs, but she would hardly speak a word to me. And then she walked away."

"Where did she go?" he again asked.

"Oh, I did not ask her," she answered. "I thought that she would be trying to get to Maribo this very night, and that it would be too pitiful to question her."

"She had come a long way," said Eitel. "Did she not want to take a rest?"

"She did so," said Mamzell Paaske. "When she took leave of me she said: 'Now there is nothing more for me to do. Now I shall take my rest.'"

"You ought not to have let her go away tonight," he said.

"I thought so myself, dear Master," said she. "But Lone always wanted to have things her own way. One did not like to go against her."

She saw that her news had made an impression on her young master, and sat on a little enjoying her own importance. But as he did not speak again she got up. "Well, good night then, my dear Master," she said. "The grace of God be with all of us. May you sleep well."

"And you yourself," said he. "It is late, too late for you."

She nodded her head in a kind of friendly assent. "Yes," she said, "it is late. Too late."

But when she had got up, she lingered. She fixed her clear eyes on his face, stretched out her small hand and touched the hem of his coat.

"My good noble Lord," she said. "My dear Master Johann August. Do not go on with this thing. There may be blood in it."

She turned the door handle without a sound.

Eitel for a second time took the candlestick from the table, went up to his father's portrait and stood still before it. He remained there till the candlestick weighed down his arm, then set it back. For a long time the two faces, the painted and the live, looked at each other.

"We heard it all, you and I," he at length said, "and it makes no difference. A good, faithful woman set her heart on avenging an injustice in a way more hideous than the injustice itself. In that hour the revenge was taken. I was your son, but she made me hers. We ourselves, my father, and these people of ours have got the roots too tightly intertwined, deep down in the ground, ever to be able to free ourselves of one another."

He went to the window and looked out. The night was clear and cold, such as nights will become at the end of summer. The full moon standing behind the house laid the shadow of the building on the broad moat below, which here in front of the windows widened into a lake, and was patterned, as in a mosaic, with broad, flat water-lily leaves. As far as the shadow reached, the water was brown as dark amber, but farther out in the moonlight its sheet was misty with delicate silver. On the other side of it, the grass of the park was silvery too with the heavy dew; the small darker spots on it were wild ducks, asleep. A feeling of deep satisfaction ran through him as he called to mind that the harvest was in.

The still moonlit landscape called up the idea of a perfect harmony to be found somewhere in the world. His thoughts went to Ulrikke, and dwelt with her for a long time. A few hours ago he had held her in his arms. Soon he might hold her so again; all the same things were over between her and him. For of what had happened tonight, of his two talks with a couple of old women, each of them in her own way somewhat off her mind, he could not speak to her. He thought of his small daughter, who in her short life he had seen but a few times. It was fortunate, he reflected, that the child was a girl. She would grow up to be like Ulrikke. "Women," he told himself, "have got another kind of happiness than we, and another kind of truth." The picture of Ulrikke as a little girl, and of her and the prisoner at Maribo in the wood, once more passed before him. It brought no pain with it; it was as if he had been an old man, content to leave the two at play in the green shades, while he himself was advancing upon another long lonesome road.

As he turned away from the window his eyes fell upon the books on the table, which a short time ago he had taken down and had meant to consult. He set them back on their shelves, one by one, and looked the shelves over, walking from one bookcase to another. Much human knowledge and wisdom were stored here in the tall, heavily bound books. Did any of them have anything to tell him tonight?

At length at the end of the room he found on a shelf an old storybook from his boyhood. He took it down and laid it on the table. He let it fall open at random, and, standing up, by the light of the candles read one of the old tales through.

Once upon a time, the story ran, there was in Portugal a proud and hasty young king. To him one day came an old knight, who in the past had led the armies of the king's father to victory. The king received him with great honors. But when the baron stood before his liege, without a word he raised his arm and struck the king's face. Angered as never before, the young king had the offender thrown into his deepest dungeon and had the scaffold raised for his execution.

But in the night the king pondered the matter and counted the great services which this same old knight had rendered his father. So early in the morning he sent for his vassal, ordered all his courtiers out of earshot, and demanded from him the true reason for the affront.

"My lord," said the white-haired warrior, "I shall tell you

the reason. Once, when I was a young man, such as you are to-day, I had an old steward who had served my family faithfully all his life. One day in a fit of unjust wrath I struck the servant who could not return my blow. My steward is dead these fifty years. I have looked for, but never found, means to atone for my blow. In the end I have decided that the best way to do so would be to strike the face of the man who, above all others, had power to return the blow. For that reason, my lord, did I strike your royal face."

"Verily," the king said, "now I understand you. You have chosen for your blow the face of your king, of the mightiest man you knew. But if your arm had been long enough, it would have been the face of your God Himself, who justly deals out reward and punishment, that you had struck."

"It is so," the old man said.

"Verily," the king said again. "This blow of yours, then, is the truest homage that I ever received from a vassal. And I shall answer you as truthfully myself.

"I shall answer you, first, in the manner of a king." With these words he loosened his gold-hilted sword from his sword-belt, held it out to the baron and said: "Take this, my good and faithful servant, as a token of your king's grace and gratitude.

"And," he went on, "I shall answer you, secondly and in accordance with your wish, in the manner of Almighty God. I tell you, then, that I cannot quench the thirst for justice within your soul. For I shall not alter my own law. Until the hour when you meet again that old servant of yours whose face you struck, you will carry the burden of your shame with you wherever you go. Till then you will be, in your castle in the mountains, by the side of your wife and in the circle of your children and grandchildren, or in the arms of a young mistress, forever lonely, the loneliest man in my kingdom."

With these words the young king of Portugal dismissed his old liegeman.

Eitel set back the book on the shelf, and seated himself in his armchair by the table, his chin in his hand.

"Forever lonely," he repeated in his thoughts. "The loneliest man in the kingdom."

For a long time his mind wandered to all sides.

"The prisoner at Maribo," he thought in the end, "is as lonely as I am. I shall go to him."

As he made this decision he felt like a man who, having lost his way in woods and moors, comes upon a road. He knows not whereto it leads, whether to salvation or destruction, but he follows it because it is a road.

"Now," he told himself, "now, after all, I shall sleep tonight."

"He alone, of all people," he continued his thoughts, "will help me to sleep tonight. All through this long evening I have been fearing or hoping, that the rumor of his flight from prison were true, and have been waiting for him. It is no good waiting for him any longer. I shall go to Maribo tomorrow."

Early on Wednesday morning the old coachman of the manor got an order to get the carriage ready. A while after he was told to take out the closed carriage. The old man was puzzled; his young master was not in the habit of using the closed carriage in fair weather. But a little later he again had a different order; he was to take out the new, light open carriage from Hamburg.

"What is the matter with Eitel today?" he asked himself. "Never before have I had, in one morning, three different orders from him."

With his foot on the hub, Eitel hesitated whether to take the reins himself, then he handed them over to the old man. "Drive quickly," he told him, "until we come into the town of Maribo. Then go slowly through the street." He thought: "I shall not try to hide my face from the people today."

The weather this morning was colder than the day before, and the landscape less rich in color and light. A wind blew in from the sea; there might be rain before evening. In the fields and above them the sea gulls were moving restlessly.

The sound of the carriage wheels changed from a softer to a louder rumble as they rolled from the high road onto the paved street of Maribo.

Eitel had the carriage stop outside the courthouse. There was a clock on the house. As on the stone stairs in front he was informed that he would find the police magistrate in his office, the clock above his head struck eight strokes.

The police magistrate himself, old Counselor Sandoe, who came out in a hurry to meet him, was a small rigid official of the old school, who still wore his little pigtailed wig. He had sat in his peaceful office in Maribo as long as the people of the town could remember, but this was his first death sentence. It made him conscious of his own high significance; at the same time the idea of it was curious and disturbing to him. He was now cheered by the prospect of discussing the event with a young nobleman whom he had known from birth.

He grew silent, pushing his lower lip over the upper lip, at Eitel's demand to see the condemned man in his cell and to speak with him alone there.

"This person," he said, "hardly seems to have any human qualities left. He has passed more years of his life in the woods and on the moors than in a house. I suppose that he has never loved any human being. I gather from our good Pastor Quist, who has sacrificed much of his time to him, that he knows no more of the word of God than of law and justice. Verba mortuo facta."

He recounted how his prisoner, when seized red-handed in the manslaughter, had defended himself with most extraordinary strength, and had knocked down three men before he was taken. The counselor had had him put in chains, but even thus did consider him dangerous.

"His mother was my nurse," said Eitel. "She came to see

me last evening. If anything can still be done for him, I shall want to see it done."

"For him?" said the old gentleman. "This person hardly has sufficient understanding of his position to take it to heart. I cannot even imagine any last wish that he might have to state. It is true, though, that this morning he asked that his hair should not be cut until on the scaffold itself, and that we would have him shaved. Out of commiseration with a man who is to die at noon, I sent for the barber. But does such a wish bespeak remorse or amendment?"

"I wish to see him," said Eitel.

"Let it be so then," said the counselor. "Possibly our humane feelings are most urgently called upon in the case of those deepest sunk. In the name of God, we will go to him."

He sent for the gaoler, and preceded by him the old and the young gentleman walked down a long whitewashed corridor and a few stone steps. The gaoler turned the heavy key in the lock.

"Beware, there is one more step inside the door," said the counselor.

The small room which they entered had one narrow grated window high up in the wall. Its stone floor was covered with straw. To Eitel, coming from his drive through the light landscape, the cell seemed almost dark.

The condemned man sat on a bench so low that his chained hands between his knees rested on the floor. His dark head dropped, so that his long brown hair was hanging down over the face. His clothes were in rags, one sleeve of his coat torn off, and he was barefooted. He made not the slightest movement at the entrance of his visitors.

"Stand up, Linnert," said the counselor. "There is a noble gentleman here who wants to see you." He gave out Eitel's name with much dignity, more in honor of Eitel than of the prisoner.

Linnert for a while sat on as if not aware that he was being spoken to. Then he rose without raising his head or his eyes, and sat down again in exactly the same position as before.

The counselor gave Eitel a short glance, confirming his statement as to the hopelessness of concerning oneself about a creature like this.

To Eitel the filth and degradation before him were so loathsome that if he had wanted to, he could not have taken another step toward the figure. After a while he saw that this poacher and murderer, of his own age, ravished by a wild lawless existence, lean and tanned by sun and wind, was beautifully built, with long limbs and rich hair. He felt that this body would be strong and supple, every muscle and sinew of it hardened and trained to the utmost. In the movements of the prisoner as he had risen and again sat down, there had been an extraordinary collectedness and grace and a kind of obstinate joy of life. In his renewed immobility now there was the calm of the wild animal, which will keep more deadly still than any domestic animal. It was to Eitel as if he had, within his own wood, come upon a fox and was now himself standing immovable to watch him.

He noticed that the wrists of the prisoner were swollen and raw from the iron round them, and a choking feeling, as at the sight of a pretty wild animal in a trap, oppressed the visitor's chest.

"Be pleased to unchain him while I talk to him," he said to the counselor.

"It will hardly be advisable," the old magistrate answered, and added in German: "He is still most unusually strong, and he is probably desperate. You may be exposing your life."

"Nay, unchain him," said Eitel.

After some hesitation the counselor made signs to the gaoler to remove the chain from the prisoner's wrists. It fell upon the stone floor with a hard clank. Linnert stretched his arms a little along his sides and lowly yawned or growled like a man waking from his sleep.

"Leave us alone," said Eitel.

The counselor threw a last glance at the two men whom he was to leave alone. "I shall be waiting just outside the door with this man here," he announced in a loud voice, and followed by the gaoler left the cell.

Eitel stood looking at the man who was to die. "I shall speak to him," he thought. "Shall I be able to make him speak? I myself may have half a century before me in which to say what I want. But what he has to say must be spoken before noon. And by the way, after noon, what will I myself find to speak of, for fifty years?"

Linnert sat motionless as before. Eitel was uncertain whether he did realize that one of his three visitors had stayed on when the others left.

"Knowest thou me, Linnert?" he at last asked.

The prisoner remained dead still for a minute. Then he looked up askance, beneath his long hair, and Eitel was surprised to see how light the eyes were in the dark face.

"Ay, thee I know well enough," he said, and after a moment added: "And thy woods too, and that long marsh that thou hast got out westward."

He spoke the dialect of the island so markedly that Eitel had some difficulty in understanding him. In the fight when he was taken, he had had his upper lip split and a tooth knocked out; he pulled his mouth awry and lisped as he spoke, and all through the conversation he hesitated a little after each of Eitel's questions, as if he had to set his mouth right before answering.

His remark had not been offered as a challenge or a jeer, although he must have realized that it would be clear to Eitel in what manner he had acquired his intimate knowledge of his woods and marshes. It fell more like a light, sprightly communication between acquaintances exchanging news. In exactly that way, Eitel reflected, the fox on the forest path, in passing, would render the farmer a quick, snappish, jovial report on his poultry yard.

"Thy mother once was nurse to me," Eitel said.

Once more Linnert hesitated a little, then asked in the same unconcerned manner as before: "What was her name now?"

"She is named Lone Bartels today," Eitel answered. "Many years ago she married the parish clerk. Thou, Linnert, art my milk-brother." The word echoed through his mind, "Brother."

"Was it so?" said Linnert. He was silent for a while and then added: "It will have been but a poor drop of milk that I ever got out of those paps."

"I have come today to see whether I can help you in any way," said Eitel.

"In what way art thou to help me?" the prisoner asked.

"Will there be nothing at all that I can do for thee?" Eitel asked.

"Nay," said Linnert. "They are going to help me here, I think, with all of it."

During the pause that followed, the prisoner a couple of times spat on the floor, stretched out his bare foot and rubbed out the spittle in the straw. No more than his remark did his gesture contain any mockery or spite of the visitor; it had all the character of some humble game or pastime, in which the guest, did he care to, might join.

In the end Linnert himself, after having twisted and writhed his mouth, took up the conversation.

"Aye, there is one thing," he said, "that thou canst help me with if thou wilt. I have got an old bitch, she is mine. She has got but one eye. She is on a rope by the wheelwright at Kramnitze. She is not wont to be chained up. Thou might send down that keeper of thine and have her done away with."

"I shall have thy bitch brought up to my house and looked after there," said Eitel.

"Nay," said Linnert, "she is no good to anybody except just me. But it might be well if thou wouldst shoot her thyself—and then, as thou takest her along with thee to do it, talk to her." After a moment he said: "She is called Rikke, after someone."

Eitel slowly put his hand to his mouth and down again.

"I will tell thee something, in return," Linnert suddenly said. "Thou hast got a brace of otters in thy mill-brook that nobody knows of but me. Early one morning last winter I saw that the rime had melted on the grass round the air-hole of their den. Since then I have kept an eye on them. I was down there, time and another, this summer, and sat by them all day. I watched the old otters teach their four young ones to swim. They are big now; they have got fine skins. The hole is below the eastern brink; it will be easy to thee to take them there."

"It is all right," said Eitel.

"Aye, but thou hast got to remember," said Linnert, "that their den is in the place where the river bends, by the five willows."

"Yes," said Eitel, "I shall remember.

"I have been thinking of thy lot in life," he said after a pause, "ever since I heard of thee. My people have wronged thy people, and it ought not to have gone so with thee. I would do justice to thee today, were it in my power."

"Justice?" said Linnert wonderingly.

Just then Eitel heard the clock on the front of the house slowly and as if pensively strike nine strokes, and wondered whether Linnert, too, counted these strokes.

"Hast thou ever been told, Linnert," he asked, "that the manor house stands where the farmstead of thy people was once standing, and has been built on top of it?"

"Nay, that I have never heard," said Linnert.

There was a long silence in the cell, and Eitel's mind was following the hands of the clock that were now slowly going on, tick, tick, marking the minutes. In the end Linnert shot up a swift glance, as if to find out whether his guest was still with him.

"Linnert," Eitel said. "Thy mother came to me last night

to tell me a curious tale. She told me that by the time that she was nurse at the manner she sent away the lord's child and put her own in its stead."

A new pause. "Is that so?" Linnert then asked. "That will have been a long time ago."

"Yes," said Eitel. "It will have been twenty-five years ago. At the time when neither of us knew who he was."

Linnert sat on, so still that Eitel could not tell if he had heard him or not.

"Was it true what the woman told thee?" he asked at last.

"No," Eitel said. "It was not true."

"Nay, it was not true," Linnert repeated. Then, suddenly, with the same kind of fox-joviality as before: "But if it had been true?"

"If it had been true," Eitel said slowly, "then thou, Linnert, wouldst today have been in my place. And I, who knows, in thine."

Linnert seemed to have once more come to rest on the bench, his eyes on the floor, and Eitel thought: "Is it all over now? Can I go away now?"

At that same instant the prisoner rose and stood up straight, face to face with his visitor. The heavy chain at this rattled a little against his foot. The sudden, unexpected, light and noiseless movement was so extraordinarily vigorous that it had all the character of an assault meant to give the attacked party no time for defense.

The two young men, now standing very close to each other, were of the same height. For the first time during their conversation they looked each other in the face meaningfully, conscious of a trial of strength. A strange, fierce light spread over Linnert's face.

"They would have been mine then," he said, "the deer and the hares and partridges that I have shot in thy fields and thy woods?"

"Yes," said Eitel, "they would have been thine then."

The prisoner's thoughts seemed to run away from the

small dark cell to those fields and woods of which he had spoken.

"And thou wouldst have owed it to me then," he said, "that thou canst go out with thy gun in a fortnight, when the young partridges are fledged, and again in three months, when the tracks of the game are on the snow, and that thou mayst troat to a buck in thy woods next spring."

"Yes," said Eitel.

As Linnert stood so, without stirring, with his eyes in Eitel's but sunk in his own thoughts, the blood mounted to his face twice in a deep dark wave. Only a short time ago, it seemed to Eitel, he had looked into a face which bore a likeness to this one. Was it the hard glint of triumph in Lone's face which here, in the shade of death, did mellow into a smile?

All at once the prisoner threw back his head, so that his long hair was flung away from his brow. He raised his right hand. It was lean, dark-stained, and earth and blood stuck under the nails. The smell of it was nauseating to Eitel.

"Wilt thou then," he asked, "go down on thy knees to kiss my hand, and thank me for my mercy?"

Eitel for a moment kept standing before him. Then he bent one knee on the stone floor, in the straw where Linnert had spat, and touched the outstretched hand with his lips.

Linnert very slowly withdrew his hand, very slowly raised it to the top of his head, and scratched deep down in his long hair. He twisted his swollen mouth into a smile or grin.

"They are biting," he said. "It was well that thou didst set me loose."

COPENHAGEN SEASON

The winter season in Copenhagen at the time of this tale, in the year 1870, opened with the big New Year's levees at court and closed on the eighth of April with the birthday celebration of King Christian IX. (This chivalrous king and fine horseman was known to the great world as "Europe's Papa-in-Law" because he was the father of lovely Alexandra, Princess of Wales, and graceful, witty Dagmar, Empress of Russia to-be.)

Climatically the season was characterized by the fact that it included the Vernal Equinox. It would thus begin with a day of seven hours and a night of seventeen, with hoar frost on the red-tiled roofs of the town and the ring of snow shovels against cobblestones, with skating on the citadel moats and torch-lighted sledge parties, with muffs, bashliks and furred boots. Then, by the time when February's carnivals were over and when legitimate matchmaking and secret love affairs, fashionable rivalries and lofty intrigues were in full blaze, it would allow days to grow longer and all pavements to be suddenly and blissfully dried by the sun and the spring wind. And before it took its leave there would be violets in the dry grass and velvety catkins for the promenaders on the old town ramparts and glass-clear green evening skies.

It was characterized socially by the invasion of the town by the country nobility.

In the streets and on the squares stately gray and red mansions, which had been blind and dumb over Christmas, stirred and opened their windows. They were cleaned and heated from basement to attics, and on festival nights would beam down, through rows of tall, rose- or crimson-curtained windows, upon a dark and icy outside world. Heavy gates, long barred, swung open before fiery pairs of horses which had been brought by sea from Jutland and all the islands of Denmark and were steered by stony, fur-caped coachmen on the boxes of landaus, clarences and coupés. The Copenhageners in the streets would know one of the shining vehicles from another by the colors of its liveries: here were the Danneskiolds, Ahlefeldts, Frijses and Reedtz-Thotts on their way to Court, to the opera or to one another, striking long sparks from the stones, and all of them with that scintillating bit of metal, which must be displayed by noble families only, in the headstalls of their horses. The big houses found their voices too; all through a winter night waltzes streamed from them; late night-walkers lingered outside, beat their fingers and listened: they were dancing in there.

A new little song was in the air of the streets too, for the country gentleman of high rank and title would preserve a clink of the dialect of his native province, and during the season promenades, theater foyers and Court halls echoed with gay and sonorous Jutland, Funen and Langeland accents, from elegantly coated and uniformed, or starch-shirted and beribboned chests. The country maidens were distinguishable at a glance from the young bourgeoises—clear-skinned, straight and supple, fresh flowers with their roots deep in the mold, undaunted by wind or rain, disciplined and risible, lithe horsewomen and indefatigable dancers, young she-bears fresh from the lair and out to make up, within three months of candlelit fairyland existence, for long autumn months of wet rides, evening needlework and early bedtime.

With the conquest of town by country, femininity, the world of woman, rose like a tide and inundated Copenhagen.

Normally the spiritual atmosphere of the city was masculine, and had been so for fifty years. The capital of Denmark held the one university of the country and the primary See of its Church, and around these venerable institutions learned and brilliant philosophers, divines and aesthetes gathered, to solve profound problems and hold sparkling discussions. Less than twenty years before the circle had had the opportunity of sharpening its wit on the edge of the wit of Magister Soren Kirkegaard; adversaries of his were still arguing. From the time when the county had got its free constitution, Parliament had resided in Copenhagen. The upholding of intellectual values fell to Adam's sons. Eve was to be found at her lace pillow or her household accounts or watering the flowerpots in her windows. She was the pure and demure guardian angel of the hearth; her mental color was white and her principal virtues more passive than active —innocence and patience and total ignorance of those demons of doubt and ambition which were supposed to harass the heart of her husband. The ladies of the wealthy bourgeoisie were solid and sensible women, consciously handling their domestic and social problems inside a restricted sphere of ideas. There was no Bohemia in Copenhagen, and no muses of a higher or lighter order. A great dazzling actress for two generations had been the idol of the people, but had had to make her choice between life and death, and had become a glorious martyr to respectability. Only within the small community of rich orthodox Jews, gifted, authoritative women for half a century had acted as patronesses of the arts.

In the great country houses it was the other way. The sons of territorial magnates, with the exception of those who had adopted the diplomatic career, were open-air people; their predominant interests were hunting, with the care of the stock of game on their estates, horses, good wine, forestry and farming, and fair women. They traveled in Europe and might feel at home in Paris and Baden-Baden, but they would come back the same as they had gone away. They consented to be considered as made of grosser material than their females, since such placing released them from the books that they disliked, and set them free to take their pleasures where they found them. Their sisters, the while, were taught at home by French, English and German governesses, had piano, singing and painting lessons and were sent to finishing schools in France; and they would keep up their proficiency by reading French novels and playing the newest composers. Religious life on the big estates was exclusively the domain of the women. While the men would agree to sit under their minister only on the great feast days, they drove to church regularly on a Sunday, and when the vicar dined at the manor it was the lady who entertained him on pious and even theological matters. In a milieu where woman is looked upon as the supporter of civilization and art, the claims on her virtue are likely to be somewhat slackened. The young country girls might still be strictly supervised, but they married—most often very early in life— into freedom. A spirited and charming hostess was a precious asset to the country house; a casual slip from virtue was condoned; and venerable old ladies with deep genealogic insight would unconcernedly state that the third or fourth child of a big house did in reality derive from the neighboring estate.

In a world to which legitimacy is the primary law and principle, woman acquires a mystic value. She is more than herself, and holds the office of the ordained priest who alone among the people possesses power to transform the grapes of common earth into that supreme fluid: the true blood. The young noble matron, at the time and in the sphere of this story, was seal-keeper to the name and ceremoniously passed it on to the coming ages (and from her mien and manner one could not tell whether she knew or knew not, that according to the world of Rome she might achieve without her lord and master what he could not achieve without her). The noble young girls were pert little priests-to-be; wise old gentlemen danced a pretty and prudent courtesy on them; they might meet them again one day as arch-bishops.

Thus the sex brought the season to town, and for three months Copenhagen laid aside its black trousers and put on a ball-frock. Old ladies from country castles opened their salons as arenas for fashionable competitions and set up their reception days as landmarks in the week. The carriages in the streets were not really meaningful until they contained a female of the higher world, floating on clouds, and in theaters the audience of the parterre no longer pointed out prominent, somber male figures in the parquet, but turned their eyes to its many-colored, sweet and vivacious flower bed. The fashionable florists received orders to send out bouquets right and left; it was as if the city were being bombarded with roses.

The world in which the invaders of wintry Copenhagen moved and thought was the world of the name. To a noble-man his name was the essence of his being, that immortal part of him which was to live on after other, lower elements had faded away. Individual talents and characteristics were sup-posed to be concerns of human beings outside his sphere. The

view did not hold water, for in actual life the genuine individ-
ualist was to be found in the country. The townsmen had been
schooled to walk, as to reason, along one line or another;
the people of the big estates would still ride cross-country,
and move unhindered in two dimensions. They had grown
up, in lonely houses with the nearest neighbor at a distance
of many hours, like trees not of forests but of parks or plains,
with room round them and freedom to unfold their particular nature. Here some of them had brought forth broad and
generous tree-crowns, while others had wriggled into ogreish
formations, or shut out highly surprising knots and excres-
cences, and it was in the big country houses of distant prov-
inces that one would find oneself face to face with otherwise
extinct species, and talk to old gentlemen like mammoths or
plesiosauri, and old ladies like the dodo. The country nobility, however, being nothing less than introspectively inclined, stuck to their view and good-naturedly accepted
Uncle Mammoth and Aunt Dodo as venerable archaic con-
sanguinaries.

Most of the noble Danish families had a particular descrip-
tive adjective attached to their name—the pious Reventlows,
the dry and faithful Frijses, the gay Scheels—and society was
at one with the young son of an ancient house himself in the
conviction that by sticking to the family characteristics—be
it but an inherited red-hairedness—he gave proof of a loyal
nature. A young man with an old name, but with no illusions
whatever as to his personal appearance or talents, would offer himself in marriage to a brilliant beauty, proudly—or
humbly—confident in the soundness of this his real self. The
country nobleman, in town as well as on his own land, was
walking, talking, riding, dancing or making love as the person-
ification of his name.

The land went with the name, the big fortunes and the
good things of the earth. All were inherited, and were destined to be passed on as inheritance. The old propertied
class had heard of—had indeed with their eyes seen—people

capable of making a fortune on their own, but they had never quite taken in a fact which to them had all the look of an abrupt, willed act of creation, a breach of the law of a cosmos wherein existence itself was obviously inherited. To be born into the world without any kind of escorting inheritance was an idea so little pleasant as to be almost unseemly; to die without leaving some sort of inheritance behind one was a sorry affair. Old unmarried daughters of great country houses would year by year lay by, out of a small—inherited—income, small amounts which might some day be flowing back into the family funds, allowing them themselves to be laid by, some day, in the family vault, with due honors.

Within this world of names and families, individual fortune or misfortune, as long as they did not touch the name, was staunchly born, and individual death had its own solemn rites as the latest repetition of a sad passus within the genealogical table. The extinction of an old name was a mournful, somehow inexplicable event, before which heads were bared and eyes for a moment turned heavenwards. The good Danish name was now up there, out of the reach of that dubious being, the individual; it had reached the ultimate, austere and immune nobility of the coral reef. But namelessness was annihilation.

A later generation will not easily conceive to what extent, to the eyes of the aristocratic classes of the past, they themselves were the one reality of the universe. Their closest vassals and dependents might be allowed into existence in the quality of retinue—and in such high quality and connection a nickname even, after all, was a sort of name—and during the season the Copenhageners in streets and theaters might come into focus as background or audience. But the vast gray masses of humanity, individuals without a name, washing beneath them and around them, remained imperceptible. The idea of the earthly pseudo-existence of such people, pervaded with want and struggle, was still acceptable to the mind. But what became of them when they died, leaving behind them nothing but nothingness? The reluctance with which, when from time to time compelled to do so, the world of names turned its eyes to the world of namelessness, was the *horror vacui*.

The country nobility was unfailingly loyal to the King and his house. There had been a time, still remembered but better not talked about, when King Frederick's morganatic marriage had kept ladies from Court. Now they came back, swarming like silver-winged bees to their hive, to pay homage to a royal family of solid magnificence and exemplary family life. The old aristocracy would even display their loyalty a little more than they felt it—in the spirit of the world of the marriage ritual: that whoever honors his wife honors himself. For in their blood they knew their own claim to the soil, climate and weather of Denmark, to its woods and its game, its language and customs, to be more validly legitimate than that of a Royal House, the members of which still spoke Danish with a German accent. Had the name of the new dynasty been called out in a valley of Jutland or Funen it would, they felt, have obtained a slower and lower answer from the Danish echo than their own.

This whole world, by the time of the following tale, was nearing its end; already it had one foot in the grave. Yet in this eleventh hour—as is often the case in the eleventh hour of conditions and states—it did bring forth an abundant flowering, equal to that of its rise. Danish estates and farms had lately changed over from grain production to cattle breeding; wealth was flowing into the land, and life in country houses sprang into a luxury unknown for three hundred years.

Within this world, at last, this tale turns upon two families, which, although closely bound by blood, were still socially widely parted.

The first of the two was at the same time almost unanimously recognized as the first in the country. Such vast areas of land spread before it to all sides that the domain had become a kingdom of its own: tall forests with deer and fallow deer in them, fields and meadows with clear streams winding through them, lakes and ponds gazing sleepily up into the sky. Seven hundred copyhold farms lay on the lee side of woods and ridges of the estate; forty-two good Lutheran churches kept a pious watch on its hills. Above the tall trees of the park the copper-roofed towers of the castle caught the golden rays of the rising and the setting sun. The centuries had soldered land and name into a unity, so that today no one could tell whether the land belonged to the name or the name to the land. Mill wheels turned in the rivers for the name; plows broke its deep soil for it behind patient, shaggy horses. The lord of the land came trotting out with his attendants to inspect the work or to take a survey of the crops; he would know the plowman, and sometimes his horses, by their humbler names, and in the good proven way of his plowmen and horses would esteem the doing of a thing once to be quite a sufficient reason for doing it again. He changed his clothes according to the hours; a while ago he had sat in his saddle under a full-bottomed wig, later in a pigtail, and again in a top hat and havelock. He was the steadfast, more or less bright, center of a solar system which could no more be what it was without him than, without it, he could have been what he was. A hundred spinning wheels whirred for the name in thatched cottages, and the lady of the manor came in a coach-and-four to make up spinning accounts and give out new orders, prim and pompous in powder and whalebone, slim in Greek draperies or voluminous in crinoline and shawl. She, too, at times would recall the names of gaping children in the small dim rooms.

The lord of the land who, at the moment of this story, kept a paternally watchful eye on the trees, animals and human beings of it, and who presided at the stately dinner table, Count Theodore Hannibal von Galen, was an upright, well-balanced personality, in conformity with the family tradition a little heavy in movement and uptake, of a genuinely patriotic and patriarchal mind. His Countess Louisa was a talented and ambitious lady, who had been a brilliant beauty and still deserved and liked compliments, and arbiter of taste and deportment to society. There were two children at the manor to serve and glorify the name, a son of twenty-four, handsome, winsome, debonair Leopold, the idolized and envied leader of Danish *jeunesse dorée*, and a daughter of nineteen: Adelaide.

"The Rose of Jutland" they called her, as if all the land of the peninsula, from the dunes of the Skague to the pastures of Friesland, had gone to make up soil for this one fragrant, fragile flower. The rose swayed pliantly to the breezes, youthfully and naïvely alluring in color and scent, but it stood on an exceedingly high hill. Her voice was as clear and sweet as a bird's, and most often low, for she had never needed to raise it to make people carry out her will. The finest objects of the earth in clothing, food and wine, beds, horses and lapdogs had been hers all her life, by right of birth and because it was felt that nothing else would go harmoniously with the bright, frank figure.

A wanderer in her father's forests, hearing clattering of hoofs on the path and watching her pass with a noble young admirer and a groom behind her, might well stand gazing after her, a little dazzled, as if he had been looking straight into the sun. Light as a feather, in her sidesaddle on her big horse, she still carried with her the whole weight of fields and forests, of the seven hundred copyhold farms and the forty-two churches. If the wanderer was a young man, filled with *weltschmerz*, or an old man stripped of illusions, he might walk on at an altered pace, his outlook on life vaguely altered; the world, in order to hold in it a being so highly and wholly favored, must be a happier kindlier place than he had hitherto believed it to be.

She had traveled in Europe with her parents, and on promenades of watering places or in theaters of big towns, people had turned to have a second glance at the long-necked, red-lipped, light-footed girl. She had done two seasons in Copenhagen and there had worn such thin soles to her dancing shoes that she had driven home soleless in the morning. She had been demanded in marriage by the three finest *épouseurs* of Denmark; many other young noblemen had held themselves back because they felt her to be out of their reach. The incense burned before her had not hardened or closed up her nature; she was so young that it only made her a little bolder in her playfulness, and not a little coquettish. She accepted the exquisite compliments paid her as she accepted her exquisite clothes, and approved of her admirers as she approved of her dressmakers, modistes and shoemakers. She had dark-brown hair and very dark eyes; her short, rounded chin gave piquancy to the classic upper face, with its clear forehead and arched, expressive eyebrows that looked as if they had been painted on by the brush of an old Chinese artist.

The second of the two families was named Angel, a name not found in the Peerage of Denmark, and its home was Ballegaard, in the north of Jutland. It was a vast estate, in its own way also a kingdom. But the soil of it was poor; it held wide stretches of moors and marches, and on top of the high ridge running diagonally across it the wind-blown trees crawled laboriously along the ground. Something in the soil, hidden layers of lime or chalk, rendered the landscape exceedingly light, colorless or bleached and as if weightless. Earth and air here had become one; it was in the air that things happened and people lived, and the whole impression was one of both sparsity and grandeur. Thus the bird life of Ballegaard was exceptionally rich; infinite lines of wild geese striped its sky; at the approach of man, clouds of ducks rose from its shallow marsh lakes, and the seasons of its year were marked by dense migrations of waders on their way north or south.

There were sheep on the moors of Ballegaard and cattle in the meadows, and a great number of horses galloping all over the grassland. There was in all the work done here something which went well with the scenery, a combination of chariness and fantasticalness not uncommon in the psyche of Jutland peasants.

The manor house, like the estate in which it stood, was large, noble and bare. A low gray stone wall fenced its grounds with their draughty groves and neglected rose garden. Visitors from more civilized tracts called it "romantic." In good keeping with the word, the long row of young people born in it, and leading a happy, wild life in its big rooms and long corridors, owed their existence to a romance.

One may imagine that a water mill, which is driven by a force ever going the same way, may feel an inclination, even an infatuation, for a windmill, which gets its orders from the four corners of the sky. Or one may imagine that a minute, indistinguishable grain of extravagance or folly in each generation of a sane and steady family, strictly subdued in everyday life, during the centuries may slowly gather into an uncontrollable power. Two hundred years ago there had been a great alchemist of the name of von Galen. In any case it happened, twenty-five years before the day of this tale, that Count Hannibal's young half-sister by his father's late second marriage, a pretty girl, the pet and hope of the family, not yet presented at Court, left her home one evening to drive away and marry a man outside her own sphere, and so unknown to it as to make it wonder where the maiden could possibly have met him.

To her relations and to the whole world of names and families the shock was hard. They felt that sans witchcraft nature could not have erred so preposterously, saw the figure of the seducer all coal black and shrank from the idea. The event was not even much talked about. The bewitched young lady's brother might have had the marriage dissolved on account of her minority, and contemplated to have it done. But he was a man of facts and reflected that he would obtain little more than breaking his young sister's heart; so he set out instead to collect information about his sinister brother-in-law. He was found to be Vitus Angel, the last of a long line of big Jutland horse-dealers, whose father, after having made a fortune on his knowledge of horseflesh, in his old age had bought Ballegaard for his only child. Vitus had been to the von Galen castle to sell its master a rare mount from his own stud; while showing the horse in the courtyard he had displayed his horsemanship to a maiden watching from a window. The family accepted what could not be undone.

The young wife brought her husband and, as they came along, her children, with her into her old circle of friends, as if innocently confident that they must love what she loved, and to their own surprise and against their own wish they came to like the stranger. He had an innate sense of soil and crops and a keen, almost uncanny eye for the quality of animals; he spoke the broad Jutland brogue of their own old nurses and keepers. It was to them as if they had been taken round behind the historic and heraldic age to which they themselves belonged, and there had been set face to face with an ancient inhabitant of Denmark, a stone-age man or a viking, the mighty, nameless ancestor. Much better, Count Galen told himself, than that his sister should have married a brilliant townsman, who would ask for an umbrella to walk out in the rain. In the course of time the happy married life of the fair young law-breaker, and in the end her early death in childbirth with her seventh child, cleansed her image of any spot of the past. She began to shine in the minds with the silvery sweetness and sadness of that heroine of an old Danish ballad who lets herself be lured away by a water-sprite.

After the death of his wife, the master of Ballegaard was but rarely seen outside his own domain; it fell to the younger generation to fulfill the reconciliation between their father's and their mother's world. They came forth from their realm of marshes, children of the god of flocks and pastures, playing on his traditional double-reed pipe, on life and death.

In the eyes of their mother's friends and relations, they were pretty and graceful, and at the same time weird, and even formidable. They were indisputably legitimate, made under the law, but the ambiguity of their birth might be more ominous than plain bastardy. They went about in society like fresh and clean carriers of some grim social bacillus threatening their softer, more exposed, pure-bred playfellows. No old uncle or aunt could help wishing them well; but was it proper, was it morally right to wish them well? The prosperity in life of these young people would imply a breach with the law concerning the sins of fathers; then why not with that concerning the merits of great-grandfathers? Even upon the straightest and firmest of high roads a film of the quagmire of lawlessness seemed to be clinging to the soles of these light feet.

The particular blood mixture had proved particularly true to breed. Among the children of Ballegaard there was an almost pathetic likeness, more of substance than of form—not homogeneous upheapings of heterogeneous atoms, but heterogeneous upheapings of homogeneous atoms, the likeness of the acorn to the oak leaf and the oaken chest. Two or three strong and strange characteristics ran through the nature of the whole brood.

One of these was a great, wild happiness at being alive, what in French is called *la joie de vivre*. Each single thing included in daily human existence—drawing breath, waking up or falling asleep, running, dancing and whistling, food and wine, animals and the four elements themselves—called forth in them a rapture like that of a very young animal, the ecstasy of a foal let loose in a paddock. They would count a flight of geese against the sun, the hours to a coming ball or their last coins of money at the gambling table, with the same intense fervor, and lose themselves in a friend's sad love tale or in the putting together of a fishing rod with the energy of a person throwing himself into the sea. They were natural connoisseurs of wine and food, but munched with equal delight the dry black bread carried about in their pockets for feeding their horses. They were quiet in their manners and least of all self-centered, but they radiated a turbulent content, and their pride in being alive was almost vainglorious. Inspired by some hidden source of energy in life, they did in their turn inspire their surroundings, and on this account were popular with the young people of their own age; the children of the law fell in love with the children of love. To their more obtuse friends amongst the nobility it was a pleasant thing to have existence proved to be a privilege; they would need to have their conviction of the fact brushed up from time to time and thus could not very well for a long time do without their mad young kinsmen of the north. When, a short time before the opening of this story, the Jockey Club of Copenhagen was founded as an Olympus for the supremely favored, it was at first stipulated that only young men of pure noble blood should be admissible, but on realizing that such a rule would exclude the brothers of Ballegaard, the committee had the paragraph altered. A good many years after the end of this tale a baldheaded old gentleman, who on account of his love of the second-eldest girl, Drude, for fifty years had remained a bachelor in his fine big castle, stated to a young girl of the family, Drude's goddaughter: "After there were no longer any Angels of Ballegaard amongst us, neither the great autumn battues, nor the hunts or hunt balls, nor the Christmas parties at the manor houses were worth participating in."

It is likely that the young Angels owed their gaiety of heart mainly to their almost perfect physique. Each organ of their bodies was flawless, so that there would be few such hearts or lungs, kidneys or bowels to be found in Denmark. Their five senses were as keen as those of wild animals. They were fine dancers, shots and anglers; from their horse-dealing ancestors they had inherited a particular relationship with horses, and on horseback would evoke the idea of a centaur even to people without a classic education. They were proof against wind and weather, could go without sleep for a week, drink deep and sleep off their drink like a bear in his lair, to wake up fresh, with a sweet breath.

They were good-looking people as well, the eldest brother almost ideally handsome and two of the sisters recognized beauties. The girls were a little over average height, the boys not tall, but exceptionally harmoniously built. All had long hands and eyelashes, short feet and teeth, a wide span between the eyebrows, and narrow hips, and all of them were light, as if airy, in their movements. Their eyelids lay loosely over the eye, casting a shade along the upper part of the iris and giving a rare limpidity and depth to the glance, such as one will see in the eyes of a young lion cub in contrast to those of the sheep, goat or hare, where the eyelid seems to be tightly drawn upon the eyeball. Five years ago, when young Princess Dagmar traveled to Russia to marry the Czarevitch Alexander, the eldest Angel brother, who was an officer in the guards, had been sent to escort her. Such a nomination against rules and reasonableness—since the young man possessed neither name, rank nor fortune—would have to be put down to his good looks, as if the Danish nation, after having delivered an exquisite specimen of its womanhood, wanted to display before its mighty neighbor and ally a fine sample of its young manhood. The officers of the Russian guards were instructed to entertain their guest; the boy came back to Copenhagen as from a dream. He might indeed, on his own and without effort, have made up such a world of bear hunts, champagne, gypsy music and gypsy girls. Now that he had seen it existing round him, sovereign and magnificently tangible, he seemed unable to take himself away from it again; he moved about in Copenhagen society, still a figure of striking beauty, to some a Tannhäuser out of the Venusberg of St. Petersburg, to others a Münchhausen of the Siberian steppes. At the time of this story he was out of Denmark, at the riding school of St. Cyr.

The last trait in the brood of Ballegaard was this: that they were doomed, each of them in advance marked down for ruin. It happens when a person dies young that his friends will tell themselves, strangely moved: "We knew that it would be so." And most often in such cases the death sentence on that young head, far from appearing as a thorny crown above it or a barrier between it and the world, will have been seen as a dim rainbow halo, the sign of a particular close pact with all things alive and with Life itself. In such a way coming disaster surrounded the young Angels with a gentle and gallant glow. People showed them particular kindness and friendship; nobody but base and coarse natures envied them their youthful successes; it was as if the world told itself: "This will not last long." Later on, when the foreboding in the case of each of the brothers and sisters had been fulfilled, their friends remembered it with wonder and sadness; the people of older generations, who had felt a misgiving concerning them and something ominous in the atmosphere round them, now felt their suspicions confirmed: they had seen the goddess Nemesis stepping forth, and the sight left them bewildered.

There was an old painter and sculptor who had observed scenery and men in all the countries of Europe, who had once come to Ballegaard to study birds and had there had the brothers and sisters, at the time not yet grown up, presented to him. He looked at them, fell into deep thought and remarked as if to himself: "This pretty litter of Ballegaard in the course of their lives will come to break most of our laws and commandments. But toward one law they will be unfailingly loyal: the law of tragedy. They have, each of them, it written in their hearts."

One particular little characteristic of the family ought to be mentioned here: they all dreamt vividly and beautifully. The moment they fell asleep in their beds, tremendous landscapes, vast deep seas, strange animals and people created themselves within their minds. They were too well brought up to entertain strangers with their dreams, but among themselves they would recount and discuss them in detail. The eldest sister, the tallest of the lot and the finest horsewoman, toward the end of her life said to her children: "When I am dead you may write on my tombstone: 'She saw many hard days. But her nights were glorious.'"

But the story-teller does not want to anticipate events. At the time of this particular Copenhagen season no dark fate had yet overtaken any of the young people; only the eldest daughter sat, far away on a big estate of the west country, curiously married to a rich man more than twice her age. The youngest children were still playing at hide-and-seek on the stairs and in the attics of Ballegaard. The second brother, Ib, who was by then twenty-three years old, and the second-eldest daughter, Drude, whose twentieth birthday fell on the day of the equinox, were out on the dancing floors of Copenhagen.

Count Hannibal, who would have been pleased to see a big family of his own around him, had been kind to his sister's children; they were as much at home in his castle as in their own house. Ib, who at the time of his mother's death was twelve years old, and who had taken his loss much to heart, was brought up with his cousin Leopold. The Countess Louisa at first had looked upon the intimacy with misgiving, for she was the most zealous partisan of pure blood in society. But she was at the same time a passionate mother. When Leopold claimed Ib as a constant companion in his studies and pleasures and Adelaide could not live without Drude, and when she noticed what a becoming contrast Drude's fair loveliness made to Adelaide's dark beauty, she gave in, and benevolently adopted her nephew and niece into her own lofty family life. To her friends she talked smilingly of the sister- and brotherhood between the young people; with her children her benevolence toward the

orphelins de mère often took on a sadder note—to Leopold
in particular, who was much like his beautiful mother and
devoted to her, she would dwell with melancholy upon the
dubious status of the young Angels and the sad outcome of
mésalliances in general.

During the season Drude resided, so to say officially, with
her old Aunt Nathalie, a former lady-in-waiting to Princess
Mariane, in the quarter of Rosenvænget. But Adelaide con-
tinually begged and implored her friend to stay overnight at
the von Galen mansion, in order that, before a ball, she
might get her advice upon her frock and hair ornaments, or
have her maid do up Drude's pale-golden tresses in a new
striking manner, and that after the ball, while brushing
their hair, the cousins might exchange confidences and laugh
together at their admirers and rivals in society. The two
girls were generally admitted to be the beauties of the season; the two young men were such close friends that the wits
of their circle had given them but one name in common,
creating a mythical figure which combined elegance and
knowledge of the world with wild, wayward talents. The
four young people rode on from crest to crest of the waves
of Copenhagen revelry, the observed of all observers, in the
happiest of relationships.

But Ib was not happy, for he was eating his heart with
unrequited love for his cousin Adelaide.

He often wondered how it came to be that, with the dagger
in the heart, one might be stabbed anew twenty times a
day. How did it come to be, he wondered, that a never-absent
picture had in it to make a fresh, overwhelming appearance
every hour, dark-eyed, white-toothed, terrible as an army
with banners.

She was altogether and hopelessly outside his reach. He
did not need the word of society to accept the fact; he had
accepted it on his own and from the beginning. He had
nothing in him of the iconoclast: the idea of Adelaide in a
setting meaner than that into which she was born was re-

volting, was nauseating to him; he turned from it, and with even more horror from the idea that such an offense against nature should have been brought about by himself. He had heard Adelaide and her girl friends, in a discussion over their needlework, maintain the theory that the saddest effect of one's hypothetical marriage to a commoner would be the vanishing of the coronet from one's handkerchief. He had not contradicted them; in his heart he had agreed with them. The picture of Adelaide, from her dark, flower-adorned hair to her little foot in its silk sandal, must include the coroneted handkerchief at the tip of her slim fingers.

Because to all of his blood, physical and mental nature were one, his longing for her was burning up his young body. His blood was escheated to Adelaide; his limbs and entrails were pledged to her; his eyes, lips, palate and tongue were devoured with the fever of her. Then again his existence held hours of incredible sweetness: she turned her half-closed smiling eyes to him; she let him button her glove, one afternoon, when she had declared that all the world was deadly dull; she had for a moment, yawning, laid her face on his shoulder.

In the end, this last autumn, he had taken a week's leave and had traveled home to Ballegaard. He had sat with his father, talking about actual, authentic things and matters; he had looked up the people of his childhood who remembered his mother and had learned from them how reluctant they had been to distress or disappoint her. He had walked out to his mother's grave. Over here, on a stormy and rainy evening, when he had been out in the fields with his old dog, which had been wild with delight to see him, an idea had come to him. He would leave the country to enlist in the army of the French, who seemed to be on the verge of a war with Germany. He had found the plan easier to hold onto than he had expected, and had seen this fact as the first lucky thing that had happened to him for a long time. But when he applied for permission, his application was turned down.

The Danish Government, in the present situation, had to keep up the strictest neutrality, even in direct opposition to the feeling of the Danish people. The volunteering of a Danish officer for the French Army, at a moment when a Franco-Prussian War seemed inevitable, would be looked upon by the Prussians as a breach of neutrality which might have fatal consequences.

For a whole day a sweet, poisonous temptation dwelt in Ib's mind: he had done what he could; he might stay at home and see Adelaide as before. But in the evening he cried to it, "Get thee behind me." He would not have Ib Angel turned into a mollusk. And still less would he himself cause the innocent Adelaide to take on the look of a Calypso. Moreover, this resolution of his had been made at Ballegaard. He would now have to resign his commission as a Danish officer; then he would be free to go wherever he liked.

Such a step would mean that he could not, in the future, return to Denmark. It did not much matter; he did not intend to return. So he made his preparations, considering in a strange way both past and future.

In order to fill out this period, he adopted a habit hitherto unknown to him: he began to pay calls and to put in an appearance on the reception days of the ruling ladies of Copenhagen. Only he himself knew that these were visits *pour prendre congé*, paid in a kind of gratitude, or in a kind of remorse, toward his Copenhagen existence. Old hostesses with an eye for a particular brightness in the boy, who till now had heard him described as a wild young person, smiled on his social conversion, and in their minds put him down as a husband for a grandniece out of a big number of sisters. His gay young friends followed his course with jesting comments and believed him to be out to hook an heiress.

On this fashionable pilgrimage of his he became skilled in balancing sword and cap, with white gloves in it, and a teacup, and there had all the looks of a gentle wild animal with big soft paws, patiently and conscientiously going through his series of tricks in a circus. In the salons he occasionally met Adelaide under the chaperonage of her beautiful and imposing mother, and amid the general talk of the groups caught her laughter and her sweet, low, clear conversation voice. It was both happiness and agony; it was, yet, a little more happiness than agony, or he would not have gone on paying visits. In a strange and vague way it did him good to see that other people were now taking in her face and figure as vividly as he himself, and for a short span of time to feel confident that he was not mad. On his way to these social functions she would also from time to time pass him in the street, in her father's carriage and with Drude by her side, on active service to the mystic rite of leaving cards, an honor shown one noble household by another entirely by means of carriage and pair, coachman and footman, in which the young daughters of the houses took part, so to say invisible and never setting foot outside the carriage. She would smile at him then in a secretive way, might even in such a way blow him a very small quick kiss, stolen too, since she was invisible.

In the reception rooms he watched her surrounded by a throng of admirers, but it did not affect him. In his love for her there was a kind of dignity which rejected jealousy: he knew his passion to be of a different quality to that of any other man.

Toward the end of this season Ib unexpectedly found himself the hero of the day in Copenhagen. One morning after a gay night, he had fought a duel with sabres with the Military Attaché to Sweden and Norway, and blood, if only in modest quantity, had been shed on both sides. Duels were prohibited, and he was sentenced to a week's barracks arrest. He was not sorry to withdraw from the world for a while; he was not proud of his exploit, for neither he himself nor Leopold, who had been his second, nor his adversary clearly remembered how the quarrel had arisen. He came out of seclusion to find that Copenhagen society, when unable to get information from the chief actors, had on its own set a series of exciting tales running, and to grin back a little, in a manner to make the tale still more exciting.

A great old lady received on Fridays.

In the square in front of her house a long line of carriages had drawn up; one by one they swung through the gate to turn in the court and swing out again, leaving room for the next in the queue. Spring was in the air today in spite of a sharp little wind running through the streets and chasing bits of paper and straw before it. The sky was a pale blue with light white clouds in it; when the ladies had left the carriages the stolid coachmen themselves sat gazing up at it. The big airy hall of the house was warm; there were oleander trees in pots on the broad stairs leading to the reception rooms, and incense was being burnt—a specialty of the house, the smell of which many years later brought back the idea of Arcadia to the guests now walking up and down. The stair itself today had become a reception room, alive with greetings, and with the rustling of silk frocks and an occasional ring of spurs.

The social functions of the epoch differed from those of later times by the circumstance that here all generations met. Pretty lively-glancing girls steered in like cygnets in the wake of heavier mother swans, and white-haired or bald gentlemen kissed the hands of young married women and cooed to debutantes. Very old ladies, whom the years had rendered small and light as dolls, displayed their wit and charm to timid youths or to ambitious young men who kept in mind the fairy tale in which the hero, when granted one wish, opts for the friendship of all old women. The wide span of age in the assembly made up for its uniformity of class and ideas.

Ib came up the stairs in his cousin Leopold's company. Out in the square the two young men had been discussing a supper party which Ib's regiment was giving to a pretty French singer on tour to Copenhagen. But the spring weather had gone to Ib's heart in a sudden little pang. He saw that the blue shadows of trees on the pavement had changed; their delicate netting was growing fuller as the buds were swelling. In the country, he thought, the coltsfoot by now would be out by the roadside, the fields, light-brown in the light air, were being harrowed, and as one rode along, the cloud of dust behind the harrow, hard and cold and with particles of manure in it, would be blown into one's eyes and mouth. One might hear the lark. He lost interest in the supper party and became silent.

On the landing the young men for a moment were held back by a mature beauty turning herself before the mirrors, and reflecting, as she shook the fringes of her mantilla into order: "Nay, mirrors are not what they used to be," then sailing on through the doors.

In the first salon a small group, encircling the wife of the Danish Minister to Paris home on a holiday, discussed the probability of a French-German war. "But can we be quite certain about Italy?" an old court functionary asked the lady. The Ministresse laughed, so to say in French. "My friend," she exclaimed, "of what are you speaking? Count Nigra is one of the Empress' most ardent admirers."

In the inner, red salon the old hostess herself, by the fireside and the samovar, while entertaining an elderly Prince of the Royal House, caught sight of Ib and, unexpectedly, in a little bright twinkle ordered him to her side. Then she held him as hostage, behind a cup of tea, for later use.

In the window recess a number of ladies had gathered round a small gentleman, a painter of European fame. He had once declared all artistic greatness to be only a higher degree of amiability, and the theory might hold good as to his own art, which was inspired by delight in taking in, and in dealing out, the beauty of the visible world. Since it seemed incongruous that such a brilliant person should have a little pink full-moon face with no hair, features or expression to speak of, and most of all like the posterior of an infant, his pupils, who idolized him, had formed the theory that there had been a shifting about in his anatomy, and that he had got an eminently expressive face in the other place. He was feted in society, but feared as well, because he would at times sit without saying a word, taking in the face and figure of a lady until she felt that she had no clothes on, and at other times, when once set upon a theme, would go on talking forever.

At the moment the group was discussing progress. The idea of evolution was in the air: Professor Darwin had made the air of England vibrate, and sent waves of echo across the North Sea. The nobility of Denmark was stirred and intrigued by his doctrine—shocked by the assumption that one's ancestors were no better than oneself, attracted by the statement that a high rank in the universe was in itself the proof of genuine fitness for that rank.

"I am with you, Eulalia, my pet," said the artist, speaking as ever very slowly, in a small creaking voice and with a series of small grimaces to make up for his lack of expression. "The world is progressing; we are all progressing and in a hundred years will be nearer a state of perfection than we are now. Still, I tell you, while we march on so gaily, improving all over, certain little traits in our nature will, so to say on their own, reach the acme of perfection to be again shed and dropped and to be gone forever. I shall name to you the one part of us, which at this very moment has reached its climax and is about to become a rudiment. We may in times to come witness wonders of scientific and social improvement. But we shall never again set eyes on a gathering of such noses as the ones which we see round us. There is not one of them that has not taken five hundred years to produce. You realize, in this salon, that the nose is the *pointe* of the whole human personality, and that the true mission of our legs, lungs and hearts is to carry about our noses."

A pretty lady of the circle here, with a glance at the speaker's own diminutive nose, burst into a little laughter, was embarrassed and held her handkerchief to her mouth.

"There are here," the artist unconcernedly continued, "muzzles of antelopes and gazelles and snouts of panthers and foxes. And as to beaks, my dear, as to beaks! There are eagles' beaks and cockatoos', small strong owls' beaks almost hidden in the soft fullness of the cheeks, pelicans' beaks with provident pouches beneath them, and long beaks of gentle, inquisitive snipes.

"Contemplate, now, the nose of our eminent hostess. There is none more delicate or refined in all Copenhagen; it will take in everything within sniffing distance with the accuracy of a seismograph. At the same time it has the strength of an elephant's trunk, which lifts up the heaviest timber of the jungle. It has lifted up the lady's own imposing purple velvet bust to the level of her chin, and is holding it there. It may at its pleasure lift up the obscurest among us into the full glare of social limelight, or it may—God help us—if disapproving of our individual smell, heave up any of us from her own shining floors, swing us about and drop us into the abyss of social darkness. And all the time," he concluded, "nobly immovable."

"But shall we really," asked a stout lady in magnificent magenta, "come to drop our good noses like so many autumn leaves? I feel my own to be quite safely nailed on." She pensively touched her nose with a short plump finger.

"It may look so," said the old man. "But it is an easy thing to drop a nose, and I have got the Punchinellos of all ages with me. Or what other particular of its anatomy has humanity to such an extent agreed to view as a detachable part?"

"Dear Master," said a thin lady in gray, "you have made me feel sinister, like a kind of werewolf running about, in the morning light of civilization, with the nose of a carnivore of the dark past. Your characterization of our noses was hardly complimentary."

"It was meant to be complimentary," said the old artist dejectedly. "Only, as you all know, I am sadly poor in words. Had I my brush here I should touch all the tips of your delicate noses with it and make myself clear in a moment. But let me tell you, in my few sorry words, that the five senses—and among them the sense of smell surely holds a high rank—make up the *savoir vivre* of wild animals and primitive people. When, in the course of progress, these innocents are blessed with a bit of security and comfort, and with a bit of education, nosing out things becomes an extravagant undertaking, noses will deteriorate and grow blunt, and with them good manners. Our domestic animals, which are used in the progress of civilization and so are procured for and somewhat educated, have lost the keenness of their senses, and our pigsties and duck yards display but little manners. The middle classes of our civilization have obtained security and a bit of education—and where, my dears, are now their noses? With them the word of smell, even, has become an unseemly word. It is only when one gets up to your own lofty social level that one will again meet with keenness of the senses as with *savoir vivre*. For what is the end of all higher education? Regained naïveté. Therefore, also, among all our domestic animals the one which comes nearest to the wild animal is the one most highly bred and educated: the thoroughbred, our *édition de luxe* of the horse.

"And look now," he went on, "at that almost luminous blonde in olive-green velvet who is talking to Count Leopold. Her knees and thighs, and that gallant back of hers, all very frankly and candidly express her nature. But is not her nose the true *pointe* of it? Alive, piquant, with a brave little tilt to it and almost circular nostrils, it can be traced back directly to the audacious and loyal profile of the Arab mare. She will not fail her rider. But one will have to look round well to find a horseman worthy of her."

"She is Drude Angel," said a lady in a toupee. "A cousin of Leopold's and Adelaide's. It has been much discussed this season whether she or Adelaide is the better-looking. And she is one of those Angel children for whom once, at Ballegaard, you predicted a future of tragedy."

The old artist at these words gave the young girl a long, deep glance, then said no more about her.

"Count Leopold," the stout lady commented, taking up her lorgnette, "in the competition seems to me to be backing his cousin."

"Ah, tragedy," said a lady who was taking a fresh cup of tea from a footman. She was a little hard of hearing and like most such people was in the habit of sticking to a particular word in the conversation after others had left it behind. "Who among us escapes tragedy? As I was getting into my carriage to go here I was handed a telegram that my poor niece at Lolland has been delivered of her ninth daughter. Tragedies of the stage are but half as exacting as those of real life. My unfortunate Anna—you all know her husband —will now have to start on the tenth act of hers."

"But surely, Charlotte," the thin lady said admonishingly, "you will keep in mind that tragedy is the outcome of the fall of man, and thus cannot possibly be easy to do away with. Our great-grandchildren will have obtained many things, but they will have no more hope than we ourselves of eliminating tragedy from human existence."

"Alas, no," said the lady who was hard of hearing.

"Alas, yes!" said the artist. "Tragedy will be an easy thing to do away with, as easy almost as the nose. I close my eyes," he went on, and actually closed his little lashless eyes, "and I see before me in a hundred years from now a gathering, just like ours, of your great-grandchildren. They will be very pleasant people, justly proud of having achieved great things in science and social conditions and, except for their noses, very nice people to look at. They will be able to fly to the moon. But not one of them, to save his life, will be able to write a tragedy.

"For tragedy," he continued, "far from being the outcome of the fall of man is on the contrary the countermeasure taken by man against the sordid and dull conditions brought upon him by his fall. Flung from heavenly glory and enjoyment into necessity and routine, in one supreme effort of his humanity he created tragedy. How pleasantly surprised was not then the Lord. 'This creature,' He exclaimed, 'was indeed worthy of being created. I have done well in making him, for he can make things for me which without him I cannot make.' "

"Preserve me!" the stout lady exclaimed. "You are very mysterious—or is it mystical? for I have never been able quite to distinguish the two words from each other—and we beg you to express yourself in plainer words. In my young days I have created a sensation on my entrance into a ballroom, and this last season, God help me, by the aid of various rare spices I have created the recipe for a Cumberland sauce. But how does one create a tragedy?"

The old man sat for a while in silence, stirring a little in his chair as if he were, in accordance with his pupils' theory, now thoughtfully and gently scratching his forehead.

"Not being good at direct answers," he said at length, "I shall answer you in riddles:

"What is it that man has not got and would on no account accept if it was offered him, and that is still the object of his adoration and desire? The divine female bust, Mesdames.

"And what is it," he asked again, "that old Professor Sivertsen has not got, and would not accept if it was offered him for himself, and that yet to him is the most picturesque attribute of a human being? What is it that to him is an absurd and preposterous thing, a ridiculous thing to carry about with you in life, and which is at the same time the rare spice by the aid of which tragedy is created? I shall give you the answer such as you want it, in plain words. It is named honor, Madame, the idea of honor.

"All tragedies," he said slowly, "from *Phaedra* and *Antigone* to *Kabale und Liebe* and *Hernani*, and to that promising work of a young Norwegian author, *Maria Stuart in Scotland*, which we saw together the other day, are determined by the idea of honor. The idea of honor does not save humanity from suffering, but it enables it to write a tragedy. An age which can prove the wounds of the hero on the battlefield to be equally painful, whether in the breast or in the back, may produce great scientists and statisticians. But a tragedy it cannot write.

"Those very pleasant people, your grandchildren," he went on, "at their tea party in a hundred years will have their troubles, but they will have no tragedy. They will have debts—troublesome things—but no debt of honor, on life and death. They will have suicides—troublesome things—but the hara-kiri will be forgotten, or smiled at. But they will be able to fly to the moon. They will be sitting round their tea table discussing their routes and tickets for the moon."

He was silent for a moment, then took up his theme again, gravely.

"I am an artist," he said, "I will not exchange the idea of honor for a flying ticket to the moon. I, who alone in society have no nose"—he shot a glance at the lady who had laughed when he talked about noses, a glance familiar to his pupils, who had even a name for it and called it: that Jehovah was putting out his tongue at one—"can yet speak with connoisseurship about noses, for, being an artist, I am myself the nose of society. And I thank God that the people whose portraits I paint have still got noses to their faces. I am an artist, I have no honor of my own, and can yet speak with connoisseurship about honor. In Paradise there was no idea of honor. ('And they saw that they were naked'—that comes in later, and would by no means have been an objectionable sight to the eye of an artist.) And I thank God that the people whose portraits I paint have still in their hearts the idea of honor, by which tragedy is created.

"Or where—" he at last concluded his long lecture, in the small, plaintive voice of a child addressing grown-up people. Two of the ladies round him by this time had got up, smiled to him and joined another group of conversationalists. "—where, this being different, would I get the black for my pictures? The *noir d'ivoire*, the *noir de fumée*, the blessed, deep *noir de pêche?* Look at my latest still life, the finest picture I ever painted"—so was always to him his latest picture the finest he had ever painted—"and tell me whether I should possibly have got any black into the crimson and scarlet of my lobster shells, or into the greenish-gray of my oysters, if I had not seen tragedy going on all round me?"

At this moment the hostess, who had by now taken leave of the Prince, released Ib and served him. She had always liked the boy; moreover it had been reported to her that his adversary of the Swedish Legation had made a remark on her figure; all the same she felt that she ought not to let Ib's irregularities pass unpunished.

"This is a young friend of mine," she said to other, more worthy friends round her, "who is doing penance for his deeds of blood by coming to see a fat old woman. But ought he not to give a thought to the reputation of the woman herself? It actually makes me jump to see him enter my door. Tell me, Ib Angel, when did you last see the sun rise without seeing it double?"

"I saw it rise quite respectably single this morning, Aunt Alvilda," he answered, addressing her in the manner used in noble circles toward one's mother's and grandmother's friends, "as I was making Bella jump in the riding ground." Bella was the mount of the old lady's granddaughter, which he had undertaken to exercise while its young mistress was in Paris on her wedding trip.

"I made her take the stone wall five times," he continued, "and she did it awfully nicely, because I was thinking of you all the time, and in my mind had you on my pommel. I feel that she does now deserve a lump of sugar from your own hand, if you will so far honor her and me."

As the old lady handed him the bit of sugar in her two fingers, he kissed her hand. In her young days she had been the greatest horsewoman of the country. Now the touch of the young lips against her fingers was like the touch of a long-gone, dear muzzle; for a moment she felt that in the midst of her lively talking salon she and this boy belonged to each other, and she drew a little sigh, wishing that his duel had been fought for her.

Ib's ear here caught the well-known rustle of a frock and the stir in the room generally accompanying it. Adelaide, slim as a reed in a new brown-and-white-striped silk frock draped, brailed up and frogged, and a small neat brown hat with ostrich feathers, had entered the room with her magnificent mother all in mauve, still crinolined and in a lace-trimmed bonnet. The art of upholstery at this period had been brought almost to perfection and had gone a little to the head of the fashionable world; the rich, symmetrical curves of all sofas, chairs and *causeuses* were smoothly and tightly enclosed in silks and satins, and ladies were made to look as much as possible like masterpieces of the craft. Adelaide was bright-eyed, with a rose in each cheek from her drive in the fresh air, filled to the brim with two equally strong emotions: the sad anticipation of the end of the season and the intoxicating consciousness of approaching spring.

The currents of the salon swerved and shifted about a little at her arrival. A minute after she had curtsied to her hostess—young girls of the nobility curtsied to married ladies, and thereby so clearly honored their own sex and class that young bourgeoises sighed at the sight and wished that custom would allow them to do the same—she was in the midst of a gay general chatter about the last ball and the next, and the first night of a new ballet at the Royal Theatre.

Ib withdrew to the window circle to look at her. The sight of her happiness filled his own heart with a happiness akin to it and differing from it—the melody in major key of a young female mind turned into the minor key of that of a young man. She had a small bouquet of violets at her bosom; it was a wonderful thing, he reflected, that those few flowers should have fragrance to fill the whole room. After he had watched her for a little while he set out for the door, as was his habit these days. Adelaide had noticed this particular maneuver of his and had commented upon it to Drude. "Ib has become very grand," she had remarked. "As soon as he sees one at a party he takes his leave, to show that the welfare of the King's army rests on his shoulders." Today she would not allow him such presumption, but as he passed her spoke airily over her shoulder. "It was wonderful luck to meet you, Ib," she said. "I must have you fetch a parcel for me at the custom house. My long gloves from Paris for the ball on Monday! It is important!"

By the door Ib was stopped by a group of elderly gentlemen, animated by the stronger refreshments served around, and was actually collared by a big figure in a red uniform, with a red face and in the midst of it a big red mustache.

"Ho, the valiant Ib!" he cried. "How goes, fire-eater? In search of a second for the next battle? I offer" he went on, striking his broad, beribboned chest, "the bosom of a true friend in defense of the virtue of Mademoiselle Fifi!"

Ib wanted to get home with Adelaide's picture in his mind and was annoyed at being held back. He remembered that this high officer, at the card tables, had a reputation of peeping into his opponents' cards.

"There was no Mademoiselle Fifi there, Uncle Joachim," he answered. "But hearts was trump. Von Rosen had not been keeping account of the trumps and when in the last trick I trumped his ace of spades he cried out that it was impossible that there should still be a trump in, so that I had to tell him that I had hidden my small heart amongst the diamonds. That, curiously enough, made him very angry."

The big man swayed a bit on his feet as if he had actually received a push, and Ib, realizing that this might be the last time he saw this old friend of his, felt a little sorry at having vexed him.

"But I may come to beg your kind offices still, Uncle Joachim," he said. "I felt uncomfortable when the swords were drawn, and some other time shall be thankful for the assistance of a man who has never in his life been afraid."

The red gentleman, who had not heard a word of Ib's chaffing but had been swaying for other reasons, laughed.

"Oho," he cried, "who has never been afraid in his life?" He glanced around him quickly to make sure that there were no ladies within earshot. "When I was your age in the garrison of Rendsburg, I got crab lice, and was shaved by the hospital orderly. Then I was afraid!"

The young man laughed at the older man's joke and walked down the stairs, out into the open air.

Ib next morning arrived at the Galen mansion with Adelaide's long gloves hidden beneath his uniform coat, since officers must not carry parcels about. In the gateway he had a short chat with the old porter, who had known him all his life and had a partiality for him, as to a talented illegitimate child of the house. Upon the stairs to the first floor he exchanged a remark with the gray-haired butler, to whom he stood in much the same relation, and from him learned that he would find the two young ladies in Countess Adelaide's private sitting room.

There was a particular scent in the air of the gallery outside the room, Adelaide's "Violette de Parme," and from behind the door came the sound of voices and laughter. Ib tarried a moment, to take in both, then turned the handle of the door.

On the threshold to Adelaide's small pale-blue, ·silk-upholstered boudoir he was met by a sight which during the years left to him he kept in his remembrance as the sweetest of his life. The two human beings whom he loved highest in the world stood close to each other, gracefully and playfully grouped, and very likely, on this same spring morning, in the zenith of their triumphant virginal beauty.

The girls were back to back, straight as grenadiers, their young bosoms defiantly pushed forward, their faces somewhat painfully screwed around toward the long mirror on the wall, measuring heights. In this undertaking the whole imposing structure of whalebone, flounces, and bows at the back, below the waist, was pushed out of place and flattened, forming a fanciful silhouette. Above the waist their torsos shot up incredibly slim, for not for nothing had Countess Louisa's private corsetière, five years ago, enjoined her to have her young ladies properly and firmly laced up and whaleboned to the armpits, since otherwise one risked that their internal parts started developing. The faces of the two cousins were demure and grave, but their chests and throats were filled with cascades of suppressed laughter. Out of the corner of their eyes they recognized the newcomer and loudly welcomed him as an arbiter of their contest.

Ib had seated himself comfortably in a chair, so as to draw out the moment. He let himself be pressed and severely scolded before he got up from it, walked twice round the competitors and stood still, gravely suggesting that he should run his sword blade through the stair-turrets of curls and tresses that crowned the dark and the fair head. At this the group, still statuesquely immovable, became acoustically highly alive in a two-voiced indignant entreaty to show due respect of coiffures. He then asked for a ruler, but there was no ruler in the room, and in the end it was agreed upon that a long ivory knitting needle from Adelaide's workbag would do for the purpose. The young ladies gave signs of nervousness as he slowly bored it into the masses of hair.

"You have only yourselves to thank, wenches," he said

coolly. "One does not manage to arrive at the skull of one's own sister or cousin for all the hair of Paris mamzelles on top of it. Still," he pronounced, as, having got the knitting needle all through and linked the two heads together, he took a step back and half closed his eyes, "there is no doubt. You are probably, both of you, a little bit beyond the height of most girls in Copenhagen, but Drude is the taller by a quarter of an inch. You, Adelaide," he added, "look taller than you are on account of your head being so small."

"It is," Adelaide replied with much dignity, "the correct size for the head of a classic statue. Professor Sivertsen, who teaches me to paint in water color, has told me that the head should make out one-seventh of the person. That is named the heroic proportion."

"A serpent's head!" said Ib. "In harmony with your serpentine curls and your serpentine back. And with that serpentine waltzing of yours at the balls."

"And I suppose," she replied, her dignity taking on a tone of lofty irony, "that you yourself will, there, be figuring as the snake charmer?"

There was nobody with whom she waltzed so well as her cousin. The two had danced together from childhood, at the balls of all Jutland country houses or at times alone in the winter dusk, in the huge hall of Ballegaard with its giant iron stove. When she slid from the arms of her other cavaliers into Ib's embrace, she was swept into her true element, like a ship launched, and the two were united in a perfect harmony all void of thought.

"Of course I am the snake charmer," he said, "and you know it well enough, and will always answer to the sound of my whistle. My charms have forced the cobra to dance, inexplicably, on a single ring. A waltz is a waltz, but each of you girls will interpret it to the world in your own way. Drude dances like a wave, Sibylla like a gale, Aletta like a rocking horse. But nobody who has seen you dancing can doubt that you are a serpent. Prince Hans himself the other night remarked upon the fact."

Adelaide felt that it was time to change the theme. "Why were you not at the ball yesterday?" she asked, adding with a grand gesture toward the bouquets on all tables and window sills of the room the haughty statement: "From my cotillion."

The girls here ordered him to take away the knitting needle, dissolved their group and, each in front of her mirror, lifted her arms to bring her hair in order. None of the two had ever been in a room with another woman with as fine a head of hair as herself, this young cousin solely excepted. The fact caused no rivalry between them because the rich hair on the two heads was so different in character: Drude's golden, like a barley field running in long waves before the breeze, Adelaide's very dark, with something dangerous in its rippling, like a deep, narrow river hurrying toward the cataract.

Ib, once more seated in the chair, kept his umpire's eye on the girls. "You are so Adelaide-ish," he said slowly. "When on entering a room I see as much as a glove's finger of you, I can point you out on the spot: Adelaide."

She asked him pertly on what occasions he had needed to point her out.

"Nay," he said thoughtfully, "nay, that is it. You have never in your life entered a room in which everybody has not known who was entering it: Adelaide."

"And have you done so?" she asked.

"O my God, me?" he said. "Do you imagine that people in Copenhagen will knock one another in the ribs as I pass and whisper: There goes Ib Angel? My soldiers know me. But I have had to paint myself red all over with blood, you know, to have Copenhagen society see me at all. At Ballegaard of course it is different."

"And has Drude done so?" Adelaide asked again, wonderingly.

"And poor Drude has done so, too, many times," said he. "On her entering a room people will first look at her indifferently, then sit up and ask: Who is she? I have sailed with Drude from Jutland to Copenhagen, and the old ship's captain has come up slyly to get out of me who that pretty girl was. But you," he added, "you have never seen the face of a person who did not know about you. You cannot drive from Kongens Nytorv to Amalienborg without people in the street being aware who sits in the coach: Adelaide. You have never traveled in a ship in which the captain and the cook and the small cabin boy himself have not known: Adelaide has come on board."

"People who did not know who I was?" Adelaide said thoughtfully. "They must be very queer people, and silly. An old ship's captain who did not know who I was—what on earth would I do with him?"

"You would make him find out soon, you mean?" Ib asked.

"No," said she. "No. And I should never try to find out who he was either. He could remain for me among the people of his own kind, undisturbed."

"You see," said Ib, "that is the difference between you and me. The world you live in is lighted up on all sides by your presence in the center of it, but I have got to strike a match every time, in order to make humanity see my face."

Beneath her long eyelashes she sent him a searching, almost suspicious glance. It was not, then, outside the bounds of possibility that Ib, who belonged to her, had a world of his own into which he might retire, away from her. There had been times when she had guessed it to be so. Under the circumstances it was right to take the offensive. She turned toward him, so lovely, her face all aglow.

"You are quite right," she said. "You will never get into the same boat with me. You will always live in the world below the boat, at the bottom of the sea. For you are a fish. I have never known such a fish as you are."

"It is perhaps a good thing to be a fish," said Ib pensively.

"You are such an incorrigible fish," said Adelaide, "that one wonders at you. Why do you not love me? All the others love me. I do not look at one of them without seeing them become happy or unhappy according to my way of looking. You have had more opportunity of falling in love with me than any of them. But you are a fish."

He had turned his eyes straight upon her face and sat looking at her without a word, and she vaguely felt that something was happening to him, and that somehow the moment was of significance. But now, she saw, the boy had become stubborn and would not answer her.

"Do you know," she said, her eyes even brighter than before, "do you know what I would do if I were you? I would be in love with my cousin Adelaide. I would be so much in love with her that I could not sleep at night. I should see her picture before me every moment of the day, so that I should look at other people to find out whether they did see her too, or whether perhaps she might be a Fata Morgana. At last, at the end of the season, I should make up my mind to die. I should resolve to join the army of the French, now that they are going to have a war down there."

She here made a pause, happy to feel that she could make up a romantic tale.

"And I should come," she went on, "to say good-bye to her, with a broken heart—riveted but too heavy to hold together much longer—and say to my cousin Adelaide: 'I love you.' But you will never come to take the word of love into your mouth. You could not spell it on a piece of paper if people asked you to. For you are a fish."

He, who used to have such a quick repartee to her quick whims, sat on in silence, as if he had not heard what she said, and had now turned his eyes away. She was inclined to let him off, for she had other things to think of. But just then, without looking up, he asked her: "Would you do that if you were me, Adelaide?"

Her thoughts had already run a bit away from him, to a new spring bonnet with cherries on it. At his words they turned and came back. Always, from the time when she had been a little girl, in their games and fancies she had come when he called her.

"Indeed I should do that," she said.

"And what would you say then, if you were me?" Ib asked.

"I would," she said, "I would in any case not be lying back in a chair while I was making a declaration of love to a lady. I should stand on my feet even if wavering on them, and I should say: 'Adelaide, my love—'" She stopped and again went on: "'My soul.'"

Ib had risen when he was told to, and now spoke as he had been ordered to do.

"Adelaide," he then said, "my love. My soul."

She once more gazed into the mirror. "I should say," she said, "if I were you: 'I die, Adelaide, because I cannot live without you. In my last moment I shall think of you, in my last moment I shall say to you: I thank you, Adelaide, because you existed and were so lovely, because you danced with me, because you talked to me and looked at me. Good-bye forever, my dear heart, my sweetheart. Good-bye.'"

She had grown really inspired, the words coming to her as if on their own, beautifully arranged. During the season she had taken part in many charades and *tableaux vivants*, with constant success. But none of all had been as meaningful as this. She felt herself to be as great an actress as that French star she had lately seen on the stage, and wished that she could have had a greater audience, the connoisseurs of Copenhagen and the Corps Diplomatique, to applaud her. Then again she told herself that she had Ib. She recalled their childhood when, with far greater experience of books and adventure than she had and with an infinity of ideas and plans, he had taken the leading part and had been content with her as his audience, she went on.

"I should say," she said: "'Give me your hand to kiss at

this moment of farewell.' I should even say—" she added very slowly "—yes, I should even say: 'Give me one kiss, one only kiss, because I am going to die.' "

There was a pause.

"I thank you, Adelaide," Ib said, "because you have existed and have been so lovely. Give me one kiss, one only kiss, because I am going to die."

Adelaide stood silent for a moment; she felt that Ib was carrying her joke somewhat far. It was a way of his; he had done the same thing when they were children and had climbed a tall tree or sailed down the river on a raft together. She had liked it in him then; it was dangerous; it was part of the fun with Ib. She liked it now too. His quiet, steady glance at such moments had had a magnetic power over her; it had so now. And besides, since this was her own joke, it was loyal of him to join into it with such energy. She drew herself up a little, put her hands behind her and looked straight at him.

"Yes," she said. "Because you are going to die."

At this moment Drude, who during the conversation between the two had seemed to be far away, turned round toward them.

The young man knew that the girl had never been kissed in her life. But he knew too that if Drude had not been with them, her clear eyes on their faces, Adelaide would not have spoken of kisses. That kiss which to him, in the row of kisses of his life—wild or light or tender kisses—should have been the one and only kiss, Adelaide's kiss, to her herself was the kiss in general, the abstract kiss, a thing out of ballads and romances. And since it was she who had asked him for a kiss, he would have to come in with her idea of it.

So Ib kissed Adelaide.

There was a silence in the pale-blue room; the rumbling of carriages in the street outside suddenly became loud. Then Ib turned and walked away, a little sideways as he would do at times.

Adelaide, who after the kiss had been left equilibrating on the top of a pole, tried to steady herself by calling out to the parting figure a quick thanks for having fetched her gloves. But already she heard the click of the door to the gallery as he closed it behind him. For a moment she stood gazing after him.

Then the two young girls stared at each other. "Why do you look like that?" Adelaide asked.

"Like what?" Drude asked back absent-mindedly.

"You are so pale," said Adelaide. She placed a finger on Drude's cheek as if to point out that paleness to her friend.

"Am I pale?" said Drude in the same way.

"And you look," Adelaide said, "as if you were omnipotent."

At this Drude seemed to come back to the actual situation. She shook her head a little. "No, I am not omnipotent," she said.

"Omniscient then," said Adelaide. To this Drude did not reply.

There was a long pause. Then Adelaide asked Drude: "What did he come here for?"

"My brother?" Drude asked, and the word rang strange to Adelaide's ear.

"Ib," Adelaide said. "What did he come here for?"

Drude turned all around toward her cousin and spoke very slowly, with her eyes on her face.

"I can tell you now," she said. "He is going away to join the French Army. He came here today to see you before he goes, and to say good-bye to you. He is going away because he loves you. And I believe that he wants to die."

Now Adelaide in the course of a few seconds could look the whole conversation over. She stood dead still; a couple of times she gazed at Drude and again away. An idea which before now had been vaguely in her mind came back to her with sudden force: that to this brother and sister life meant more than it did to her, and that they could draw upon some great, unknown powers of existence. There was in Drude's deep emotion at the moment more than could be fully explained by sisterly pity. She had something else on her mind, a secret of her own. But whatever that might be, Adelaide for the time had to leave it alone; her own affairs gave her enough to think about.

She might have said to Drude, in conformity with truth: "But I knew nothing of what you now tell me, and Ib himself knows that I knew nothing of it. I am innocent of his misery now."

But young girls do not reason in such a way. They have in their nature a particular honesty and self-respect which makes them accept the responsibility even for the sufferings brought about through them without their knowledge or consent. Adelaide before now had broken young men's hearts and thought light of it. But she would never have excused herself by declaring: It was not I; it was my beauty; it was the music, the moon, the wine that did it. For her beauty was herself; the music, the moon and the wine were herself; and she accepted the responsibility for them all. It was, now, a cruel thing, a vulgar thing even, to make Ib pronounce in fun the declaration of love which with death in his heart he had come to make her. It was a cruel and vulgar thing to receive in the manner and mood of a great French actress on the stage his kiss on life and death.

She felt Drude's glance still resting on her, and it was a strange glance. There was neither anger nor indignation in it, but there was grief in it; there was a deeper tenderness than Drude had ever before shown her, and there was more: an inexplicable pity. Beneath this glance Adelaide became confused, or a little giddy.

Drude suddenly said: "He has loved you all his life."

"Me? He?" Adelaide exclaimed, the first word in sheer amazement, the second in the voice of a person on whom light is dawning.

"Ill-fated Ib," said Drude.

The unfamiliar word attached to Ib's name, which at the moment came natural to Drude's lips, at the moment came natural to Adelaide's ear. In the light of it the grotesque hopelessness of Ib's love became only pathetic; tears filled the big dark eyes which met Drude's big, light, tearless eyes.

Now the proud Lady Adelaide was nothing if not generous. For the sake of her own dignity she must refuse ever to set foot on the defeated.

"Drude," she said after but a short pause, "I know what we will do. You will send a letter to Ib."

"A letter?" Drude asked. "What am I to write to him?"

"You are to write to him," Adelaide answered, "that he must come to Aunt Nathalie's house tomorrow, Sunday afternoon."

"To Aunt Nathalie's house?" Drude repeated, and at the name of that honest old woman her young blood unexpectedly rose to her face. "Aunt Nathalie will not be in tomorrow afternoon."

"I know," said Adelaide. "Aunt Nathalie is going to the christening of Clara's baby tomorrow, and will be there all afternoon. Mama is going to be there as well. That is just why you must tell him to come to Aunt Nathalie's house. You will write that you have something of great importance to talk with him about, and that he must be sure to meet you there."

"Something of great importance to talk with him about?" Drude repeated as before, her blush deepening.

Adelaide continued, her mind concentrating on her scheme.

"I shall tell Mama," she said, "that I am going to bed with a headache, and that I want nobody but Kirstine to come into my room." She continued, quickening her speech, with contempt of death: "And it will be I who will meet him at Aunt Nathalie's house. I am going to beg his pardon.

"Kirstine will help me," she went on after a moment, forming the details of her plan. "I shall borrow her shawl and bonnet. I shall go out at the back door and make Kirstine get me a droshky for a bit of the way. And then I shall walk to

Aunt Nathalie's house." She emphasized the word walk because she had never till now walked alone in the street.

"But I will not," she concluded after a short pause, "sit and wait for him in an empty house. You must see to it that he comes there before me."

The blood had again sunk from Drude's face; she was even paler than before. "Yes," she said. She turned away her eyes, and her slim straight torso followed the movement. "I shall not be in tomorrow afternoon myself either," she said.

Maybe Adelaide had expected Drude to question her or to express alarm at the suggested audacious undertaking; this mute assent of hers was curiously meaningful. A recollection flashed through Adelaide's mind. It had happened that the two cousins, riding together in the woods, had jumped a windfall at the same time, so that for a moment both had been without contact with the ground. Such experiences had united them closely. Was the approaching hour, Adelaide now wondered, to be that same thing over again, a leap taking them both off the ground, a flight in the air which, this time, was to unite them forever?

Shortly afterward the two young ladies took leave of each other.

Ib had a mistress in town, a big, handsome, savage daughter of the people named Petra, who loved him with both passion and tenderness. Her mother ran a laundry business in a basement at Christianshavn. Old Professor Sivertsen, the same who had instructed Adelaide about the heroic proportions and upheld the cause of noses at the tea party, lived on the first floor of the house. The artist, when passing the girl in the gateway, had been struck by the classic beauty of her body beneath its respectable 1870 attire, and cajoled her mother to allow her to pose for him in the nude for his big picture of Susannah. Petra had created a furore among his young painters and sculptors and had soon come to be known as the loveliest model of the town. In the atmosphere of the studio a native boldness in the girl caught headway;

she came to think not a little of herself. She did not, however, fall to any of the youthful aesthetes who worshipped her, but she had run straight into the arms of the young lieutenant, by virtue of a kind of genius common to their two natures.

There was in this love affair something both grotesque and pathetic, inasmuch as Ib's devotion to his mistress and his dependence upon her arose from the similarity between her unhappy love for him and his own unhappy love for Adelaide. The girl was not intelligent enough, or not experienced enough, to realize her situation; all the same she sensed that a sword was hanging over her happiness. It was at the moment when she gave him free rein to her alarm and grief and when she accused him of not loving her that she became indeed precious to him, for then he heard his own misfortune voiced in a fresh, coarse young mouth which gave tit for tat. When her passion did not run parallel to his own, when she accused him of having seduced her or when she tried to stir his feelings by haranguing him upon some richer lover keen to marry her, she bored him and he found it difficult to keep his attention with her. He was an honest boy; he was unpleasantly aware of his ambiguous position, and endeavored to make up for it by flatteries and kisses or by presents of gloves and silk ribbons, even once of a gold watch and chain which he could but ill afford. Then again her laments would ring true to him, as coming from the depths of his own sad heart, and he would go down on his knees before her and press her hands to his lips out of deep, genuine gratitude toward her for shedding his own salt tears.

With time Petra had worked out for herself the surest method of mastering her lover. They had been closest to each other and she had had, so to say, her happiest time at a period when she had been threatening to commit suicide, and when he had considered leaving the world with her as with the one human being unhappy as himself. Their melancholic plan got no further, since at his resolve to join her her reason for dying was done away with. In spite of his pity and his friendly feelings, the liaison had developed into a long row of wild scenes, so that it was only in the actual embrace, in which no personal element was staked, that the lovers melted into harmony.

She said to him: "An evening will come when I shall tell myself that all day I have not once thought of Ib. And that will be the worst misery of all." And her words would set him wondering whether an evening would ever come when the whole day he would not once have thought of Adelaide, and he agreed with his bitter mistress that this would be the worst misery of all. She said: "I do not believe that you have ever really meant to make me miserable. But it would have been better if you had. For then in any case you would have behaved differently from what you have done, and nothing could have been harder than this!" And again he thought of Adelaide, who had never meant to make him miserable, and again in his heart admired Petra for her perspicacity.

At times he grew afraid of her because the irises of her eyes were so peculiarly small; her glance when she turned against him could be piercing as a needle.

The fair weather held, on Sunday morning the sky's big cupola over Copenhagen was filled with sweet blurred light and with a foreboding of summer days intoxicating to all hearts. The fashionable world of the town kept indoors on Sundays; it was the people who had only this one day of leisure, who were out to take the air from Amagerport to Østerport. On this Sunday one might for the first time walk on the pavements in thin-soled shoes; after long winter months of galoshes, the promenade itself to all the young women of Copenhagen was like a polka. The walls of the houses facing south had imbibed a little warmth from the sun and gave it out again to the touch of a palm. Boys in the streets were offering garlands of woodruff for sale.

In this light air and among this light-hearted crowd, Ib

crossed the Knippelsbro on his way home from a visit to Petra. He was held up by the bridge being raised to let through a tugboat with a heavy barge behind it. He looked at the name of the boat: *Olivia Svendsen.* There was a haze above the surface of the water as high up as pillars of the bridge, through it *Olivia's* red funnel-marking shone like a wax seal on a faded letter, and gave the impression that she was a lusty woman. As he turned round to take a farewell look at the old borough of Christianshavn, the golden spire of Our Saviour's Church suddenly glinted in the sun like a fish leaping in opaque water.

While he waited Ib's thoughts were still with Petra. He had known, what the girl could not guess: that this meeting of theirs was the last. In itself it was short, for she had had to go to church with her mother in the morning; they had sat together in that small apartment of his which was their usual meeting place, he on the bed and she on the chair, talking about things. It seemed to him that in the course of this talk he had seen Petra's face for the first time, for till now he had been, like Professor Sivertsen himself, mainly fascinated by the beauty of her body. Her coarse young face, with its thick lips and eyebrows, today had revealed a new side of her being to him; she looked, he thought, like a brent goose of the fields of Ballegaard. It was as if he had been talking not to a beautiful woman but to a young man, his friend, to whom he might confide his plans, his unhappy love and even his feeling of uneasiness about a mistress from whom he received more than he gave back. They had not, though, talked about any concerns of his, but had been discussing problems of Petra's life, her mother's tyranny and a project of hers to learn millinery, and, except for his regret at not being able to beg Adelaide or Drude to recommend his sweetheart to the milliner who made their own hats, the meeting had been pleasant. He had left Petra with a relief akin to that of the Copenhagen girls who had set away their galoshes. "If only," he reflected, "one might have a guarantee that each rendezvous was the last, one might keep up a love affair almost forever."

On his return to the barracks he was handed a letter and informed that it had been brought an hour ago by a footman in the Galen livery. It ran:

Dear Ib,

I want you to come to Aunt Nathalie's house at four o'clock this afternoon. Aunt Nathalie will not be in, nor Oline either, so I am enclosing the front-door key, and you will let yourself in. You must be sure to come. Good-bye, my dear Ib. Your sister,

Drude.

Now this short note might strike a sober-minded reader as in more than one way somewhat out of the ordinary. For why would Drude, whom one must suppose to be inside Aunt Nathalie's house and in a position to open the door to him, enclose the key to it in her letter? The reason for the arrangement, which was Adelaide's reluctance to sit waiting in an empty house, the letter did not give. Why, next, did not Drude, in inviting Ib to Aunt Nathalie's house, state that she herself meant to come there? The explanation of the evasion was that Drude was an honest girl, and, even in an intrigue like the present, averse to telling a direct lie. And was there not, lastly, an incongruity in style between the laconic note itself and its tender, pathetic farewell greeting? These peculiarities, however, with the three young people involved in the matter passed unnoticed, since they were none of them sober-minded and to all of them, at the moment, all things were out of the ordinary.

It had not often happened in the life of the brother and sister that Drude had asked Ib for advice or help; it did not occur to him to disobey.

So he brought the key with him and let himself into the

house in Rosenvænget even a while before four. It might be a good thing to sit in Aunt Nathalie's room waiting for Drude. The blinds were down, for the old lady was afraid of her covers fading in the sun, but the familiar smell of ancient books, hyacinths and the dog basket, the inhabitant of which was out with old Oline, received him as mildly and vivaciously as if it had been Aunt Nathalie herself kissing him on both cheeks. He pulled up the blinds, lighted a cigar and sat down. As he looked around the rooms it was brought home to him that they were furnished not so much with tangible objects as with the emotional experiences of an old maid's long life: girlhood friendships, travels to Germany and Rome, two wars, possibly a virginal heartache of long ago. The things began to speak to him. "Why," they asked, "have you and all your brothers and sisters run away from rooms furnished by the heart to halls filled with objects purchased in foreign cities, designed and manufactured after the taste of great foreign people, according to the taste of the Empress of France?" He thought for a long time of his home at Ballegaard, in which things had likewise grown up on their own.

Ib was perhaps a bit clairvoyant this afternoon. As he tried to explain matters to Aunt Nathalie's armchairs, potted plants and sofa cushions, he viewed distant things and events with great lucidity. First, that glittering and dazzling Second Empire of France of which he had seen a glimpse when two years ago he had been on a visit to France with Leopold. The great, terrible downfall of it was to come; it was not far away; he was, he surmised, to witness it with his own eyes. Like avalanches in a mountain landslide, one thundering down on the heels of the other, the coming falls of other radiant worlds began to echo around him. The golden world of Russia, that had held his brother captive, would fall too, and it would look like the end of time. Other, later glories would follow it. The while the quiet world of simple, innocent human hearts might still remain. "Why, then," he repeated the question put to him, "have we been running away from safe things, which wished us well, to golden halls in which we were risking our peace of heart?" He sat on for a time, smoking his cigar. "You see," he answered, "it could not be helped; we had to go. Those golden halls did not attract my brothers and sisters or me myself, on account of their luxury and comfort, their food and wine and soft beds. For you know that we are none of us soft-skinned, and poverty to us holds nothing at all frightening. We have been drawn to the world of splendor—irresistibly like moths to the flame— not because it was rich, but because its riches were boundless. The quality of boundlessness in any sphere would have drawn us in the same manner."

As still Drude did not come he walked from the sitting room into the small study beside it, which during the season served as Drude's private salon. By the window stood a lady's escritoire with a number of old friends, framed and under glass, upon its shelves. He himself was there, a grave boy of twelve with his first gun. Drude and Adelaide were there, lanky lasses of twelve and thirteen, twined together, with their hair down their backs. As again he set away the picture, his eyes fell on a sheet of paper in Leopold's handwriting. It was half covered by a book, as if Drude had been leaving to chance whether he should catch sight of it or not. He let his gaze run over that well-known, ever-welcome hand until it was caught by five lines of a verse:

> "Qui les saura, mes secrètes amours?
> Je me ris des soupçons, je me ris des discours,
> Quoique l'on parle et que l'on cause.
> Nul ne les saura, mes secrètes amours,
> Que celle qui les cause."

He recognized it; it was an old French poem that he himself had struck upon in an ancient book of poetry; it was supposed to have been written by the King of France to a maid-of-honor, Mademoiselle de la Vallière. He had scratched it, with the diamond of the ring that Leopold was presenting to

Mademoiselle Fifi, upon a pane of Leopold's dressing room, and his cousin, who was no great reader of poetry, had been attracted by it and had questioned him about it. Why, now, had he taken it up, and what use was he making of it? Ib's proprietorship in the verse seemed to give him a right to read the letter through.

It was a love letter, preparing an elopement. He read the burning words of longing, the vows and the ecstatic terms of adoration. "As I dare not send my own carriage, the droshky will be waiting for you by Østerport. The coachman is well known to me and loyal. Be not afraid, my wild rose, he will drive you safely to the place where he who loves you most in the world is waiting for you." He turned the letter over and gazed at the first line and then at the signature. The letter was to Drude from Leopold.

He grew a little giddy in the reading; he had to read the whole note over again. This time he was well aware that he was committing a breach of the law of honesty, but the depth of dishonesty revealed justified his action. He read it all through for a third time. Then he became very pale.

Ib was in uniform, his sword by his side. It could not be but that he must feel and reason like an officer. Even before he had arranged his ideas about the extent and the consequences of the treachery, his hand went to his sword hilt, and his whole being cried out for revenge, for blood. It was a good thing that one had a sword, sharp-edged, within reach of hand. It was a good thing that one could kill, and kill soon, at once. His own blood mounted to his head, behind his eyes; Aunt Nathalie's bookshelves, embroidered cushions and hyacinths all turned a deep scarlet.

A number of old tales of seduction, at which he and Leopold had laughed between them, came back to him. The two cousins had been hunting together in this field as in others, and had seen fair women as the noblest game of all. But the hunting of a friend's sister, the purest and proudest maiden in the country, was no longer a gay, gallant venture, but black and base treason. The hunting of her in words borrowed from that friend himself was a breach of sworn brotherhood.

He once more took up the letter—which by now was scarlet, like the room itself—and looked at the date. It had been written on the previous day. Thus the hour of the flight, which in the letter was "tomorrow afternoon at six," was in reality today, within two hours. Within an hour the droshky would be waiting by Østerport; if he went there he would find it. He would force the coachman to drive it to its destination, wherever that would be; in less than three hours Leopold would find himself face to face with the revenger. He should be forced to draw then, and Ib was a fine swordsman. It was a good thing to know that within two hours the world would have been cleansed of a traitor. Only the waiting time was long; how was he to make it pass? He went to the window, in need of the sight of open air.

By and by, in self-preservation his mind turned from the hideous and contemptible in search of something pure and good. He thought of Drude.

He and she had always been such friends. It could not be that she had written her note to him, to the barracks, just in order to get him out of her way. Or if it was so, what power must not her lover, and her passion for him, have over her! He knew that power well himself; he grieved for his sister's sake, and his thoughts again fled from his theme. Then after a long time he found himself wondering deeply at the fact that this sister, up till now so close to him, a second self, was today in a position so different from his own.

"Women," he reflected, "have been strangely favored in life. A young girl, solely by abandoning her honor, will be sure to find herself, even within the next hour, in the arms of the beloved."

As in his mind he pronounced the word "arms," and again the words "arms of the beloved," his course of thought switched. Adelaide's cool, slender arms, springing from the white rounded shoulders and flowing into the graceful delta of ten rosy fingertips. Smooth arms, with a silky swirl at the elbow, yet strong enough to sweep along and bear down the strongest of swimmers. "In the arms of the beloved."

His mind felt its way as in the dark, step by step, itself wondering at the places to which it was taken. Yes, he might be in time to save his sister and kill the offender. He might be in time to prevent that embrace from which his thoughts had shrunk. To which, even while he was standing here immovable by the window, the thoughts of the lovers were turned, he himself best knew with what yearning and transport and trembling. She would never find herself in the arms of the beloved.

And what, then, would he have done for his fair sister? She would be left for the remaining years of her life—Drude—with the one remembrance: that there was nothing to remember.

Ib was no moralist; very rarely in his life had he given thought to the problems of guilt or innocence. His indignation and abhorrence at the reading of Leopold's letter a quarter of an hour ago had been a new experience, surprising to himself. It now came upon him that he had come near to committing what is called a sin. That he had been, and that he was still, in danger of committing a sin against a higher law than that broken by Leopold. He found that he could not name this supreme law, but he knew that it was there, and must be obeyed.

When he had got so far, his hand let go of the sword hilt.

The bell of the street door rang. Still in his own thoughts he went out into the small dim hall to open the door to Kirstine, Adelaide's maid, in a black shawl and a small black bonnet. She would, he reflected, have come with a message from Adelaide to Drude, and he would have to find, and to give her, an explanation of Drude's absence. Ib was courteous to all women. He held open the door to her, so that she might deliver her message in the sitting room, then closed it behind her. And it was Adelaide.

The late afternoon sun for a moment came out in the dim sky. In its rays he saw her mouth and shoulders close to him.

Kirstine's small black bonnet with its black strings, a chambermaid's bonnet, looked queer upon Adelaide's head. If Adelaide herself had not felt the significance of the situation so deeply, upon her entrance into the room she would have undone the strings and laid the bonnet on the table. Ib understood the negative gesture; the cataclysmic character of Adelaide's appearance in Aunt Nathalie's house was finally affirmed by the fact that she was looking at him, and speaking to him, beneath Kirstine's hat.

He had not thought that he should see her again; now he saw her again. For the first time this winter he saw her and was, without any confirming testimony from other people, convinced of her absolute and indisputable reality. And together with this certainty there came upon him another, profounder conviction of the strangest kind: that on her coming here all things had—like a river which at last falls into the sea—arrived at their end and aim, and that this meeting of theirs was to last forever. All the same, since that universal solution had been brought about by her, he would have to let her speak first.

She put up Kirstine's veil, looked him in the face and said: "I have come to beg you to forgive me."

It was an unexpected opening and seemed an extraordinary thing for her to say, but she would know best. He answered: "That was good of you."

"To beg you to forgive me," she said, "for making you speak to me in such a way. I did not know that the things I made you say to me were true."

He very rarely needed any explanations from her; he knew of what she was talking. He said: "Yes, they were true."

"I did not know," she repeated.

"It is of no consequence," he said.

"I have been thinking about it since," said she. "I have been thinking that the best way would be to have you say the same things over again, now that I know them to be true."

"That I came to say good-bye?" he said. "Yes, it was true, I came yesterday, to say good-bye."

"No, not that," said she. "The first thing you said."

"That I love you?" he said.

"Yes," said she.

"I love you," he said.

There was a short silence; things grew in it.

"Do you want these words spoken for the third time?" he asked her. "They have been spoken a hundred times, a thousand times. Just now I wonder whether they are not the only words I have ever spoken."

"Tell me more about it," she said. "Speak to me, Ib, now that I know that you speak the truth."

She pressed him to speak for a particular reason. She had never quite believed in the declarations of love that young men had made her. It was natural, she knew, that they should love her, yet she had never been altogether convinced that they did. The declarations, too, in themselves had been maladroit and insipid compared to those that one read in verse or heard in songs. Now with Ib it would be different. He had words of his own, much like those of verse and songs. And to know for certain that she was loved as she ought to be would make a difference in her life. All the difference.

"What will I tell you, Adelaide?" he again asked her, and laughed a little, lowly and gently. The laughter to her was not quite that of a human being, but more like a sound you will hear in the woods, without knowing where it comes from or whether it is the cooing of a wood pigeon or a rustle in the tree crowns. "I am not good at finding words. Neither you or I are good at finding words, are we? And it is nothing to speak of, either. All fine, sweet things in the world have been either signals of Adelaide's arrival: Adelaide is coming—or otherwise echoes of Adelaide's presence: she has passed here. Is that any good to you?

"Once," he went on slowly, "you had a pale-blue frock. I sailed on the bay on a summer day, and there was a gust, the boat careened, and I thought that I was going down. The water was pale blue, I thought: now Adelaide is closing over me.

"Or which are the words you want to have repeated for a third time? You ordered me yesterday to tell you that in the last moment of my life I shall thank you because you existed and were so lovely. Hear it, then, for the third time, although this is not the last moment of my life. I thank you, Adelaide, because you exist and are so lovely. And are so lovely."

If now the two young people had gone on with a repetition of yesterday's dialogue in the blue boudoir until they had come to the kiss, their problem would have solved itself, and no further choice would have been left them. The kiss was in the boy's mind, unnamed but very near, the seal upon the everlasting meeting.

Undoubtedly the girl had it in her mind too; only she was not at all aware of it being there, and it was still a little away, a little ahead. She was not a tender nature and not given to caresses; she had come here to speak and was collecting her whole being on speaking.

"Nobody knows that I am here," she said.

He did not answer her, but his face answered her.

"I could come here again," she said in the same way. "And nobody would know."

For a second her total and absolute ignorance of the coarser facts of life, which was the *fine fleur* of her education and upbringing—as of the education and upbringing of all noble young girls of her day—and had been obtained with such tenacity of purpose and such continuous watchfulness as later ages cannot imagine or believe, awakened in him the reverence which was the highest product of the education of all noble young men. In the light of her dovelike purity, his own past looked somewhat sordid; he would have to turn away his gaze from it. It was a paradoxical fact that she should stand so high above him, and that yet the responsibility in the situation should lie with him. He knew well enough what, according to the code of orthodox morality, he ought to say to her. "Adelaide," he should say, "it is not right that you have come here; it is not right that nobody should know you to be here. Let me take you home." But orthodox morality had become a thing of a vanished past. The law sacred to his surroundings and hers, to their community and their era sank below the horizon; the people who loved them and trusted them and on whom they were dependent sank and were gone. Here at last were Ib and Adelaide, alone in the universe. The young rich blood within his veins and hers rose like a wave to fling them together.

And then, just then, at the moment when he had quashed all outside laws, the law of his own being spoke out and passed sentence on him.

He was not well read, and his mind was not schooled in abstraction. He could never have formulated in thoughts or in words the theory: that tragedy will allow its young maiden to sacrifice her honor to her love and with quiet eyes will consent to the ruin of Gretchen, Ophelia and Héloise. He did not guess that it was in obedience to the law of tragedy that less than an hour ago he himself had consented to the ruin of his sister. No more could he have formulated in thoughts or in words the theory that tragedy forbids its young man to do the same thing.

To be a great young lady's secret lover. To meet her in the ballrooms, in the full light of their chandeliers, and receive a furtive smile, a smile in a mirror, in remembrance of a last secret meeting. *Billets doux* written with trembling hands and sent off clandestinely by the hands of bribed servants. The trembling of her young body in his arms with the fear of discovery. His own, mean smile of triumph at the rivals dancing with her and openly wooing the legitimate possession of her.

All these things, with the future that together they would make up for him, passed before his mind. He did not call them forth, they came on their own, one by one, and one by one he inspected them, earnestly, without bias. In the end his situation, unexpectedly, also seemed to have got a voice, it spoke to him, quoting a line from a play which a year ago he had seen with Leopold at the Comédie Française:

> *"Je m'appelle Ruy Blas, et je suis un laquais."*

Slowly, slowly the blood with which his face had flamed toward hers again sank back until his eyes themselves faded away.

"No, Adelaide," he said, "I would rather die."

One uses the phrase, in everyday life, in a light, trivial or jesting way, one says: "I would rather die than go to bed with that woman." Here the words fell more heavily, in the way in which an axe falls. They were to be taken literally; they expressed a young man's delicate choice on life and death.

She knew him too well to be in danger of misunderstanding him; it was the everyday conception of the phrase which to her—had anybody tried to make her accept it—would have seemed senseless. These words, which came straight from his heart with less intervention of will or reason perhaps than any he had spoken till now, went straight to hers, through it even, as it is said that a very keen, thin instrument may pierce a heart without the victim sensing it. To her herself it felt as if she had been handed an object much too heavy to hold, with no place within reach in which to set it. Till today things had happened to her as she had expected them, or most often a little more happily. She let her eyes wander round the room, vaguely, wildly. Till now there had always been in a room somebody eager to uphold and comfort her. Here there was none such.

As she did not speak or move he repeated his phrase: "I would rather die."

She looked at him. At this one, conclusive moment she felt that if she could but speak one word or make one movement toward him she might still defeat him. But she could not speak a word or make a movement.

So, after a silence, the fair Adelaide spoke for the last time to her friend and lover.

"You," she said slowly. "And I."

Ib was to keep these words in his mind all his life. But they had, there, a mysterious quality to him: they evaded definition, when looked at straightly they changed and vanished. As, in Aunt Nathalie's room, he heard them for this first time, they were a verdict, the placing of her and him with the unbridgeable distance between them. At a later time, when he thought them over, there was, surprisingly, in the word of "You," a note of compassion and in the word of "I" a plaintive note, like the lament of a child. In Jutland, when in rainy spring nights the complaint of the curlew is heard, first from one side and then from another, the peasants will tell you that this is the dialogue of two dead lovers who long ago have forfeited their happiness and are now wailingly reproaching each other with their loss. There were hours in which Adelaide sang to Ib in the voice of the curlew. In the end, at that moment in which he was to thank her for having existed, the words took on the ring of a magic spell, uniting her and him for eternity.

She had no more to do here; so she walked away.

She passed him with her head high, Kirstine's bonnet like a tiara on it, and he could not know that beneath the folds of Kirstine's skirt her knees were failing her. As he held open the street door to her, the freshness of the spring afternoon struck them both, as if till now they had never been out of a room. She walked away, down the street, and he felt it somehow not right that he should be standing there, watching her slim, straight back moving away. He went in.

Back in the house, going from the sitting room into the study, he once more came upon Leopold's letter—he did not remember having seen it before—took it up and read it but could not make the words make sense.

The echo of his own voice came back to him: I would rather die. "Yes, I said that," he told himself. "I should not go about here now, wondering how it is that I am dead." In the end he said to himself: "I shall go and see Drude."

Now, while Ib lingered in the house of Rosenvænget—for a few minutes in a dead silence, in which no sound could break, then again, for a few minutes, with the laughing and shouting of children playing pitch-and-toss on the pavement outside very clear to his ears—in Copenhagen streets a mighty theme was being played out with full orchestration: Adelaide's *Liebesflucht*.

Till today she had not walked alone in a street. On her way to Rosenvænget the walking had been an adventure and the unknown people meeting or passing her at such ludicrously close distance strangely important. On her way back she saw none of them.

While all the time walking exceedingly slowly, like an old woman, she herself believed that she was storming forth in a wild and mad flight. A flight in very truth mad and contrary to nature, since she was, at breathless speed, running away from the one place in the world where she craved to be, like a piece of iron flung off by the magnet itself. Or she was, at breathless speed, climbing to zenith and darkening the sun, a mighty thunderstorm mounting against the wind.

When she had walked about a hundred steps, all the scattered sensations of her mind consolidated into a furious wrath. She had been insulted, and she must be revenged. Or, if she was not revenged, she must die. Her thoughts ran in a course parallel to that of Ib's thoughts an hour ago, when he had been reading the letter from her brother to his sister. She called on that brother to bring about reparation for the deadly affront she had suffered; she called on her father and the young men who adored her. She must have the offender vanish from the world, or how could she possibly live on in it? She cried out for blood, as Ib had done, and, like to Aunt Nathalie's rooms to his eyes, the street in front of her, with its droshkies and its tired, stiff-legged horses, took on a scarlet hue.

Her indignation and anger were felt physically, as an unbearable pain in the abdomen. The center of her fair body, from which sweet content should have flowed into all her limbs, was clenched like a fist, and she bent double under the pangs like a dry leaf crumbling in the frost, and with all her strength had to hold back a long cry—*"Es schwindelt mir, mir brennt mein Eingeweide!"*

After a further hundred steps, Ib's face suddenly mounted before her as she had seen it when they had taken leave of each other. At that the suffering changed place and character. In a big leap it mounted to her breast, constricting her heart and sending out tentacles into her shoulders and arms, to her elbows and wrists and to her little hands.

That even more terrible pain was no longer anger or thirst for revenge, but had been turned into pity of the friend she had left. Ib must be consoled and comforted, or if he could not be consoled and comforted, she must die.

For Ib was good; he was all that was good in the world, gentle, soothing, strong and deep. It was she, it was Adelaide who was hard and sharp as a knife; it was she who must vanish from the world, in order that good things might still exist in it. Or it must be proved, if that was still possible, that she was not as hard, sharp and cold as she looked. For this task it was no good calling on the men of her name, or her admirers—to whom or to what, then, would she call for help? The present being so dark and evil, she turned to the past. But the past, the door to it once opened, ran in upon her to crush her in a hundred pictures.

She kept Ib company in the autumn battues, in a multicolored beechwood, and watched him bringing down the

glowing birds from the clear frosty air. Ib, a boy of fifteen,
doctored the paw of her dog. Ib, out with her and Leopold
to find wild raspberries in the wood, had stolen a bottle of
port from the cellar and got tight on it, first wildly dancing
and singing on the sward, and at last falling asleep, in the
hot afternoon, in the raspberry shrub. Ib read *The Odyssey*
to her, so deeply seized that he made her feel the vicissitudes
of Odysseus with a palpitating heart.

One summer evening came out of the past particularly
clearly. Ib had got her father's permission to shoot a roebuck
in the meadow, and she had sneaked from the castle to go
with him. In the meadow the long grass was heavy with dew;
soon her shoes and stockings, and her white petticoats up to
the knee, had been drenched. While they waited down here,
he pointed out to her the new moon, sitting like a thin silver
sickle in the evening sky, and this sky's bath of roses seemed
reflected in the roseate and pale-purple flowering grasses
round them as in a mirror. Ib had told her the names of the
grasses: velvet grass, quaking grass, meadow foxtail, bird
grass, onion couch. She had been very near a mystic experience then; never before had she come so close to being made
one with the earth and the sky, the trees and the moon. Yet
the miracle had not been altogether fulfilled, and now she
knew why: she ought to have kissed Ib.

She looked in front of her as she walked, and there was
nothing there but the flat, hard pavement of the streets. That
street now was the picture of her own path in life. Flat and
hard, what people name a smooth path, a walk on lifeless
ground: polished floors, marble stairs, new pavements of new
cities. From now she would have to follow her road; she
would make a great match and be surrounded with lifeless,
smooth and hard things: gold and silver, diamonds and crys-
tal. Ib's path in life from now would be rough. In the
meadow, in the long velvet grass, bird grass and onion couch
the walking was rough, in the muddy field roads the hoofs of
one's horse splashed mire and water about, and in the winter

woods the dead rustling leaves, with hoarfrost on them, through which one had to wade, lay knee-high. But the things round him would belong to the earth and would not have been made by flat, smooth and hard people. The mold in the world was left with Ib, upon his dirty boy's hands that were sticky with fish scales as he took the trout from the hook and handed it to her, that were red with the juice of wild blackberries or stained with blood and fouling.

Once more the pain in her body mounted. For a few moments it squeezed her throat so that she did really believe that she was going to die; then it went up still higher and settled behind her eyes. It was no longer her own grief only or Ib's grief; it was the sadness of life itself and of all living things. It pressed against her eyelids; it filled her with tears like a vessel overflowing. If she did not weep, she must die.

The agonizing ache at the back of her nose brought to her recollections of Ib's remarkable sense of smell, keen like the sense of smell of a rare, trained dog. In their wanderings he would suddenly stand still, sniffing the air, wrinkle his nose and pass on to her its discoveries of fungi in the undergrowth not far away. At this sorry moment, in the street, it came upon her with deadly certainty, as the culmination of bereavement and forlornness: "I have lost my sense of smell! The long, long row of years lying before me will be scentless. During all of them I shall walk in vain in the lime avenues at home, or past the stock beds and the overripe strawberry beds. I shall come into the stable to feed sweet-smelling Khamar with sweet-smelling black bread, and none of them will have anything to tell me!"

She clung to the idea of smell like a drowning person to a raft for two reasons. First because she was holding on to memory as to the one thing still left to her, and among the five senses the sense of smell is the most loyal servant to memory, and will carry the past straight to the heart. "*Le nez,*" it has been said, "*c'est la memoire.*" Secondly, because the scents and smells of this world cannot be described in words, but do evade the supremacy of language, their realm in human nature lies outside that of speech or writing. And she did in this hour hate and fear words beyond all other things.

If Professor Sivertsen had been present, who taught her to paint in water color and who was such an expert on tragedy and on noses, he would have said to her:

"You imagine, poor child, that you are bewailing your sense of smell, and that if you do not get it back you must die. For you are an unlearned girl—like all girls of your class—and cannot know that you are in reality grieving because tragedy has gone out of your life. You have left tragedy with your friend, in the room of Rosenvænget, and you yourself, upon a flat, smooth path of life, have been handed over to comedy, to the drawing-room play or possibly to the operetta. You are in reality at this hour feeling that if you cannot shed tears—the last tears of your life—over the loss of tragedy, you must die. But weep you, Adelaide, poor simple child, over the loss of your nose."

But where, but in what place could Adelaide weep? If she gave course to her tears in the street the passers-by would turn, alarmed at the sight, would question her and might even possibly touch her, and the idea of people behaving in such a manner to a girl lamenting her sense of smell was terrible. If she succeeded in forcing back her tears until she was once more in her own room—which was hardly possible, for they were by now burning her brain—Kirstine, probably already nervous about the situation, would be frightened and would notify her mother, and her mother would be frightened and would send for the family doctor, and they would all of them question her and lay their hands on her shoulders and cheeks.

This, then, was what the world was like: there was no place in it for the people who must weep. The people who wanted to eat or drink would find, not far away, a place in which to eat and drink. The people who wanted to dance would find,

she knew, not far away a place in which to dance. Those
who wanted to buy a new hat would find, at least tomorrow
morning when the shops opened, a place wherein to buy it.
But in all Copenhagen there was not a single place in which
a human being could weep. The fact, when evident, to her
meant death. For if she could not weep she must die.

As she was thus walking on, alone in all the world, her
course took her past a churchyard which she had not noticed
on her way out. She was proceeding so slowly that each
step was almost a halt; as she found herself outside the
churchyard gate she stood still altogether, and thought matters over, then walked in.

She had never before given much thought to churchyards.
They were dreary places with dead people under the surface,
stones and tablets on them, and railings and hedges fencing
them in. In her day ladies did not attend funerals, and most
of her relations had their family vaults near their houses.
She did not remember ever to have set foot in a town churchyard. Now, surprisingly, this unknown churchyard of Copenhagen received her in silent understanding and compassion;
even at the moment she came through the gate, it seemed to
put its arms around her. Tears began to drip from the lashes
of her half-closed eyes; soon, soon she might allow them to
flow without restraint.

Since the day was Sunday, people were still walking among
the graves or attending to them, clearing away the evergreen
of winter and raking round the spring shoots, or laying
down wreaths. Everybody here was in black, like Adelaide
herself. A woman in widow's weeds who had been weeping, at the gate was drying her last tears off with her handkerchief, so that Adelaide remembered that she too had a
handkerchief. Her tears at this came quicker, but she dared
not yet let out any sound. She walked on at random, gazing
right and left to find an old grave to sit down on, since she
was afraid to choose a grave belonging to other people, who
might find her there. At length she caught sight of a grave

which to her looked altogether forgotten, grass-grown, without a flower on it, with a headstone and an iron stool. She went in there, sat down on the seat and burst into tears. So there was after all some kind of relief and happiness in the world, and she was fortunate to have found the place of it.

She was so filled with gratitude at the fact, that after a while she let herself glide from the seat down on the grass, pressed her young shoulder and her soft cheek against the hard surface of the stone and sobbed loudly and wildly. She had carried a heavy load of sorrows with her a long way—Ib and his unhappiness, her own joyless future and the sad condition of the world; she was laying them down now, at the foot of this stone, in the keeping of a friend.

A few more women in black passed her on their way out, since the churchyard would soon be closed up; when they heard her weeping they lowered their voices a little. Some children accompanying them stopped and looked at her, but were reprimanded by their mothers and ran on.

After a long time a very old gentleman came along the path, and as he passed her stone and caught sight of her crouching against it stopped for a moment. She grew deadly afraid that he might know who she was. Then she reflected that he would be more likely to know the grave, that he might even have known the person buried in it. He might be wondering that a young woman should be weeping so desperately there.

This was the last time that Adelaide ever wept. At her mother's death, which to her was a deep grief, she shed no tear. An old relation, who had come over to Jutland for the funeral, then said: "Adelaide has always been a curious girl. I do not remember that she has ever wept, even as a child." The old lady's memory was deceiving her; Adelaide like other girls had wept when thwarted. But to the girl herself the Sunday of this tale drew a dividing line in her existence. Later on she would think of her youth, up to the age of nineteen, as of the time when she had wept.

She sat on the grave for a long time, resting in the one kind of happiness still possible to her: avowing to the whole world that she was a human being who had lost all.

In the end she felt that she was getting cold and that her eyes were running dry. She took up her handkerchief and wiped off her last tears, as the lady by the gate had done. As she rose from the ground she turned toward the stone in order to get to know, before she left the place to which she would never come back, at whose bosom she had been weeping. There was still enough of the afternoon light for her to read the inscription:

Here lie the remains of

JONAS ANDERSEN TODE

Sea Captain
who died on December 31, 1815
born March 25, 1740
Loyal to his King and Country he sailed his ship steadily
from coast to coast. Faithful in friendship, a helper of the
afflicted, steadfast in adversity.
Through Thy precepts I get understanding.
Ps. 119

King Christian VII of Denmark (1749-1808)—son of the much-beloved Louise, daughter of George II of England, and married, at the age of seventeen, to fifteen-year-old Caroline Mathilde, sister of George III—as a boy gave promise of capacity and talent, but was both physically and mentally degenerate and did further ruin his health by debauch. At his accession to the throne, in 1766, he declared to his tutors and ministers that he would now "rage" for a year; in this task he was assisted by his mistress Katrine, a former prostitute. A few years later his mind gave way altogether, and he lived for the rest of his life almost entirely shut off from the world.

Johannes Ewald (1743-1781), now acknowledged Denmark's greatest lyrical poet, was the son of a pietistic clergyman, but at the age of sixteen ran away from home to try his luck as a drummer and soldier in the Seven Years' War, and later for a while led the life of a Bohemian and "cavalier" in Copenhagen. From 1773 to 1776, ill and destitute, he lived as a lodger at the inn at Rungsted, the present Rungstedlund, and there wrote some of his finest poetry.

CONVERSE AT NIGHT IN COPENHAGEN

It rained in Copenhagen on a November night of the year 1767. The moon was up, and a good way gone in its second quarter; from time to time, when the rain made a short pause, as if between two verses of an endlessly long song, its pale, distressful, backward-flung mask came in sight high up in the sky, behind layer upon layer of shifting, verdigris-green mists. Then the rain tuned up again, the moon-mask withdrew into the heavens, and only the street lights and a window here and there in the dark maze below revealed themselves, like phosphoric jellyfish on the bottom of the sea.

There was still some scanty night traffic in the streets. A few steady-going sailing vessels kept their course for home, and unruly privateers and buccaneers beat up against the wind on doubtful voyages between black rock walls down which the moisture streamed. A sedan chair was hailed, took up its load, and swayed on upon its way to some unknown goal in the town and the night. A coach with heavy, gilt ornaments and winking lamps, with coachman on box, lackeys behind and precious contents, came from an assembly, the wheels squirted rain water and street mire in all directions, and the high-stepping horses' hoofs struck long sparks from the cobblestones.

In the small streets and alleys Copenhagen night life was still in high spirits. From them was wafted music and song, with a steady accompaniment of rowdy merriment and scuffle.

Suddenly the noise increased; a din burst out like a conflagration. There was shouting of many voices, smashed windowpanes clinked on the cobbles, and heavy objects, hurled from the first or second story, boomed and banged against them. Roars and bellows of laughter were hurled together in a whirlpool, and from the midst of it cascades of women's squeals rose high in the air.

Two Copenhagen burghers, one long and thin, the other a short figure with a heavy belly—the collars of their greatcoats turned up, their hats rammed down over their ears, and a servant with a lantern on a pole preceding them—came to a halt a little way down an alley. The rain had made them take this short cut home, and they had fallen into talk about ships going round the Cape of Good Hope with spices for Copenhagen, until they seemed to draw a tiny sweet wake of cinnamon and vanilla through the fluctuating swell of the alley's reek. As the hubbub in front of them grew, and the shouting came straight toward them, they made their man with the lantern halt, spied thoughtfully at a house, the door of which stood open, and round which a crowd of people thronged and broke, and grew long in the face, and in the limbs, at the sight. But they said not a word.

For it was not certain that the offense going on over there

was an ordinary night riot, against which one could call upon the help of law and order and the wrath of the Lord. Nay, it might quite possibly be exactly the opposite: their own shame and sorrow. The gang in the alley was not canaille; fine gentlemen from the court were raging here. It was not impossible, it was even credible, that the land's young King himself, a child in years, was running at the head of them.

Aye, he was a child in years, and it was told that he had been much too strictly kept in his boyhood, even ill-treated by his tutor, old Count Ditlev Reventlow, so that the mothers of Denmark had wept over the motherless boy. Surely a loyal people might shut their eyes to a youthful king's excesses. But he had got his young, pink and white English Queen up at his palace; within two months, under God's will, she would be delivered of a crown prince to both of his father's hereditary kingdoms. And here he was, kicking up an uproar in the dark, fuddled and mad with wine, assisting his mistress in wiping off old scores of hers against other women of the profession. What bad people were not the King's servants and favorites—the counts, Masters of the Horse and King's Counsels—alluring the young Anointed of the Lord, a beloved mother's son, into evil ways! The two Copenhageners remembered, their feet growing cold where they stood, a story told in town, of how, recently and in a night like this, the King by the grace of God in a hand-to-hand tussle with the night watchmen had got himself a black eye, and in revenge had carried back to his palace the trophy of a spiked mace. What would they be thinking, now, in foreign kingdoms and principalities, of the Majesty of Denmark and Norway? And as to his own people, who for many hundred years had prided themselves upon their loyalty to the King and his house, how might they now, with unbroken hearts, submit themselves to so great a distress?

Still they said not a word; they swallowed down their own and their country's grief in silence. With them, in any case, it would be preserved as in a grave.

The long masterful shrill of a watchman's whistle cut through the noise. The tumult exploded and in a few minutes burst asunder in all directions. Shouts and screams, the crash of a heavy door banging to and the whirl of quick-running feet followed the explosion. The light from a window for an instant caught the rosy lining of a cloak and caressed a hurrying turquoise-colored silk ribbon; immediately after the street lights glimmered on the braid of a naval officer's uniform which seemed to enclose very round young forms. A laughing French exclamation was flung over a retreating shoulder, and a handful of biting, bitter Danish oaths were hurled back in retaliation. Then colors and voices washed away through the side streets, and the adventure was over. Only a few heavy watchman's cloaks were outlined against the luminous mist round the open street doors.

The two burghers set off again, turning their steps round the first corner and their minds back to happier fairways and the price of pepper and nutmeg. The thin twirl of fragrance behind them was seasoned with an odor of resigned sanctity.

A very young man, a small frail figure in a large cloak, during the disturbance had become separated from his companions, and had now lost himself in row upon row of backyards, passages and steps. He gazed round him, ran on, gazed round him again, and at last was stuck on the topmost landing of a steep, narrow, moldering stairway. Here he stopped, breathless after his ascent, and remained standing, with the slim person pressed into a corner. When he had regained his breath a little, his hands moved to his throat to loosen the clasp of his cloak. He held a naked rapier in his hand, the sheath was gone, and the weapon was in his way. He put it down, and reeled a little as he did so. But still he could not get the clasp undone, and now had to fumble for a while with his stretched-out fingers on the filthy floor before he again got hold of the rapier's hilt. When once more he had it in his hand, he made a few passes with the blade straight forward in the air. All the time he was as silent as a fish; not a cry, not an oath, no sound whatever came from him.

But in the dark, in the silent house, his eyes stood wide open. He did not know—and he felt that in this spot he could not possibly come to know—whether his mad run was a superb joke, a game of puss-in-the-corner up and down through the houses, or whether it was a flight, deadly danger, the Evil One himself out after him. There was no one to tell him whether next moment he would be hailed and embraced by flushed, laughing friends, or whether a relentless hand, dreaded in dreams as in reality, would suddenly descend upon him. He was alone.

He was alone, and he did not remember ever having been alone in his life before. The consciousness of his complete isolation came upon him slowly and powerfully; at first he was a bit giddy or seasick with it, then it lifted him up like a wave. It grew to be a great and just revenge on all who till now had surrounded him, a triumph—at last, at last the promised apotheosis! He held onto the idea fanatically. Here, in the dark, he became a statue of himself, one single piece of pure hard marble, invulnerable and imperishable. But after a while he began to shake until the teeth chattered in his mouth.

A little higher up, where the stairs ended, a light shone out beneath a door. The narrow, clear streak of fire which went up and down and multiplied itself must mean something. Slowly he came to the conclusion that behind this door and within that light there would be someone. But who was in there? There were many hundred faces in the dark city around him. There were people, he remembered having been told, who starved and were set on plundering, people who murdered, people who gave themselves up to secret witchcraft. Phantoms from old nightmares came upon him, and it was possible, indeed probable, that they were living just here, where he himself had never been.

Noises, too, now entered his sphere of consciousness: behind the door a woman was crying, and a young man was comforting her. All at once—surprisingly sure and dignified, and avoiding the while to put his hand on the greasy banister —he mounted the last steps, put two fingers on the door handle, and pressed it down. The door was not locked; it opened.

The room he entered was small, peat-brown in the corners, because only lit by a tallow-dip on the table, but with a play of live colors as far as the dip's power reached. Beside the candle stood a clear brandy flask and a couple of glasses. Apart from the table and a three-legged wooden chair next to it, there were in the room an old chest, an armchair with worn gilding and shabby silk upholstery, and a large four-poster with hangings of faded crimson. The whole of the little chamber glowed with the heat of a fat-bellied stove by the wall, and there was quite a pleasant smell of apples, roasting on the top of the stove and at intervals sizzling and spitting.

The hostess of the room, a big fair-haired girl, painted white and red and stark naked under a negligee with pink bows, sat on the three-legged chair and rocked it a little as she examined a white stocking that she had drawn over the outspread fingers of her left hand and up her arm. As the door opened she stopped her movements and turned a swollen, sulky face toward it. A young man in shirt and breeches, with buckled shoes and a bare leg in one of them, lay on the bed and stared up in the canopy. He lazily turned his eyes toward the visitor.

"Hallo, my sweet," he said. "We are no longer allowed to discuss the nature of love in privacy. We have a visitor." He glanced at his guest. "An elegant visitor, too," he continued slowly as he sat up. "A gentleman, a fine courtier from the royal palace. We are . . ." he broke off his speech suddenly, paused, swung his legs over the edge of the bed and stood up. "We are," he exclaimed, "honored by a visit from the Ruler of all faithful Moslems, the great Soudane Oros-

mane himself! Well is it known to everyone that this glorious
Majesty from time to time visits even the meanest lodgings
in his good town of Solyme in order that, himself unknown,
he may learn to know his people. Sire, you could never have
come to a place better suited to such investigations than this
one!"

The stranger blinked at the light and the faces. The next
instant he stiffened and turned pale.

"*L'on vient,*" he whispered.

"*Non,*" cried the young man in the one stocking, "*jusqu'ici
nul mortel ne s'avance!*"

He brushed past his guest and turned the key in the door.
The faint grating of the iron sent a shiver through the youth
in the cloak, but presently the certainty of a locked door behind him seemed to set him at ease. He drew his breath
deeply.

"*O mon Soudane,*" said his host. "You see that Venus and
Bacchus hold equal sway in our little temple—and even if it
be not their most noble grapes we press here, it is in any case
the unadulterated fluid—the thing itself! Those two are the
most honest of all godheads, and we in here put our trust
entirely in them. You must now do likewise."

The newcomer looked round the room. When he realized
into what kind of milieu he had made his way, a feeble,
lascivious smile flitted over his face.

"Does he take me for a poltroon?" he asked, the smile
still on his lips.

"For a poltroon?" his host answered. "By no means. Nay,
for a sentimental traveler, Your Mightiness. What does not
a wise and beloved master of mine announce: 'The man who
either disdains or fears to walk up a dark entry may be an
excellent good man, and fit for a hundred things, but he will
not do to make a good sentimental traveler.' I feel that, just
like me myself, you will before tonight have set foot—alas, I
feel that, just like me myself, you will also after tonight set
foot in many a dark and unknown entry. I furthermore feel

that you and I will tonight make a true sentimental journey together!"

There was a short silence in the room. The girl still sat with the stocking in her hand and gazed from one of the two young men to the other.

"What are your names, you two?" asked the guest.

"Indeed," his host answered, "forgive me that I did not immediately, in accordance with all good breeding, present to Your Majesty your humble servants so near heaven. Even though you yourself choose to remain unknown, it is evidently not seemly for us to hold back from you anything whatever of our nature or condition."

The host was at about the same stage of intoxication as the guest. It had made him a trifle uncertain on his feet, and seemed somewhat to encumber his tongue; he lisped a little as he spoke. But it had, at the same time, given wings to his speech and opened his soul to strong and happy emotions. He met his guest with an open, bright and tender look, and as he realized that more time and palaver were needed before the fugitive could feel at home in the room and the company, he went on.

"The name of our sweet hostess, then," he said, "is Lise. I myself have called her Fleur-de-Lys, after that lily-pure heroine of the old troubadours whom she resembles. Other adorers of hers, though, name her Ticklish Lise, that being their blunt way of acknowledging her aloofness and the sensitiveness of her skin. These names, however, I mention entirely *en passant* and as a matter of no consequence whatever. For she may in fact be addressed by any woman's name which a young man of Copenhagen may have imprinted in his heart, and thuswise in her own small person may be said to represent the whole sex. My recently quoted master has said: 'The man who has not a sort of affection for the whole sex is incapable of ever loving a single one as he ought.' Lise, therefore, is the genuine and worthy priestess of our goddess.

"And I myself," he continued, "I myself! Your Majesty—I

venture to believe—will already have noticed that I am a cavalier. Apart from that I am, *sauf votre respect*, a poet, which is to say: a fool. My name? As a poet—may God forgive the readers of Denmark—I have today no name. But in my quality of fool I can, like the master whom I have twice quoted, take the liberty of calling myself Yorick. Alas, poor Yorick! A fellow of infinite jest, of most excellent fancy. And now—in such a place and under such conditions!—to what base uses, my friend and brother, we may return!"

For a moment he was sunk in his own thoughts. "Return," he repeated to himself, then burst out with deep bitterness: "You intended to return in time for my father's funeral, and you arrived instead just in time for my mother's wedding!"

Then he collected himself and shook the sourness off him.

"And now, Sire," said he, "now you must feel at home and at ease with us, as in heaven—or in the grave. For taking all in all, who will ever be less likely to betray a king *par la grâce de Dieu* than—by that same grace—a poet? And, by the same, once more—but Lise does not like the word, and I shall not speak it."

Again he stood silent, but alive, observant, with the whole of his being concentrated upon the present moment, and then took a step forward. He grasped the flask, filled the glasses, and solemnly and happily in his outstretched hand presented one of them to the stranger.

"A toast," he cried. "A toast for this hour! It is by its very nature everlasting, and at the same time, and once more in accordance with its nature, nonexistent! Our door is bolted—hear how it rains!—and nobody in the whole world knows that we are inside it! We three, too, are all of us in such a way favored that tomorrow we shall have forgotten the hour and shall never, never again bethink ourselves of it. In this hour, then, the poor speaks freely to the rich, and the poet conjures up his fancy to the Prince. The Soudane Orosmane himself can here—as he has never before been able to, as, alas, he will never be able to again—sink his lofty burden of grief, incomprehensible to the common mortal, into human hearts, into the hearts of a poet and a whore. So be this hour a pearl in an oyster shell, on the bottom of dark Copenhagen swaying all around us. *Vivat,* my master and my mistress. *Vivat* this our stillborn, death-doomed hour!"

He raised his glass high up in the air, emptied it and stood immovable. His guest, obedient as a reflection in a mirror, followed every one of his movements.

This last glass, over and above what earlier in the evening the two had gulped down, had a powerful and mysterious effect upon them. It caused both small figures to grow, and sent a deep, noble flush into both pale faces and a radiating light into two pairs of big eyes. Host and guest beamed on each other, and for a moment came so close together as if they were in for a wrestling match or an embrace.

"*Ôtez-moi donc,*" the guest said suddenly in a low voice, "*ce manteau qui me pèse!*"

He stood still, his chin a little in the air, his eyes on his host's face, while the latter fumbled with the clasp and got the heavy cloak off him. Under the cloak the stranger wore a pearl-gray silk coat and waistcoat with water-blue embroidery; the lace at the neck and wrists was torn. The pale costume gave to his whole figure something immaterial and flickering, as if he were a young angel on a visit to the hot and close room. But as, in its fall backwards, the cloak unfolded itself over the back and seat of the armchair, its deep-golden velvet lining seemed to collect in it all the colors of the room and to uplift them into a glow and gleam of pure ore. The young man who had called himself Yorick saw the room round him suddenly gilt, and in a kind of rapture squeezed his guest's delicate fingers.

"O you most welcome!" he cried out. "You long hoped for! Our lord and master, we are yours! See, we offer you now our best chair, and can then offer you none better. Lise never allows herself to sit in it, so as not to weigh down the upholstering with her charms. Deign now, Sire, for this one night to turn it into a throne!"

Under the speaker's mighty gaze the hearer's features for a second shivered, then cleared into serene composure. His being, which lately, in its search for a foothold, had run so wildly in all directions, was collected and uplifted into sublime harmony. Yes, he was among friends—such as he had read about and looked for but had never found, such as would understand who he really was. He allowed himself to be led, by the ceremoniously raised hand of his host, a step backwards toward the chair, and sat down in it somewhat abruptly, but without his dignity being in any way impinged upon. Erect against the golden velvet, with his exquisite hands on the arms of the chair, as if he did indeed hold the scepter and orb, he turned his gaze toward the room as from a great height.

Yet as he spoke he was changed once more. He had uttered his short French sentences in a particularly melodious and sonorous voice. As now he changed into Danish, it became evident that he had been learning the language principally from valets and hound-boys, and in their company had mimicked and mocked his tutors.

"Indeed," he said, "indeed, Poet! That is what I want. I want to hear with my own ears the complaints of my people. But I never could get at you, with the old foxes spying on me on all sides. Tonight I have had to run a long way, through dark, stinking places and up dreadful stairs to find you. It was good that you locked the door, so that we can keep them out."

He had spoken quickly, now for a moment he searched for his words, then went on, slowly and in a raised voice:

> "Dans ces lieux, sans manquer de respect,
> chacun peut désormais jouir de mon aspect,
> car je vois avec mépris ces maximes terribles,
> qui font de tant de rois des tyrans invisibles!"

"Come along then," he said again, "complain away. Are you unhappy?"

The young man who had called himself Yorick considered for a moment, then raised his hand and pressed it against his collarbone, where his shirt lay open.

"Unhappy," he repeated slowly, "unhappy we shall certainly never be, after tonight. Neither do we, in our relation to you, wish to make ourselves pitiable. A true courtier does not insult his King by depreciating himself in his presence, as if such a thing were needed to uphold a monarch's dignity! Nay, he makes himself as tall as possible, and says to the world: 'Look what grand people are the servants of this master!' It furthers the glory of his Catholic Majesty of Spain to have got servants grand enough to have the right to remain covered before his throne, just as we further the glory of our God, not by crouching, but by holding up our heads!

"All the same," he continued, "a few small human, foolish griefs we have still got, seeing that we are both humans and fools. Do you want to hear of them?"

"Yes, that is what I told you," said he who had been called Orosmane.

"Hear then," said Yorick, "our first grief. You would find, if you looked closer, that Lise's salt tears have drawn two noble gutters down through that rose-red of her cheeks which has lately, with so much care, been laid upon them. And this only because another maiden in the house, in a squabble, has called her an alabaster whore! Had I but now got two florins —but I have them not—I should this very night go down in the town to procure some object of alabaster for my Lise, in order that she might realize with what true feminine genius this friend of hers, Nille, has portrayed her person. Fain would I like to console Lise. For verily, Orosmane, I owe this maiden much, and more than the paltry four shillings which her goodness had allowed me to have chalked up against me. It is a good and blessed thing for such people as

me—it is balm to our souls as to our bodies—that there are
such people as she!"

Orosmane looked at Lise, who tossed her head and looked
the other way.

"Your debt to Lise, Poet," he said with a noble movement
of the hand, "we herewith take upon ourselves. She will tomorrow receive an alabaster jar with a hundred florins in it.
For never shall a whore weep in our kingdoms. Nay, they
shall hold there a high official station—*comme d'un peuple
poli des femmes adorées*. It is a good and blessed thing for
such as us, too, that there be such as she."

"*Bénissons le Seigneur*, Lise," said Yorick.

"And let, then," said Orosmane, "the prudes, the virtuous
ladies shed their tears into their prayer books in resentment
of our goodness to Lise. For they have themselves no
goodness whatever in them. They mince and wag their rumps
and smirk, only to dupe and ruin us. And," he exclaimed, his
face suddenly distorted with rage, "and in a bed they will
talk!"

"You have said it, Sire," said Yorick. "In a bed they will
talk, the furies out of hell! At the moment when up to,
and above, the limit of our strength we have gifted them
with our full being, our life and our eternity, then they will
talk! Then, full-fed and complacently ignorant of man's, of
the human being's infinite longing for silence, they insist on
being told whether the *adrienne* they had on yesterday did
become them, and whether there is life after death!"

Orosmane thought the matter over, and again the little
grin ran over his face.

"I will tell you something, you there," he said, "which I
myself have been told by Kirchhoff. In Paradise Adam and
Eve did walk on all fours, even as the dumb animals they
lived among. In those days Adam hid his sex beneath him,
in the shelter of his body, such as was in accordance with his
sense of *les décences*, which by a long way exceeds that of a

female. But his lady wife could hide nothing, and was entirely bared and exposed to his gaze. Therefore one day Madame Eve raised herself up on her two legs, and assured her husband that only such carriage and gait was consistent with the dignity of human beings. From that same moment she concealed her own sex, and was in a position to deny all knowledge of it. But see now! Adam from that day had to make a full display of his, and to proclaim and acknowledge before the whole world how accurately his creator had cast and adjusted him to his wife's little secret crucible. So Madame could at her ease strut and swoon and shriek out: '*Um Gottes willen, was bedeutet dies!*'— What, what, is it not so? And therefore," he finished with a quick, keen grimace, "therefore: the more a female, in the goodness of her heart, is prepared to resemble the dumb animal, and to go down upon all fours, the greater ease does man find in her company. Is it not so, Poet?"

"Why, of course it is so," Yorick answered with a laugh. "You have said it! And in fact I have thought of the same thing before tonight. For see now you, Orosmane! I have never had the honor of contemplating Lise at her meals. But to myself I have pictured her at them, and I have clearly realized the impossibility of that sweet creature taking dinner or supper like the rest of us. Nay, she must of necessity graze daintily, like a little white lamb in a meadow—down by the babbling brook, down in the live, green shades."

Orosmane looked at Yorick for a while, and his young face smoothened.

"Not in this place," he said with dignity, "Not tonight will we speak of Kirchhoff. He is a Schlingel, a *valet de chambre*. No word of his shall be laid in Lise's, in yours or in our own ear! What were we speaking of?"

"Of our griefs," said Yorick, "and of your loving-kindness, which has wiped away Lise's grief."

"Why, yes," said Orosmane, "Lise's grief. And now yours. How many griefs have you?"

"I have but two griefs," answered Yorick, "since now Lise has nearly finished darning my stocking, and has thus kindly rid me of the third one. One of the two is that the sole of my shoe has a hole in it and lets in water badly. And yet to that I have almost got accustomed. But my second grief, Orosmane, is this: that I am not almighty."

"Almighty," Orosmane repeated slowly. "Do you want to be almighty?"

"Alas," said Yorick. "Forgive me, Sire, that I come to you with such a trite and commonplace complaint. For all we sons of Adam have an infinite longing for almightiness, just as if we had been born and bred to it, and then, cruelly and tragically, had had it taken away from us."

"Do you want almightiness, you?" Orosmane asked as before and stared hard at his host. "Ha, come to me, I have got it. I have got it, according to what they all assure me. Did they not set a crown on my head and a scepter in my hand. Danneskiold and the Lord High Chamberlain bore up the train of the robe! They vowed it in verse too. Wait a moment, and I shall recite it to you!"

He considered for a few seconds and then quietly and clearly declaimed:

"How shall I name you now, our youthful Solomon?
A king? or are you God? ah, you are both of these!
See, stamped within your seal: almightiness and wisdom!
A Monarch Absolute, with character of God."

"Did you perhaps make that verse yourself, you who are a poet?"

"No, that verse I did not make," said the poet.

"Will you be me?" Orosmane exclaimed in a high clear voice. "Shall we exchange parts tonight, and see whether we will notice any difference? For look you here: a little while ago, as you were handing me the glass, it came upon me that it was you that were almighty."

"You are right again, Sire," said Yorick. "Of all people in

Copenhagen, very likely you and I, the monarch and the poet, are the two who come nearest to being almighty. Nay, we probably should not notice any difference."

At this point of the conversation Lise got up to take the apples off the stove so that they should not be burnt. She set them on the table and sprinkled sugar on them with her fingers, so that her guests could enjoy them when they wished. From time to time, while the two others talked on, she herself took a mouthful, left a little crimson fard on the flesh of the apple, and carefully licked her fingers. Orosmane followed her movements absent-mindedly, as if he did only half see her.

"All Adam's sons, you said!" he exclaimed. "What about Mistress Eve's brood? What about womenfolk? You are not going to tell me that they do not long to be almighty? You may be certain that my sweet Katrine should like to rule the whole world—just as our royal consort's good Lady of the Bedchamber and *Preneuse de Puces* means to fix the time for us to go to bed."

"No, they may not exactly long for almightiness," said Yorick. "But that comes from the fact that every woman already, in her heart, does hold herself to be almighty. And indeed they are right in thinking so. Look at Lise now; she has not said a word during this conversation of ours and will not come to do so either. And yet it is she who has allowed the whole conversation to come into existence, and had she not been in the room with us, it would not have been held at all."

"Well now," said Orosmane after a short pause. "What do you want to do with your almightiness? For I myself know well enough," he declared, his young face for a few seconds strangely wild and snappish, "what I should like to do with mine."

"*Mon Soudane*," said Yorick humbly, "I should like to live."

Orosmane was silent for an instant. "Why?" he asked.

"Well," said Yorick. "*Sauf votre respect*, Sire, the fact is that people do want to live.

"First of all they want to keep alive from today till tomorrow, and what they need to this purpose is something to eat. It is not always easy to get something to eat. And when we are hungry we moan and scream, not precisely from pain, but because we feel in our stomachs that our life is threatened. The baby, even, cries for the nipple because it claims to keep alive till tomorrow; poor puss, it does not know what life means.

"But next," he continued, "we desire to live for a longer space of time than from today till tomorrow, and for a longer time than those scanty years which are called a span of human life. We desire to live down through the ages. To that purpose we claim the embrace! To that purpose we claim the beloved, the mate who will receive, house and bring forth this our never-ending life on earth. This, now, is why the youth moans and storms—in verse even, some of us— because he wills his own blood to greet, in a hundred years' time, the dawn and the moonrise. And because he feels, in all this blood of his and in every limb, that should the embrace of love be denied him, life itself is denied him.

"But finally," he finished very slowly, "finally and most powerfully man desires life everlasting."

"Go on," said Orosmane, "I know all about life everlasting. My tutor, old Court-chaplain Nielsen, got much credit because I did so well in my catechism." He rattled on quickly: "The forgiveness of sins, the resurrection of the body and the life everlasting. Is that what you want?"

"More or less," said Yorick. "Although my body is not exactly the part of me on which I pride myself most. Light it is, and yet often heavy and painful to carry about. Let it remain where it is. Still, my spirit yearns for that everlasting life, and will not be dismissed.

"You yourself, the Lord's Anointed," he continued, "are on the safe side, and will take your seat, *hochselig* amidst your *hochselig* ancestors. But my own dear soul roams in uncertainty, now striving toward light, now shrinking from the dark and thus, in all this matter, bound to suffer both the pangs of hunger and the infinite longing for the embrace. And indeed I should much like to help it on!"

Orosmane, his happy memory of former triumphs once awakened, recited a stanza from an old Danish hymn:

> *"How sweet it is to taste the flavor*
> *Of what the house may call its own,*
> *And of one's due inhale the savor*
> *Mid those who stand before the throne.*
> > *Oh, there to see*
> > *The Persons Three*
> *Is risen humans' greatest favor."*

He lost the thread of the stanza, broke off, and gazed fixedly first at his own hand and then at Lise and Yorick. Yorick too became thoughtful, waited and sipped a little gin from his glass.

"Yes," he said and smacked his lips a little, "it will certainly be very sweet to taste, and the house, without doubt, will call a great deal its own. But I will confide to you, Orosmane, what I have not dared to confide to anyone else, because you understand all that one says to you! I shall never entirely turn away from this earth. I have, you see, continuously kept it alive in my thought, just as, when I was a child, I kept alive a bird in its cage or a plant in my window, by giving them water when they were thirsty, by shifting them toward the sun and by covering them up at night. This earth of ours has been most dear and precious to me. Even up above there, I certainly could not help peering out from time to time to find out whether it were able to go on without me. Aye, I should, even up there, cry to it to preserve me! I should long to see my state of heavenly bliss reflected, far away down on earth, as in a mirror. Do you know, Sire, what such a reflection is called?"

"No, I do not," said Orosmane.

"It is called *mythos!*" Yorick cried out, transported. "My *mythos!* It is the earthly reflection of my heavenly existence. Mythos, in Greek, means speech, or, since I was never good at Greek," he added as in parentheses, "and since great scholars may consider me mistaken—you and I, at any rate, for tonight will agree to take it in such a sense. Highly pleasant and delightful is speech, Orosmane; we have experienced it tonight. Yet, previous to speech, and higher than speech, we acknowledge another idea: *logos*. Logos, in the Greek, means *Word*, and by the Word all things were created."

A rhythm in their common, happy intoxication, like to a noble, precise law, throughout their talk had led on and borne up the talkers. The same law now appeared gently and formally to force them apart, as when two dancers in a ballet separate, and the one, although still close at hand and indispensable to the figure, remains inactive, observing his partner's great solo. The host in a mighty movement swung away from his guest and figured alone.

"Verily, verily," he cried, "all my life I have loved the Word. Few men have loved it as deeply as I. Its innermost secrets are laid open to me. Therefore, also, a knowledge has been communicated to me. At the moment when my Almighty Father first created me by His word, He demanded and expected from me that I should one day return to Him and bring Him back His word, as speech. That is the one task allotted to me, to fulfill during my time and my course on earth. From His divine Logos—the creative force, the beginning—I shall work out my human mythos—the abiding substance, remembrance. And in time to come, when by His infinite grace I shall once more have become one with Him, then will we look down together from heaven—I myself with tears, but my God with a smile—demanding and expecting that this mythos of mine shall remain after me on earth.

"Terrible," he continued, in a changed, slower rhythm, "terrible is the comprehension of this our obligation toward the Lord. Terrible in its weight and incessancy is the obligation of the acorn to yield Him the oak tree—and yet it is exquisite, too, and sweet and pleasant is the young verdure after a summer rain. Crushing in its weight is my own covenant with the Lord, yet it is, at the same time, highly gay and glorious! For if I do only hold onto it myself, no adversity and no distress shall compel me, but it is I who shall compel adversity and distress, poverty and sickness, and the harshness even of my enemies, and force those to labor with me for my benefit. And all things shall work together for good to me!"

He came back to his partner in the dance, and in front of the latter's figure, which had remained immovable on the spot, he made ready for their *pas de deux*.

"What good luck," he cried, "that I have tonight got you here to talk to, Orosmane. All other people might think that I am drunk and am talking wildly. But you are a king, and I once more bless you for your kingly understanding. Your sympathy convinces me that this mythos of mine will indeed some day be found on earth. In two hundred years' time the people of Copenhagen will know nothing at all about me; yet when they meet me they will recognize me. Terrifying and joyous is my covenant with the King of Heaven—*dignum et justum est*, that the hand of an earthly king shall seal it."

Orosmane received him gracefully and harmoniously as a dancer, and fell in with his rhythm.

"*Ainsi soit-il!*" he said. "My hand shall seal your covenant."

For a moment, as in confirmation of what had been spoken, both speakers were at rest and expectant.

"But what of me?" Orosmane exclaimed in a new movement. "What of me? Will I myself, some day, obtain that reflection on earth of my heavenly glorification, which you tell me is called mythos? Do you think so?"

"Yes, I think so," said Yorick.

"O la la," cried Orosmane. "You think so, because all your

life you have associated with decent people and have never met tutors, teachers of religion or advisers of kings, and so have no knowledge of genuine *canaillerie*. For all that you have said tonight, Poet, is but what I myself have long known, and what all my life I have wanted. What other thing have I ever longed for but that which you have named, and which you call—what did you call it?"

"Mythos," said Yorick.

"—but mythos! I have wished to harden myself—and surely a mythos is hard, and surely an oak tree is hard—and I have wanted to be all in one piece, like them. But I shall tell you something, you! At Court, and in council meetings, people fear! Everybody fears, although none of them will ever let out what it is they fear. They may tell you that they fear God—but they fear not God!—or that they fear the King—but they fear not the King! Nay, they run about, they tattle, they bow and scrape and rig themselves out in uniforms and robes, they chop up a king's mind and life into kindling wood, all for fear of one thing, which is named . . ."

"Mythos," said Yorick.

"Mythos," said Orosmane. "Womenfolk they will get for me in plenty, both of the blood royal and out of the Danish stud-book—in order to have me henpecked. They wish a king's mythos to be danced on by silk slippers, but not one of them will bring a cothurnus for it to march in. They would consent to honor me with a pompous enough monument—and the sooner the better too—they will be all at one in setting up an equestrian statue for me. But they are all at one, take my word for it, in grudging me the—say it again!"

"The mythos," said Yorick.

"The mythos," said Orosmane. "*Tu l'as dit!* My seat amidst my *hochselig* ancestors I cannot fail to get. But the clear and deep reflection of my *Hochseligkeit* here, here in Copenhagen, they are smashing up before it has come into existence—into a thousand pieces, so that even now, while still alive, I hear the splinters of glass clatter round my ears!"

Yorick looked at his guest for a long time. At last he spoke. "No," he said with great authority. "You are wrong, Sire. You will have your mythos.

"For your mythos will be this, that you have got none. Your people of Denmark, of Copenhagen, in two hundred years will know but little about you—and maybe nothing at all. Yet within the long row of kings of Denmark, of Christians and Fredericks, the one whom they will first of all recognize will be you."

Orosmane was now silent for a while, with all his powers of observation turned inwards, onto something in himself.

"Fill my glass," he said.

The gin, which might be said to have been the music to the scene, lifted up his being into high earnestness and energy. Now was the time for his own solo. Strangely free and erect and light as a bird, he rose, spiritually, on tiptoe. No movement of his was over-hasty or disconnected, in his most daring airiness there was abundance and equilibrium. He glided across the pause as across a stage, straight towards Yorick.

"You praised your luck, Yorick, my poet and my friend," he said, "in having me to speak to tonight. Now hear! Your luck is greater than you know of. I will share my wisdom with you. I will tell you who I am, and who you are!

"For there are," he went on, "upon this earth a few people—and to my belief we are only seven in all—who see into the true and essential nature of the world. The others incessantly distort it to us because they want nobody to understand its proportions and harmony. And those others will be working tirelessly to separate us and to keep us apart—since they are aware that if we are united, we should overcome our foes. All my life I have looked out for the six others of my own kind, but my jailers have not allowed me to find them. Ha, they do not know that tonight, I have all by myself found my way up here, to you! And alas—soon, very

soon, they will be on my track to tear us asunder. At this
very moment they are out after me, scurrying through backyards, up alleys and steep stairs. Well may you now think,
and cry out:

> . . . *o nuit, nuit effroyable,*
> *peux-tu prêter ton voile à de pareils forfaits!*

"But in that hour of which you spoke, and which you
toasted, we can still be together and speak the truth to each
other. Let me then, as I speak truly to you, have your true
answers."

"Aye," said Yorick. "Speak, Sire, your Poet and Fool lis-
tens."

"Listen, my Poet and my Fool," said Orosmane. "The
world, I tell you, is far nobler and more beautiful than our
enemies will ever allow us to see."

"It is so," said Yorick.

"Human beings," Orosmane continued, "are all created
greater, finer and more lovable than they look."

"They are so," said Yorick.

"And are not our pleasures," Orosmane cried, "much
greater fun than they allow us to perceive?"

"Why, yes," said Yorick.

"Are not our actors of the stage," Orosmane cried again,
"far less wretched than they appear to us?"

"Certainly they are," said Yorick.

"And is it not," said Orosmane, "a great deal more pleasant to go to bed with a woman than we can know by now?"

"Of that I can assure you, *mon Soudane*," said Yorick.

"We three then do know!" said Orosmane. "We do know,
you and I and Lise—even if, the night over, we must keep our
knowledge to ourselves. We know, tonight, how sweet and
of what excellent quality is our gin. Aye, we know," he exclaimed, slipping over into a graceful repetition of an earlier
passage of the conversation:

> *"How sweet it is to taste the flavor*
> *Of what the house may call its own,*
> *And of one's due inhale the savor*
> *Mid those who stand before the throne.*
> *Oh, there to see*
> *The Persons Three*
> *Is risen human's greatest favor."*

He gracefully stretched out a hand, slim, pointed fingers collected—to each side, toward the two others. The hand was not meant to be touched, nor did either of them stir to touch it. Yet this gesture of high kingly favor made the three people in the room one.

"And," he said very slowly, "*Il y a dans ce monde un bonheur parfait.*"

Yorick rose and fell into step with his partner.

"Yes, Sire," he agreed, speaking as slowly and weightily as he. "There are, upon this earth and in this our existence, three kinds of perfect happiness. And there are human beings so highly favored as to come to taste all three."

"Even three!" Orosmane cried out joyfully. "There you see how, when we three are together, good things double and treble themselves. Now set words to my thoughts, you who tell me that you love the word. Nothing further shall I demand of you. Name the three."

"The first *bonheur parfait*," said Yorick, "is this: to feel in oneself an excess of strength."

"As we do now!" said Orosmane and laughed. "As now, blissfully united, we are able to soar into the air, like to three kites made fast with slim strings only to wet Copenhagen beneath us. You are a real poet, you! Your words turn my thoughts into pictures. At this moment I see before me a glass filled to the brim with wine from Bouzy or Epernay, foaming down its stem, and in its abundance frothing even in the dust! When, at the time of my accession to the throne, I informed the wig-blocks that I would now rage for a year, then did I foam and froth like that. An access of strength—ha, those are sweet-sounding words, like a song. And verily, during that one year the entire Court-ceremonial was turned into a drinking song, which rang in the halls of our palace and resounded in our streets of Copenhagen! But you tell me," he went on after a short pause, "that there is a second happiness as perfect as the first. Name it!"

"The second perfect happiness," said Yorick, "is this: to know for certain that you are fulfilling the will of God."

There was a short pause.

"*Mais oui!*" said Orosmane proudly. "You are there speaking rightly and seemly to a king *par la grâce de Dieu.* The burden of the crown, you must know, is a heavy one, but our insight and knowledge—by the grace of God—will swing the balance. Your second supreme happiness, Poet, is my inheritance and my element, and cannot fail me. But see you here: since tonight we have met and have been united, I will share that happiness with you. From now on you will, both of you, in your separate callings, the poet and the whore, be fulfilling the will of God. You will, in hours of despondency, remember these my words and be comforted, and never again will you weep—as Lise wept, the while I was tarrying outside your door.

"But now, my soothsayer, good Athenian—now to the third perfect happiness of which you spoke."

As Yorick did not answer at once he repeated: "The third, what is it?"

Yorick answered: "The cessation of pain."

Orosmane's face became clear with an almost luminous pallor. In a last, flying, completely weightless leap—as in the language of the ballet is called *grand jeté*—he finished off his solo.

"Ha!" he cried. "There you hit the nail on the head! There you speak from my own heart! Would that you knew how many times I have experienced your third perfect happiness! And indeed, that was why, first of all, even as a child, I demanded to be made almighty—in order that I should no longer feel the cane—old Ditlevs' cane!"

Yorick took a step back, as if in his flying leap Orosmane had knocked him over. Slowly his own face whitened and lit up like that of his *vis-à-vis*. His intoxication fell from him, or it increased to the point of steadying him.

The stillness that now filled the room was not the absence of speech; it was a vital affirmation superseding words.

Finally the host took a step forward, as he had before taken a step back, and bent a knee before the armchair. He raised his guest's noble hand from the arm of the chair, brought it to his lips, and for a long time kept his mouth pressed upon it. Orosmane, immovable as he, lowered his gaze to the lowered head before him.

The kneeling man stood up, went and sat down on the bed, and pulled on his stocking and his shoe.

"Are you not staying on?" asked Orosmane.

"Nay, I am going," said Yorick. "My business here was finished already before you came. But do you stay a while with Lise. In the lap of the people," he added after a short pause, "King and Poet can mingle their innermost being— just as in times of old the Nordic vikings in confirmation of sworn brotherhood—a pact of life and death—let their blood mingle, to soak into the earth's mute, bounteous womb."

"Good night, Sire," he said. "Good night, Lise."

He took from a peg on the wall an old cloak, which had once been black, but now after many years of service showed shades of green and gray. He buttoned it, listened for the rain outside, and turned up his collar. His hat had fallen to the floor, he found it, pressed it down upon his head, and went out of the door and shut it after him.

As he descended the steep stairway, he heard muffled voices from below. On the next landing he encountered a small company mounting in single file. At the head was a young man wearing a livery under his cloak, with a lantern in his hand. An old gentleman, who had some difficulty with the uneven stairs, and two more persons followed. All faces in the gleam from the lantern were pale and anxious.

As the group met him on his way down, they halted, and thereby halted him too, since in the narrow space he could not get round them.

They looked at him doubtfully for a few seconds, and seemed to wish to put a question to him, but to be somehow puzzled as to how to shape it. Yorick forestalled them by whistling softly, and by pointing upwards over his shoulder with his thumb.

"Yes, that is where Lise lives," he said. "An horest wench. I have just paid her off and left her."

The little ascending procession pressed themselves against the wall so that he could pass. But as he went by him, the old gentleman said in a low and hoarse voice:

"And there *ist kein anderer daoben?*"

"*Kein anderer,*" answered Yorick and whistled again, this time a snatch of a ditty.

He continued his somewhat uncertain way to the ground, and before he had quite reached the bottom of the stairs, he heard the company above him turn round and follow him downwards.

About the Author

ISAK DINESEN is the pseudonym of Karen Blixen, born in Denmark in 1885. After her marriage in 1914 to Baron Bror Blixen, she and her husband went to live in British East Africa, where they established a coffee plantation. She was divorced from her husband in 1921 but continued to manage the plantation for another ten years, until the collapse of the coffee market forced her to sell the property and return to Denmark in 1931. There she began to write in English under the *nom de plume* Isak Dinesen. Her first book, and literary success, was *Seven Gothic Tales* (available in Vintage Books). It was followed by *Out of Africa* (also available in Vintage Books in a facsimile edition of the first printing), *The Angelic Avengers* (written under the pseudonym Pierre Andrézel). Also available in Vintage Books: *Winter's Tales, Last Tales, Anecdotes of Destiny,* and *Ehrengard.* Isak Dinesen died in 1962.